THE SUMMIT BY THE SEA

The Summit by the Sea

MICHAEL LAJOIE

Reddington Press

To Jason and Melissa, for encouraging me
to ramble;

To Lisa and David, for blazing the trail;

And to Shackiel, for helping me keep the
summit in sight.

CONTENTS

~ ~

~ ~

Chapter Fifteen

~ ~

Chapter Sixteen

~ ~

Chapter Seventeen

~ ~

Chapter Eighteen

CHAPTER ONE

Abilene reared her sweat-streaked face to the sky, her eyes closed and heart pounding. The sunlight suffused her upturned cheeks, red-orange through her eyelids and warm against her flushed skin. She squinted at the swaying canopy of leaves overhead and inhaled deeply. Cool mountain air rushed to her core, fueling her resolve. Spirits elevated, she lowered her head. Mud caked her legs and stained the ragged hem of her deerskin dress. She clasped the scallop shell that dangled from her neck and set her gaze on the mossy trail before her.

Her bare feet sank into the damp earth. They had come to know the essence of this winding path—every papery fern, jagged stone, and smooth serpentine root was stamped into her soul. She had been hiking for three weeks and had lost count of the miles somewhere along the way. Three weeks, and her journey was far from over. She was rambling toward uncertainty.

The trail, a gravelly slope framed by looming firs, progressed steeply upward. Abilene brushed her black curls out of her eyes and began to climb. Her muscles blazed in protest. Each step was careful, deliberate, and increasingly weary. The trees on either side of the trail recognized her plight and reached out to her cajolingly. She gripped their boughs for support and heaved herself onto level ground.

She sighed, grateful for the break the flatness offered—even though she knew it was brief. The trail had established a pattern of long days over level ground permeated by steep scrambles up and over lofty hills. The ascents broke the monotony but routinely slowed her to a snail's pace. Abilene managed a laugh—she knew better than to scoff at a snail's pace.

Many months ago, she had walked with her mother by the sea. They came from a little village of wigwams overlooking the coast. The ocean was their neighbor, their teacher, and their everlasting companion. They were Pax—sentinels of forest, crag, and sea.

Her mother had pointed to a glistening line in the sand, which Abilene came to recognize as the trail of a snail the size of a pebble. She had leaned down, positioning herself at eyeline with the tiny creature, fascinated by its determination. "Where do you think he's going?" she asked.

Abilene's mother shrugged. "I don't know," she said. "He may not even know. Maybe he'll find out along the way."

Abilene considered the snail with pursed lips. "He looks lost."

"That doesn't matter," her mother said dismissively. "What matters is that he has the will to keep moving forward."

"He still has a long way to go."

Her mother nodded. "Yes, but look at how far he's come."

Abilene traced the snail's slick trail with her eyes. It measured only about as long as her forearm.

"It doesn't look like much to us," her mother admitted, taking note of her unimpressed expression. "But from our friend's perspective, he's no doubt traveled a great distance."

They watched in silence as the snail approached a cluster of shells strewn in his path. He scaled them with apparent ease, continuing on his way. But just as the snail surmounted the obstacle, the ocean heaved a sigh and he was lost in the foaming surf.

Abilene winced. Her mother squinted at the receding water ruefully. At length, they found the snail half-buried and upside-down, embedded in the glassy shore like a knob in a plank of petrified wood. Abilene freed him sympathetically, washing the sand from his shell and placing him on his stomach. The snail was still for a moment, as though gathering his bearings, before inching forward with sluggish fervor. On the freshly-smoothed surface of the shore, he began blazing a new path into the un-known.

Abilene's mother broke into a grin. "You see? Slowly, pen-sively, resiliently—our friend perseveres."

So, too, would Abilene persevere. The trail broke into a clear-ing. She smiled musingly, knowing she'd finally reached the top of this undistinguished hump in the wilderness. She peered through a gap in the evergreen walls of the glade, looking out across the vast forested expanse. It was the first view she'd seen in days, so she savored it. A cavalcade of crags was stretched out before her, each one wooded to the crest. To the north, she dis-cerned the next hill she'd traverse, and the next.

Several peaks down the line she spotted her ultimate desti-nation, the culmination of her efforts: the highest peak in the land. The Pax called it Spero. It was a sheer horn of a mountain with ravine-scarred flanks and a summit enveloped in a realm of clouds. It was said that those who reached the summit were true Pax—true stewards of forest, crag, and sea.

Stepping back from the view, Abilene kissed her scallop shell necklace and beamed at the reality of her accomplishment. She knew in the back of her mind that this was hardly the most dif-ficult part of her journey, but reminded herself that even the

smallest summits signified her success. Every step she took toward Spero was a victory.

The trail beckoned to her. There were more mountains to explore. It was time to move on.

She descended the hill quickly, hiking alongside a trickling
stream that awakened her thirst. As she knelt over the sparkling
water, she caught a glimpse of her bedraggled reflection. Her
skin was the color of the streambed, of rich dark silt, while her
hair resembled a tangled mass of sunbaked seaweed. She had
eyes like a pair of freshly extinguished embers that still radiated
warmth, eyes that burned with determination through a mounting fog of fatigue. There were sagging craters beneath them that
she tried in vain to rub away. She laughed to herself. Barely
noon and she looked as though she hadn't slept in days...

Abilene's gaze dropped to her necklace, and her thoughts
drifted to its origins. She recalled her last conversation with her
mother on the eve of her journey north. They had been wandering through the pale bands of shells that adorned the shore,
oceanic treasures that marked a threshold between worlds. The
ocean was ever-giving. With every breath, it deposited the bone-
white abodes of oysters, crabs, muscles, and snails onto the sand.
They were innumerable—fragmented and full; spiraled and
smooth.

Abilene's mother had stooped down and plucked a single
shell from the shore. She passed it through a sinew thread, tied
the two ends together, and presented the gift to her daughter.
It was a scallop shell, a true relic of the sea—full, unbroken, and
the size of Abilene's palm. The sun and surf had left it weathered, and traces of sand still lingered in its faded blue grooves.

Abilene donned the necklace, smiling as the pendant settled
over her heart. She hugged her mother tightly.

"I wish you could come," she said. Her hike to the summit of Spero was a coming-of-age ritual that had to be completed alone. Her people called it the Rambling. She would be celebrated upon her return.

Her mother pointed to the scallop shell with a smile. "I'll be with you through it all," she said. "My girl...I'm so proud of you." There was love in her eyes, love as soft and tender as moonlight. Love that lined the creases of her face and radiated from her smile. "You're ready."

Abilene sighed. The Rambling had long been a distant ambition, a task to prepare herself for—but now that it was time for her to go, she felt daunted by the trip ahead. "I know I am," she said.

"You'll have to convince yourself of that before you can convince me."

The unexplainable truth made its way to Abilene's lips. "I'm afraid," she said.

"Of?"

She thought for a moment. "The unknown," she decided, remembering the snail's path through the sand.

Her mother's eyes were lunar spheres of conscience. "This journey will shape you," she said. "Never forget to look back from time to time on the trail you've blazed. Don't be discouraged if you don't like what you see. Learn from it and use that knowledge to plot your course for the future."

"I'm still afraid," Abilene said stubbornly.

"Good," her mother said. "The further you explore, the less you will be. Look at me, Abilene."

She stared into those lunar eyes.

"Remember, my girl, that you are never truly alone. Savor this time. Savor every toil, every storm, every experience. All of it will make you stronger."

CHAPTER TWO

Around mid-afternoon, Abilene passed into a fragrant stretch of woods. Among the green blankets of moss, she detected the source of the lovely aroma: dozens of tiny white flowers. Her people called them twinflower; as a girl, her mother used to weave the sweet-smelling buds into her braids. She knelt down to get a closer look at the aromatic underbrush. From a single stalk of the plant, two identical blossoms hung like a pair of ephemeral bells. Twinflower only bloomed during the onset of summer—in a few weeks, the delicate scent would be gone. She inhaled it gratefully and admired the silky petals before straightening and continuing on her way.

Before long, she came across a man standing in the middle of the trail. He was, as she soon realized, staring unblinkingly at a patch of twinflower nestled at the base of a log. As Abilene approached him curiously, he made no acknowledgement of her presence.

The man clutched a pen in his white-knuckled fist. He gripped it so tightly that she wondered how the thin wooden shaft didn't snap between his fingers. A small leather-bound notebook lay open in his other hand. Amid his scribbles, she observed a meticulous sketch of the flowers before him. The tip of the artist's pen hovered over the page as he considered his subject carefully.

"I like your drawing," Abilene said. "It's very good."

"It's not a drawing," the man replied without looking up. "It's an illustration."

"Oh," she said, a little confused. "I like your illustration then."

"Thank you. Now, hurry along. I'm busy."

She stood her ground. "What are you busy with?" she asked.

"Field work," the man said. "Notes. Observations."

"And illustrations?"

"Yes." He made a mark beside his sketch, then drew a short measuring stick from his satchel. Abilene watched as the man positioned it at the base of the clump of twinflower and studied the results. In the presence of his stick, the flowers seemed to slouch like restless children. He pinned the stalks against the log and stretched them to their full height, then returned to his notebook and began muttering to himself.

"*Linnaea borealis*," he said as he wrote. "Short, insignificant, and characteristically unimpressive..."

"What's that you called them?" Abilene interrupted with a frown.

"*Linnaea borealis*. A resident of deciduous undergrowth during the early summer months."

"Yes, that!" she said. "I think you made a mistake. That's twinflower."

The man looked up from his notebook for the first time. His spectacles magnified his scrutinizing gaze. He had the demeanor of an owl so lost in a cloud of fog that it had started to mistake pinecones for mice. "That's simply incorrect," he told her.

"What do you mean?" she said. "I've known those as twinflower my entire life!"

The man chuckled, shaking his head. "That just makes you ignorant," he sneered. "This is *Linnaea borealis*. It's been documented in these woods for years."

"How do you know that?"

"Because I'm a learned man," he said, seeming to puff his feathers.

"What's that mean?"

"It means I know things and you don't," he said matter-of-factly. "Don't take it too harshly, though. Ignorance is hardly a choice for your kind." He studied her up and down, then held his notebook out for her to see. "Tell me, what does this say?"

Abilene scanned his drawing. On the page opposite his twin-flower rendition, she noticed a mass of scribbles and loops. She saw no words. "Where?"

"Here, or here, anywhere." He patted the chaotic scrawl impatiently.

"I don't know," she said.

"I knew it!" His eyes grew brighter, but the fog before them thickened. "You don't know what that says because you can't read! I don't know why I assumed you could." He patted her shoulder condescendingly, but she shrugged his hand away.

"I *can* read," she said. "I've read plenty of things."

The learned man raised an eyebrow. "Your lies only accentuate your ignorance," he chided. "And besides, your savage texts don't count."

"I know how to read," Abilene said.

He studied her again. "You *are* an amusing specimen, aren't you?" he mused. "But something doesn't feel right. Where's your hatchet? What about your bow and arrows? Did you lose them?"

She shook her head. "I never had them to begin with," she said. Weapons, after all, were a cumbersome burden to bear.

"I see," he said. "You evidently have much to learn, even from your own kin."

"I don't know what that's supposed to mean," Abilene told him indignantly, "but listen, you've got it all wrong. I'm not ignorant, I can read, and that is not called *Linnaea borealis*. That's twinflower."

The learned man endured her displeasure with a smirk. "I really should return to my work," he said, "but you've amused me. I'll entertain your argument. Go on."

Slowly and carefully so he could comprehend, Abilene explained to him that the plant in question was called twinflower because of its sister-like blossoms.

"Fascinating," he said when she was finished, making no effort to stifle a yawn. "Does every understory plant in this forest lay at the center of one of your savage origin stories?"

Abilene declined to answer, knowing full well that the learned man would belittle her reply. "You call that *Linnaea borealis*," she said instead, gesturing at the subject of their debate, which swayed innocently in the breeze.

"Yes," the learned man said. "All of Christendom does."

So, he was Christian—she should have known. It was clear now there would be no convincing him, but she pressed her luck anyway. "And I call it twinflower," she said.

The learned man sighed. "Will you get on with it? I'm a very busy man."

Abilene ignored him. "I call it twinflower," she repeated. "But the salamander that uses its leaves as shelter from the sun, it calls it 'home.'"

"Yes, I suppose so."

"And the neighboring flowers, the moss, the log—they know it differently than we do, too. They call it 'friend.'"

"Flowers, mosses, and logs are not sentient," the learned man corrected her sharply, "but if they were...then, yes, I'm certain they would harbor some sort of relationship with each other."

"So," said Abilene, watching his owl-eyes carefully. "It seems we all know that flower by different names, but is it not the same plant? Doesn't its identity remain the same?"

The learned man considered this for some time and it appeared that the fog before his eyes was about to lift. But alas, Abilene concluded she was only imagining things—the fog resettled and the learned man hooted with laughter.

"I think you misjudge your role in comparison to mine," he said. "You are an ignoramus, a savage, a foolish girl. In short, you exist to be taught. I, on the other hand, am a learned man. I exist to teach—not to be taught." He studied her scornfully. "Your logic is feeble in the face of fact. That plant is called *Linnaea borealis*."

She couldn't believe the tenacity of his ignorance. "Am I wrong?" she demanded.

"Not wrong, just misdirected," the learned man replied wryly. "But as I said, it's not your fault. For your kind, stupidity is not a choice..."

"And for yours, it most certainly is," Abilene snapped, stepping around him. She set her eyes on the bright path ahead and left the owl floundering in his fog.

CHAPTER THREE

She walked several miles before a gruff-looking man on horseback came trotting down the trail. He was dressed almost entirely in furs, and the long, tarnished barrel of his musket was resting against his shoulder. A small silver cross hung from his neck.

"Hello," said Abilene, somewhat cautiously.

"Afternoon," the man wheezed. "Where you headed?"

"North," she replied simply.

"Alone?"

"Yes."

The man stared at her, massaging his forehead with his hand. "I see."

"What about you?" Abilene asked, glancing at his gun. "Where are you going?"

"Home," he grumbled. "I've had rotten luck in these god-forsaken woods. A pair of miserable rabbits, but that's it." The hunter brusquely adjusted his saddlebags, giving her a glimpse of the two bloodied pelts. "Pitiful, just pitiful..."

"Maybe it's your horse," Abilene suggested. "If I could hear you coming, then I'm sure the animals could, too."

The horse flared its cavernous nostrils and exhaled loudly. "I don't think so," the hunter said, patting its neck. He looked down at her bare feet and smirked. "You're a fool for walking this far. Don't you have a horse?"

"No," said Abilene, but she felt no envy. She preferred experiencing her Rambling on foot.

He squinted down at her. "Doesn't look like you're carrying anything," he observed. "You'd be better off just turning back."

"I have everything I need," Abilene told him.

"Silly girl," the hunter scoffed. "You don't know what you need."

"Yes, I do," Abilene said, a little annoyed.

"No, you don't," the hunter said. "You don't even have a tent."

Abilene shrugged. "The trees are my shelter," she said.

"You don't have food," the hunter persisted.

Abilene gestured to her waist, where a length of sinew fishing line doubled as her belt. "I'll catch something when I'm hungry."

"You don't have water."

"There are many streams in these woods," she informed him patiently.

"Hm," the hunter said. "And where's your map?"

She tapped her temple. "In here."

He studied her fiercely, then raised an eyebrow. "Where's your hatchet? Your bow? Your quiver of arrows?"

"I don't have them."

The hunter narrowed his eyes. "Don't tell me you're wandering alone out here without a weapon."

"I am," Abilene reiterated flatly.

"You're a damned fool," he said, shaking his head in disbelief. "What would you do if you came across an animal out here?"

She thought for a moment. Her mother had taught her that most animals were good-natured and generally avoided people.

"I'd probably wait for it to pass," she said. "If it didn't, then I'd hike in the other direction."

He gaped at her. "You'd let it live?"

Abilene nodded. "Why wouldn't I?"

"The only good animal is a dead animal," the hunter grunted. "Remember that."

"If you say so," Abilene said.

He swatted the air scornfully. "I wouldn't expect someone like you to understand. You're practically an animal, anyway."

"What's that supposed to mean?"

"Well, you're a savage, aren't you?"

"I'm not an animal," Abilene snapped, "and I'm not a savage, either. I'm Pax, and—" She was cut off by a loud rustling in the underbrush. The hunter, eyes ablaze, fumbled with his gun and fired a shot into the ferns. There was a piercing chirp, and a single chipmunk scampered across the trail in a panic.

"What are you *doing*?" Abilene yelped, covering her ears.

"I thought it was another rabbit," he growled, shouldering his smoking weapon. "*Rotten* luck, I'm telling you..."

She left him without another word, the stink of fear and gunpowder still lingering in her nostrils.

CHAPTER FOUR

The next day, Abilene enjoyed the good fortune of not coming across anyone on the trail. It was refreshing to hike alone again, serenaded by only the chattering nuthatches and the whistling breeze. The forest was a welcome companion that emulated solace instead of scrutiny, and for that, she was grateful. It wasn't so much that she disliked people or their curiosity about her journey north—she was always happy to pursue a meaningful conversation. It was the learned man's arrogance and the hunter's condescension that she detested, the raised eyebrows and pitied smirks that shoved her dignity into the mud.

She passed a wizened maple, patting its thick trunk kindly. A weathered stripe of white paint on its gnarled surface barely caught her attention. To the haughty Christian, it may as well have been a washed-out variety of lichen. To her, however, the white paint was the subtle sense of reassurance that she was headed in the right direction. She gazed up the trail, picking out several other white blazes among the towering trees. Nature itself was her guide.

This was an ancient route, forged generations ago by the ancestors of her ancestors. It climbed from the seaside high into the mountains, coming to an end atop Spero's lofty summit. To ramble the age-old trail from start to finish was a Pax tradition, a preservation of her people's legacy that was well-revered throughout her village. It was a test of strength, endurance, purpose, and self. Boys left for the Rambling and returned men; girls left for the Rambling and returned women. Both, through the completion of their journey, earned the right to call themselves Pax.

The Rambling was integral to the Pax identity. It allowed Abilene to wander in the footsteps of her heritage, to roam alongside her roots, and to experience life from an unrestrained perspective. Nomadic blood flowed through her veins. Her soul, true to her people's oceanic origins, resonated with perpetual movement. She was the sea in all of its nuances. In times of strife, she stormed. In times of peace, she mellowed. But she was always moving. For the ocean, even in its calmest moments, is never still.

At home, whenever Abilene needed to clear her head, she would clamber into a birch canoe and spend the day beneath the sun, bobbing among the waves. She didn't need to paddle very far offshore to begin to feel at peace. She liked to sit with her back against the horizon, tracing the craggy coastline with her eyes. From her broad vantage point, she could discern the blurry area where the forest met the shore, and where the shore faded into a vast swathe of marsh. To the left of the marsh lay Abilene's village. To the right of the marsh lay the Christian settlement: a formidable collection of log houses, dwarfed by a curious white building with a tower pointing to the sky. Left and right, separated by a boundary—that's the way Abilene had always known it to be.

Even so, the concept of the marsh as a border was admittedly strange to her. The world, she had been raised to believe, was a wild place that merited boundless exploration—her Rambling was a ready testament to that. As a girl, her mother had widely encouraged her wandering impulses and had let her investigate almost any place that piqued her curiosity. The other side of the marsh was the only exception. There were snakes that lived there, her mother said, so it was best to keep away.

"Please?" Abilene had begged one day, looking wistfully toward the sprawling bog. "I won't be gone long, I promise!"

"No," her mother had said. "It's far too dangerous. But there are countless other places to explore—what about the forest?"

"I've already explored the forest," Abilene mumbled. "And besides, there are snakes there, too."

"The snakes on the other side of the marsh are different," Abilene's mother said. "They're spiteful creatures that wear crosses on their necks. They don't take kindly to people like us."

Abilene frowned. "Why?"

"It's very complicated," her mother said.

"Have they always been that way?"

"Not always. They were kind to us once, and humble, too. We helped them understand the land and taught them how to fish."

"When was that?"

"Oh, years and years ago," Abilene's mother said. "I was younger than you when the sea brought them here." She laughed. "I was told they were swept ashore in a boat with red, white, and blue sails."

Abilene pursed her lips. "What changed? Why aren't they kind to us anymore?"

"Sometimes I wonder if it's because we were too generous," her mother said. "We taught them how to keep their hunger at bay, but their appetites were insatiable. Over time, they started to claim more and more for themselves, but we were too blind to realize it."

"More and more of what?" Abilene said.

"Land and fish, mainly," her mother replied. "They convinced us that they needed more of both to satisfy the needs of their growing village, and we were foolish enough to believe them. We agreed to a treaty devised by a forked tongue and suffered the venomous consequences." She shook her head regretfully. "Soon after we signed the treaty, the snakes began to lose their sense of humility. They seemed to forget that we had showed them how to survive. They stopped treating us with deference and began treating us with disdain."

Abilene sighed. "I wish I knew why."

"The Christians are a conceited and condescending people," her mother said bitterly. "They believe themselves to be superior to us, and so they see no wrong in treating us poorly. They inhabit a senseless distortion of the truth."

"There must be other reasons, too," Abilene said.

"There are always other reasons," her mother said. "A bird cannot fly without both of its wings and all of its feathers."

Abilene crossed her arms. "I don't understand."

"We live beneath the gaze of a great white bird," her mother said, lunar eyes twinkling. "Our truth resides on the wing that is clearly visible to us. Their truth resides on the other side of the marsh, on the wing that is folded and tucked out of sight."

Abilene gestured to the sparkling horizon. "Why don't we cross the marsh and see the other wing for ourselves?"

"I wish it were that simple," her mother said sadly. "But you forget that the Christians are snakes. They'll lash out at us if we wander too closely. Not all snakes are poisonous, and some are more agreeable than others, but still..." Her gaze was insistent. "It's best to stay away."

Overhead, a brilliant white seagull flapped its wings and let out a piercing *scree*. Abilene watched it soar toward the marsh and vanish, at length, into the fog. "I'm not afraid of snakes," she said, jealous of the bird's elevated perspective.

"That's what worries me," her mother said.

CHAPTER FIVE

Abilene awoke the following morning to the unmistakable cacophony of rushing water. She had spent the night atop a little hill and rambled down the trail to witness a coursing river. A white blaze stood out to her among the trees on the other side. She clambered down to the gravelly bank with a grin and began to wade across. The river jolted her awake. The icy water reached her knees and the current was swift, but she stood her ground.

She reached the opposite side with triumph and set her sights on the trail ahead. But before she left the river, she heard a faint voice calling to her.

"Help...please help me..."

Abilene looked about and soon found herself staring at an old man sprawled at the riverside. She hurried to help him sit up.

"Are you all right?" she asked him. "What happened?"

The old man sighed heavily. "I was fording this brook when I slipped on a rock and fell," he recounted. "I've been feeling very unbalanced today."

"Accidents keep us humble," Abilene said, offering him her hand. "Are you hurt?"

"I don't need to be humble," the old man scoffed. "I'm a doctor, for God's sake." He lifted the leg of his trousers, scowled at the plum-colored bruise on his shin, and then scoured the rest of his body for injuries. At the end of his impromptu self-evaluation, he adjusted his tricornered hat and grimaced. "If that's the worst of it, I'll manage," he assured her.

But as the breeze ruffled his wispy hairline, Abilene noticed a splotch of dark purple peeking out from beneath his hat. The doctor took it off at her request, revealing a nasty bump protruding from his forehead. He pressed it deliberately and winced. "I'll manage," he said again. "But you, on the other hand—I imagine you would've snapped like a twig if you'd taken the same fall!"

Abilene took pity on the old doctor, despite his obvious lack of modesty. She left him for a moment, scanning the nearby underbrush intently. In no time, her eyes settled on a little yellow flower among the drooping ferns. She tore a few leaves from the base of the stem and returned to the doctor's side.

"What's *that*?" he demanded, eying her distastefully.

"Something to help with the bruising," she replied, chewing the leaves thoroughly. She deposited the astringent paste into her palm and held it out for the doctor to see. "It's called arnica," she told him. "The healers in my village use it. It'll soothe the tenderness and speed up the healing. Trust me."

The doctor wrinkled his nose at the leaf-paste. "So primitive," he shuddered. "I'd feel much safer using one of the treatments in my medical bag." He felt the empty ground around him and sighed. "Help me find it, will you? I must've dropped it when I fell."

Somewhat offended, Abilene smeared the dollop of paste onto a flat stone and reluctantly wandered along the riverbank. She located the sopping bag with ease and dropped it into the doctor's lap.

"Thank heavens!" he exclaimed, clutching the bag to his chest as though reunited with a lost child. "Now, let's see..."

He dumped its soaked contents onto the ground and rummaged through them with a frown. "Well," he huffed, "how unfortunate."

"What is it?"

"It looks like most of my supplies—including my pain-reliever tonic—was swept away." He picked through the cracked vials, crestfallen, and seized a handful of muddy gauze with a *squelch.* "Hopeless, so hopeless..."

Abilene pushed the arnica paste toward him gently. "It works," she insisted. "Trust me."

"Trust a savage with medical care? Not a chance!" The doctor appeared insulted. "I'd be better off dead!"

Abilene took a deep breath and pointed to the heap of soiled gauze. "Listen," she said. "Let me wash that out and dress up those bruises. You'll feel better after, I promise."

But the doctor pushed the paste away, repulsed. "I don't need that slop or your uncouth advice," he said. "All I need is a blade to set things right."

Abilene blinked. "A blade?"

"Yes, you foolish girl, a blade. A proper blade, too—not some crudely-assembled hatchet."

"What can a blade do that arnica can't?"

"A blade is a sophisticated medical instrument," the doctor said sharply. "That paste could be poison, for all I know."

"It's not poison," Abilene sighed. "It's a remedy, I told you."

"It's repugnant," the doctor retorted, "and I don't want it." He felt around on his belt and drew a stubby knife from a faded sheath. "Sophistication," he mused, admiring its tarnished surface. "That's something you savages know nothing about."

Abilene watched silently as the doctor carefully pulled up his sleeves and extended one of his arms. "A blade is the only thing that can rectify this humorous imbalance," he continued, making a fist. "It draws out the bad blood and restores the peace."

Abilene watched him warily. "I don't know about that," she said.

"You're a savage," the doctor jeered. "You don't know about anything." He raised the knife with a deep breath and then very deliberately sliced the fattest vein in his forearm.

Abilene gasped as blood spouted from the severed vein, staring in nauseous shock as the doctor groaned and clenched his fist. "That's it," he murmured. "I can feel the balance returning."

"Are you insane?" she cried.

The doctor appeared not to hear her. "Very good," he whispered, setting the knife down in the red puddle rapidly forming around him. He eased himself onto his back, bloody arm still spurting, and closed his eyes. He was turning pale as quickly as Abilene was turning green.

She departed at once, hurrying down the trail as quickly as she could. *I'll never understand,* she thought, *and that's fine by me.*

CHAPTER SIX

The trail rounded a bend and emerged in a clearing of cut down trees. It looked like the scene of a massacre. Crumpled leaves and severed limbs lay strewn about the forest floor, which was coated in trampled white dust. Scores of stumps gazed up at Abilene somberly. Her eyes rested upon the bones of the fallen, stacked nearby in a neat pyramid. A sap-stained axe, undoubtedly the property of a Christian, was propped up against the pile. She expected nothing less.

As she surveyed the carnage, she remembered the words of her mother. *It is better to plant a tree out of goodwill,* she often said, *than to fell one out of spite.*

Abilene frowned. She thought about the learned man, the hunter, and the old doctor. During her encounter with each of them, she had planted a tree that was doomed to die. It was hard work—why had she wasted the effort? What difference had any of it made? She could plant an entire forest of trees, and some axe-wielding Christian would soon come along to chop it down. Her attempts at sowing goodwill would always be met with spite.

To her left, a branch snapped. Her gaze darted from the clearing and gradually discerned a length of rope tied around two trees. Draped over this thin demarcation was a miscellany of wrinkled shirts, damp trousers, and puffy gowns. She detected movement at one end of the rope—a woman in a coif was pinning more clothes to her billowing barrier. She glanced timidly at Abilene, then back at the line.

"Hello," said Abilene, approaching the woman curiously.

The woman started with a small squeak. "Good heavens!" she gasped. "You frightened me!"

"Sorry," said Abilene, puzzled. "I thought you saw me."

"I've been up since sunrise, so I assumed I was seeing things," the woman replied, smoothing down her dress and tucking a loose strand of hair beneath her coif.

"So have I," Abilene said, recalling the brilliant spectacle with a smile. "Did you see it this morning? It was absolutely beautiful!"

"I had no time!" the woman said.

"No time?"

"No, none at all!" the woman said. "I had to tend to the fire—quietly, of course, so as to not wake my husband. I tiptoed out to the barn and milked the cow, fed the hens, and collected eggs for breakfast. Then, I crept back into the house to boil a cauldron of water for my husband's morning bath—he likes to bathe before he eats, you know. I set out his clothes at the foot of our bed and went down to the river to wash the laundry. Now, I'm hanging it up to dry, and once I finish, I'll go back to the house to cook my husband's breakfast. He likes it to be on the table for him when he finishes his bath. He's a wonderful man—he knows just what he likes and he loves me with all his heart."

Abilene nodded. "You're a very busy person."

The woman grinned exultantly. "Yes, I am!"

"I've been hiking since sunrise," Abilene said. "I'm headed north."

The woman placed a hand on her chest in shock. "You're so brave! Your husband must be even braver. Big, burly, and bearded—I know just the type," she said with a wink.

Abilene laughed. "I don't have a husband," she said. In her village, marriage came long after the Rambling.

"Silly me," the woman said. "Your brother, then!" She craned her neck past Abilene, peering down the trail. "How far back is he? I'm eager to meet him!"

Again, Abilene laughed. "I don't have a brother, either," she said. "I'm hiking alone."

The woman giggled—albeit with restraint, for fear of acting unladylike. When she composed herself, she noticed Abilene's earnest expression and raised an eyebrow. "Wait...are you telling the truth?"

"Of course."

She immediately looked sympathetic. "You poor, lost soul," she said gravely.

"What do you mean?"

"You're one of them, aren't you? I mean, you're really one of them, aren't you?"

"A what?"

The woman looked around, as though afraid that her husband might hear. "A savage?" she whispered.

"I'm Pax. I come from a village by the sea." Abilene faltered, taking note of the woman's blank face. "My name is Abilene," she said instead.

The woman curtsied. "Mrs. John Torvus," she said. Her gaze flitted to the trail again. "You're really out here on your own, then?"

"Yes," Abilene said, "and I love it. It's very peaceful."

"Peaceful?" Mrs. Torvus made a face. "It's dangerous! You're a fool for wandering out here alone!"

Abilene sighed, thinking halfheartedly of her past trailside encounters. "A lot of people tell me that," she said.

"That doesn't surprise me," Mrs. Torvus said. She stared at Abilene as so many others had done. "The woods are no place for a woman."

Abilene narrowed her eyes. "But you're out here, too—alone, just the same as I am."

"Yes, but I'd never go anywhere without my husband nearby to protect me!"

Abilene shrugged. "I suppose that's where you and I are different."

Mrs. Torvus nodded, already having lost interest in their conversation. She was surveying Abilene's deerskin dress, eying her with the air of a hen sizing up an odd-looking insect. She appeared to be trying to determine whether the girl before her was a moth or a butterfly. "So primitive, so simple," she muttered to herself. She scrutinized Abilene's scallop shell necklace. "This is nice," she admitted.

"I think so, too," Abilene said. "My mother gave it to me."

"That's very sweet," Mrs. Torvus said. "But I'm afraid it's nothing compared to this." She lifted her chin so that Abilene could see her own necklace: a gleaming chunk of transparent stone suspended from a silver chain.

"That's a pretty rock," Abilene agreed, although she was secretly never impressed by shiny stones. She much preferred the shimmering waves or the dazzling glow of the setting sun.

"A rock? This is hardly a rock!" exclaimed Mrs. Torvus. "Don't you know a diamond when you see one, you silly girl?"

Abilene was vaguely reminded of her debate with the learned man. "Right," she said, avoiding the imminent argument. "It's very nice. Where did you get it?"

"My husband bought it for me as a wedding present. That's how he shows his love, you know. Isn't he just the sweetest man alive?" Mrs. Torvus smirked. "Do you know how much this diamond costed him?"

Abilene shrugged. She really didn't care.

"Well, far more than that shell. More than your entire village, I'm sure!" She swelled with joy over the little diamond hanging from her neck. "I don't know of a more romantic gesture!"

Again, Abilene shrugged. She wasn't quite sure what to say.

Mrs. Torvus pursed her lips, silently reaching a verdict. She regarded the moth before her spitefully. "You're really not much of a woman, are you?"

They were interrupted by a thunderous shout that came from the direction of the woman's house:

"HANNAH!"

Immediately, Mrs. Torvus froze like a child caught in the act. There was a boisterous crashing, like the sound of a bear bounding through the underbrush, and a fuming man with a boulder of a stomach lumbered into view.

"John, darling," she stammered. "You're out of your bath."

"You're damned right I am!" John Torvus growled. "And I'm starving! How long does it take to hang the damned wash?"

"Not long, I—"

"Not long? Not long?" he roared. "I sat in that tub so long the water got cold and the suds disappeared! Come make my breakfast, woman! It's not going to make itself!"

"I'm sorry," Mrs. Torvus demurred, fumbling with her diamond necklace. "I'm almost done hanging the wash—I promise."

"Well hurry up, you lazy bitch! What are you doing out here, talking to the damned trees?"

Abilene held her breath. Mrs. Torvus was silent.

John Torvus clawed at the clothesline irritably before storming back to his house. Abilene stared. She'd never laid eyes on a more contemptible man.

As her husband's heavy footfalls faded away, Mrs. Torvus wiped tears from her cheeks. She was trembling. "He's right, you know," she whimpered at last. "I am lazy. I knew I had work to do and I let myself get distracted."

Abilene stared at her in disbelief. "Do you always let him treat you like that?"

She nodded, clasping her necklace in her fist. "I need his direction. Sometimes I feel lost, but he helps me back onto the right path again with his love." She drew in a quivering breath, smiling back in the direction of his house. "I don't know what I would do without that man..."

Abilene could think of a lot of things.

Mrs. Torvus resumed hanging clothes from her rope demarcation. "Now, leave me alone," she sniffed. "I can't have you distracting me."

"I understand," Abilene said, even though she really didn't. She glanced at the trail, pinpointing her next blaze amid the foliage. She turned to go, but found herself unwilling to leave without first speaking the truth. "Hannah?"

Mrs. Torvus had occupied herself with the diamond in her grasp. She didn't answer.

"You're worth more than that piece of rock." The words left her lips with the unexpected grace of a moth in flight.

Mrs. Torvus chose not to correct her, or maybe she didn't hear. Abilene was too far down the trail to tell.

CHAPTER SEVEN

You're really not much of a woman, are you?

The bleating voice of Mrs. Torvus reverberated throughout Abilene's conscience. She cringed at the punctuated disgust in the sentence. It wasn't a question at all—it was a statement, an assertion, a condescending fact. The insult stung like the slap of a porcupine's tail. Abilene had survived the thrashing, but it had left her bristling with a dozen lingering barbs.

Are you? Are you? Are you? The echo was unrelenting.

I am! she shouted back. But soon, a small voice in the back of her mind spoke up fearfully. *Are you?* it wondered.

Am I? Abilene repeated, beginning to doubt herself.

She found herself at the bottom of yet another uphill struggle, staring up a steep chute of dark and slippery rock. She inhaled deeply and took her first step toward the top.

She was a woman—wasn't she? What did it matter that she couldn't sew or prepare a man's breakfast? If her shortcomings lengthened the distance between her and a man like John Torvus, she was hardly disappointed. She thought sadly of Mrs. Torvus, of her timid demeanor and servile relationship with her brutish husband. If that was what it meant to be a woman, she didn't want to be one at all.

Abilene trekked up the slope, grasping absentmindedly at her scallop shell necklace. As she traced its curves with her weary fingers, she remembered her mother with a smile. She was a real woman, strong and undaunted in the face of adversity. There was unparalleled wisdom and confidence in her lunar eyes. Independence and rationality surrounded her presence.

She had learned nearly all she knew from her mother, especially how to fish. Given their village's close proximity to the ocean, fishing was an essential part of Pax life. As a girl, her mother had taught her how to render a fishing hook from a shard of bone and had shown her how to weave a net from resilient marsh grasses. The two of them often accompanied the Pax fishermen on their weekly seafaring excursions. During low tide, they would comb the craggy coves with nets strung between their canoes. During high tide, when the ocean gushed into the reed-choked estuaries, they would cast their lines into the shallows until the great flood retreated. Then, after a long day out on the water, their fish-laden canoes would be hauled ashore by countless pairs of waiting hands.

On one occasion, Abilene recalled their modest fleet of fishermen had returned home with a remarkable bounty of fish. They were in the midst of lugging their swollen nets up the shore when she observed a throng of Christians emerging from the marsh. They were not smiling.

Their leader was clad in a muddy waistcoat and a tricornered hat. A long saber dangled from his hip. "Hold it!" he barked. "Hold it right there!"

Abilene and the other Pax fishermen stopped, setting their nets down on the sand.

"I don't know what you think you're doing," the man snarled, coming to a halt before them.

Abilene's mother grasped her net firmly and met the man with a levelheaded gaze. "I think it's pretty clear, Captain Armand," she said. "We're hauling in today's catch."

Captain Armand jabbed a calloused finger at her bulging net of fish. "Half of that belongs to us."

"That's a bold claim," she remarked. "Especially considering neither you nor your men helped us catch any of it."

"You ought to know, savage," Captain Armand said, nostrils flaring, "that my men and I have been watching you all day. We saw everything."

Abilene's mother smirked. "Perhaps you would've had better luck if you had been watching your nets instead."

The captain scowled. "It had nothing to do with luck."

"Say what you will," Abilene's mother said, "but at the end of the day, our hands are full and yours are empty."

"Not for long," Captain Armand snapped. "We watched you pull in those fish from *our* waters. Half of them belong to us."

Abilene's mother rolled her eyes. "We've already debated this," she said. "The sea is as wild as the wind or the clouds or the rain. It cannot be contained to a border."

"It can, and it is," Captain Armand said.

"That's ridiculous."

"What's ridiculous," he fumed, "is your refusal to adhere to the rules of our fishing treaty. Everything north of Bound Rock belongs to us."

Abilene's mother frowned. "Bound Rock?"

"Yes, you incompetent heathen, Bound Rock!"

"I can't say I've ever heard of Bound Rock." She turned to the rest of the Pax fishing party, who shook their heads. "I'm afraid none of us have."

Captain Armand narrowed his eyes. "Is that so?"

She nodded. "Where is it, exactly?"

He drew his saber indignantly, thrusting its point at the horizon. "There," he said. "About a mile out."

Abilene followed the path of the sword, eyes settling on a tiny speck of rock protruding above the waves. She identified it immediately, albeit by a different name.

Her mother shaded her squinting eyes from the sun. "That's not Bound Rock," she said.

"What are you talking about?" Captain Armand cried. "Of course, it is!"

"No, it isn't," she said. "That's Turtleback Rock. It's marked the best fishing spot on the coast for generations."

"It *was* Turtleback Rock," Captain Armand corrected her. "It was rechristened after the signing of our treaty."

Abilene's mother sighed. "Tell me, Captain, are you familiar with the creatures that slither about on their bellies and bite those who wander too close?"

"Snakes?" he said. "Of course, I am."

"Well," Abilene's mother said, "what if I were to point at a snake and call it an owl. Would it still be a snake?"

"Yes," said Captain Armand. "An incorrectly-labeled snake, but still a snake."

"What if I were to call it a frog instead? Would it still be a snake?"

"I don't see why not."

"And if I called it a snail, a fish, or a salamander?"

"You're pushing the bounds of your stupidity! It would still be a snake!"

"What if," Abilene's mother said, "I was to capture one of these creatures, dress it up in a hat and a waistcoat, and give it a cross necklace? Would you still call it a snake?"

"Enough of this!" Captain Armand hissed, brandishing his saber impatiently. "The terms of our treaty still stand!"

"If that's the case," Abilene's mother said, "then we're sure to have many more meetings like this."

"Oh, are we?"

"Without a doubt, Captain."

"And why is that, savage?"

"Because," Abilene's mother said, "whoever wrote the treaty clearly didn't know that Turtleback Rock only reveals its back during high tide."

"That hardly makes any difference," Captain Armand scoffed.

"But it does," Abilene's mother said. "While we fished, there was no boundary to cross."

"Stupid woman! The boundary doesn't cease to be with the changing tides!"

"Apparently, it does," she countered coolly. "But as you say, the terms of our treaty still stand."

Captain Armand blinked, outmaneuvered in front of his men. He glared at Abilene's mother, then seemed to remember the sword in his hand. "No matter," he sneered, leveling the blade at her face. "We'll take half of your catch just the same."

Abilene and the other Pax fishermen leapt to her defense, fists raised. A few of the Christians drew knives from their belts. Captain Armand grinned. "Half of your catch," he repeated, nudging one of the nets with his boot.

An unprecedented combination of fear and defiance compelled Abilene to stand her ground. She held her breath as the other fishermen, who had planted themselves in front of their nets, refused to budge.

Captain Armand slashed at the air impatiently, then once more pointed his sword at Abilene's mother. "Now!" he barked.

She stared back at him, unscathed. "No."

"Filthy savage," he spat, pressing the tip of his saber into her cheek.

Abilene's mother did not flinch, did not turn away. Her lunar eyes flashed. "Are you going to kill me, Captain?" she asked quietly. "Are you going to kill an unarmed woman over a sack of fish?"

Captain Armand was still for a moment, holding his sword steadily. Then, suddenly, a flicker of guilt softened his seething face and his arm wavered. He spat on the sand bitterly, then lowered his saber and backed away. Wearily, he turned on his heel and told his men to sheath their knives.

Abilene's mother wiped a droplet of blood from her cheek as the Christians stalked back to the marsh. She watched them go, then took a deep breath and resumed dragging her net up the shore. Abilene and the others stared after her, awestruck, until the wind shook them from their stupor and hastened them to join her.

CHAPTER EIGHT

The sun was hanging low in the sky when Abilene ventured off-trail and made for the riverside, smiling as she unwound her sinew fishing line from her waist. She enjoyed the nightly battle of wits between her and her dinner, the strategic method of obtaining food that surged through her people's history. Her vitality didn't rest on some hatchet or bow, but instead on the tenacity of her line.

She reached the bank and tied one end of her line around her ankle, setting her aim on the swirling eddies. She flicked her wrist, sending the bone hook arcing through the air. It disappeared into the water soundlessly.

A few minutes passed before she felt the telltale tugging on her line. She yanked back sharply, gave the line some slack, and then pulled a wriggling salmon ashore. She cast again and again, reeling in two others in quick succession. Abilene laid the fish in a row, admiring the way the sinking sun played along their luminescent scales.

She gradually became aware of a splashing commotion across the river. Her curious gaze fell upon a bearded man in a long robe wading about in the shallows. He was scanning the water intently, his makeshift net poised. Every now and then he would bring it crashing down into the water, scooping around frantically—only to bring it back up again, empty. His face grew even more anguished with each failed attempt.

Abilene took pity on him. Fishing with a net was far more difficult than fishing with a hook and line. She considered taking her three fish and leaving the man to his floundering failures, but something halted her. She urged her feet to move, but they wouldn't budge. She had to help him. He would turn her away if he was anything like the other Christians she had encountered, but she couldn't leave him without at least trying her luck.

She crossed the river, traversing the golden boundary with caution. The man raised his head as she approached. Abilene studied him with interest. His gangly figure was draped in a threadbare cloak that reached his bloodied shins. A tumultuous thicket of brown hair and a matted beard framed his bright blue eyes. A small wooden cross hung meekly from a thin cord around his neck. He was a wild man—an emaciated brown bear with an inquisitive stare.

"Have you had much luck?" she asked him.

The man shook his head. "I've been vying for the same fish for an hour. I think it's my net." He held it aloft. It was a crude thing, a two-pronged branch supplemented by a hurried cross-hatching of riverside grasses.

Abilene pursed her lips. "I could give it a try," she offered.

To her surprise, the man handed her the net. "Good luck," he said, staring into the shallows with a furrowed brow.

She waded into the water slowly. Above the pebbled riverbed, she spotted a plucky little minnow zigzagging about gleefully. In the age-old game of predator and prey, it was blithefully prevailing. *Not for long*, Abilene mused. She took note of its swimming pattern carefully, her net darkening the water like the shadow of an approaching eclipse, and struck swiftly.

The man searched the water eagerly, squinting through the murky gloom with a fading grin. "Ah well," he said. "It looks like the little fellow outsmarted us both."

But Abilene beamed, cupping her hand against the net. The minnow squirmed between her fingers.

The man's grin returned in an instant. "You did it!" he exclaimed. "Excellent!" She deposited the fish into his grateful hands. The minnow, finally accepting defeat, ceased resisting.

She admired his net. It was crude, but there was something familiar about its construction. It bore a peculiar resemblance to the nets that the fishermen of her village used. "Where did you get this?" she wondered aloud.

"I built it myself," the man said proudly. "I'm rather pleased with it, too—although I'll admit the netting is a little weak. Marsh grasses work much better."

"You've made these before?"

"A few times. Haven't had much practice with them, though. I'm not much of a fisherman." He grinned sheepishly. "This was my first attempt in a while. Up until now, I've sustained myself off of pinecones and dandelion greens."

Abilene was impressed. "That's not much," she said.

"I don't need much. I'm a simple man."

"You mentioned marsh grasses," she recalled. "Where are you from?"

"I was raised in a small village beside the sea."

Her heart leaped. "Really? So was I."

The man examined her closely and his eyes grew brighter with realization. "You live on the other side of the marsh, don't you?"

Abilene nodded, silently bracing herself for his imminent condescension.

"I can't say I didn't suspect it from the beginning," the man admitted. "The woman who taught me how to weave a fishing net wore a dress quite similar to yours. She was endlessly generous, even when I realize now that I did very little to return her kind gesture." He tugged at his beard pensively. "I've always found it rather curious that we look upon your people with so much disdain. It's a shame, really."

Abilene was speechless. Immediately, she focused on the cross dangling from his neck. "What's the significance of your necklace?" she inquired.

The man patted the simple pendant. "It reminds me of who I am."

"And who are you?"

"I'm a Man of God," he replied humbly. "And you, sister? What do you call yourself?"

"I'm Abilene."

"It's a pleasure to meet you, Abilene," the Man of God said. "I see you wear a necklace, too."

She held her scallop shell in her palm. "Its purpose is the same as yours," she said. "As we branch out, it's essential that we remember our roots."

The Man of God smiled. "I like that. Is that from the scripture?"

She shook her head. "It's an old Pax saying."

"Pax," he repeated interestedly. "That's a fine name, but I'm sure you're aware that my Christian kinsmen insist on calling you something different. They label you a savage just the same way they label me a lunatic. But that hardly matters," he said with a wave of his hand. "We are who we are, regardless of what they choose to call us."

"Very true," Abilene said, dumbfounded. She really didn't know what to make of this strange man. He was, without a doubt, the most unchristian Christian she had ever met. Her attention turned to the blackening sky. "We'd best light a fire," she advised, beckoning for him to follow her back across the river. "These fish are no good to us raw."

The Man of God chuckled at the minnow in his grasp. "This little fellow isn't much of a contribution," he acknowledged, "but I'd be happy to share some of my bread and wine."

Abilene assured him that his contribution was sufficient. She would have shared her food with him even if he had nothing to offer her in return. They crossed the river and selected a spot for the fire on the opposing bank. The Man of God gathered sticks from the underbrush while Abilene cleaned their fish with a sharp rock. They assembled a wooden pyramid together, and with a clap of two river stones, Abilene provided the spark. Soon enough, the two sat alongside a growing blaze that burned brightly in the face of the impending night.

Abilene prodded the fire meditatively, clearing a space among the embers for the fish. She placed the pink fillets at the base of the flames; they settled over the glimmering coals with a low hiss. She sensed the Man of God's gaze upon her and registered that he was contemplating her necklace.

"We're so far from home," he said. "Further and further we walk, led by the Spirit into the wilderness."

He really was a peculiar man. "I take it you're walking this trail alone?" she asked.

"I am," he said. "On this solitary exodus, God is my only companion."

"I'm hiking alone, too," she said.

"Ah," the Man of God said. "On a mountain-bound pilgrimage of your own?"

"I suppose," Abilene said. "This journey is something of a tradition in my village. I'm rambling to the summit of the highest peak."

"It seems we share a destination," observed the Man of God.

"Really?" said Abilene, surprised. "I didn't think Christians cared much for the mountains."

"Many don't," he admitted. "But I'm not sure why. The mountains are a sacred, magnificent place. Abraham, Moses, Joshua, Elijah, Jesus—each of them found peace atop mountain peaks. I hope to do the same."

"I'm assuming those men are your friends?"

"You could say that," the Man of God replied.

Abilene flipped the pieces of fish, which sizzled and smoked slightly. "I have to ask," she said, surveying his smiling face. "Why do your people call you a lunatic?"

He laughed. "I'm certain a large part of it has to do with the way I dress," he said, referring to his shabby robe and wild hair.

"There must be more to it than that," she insisted.

"Well, to put it plainly, they label me a lunatic for the same reason they label you a savage."

"What's that?" she said.

"Because I'm different." The Man of God shrugged. "That's the best answer I have."

Abilene thought of the learned man, Mrs. Torvus, and the other unpleasant Christians she had met on the trail. The Man of God was right—he was nothing like them. "Is it so bad to be different?" she said.

"I suppose not," the Man of God said thoughtfully. He drew a leather flask and a loaf of bread from his robe, then took a sip from the flask before offering it to Abilene.

She accepted it and drank. The stinging liquid numbed her mouth. It was dry, ancient, and foreign—and yet she liked it. It was as simultaneously harsh and pleasing as the truth.

"The churchmen in my village call these the body and blood," the Man of God explained, tearing her off a chunk of the loaf.

Abilene chewed serenely. "They taste like bread and wine to me."

"Yes, but—oh, never mind. We eat in your Spirit, Lord," he said, making a funny gesture with his hand over his face and chest.

"What was that?" Abilene asked him.

"The sign of the cross," he said. "It's a sort of prayer, a silent declaration of my faith. It's a way of showing thanks to God."

"Your faith?"

"Yes, my commitment to the beliefs that make me a Christian."

"I don't understand," Abilene said. She had long assumed the word "Christian" referred to an ancient homeland.

The Man of God took a deep breath. "Long ago, in a faraway land," he started, "a child was born to a virgin. It is said He was God's son on Earth, both human and divine. Forgive me," he said, noting Abilene's confused expression. "It's a fanciful tale, but it is within this story that our truth resides."

"Oh, of course," she said. "Please continue."

"In time," the Man of God went on, "this child grew into a man. He was a benevolent man, virtuous and charitable in every endeavor. He healed the sick, nourished the starved, gave to the poor, and counseled the ignorant. This man was capable of wonderful things—miracles of the purest design. He is said to have walked on water, cured blindness, and even brought a man back from the dead."

Abilene was intrigued. "What happened to him?"

"He encountered fierce adversity, but persevered with God's guidance and preached compassion to all he met. But alas, He was betrayed by one of his followers. He was captured, tortured, nailed to a cross, and left to die." The Man of God touched his little wooden crucifix broodingly. "He died in the name of injustice so that humanity, in turn, could be saved."

"That's terrible," Abilene said solemnly.

"It was," agreed the Man of God. "The man's followers mourned the loss of their friend. They visited His tomb to properly tend to His body, but found the chamber empty. All that remained of Him were the garments in which He was interred."

"You're suggesting he rose from the dead," she gathered, wide-eyed.

"Precisely," said the Man of God.

"But...how?"

His blue eyes twinkled in the firelight. "God's grace is a beautiful, mysterious thing."

"Impossible..."

"So it would seem," he confessed. "But the scripture does not lie."

Abilene stared into the fire, nonplussed. "Who was this man?" she asked.

"We call him Christ."

She finally glimpsed the truth. "Your people bear his name."

The Man of God nodded. "And some of us follow in His footsteps."

"You mean you worship him?"

"We revere him for His sacrifice. Through Him, we can grow closer to God."

"That's very interesting," Abilene said.

The Man of God eyed her amusedly.

"What?"

"You've listened, but you don't believe."

"I don't need to believe to understand."

"True," the Man of God concurred. "But doesn't it bother you that you don't believe?"

Abilene shook her head.

"May I ask why?"

"I stand by my beliefs," she said simply. "Just as you stand by yours."

The Man of God stroked his beard reticently.

"But," Abilene added, "through our combined perspectives, I can see much more clearly. After all—a bird cannot fly without both of its wings and all of its feathers." She skewered the charred fillets, lifting them from the embers and setting them on a flat stone to cool. She then fed a sizeable log to the flames, which flickered ravenously in response.

The Man of God gazed into the fire expressionlessly.

"What are you thinking?" Abilene asked, fearing she had angered him.

"Just...remembering my roots," he said.

"We can't change where we've been," Abilene said, recalling her mother's words. "But we can use those experiences to plot our course on the journey ahead."

"A sage observation, sister," said the Man of God. "Forward is the best direction a person can move."

She handed him a skewered fillet and took a bite from her own. The smoky taste consoled her growling stomach.

The Man of God ate reservedly, eyes closed. "I was raised to believe that the church was the epitome of God's word, a perfect representation of the scripture," he said suddenly. "But it isn't. A few months ago, I discovered I was wrong."

Abilene looked up from her fish. "What do you mean?"

"The scripture teaches tolerance," he said, "and yet the church defines heresy and persecutes nonbelievers. The scripture teaches generosity, yet the church grows fat on tithe. The scripture teaches equality, yet the church suppresses women in favor of men." His tone grew increasingly pained; every word seemed to torment his conscience. "And the most glaring hypocrisy of them all," he seethed. "The church claims descendancy from Peter, but disregards the ideals of an apostolic life."

"An apostolic life?"

"The manner in which Christ and His followers lived," the Man of God explained. "A lifestyle of voluntary poverty, of humility. The path of the righteous is defined by the Gospels, and yet I'm scorned by the priest in my village for my appearance. Because I'm not inclined to dress in white, to adorn myself with a bejeweled crucifix, or to look down at my equals from a horse's back."

"I don't see why you would be," Abilene said. It all seemed very contradictory to her.

The Man of God continued, expelling the words in a frenzy as though they were scalding his mouth. "I consulted the priest about the inconsistencies in church practices, pointing to the Gospels as evidence for my concern. But he sent me away, told me not to trifle myself with the matters of the church. I felt disillusioned, betrayed. I began telling others about the church's hypocrisies. To most, I was a lunatic—but I would much rather be a lunatic than a blind believer." The fire popped and sparked, throwing shadows over his face. "When the priest received word of my preaching, he rebuked me for my defiance and forbade me from spreading the truth." He trembled ardently. "Seeing there was no convincing him, I renounced my affiliation with the church."

Abilene admired his tenacity. "I can't imagine the priest liked that very much," she said.

"He was livid," the Man of God spat. "He rallied the village garrison and presented me with my fate: I would leave, or I would die. And so, I left it all behind. The woods were a welcome sanctuary."

"They have that effect," Abilene agreed. "Does that mean you're hiking into exile?"

"I like to think I'm following the route that I was meant to follow," the Man of God said. "I'm not accustomed to this life, but I'm eager to make it my own. On the first night away from my village, I was blessed by a vision of God's path for me. In a dream, I witnessed a lamb wandering about at the summit of an enormous mountain. I believe it was the highest peak in the land."

"Spero," she whispered in awe. "It sounds like we're both destined to ramble."

"It's no mistake that our paths have crossed, Abilene. With God as our shepherd, we will answer the mountain's call."

"With God as *your* shepherd," she corrected him delicately. "The trail is my guide."

His blue eyes gleamed. "Your resolve is everlasting," he said. "I'm beginning to believe that you and I aren't so different."

Abilene licked her fingers clean of fish. "What makes you say that?"

"As a heretic," he said, "I am assailed for my beliefs. As a heathen, you are ridiculed for yours. Together, we represent both sides of an unfortunate reality."

She knew he was right. "A bird cannot fly without both of its wings and all of its feathers," she concluded, tossing her skewer to the flames.

As the Man of God studied her silently, a smile slowly surfaced from beneath his beard.

"What is it?" she asked him.

"Call me a lunatic," he said, "but one day, I'd like to see that bird fly."

She smiled back, and the fire burned brighter. "So would I."

CHAPTER NINE

Another week came and went. Abilene relived the cycle, but this time with a companion: rise, ramble, rest, then repeat. Step by step, further and further down the ridgeline, closer and closer to the slopes of Spero. Every step reminded her of how far she was from home—but a quick glance down at her scallop shell refocused her thoughts on the trail ahead. The two of them hiked on with eager strides.

They followed the trail out of the dark forest and into the morning sunlight. It wove like a sallow ribbon through a mountainside meadow that swept over the leeward side of the ridge. Among the waist-high grass, Abilene noted the flat slabs of white-blazed rock that marked their way. They resembled the backs of sleeping turtles, and she stepped over them carefully, the Man of God trailing behind her. The wind rushed down the slope, causing the grass to ripple around them. Crickets and cicadas buzzed shrilly as the sun struggled through the clouds overhead.

Over the meadow, a spectacular vista provided a constant backdrop: mountains upon mountains, a sea of them rising and falling amid the emerald expanse like waves. Spero, stately and gray, loomed above them all. Abilene could just make out the hair-like trail winding up to the lofty summit—their inevitable route. The end was palpable. "Beautiful," she murmured.

"Truly," the Man of God grunted. She turned to see him cradling his foot as though it were a wounded animal.

"Are you all right?" she asked.

He dismissed her concern with a grimace. "It's nothing."

Immediately, Abilene recognized the lie: the Man of God's dark red footsteps were pressed into the dew of the trodden grass. She knelt beside him and gingerly examined his foot in spite of his meager protests. Since their meeting, his beaten leather shoes had succumbed to the trail, shrinking and shriveling from his feet like an old snake skin. To Abilene's surprise, he had neither lamented their absence nor mentioned wanting to turn back. He had trudged on, albeit at a slower pace, with tight-lipped resolve. But his shoe-spawned callouses had proved no match for the trail's jagged terrain. The flesh of his soles resembled a tree hacked bare of its bark—shredded, dangling in defeat, steadily oozing blood like tears.

The Man of God pulled away. "It's nothing, I said. They'll get stronger with time."

"Not unless they're cleaned first," Abilene said flatly. Conditioning bare feet was a painful process—her own soles, scarred with scrapes and gashes, were a ready testament to that.

She perused the tall grass around them, eyes passing over swaying stalks of goldenrod and aster. Finally, she found it: a bright orange flower that beckoned to her above the rest. It looked to be a cross between a daisy and a dandelion, with narrow petals that emanated from the middle of the bud like sunrays. She pinched several of the flowers into her palm. "Marigold," she answered before he could ask. "This'll clean the cuts and help them heal. I promise."

His expression was doubtful. "Are you *absolutely* certain?"

She lifted each of her feet to show him her scarred but calloused soles.

He inhaled and puffed his cheeks. "You know better than I do," he sighed at last. "I'm trusting you."

"Good," she replied, gesturing for him to sit. The Man of God eased himself down onto the damp grass, allowing her to prop his feet up on one of the blazed rocks. Abilene mashed and ground the marigold petals beneath her fingernails, looking around for something to apply it to.

"I'll need some of your robe," she said and again, he complied. She tore the hem of it in a long strip, leaving the fabric frayed over his knees, and ripped the strip into two pieces. She smeared the pungent paste over them and pressed the makeshift bandages into the Man of God's soles. He winced as Abilene wrapped his feet, one after the other, like ragged caterpillars in crude cocoons. She knotted them tightly, patting his ankles when she finished. "Better?"

He nodded. "Thank you."

Abilene pulled him to his feet, admiring her rudimentary handiwork. "Your wisdom is a blessing, sister," he said, patting her shoulder. "Marigold...I would've never thought."

"You're the first Christian to tell me that," she said, thinking disdainfully of the old doctor.

"Really?"

"Usually, whenever I come across someone in need of help, they turn me away without a second thought. They act like I don't know what I'm talking about."

"Too many people mistake an open hand for a closed fist," the Man of God said. "They don't truly see what's in front of them. Unfortunate, isn't it?"

Abilene remembered the doctor's scornful remark that he would be better off dead than under the care of a "savage" like her. It had left a gash on her conscience that stung and festered with neglect. She felt the pain rising to the surface—all of the jeering criticisms, condescending comments, and pitied stares. "It's frustrating," she mumbled.

The Man of God was watching her curiously. "You have more to say. I can see it in your eyes."

"I just don't understand it," she said.

"Understand what?"

"Why Christians see me the way they do. According to learned men, I'm ignorant. According to hunters and doctors, I'm incapable. According to married women, I'm insufficient. To all of them, I'm inferior. Why?"

He was silent, his expression pained.

"Why?" she demanded once more.

"It's because you're different," he said at last.

Abilene blinked. She hadn't expected him to answer.

"It's because you're Pax and it's because you're a woman," he continued. "It's because you're the opposite of what they've been taught to expect, and that scares them."

"What does that matter?" she said. "You said it yourself: we are who we are, regardless of the way we're labeled."

"Labels are powerful things, Abilene. If used long enough, they create the illusion of truth. To the indoctrinated soul, you are nothing but a savage. To the shallow mind, you are nothing but a woman. By that ill-fated extension, you are an inferior being."

"*But I'm not*," she protested. "That's not the truth!"

"It may as well be," the Man of God said. "The people you've encountered have known those labels their entire lives. They knew of nothing different—until they met you."

His gait was slow and delicate, as though inspired by the fear that the trail was made of glass. He walked on his heels, clenching Abilene's arm for support. She helped him along, walking at his side.

"Where do those labels come from?" she asked.

"Oh, from a variety of things," the Man of God said. "Upbringings, opinions, experiences—the scripture, almost certainly."

"The scripture mentions my people?"

"Well, not exclusively, no. But it says a fair deal about women."

"What does it say?"

The Man of God suddenly became very interested in the view beyond. "I don't think I've ever seen something so beautiful," he said. "Have you?"

"The scripture," Abilene persisted. "What does it say?"

"It sets standards on how a woman should behave." He shielded his eyes from the sun. "Look there! I can see the trail winding up the summit of the highest peak."

"And how should a woman behave?" she pressed.

"Is it really that important?"

Abilene nodded.

He declined to meet her gaze. "According to the scripture," he said at last. "A woman should never usurp authority over a man. She should serve him and exist in silence."

His words were a sharp blow to the face. She reeled, stunned.

"That's not to say I agree with everything written in the Bible," the Man of God added hastily. "For a time, I did. But that was before I opened my eyes and left the church."

"So that's why they cast you out?" Abilene said. "Because you disagreed?"

"Because I recognized that nothing is impervious to flaws—not even God's word."

"What else does the scripture say about women?" Abilene asked miserably.

"Many things of the same nature," he confessed. "But no verdict is absolute. There is, for instance, a proverb that tells us a woman's works will praise her at the gates of God's kingdom."

"What does that mean?"

"I'd long thought it defined a woman's legacy as her family, but I've begun to reconsider. Perhaps a woman's true legacy lies instead in the fruits of her own endeavors—in the successes she has achieved herself."

A white-blazed rock embedded in the trail caught Abilene's eye. She thought of her mother and the generations of other Pax women who had rambled here before her. "I think you're right," she said. "This is my legacy—this journey. The trees I've planted, the rivers I've crossed, the mountains I've climbed. All of it."

She evaluated his expression. There was a smile buried beneath his beard. "I mean that," she said.

"I know you do," the Man of God said, and his smile surfaced. "It's a wonder why more women don't share your confidence."

"Is it, though?" Abilene countered. "Girls in your village are brought up to believe that men are their superiors. Your scripture teaches them to have faith in a lie." She faltered; the Man of God's smile had vanished. "With respect," she began anew, "how can you expect a bird to learn how to fly if it's always been told it'll never leave the ground?"

The Man of God scratched his beard ruefully. "It's lunacy," he admitted quietly.

"Then you agree?"

"Of course, I do."

She frowned. "But the scripture..."

"I know what is written in the scripture, and I resent it. Women do not exist to serve men. They exist to serve God and themselves."

"Why don't other Christians see it that way?"

"For the very same reason they view you as inferior," the Man of God said. "They adhere to the labels they've always known. They take shelter in their ignorance."

"I had a conversation with a learned man a week before meeting you," Abilene recounted halfheartedly. "He told me that for my people, ignorance was a given."

"That sounds considerably less than learned," the Man of God remarked.

"I thought it was nonsense, too," she said. "But now I wonder if there's a shred of truth in what he said. My people are bound by labels, too. I doubt many of them will believe me when I tell them I hiked willingly alongside a Christian. I wouldn't have believed myself. But is that my fault? You're the first one who's treated me as an equal, after all. If we hadn't met, I wouldn't have known any different."

"I wouldn't have, either," he agreed. "It's like you say, sister: without both of its wings and all of its feathers, a bird cannot fly."

"Exactly!"

He pursed his lips. "Are you suggesting another reason why some birds remain flightless? That their ability to learn how to fly has been hindered, perhaps?"

"Partly," she said, recalling the owlish learned man once more. "I think some birds know how to fly but are reluctant to because they'd consider it a blow to their pride. I don't understand why."

The Man of God stumbled over his cocooned feet, squeezing her arm gratefully. "That, my friend, is the crux of life. Seeing both sides is imperative, but too often we are willfully blind. The only cure to our blindness is wisdom." He looked off into the distance, toward Spero's craggy summit. "And there is wisdom to be found in high places."

Abilene regarded him fondly. There certainly was.

His figure seemed to droop at the sight of the highest peak. "There are still so many miles to walk…"

She patted his hand. "We'll walk them together," she assured him.

CHAPTER TEN

The trail wandered in and out of the forest for many miles before climbing to the top of a knoll and suddenly disappearing over the edge. The white blazes led down, down, down into a ravine. Their precarious descent was a sluggish affair marked by cautious steps and many close calls.

The base of the ravine was a welcome stretch of flat ground, where the trail weaved through a boulder field. It was an eerily quiet place, devoid of birds and trees and wind. The only sound was the faint trickling of a thin stream that had followed them down the sweeping headwalls. Through gaps in the gargantuan boulders, a wretched congregation of pale green shrubs raised their crooked arms to the sun. The ravine itself felt paralyzed, holding its breath beneath Spero's looming gaze.

When they were about midway through the ravine, they paused for lunch. The sun shone directly above their heads. With sweat running down their faces, they sought shade beside a hulking rock. The Man of God set his loaf of bread and flask of wine between them, alongside Abilene's parcel of smoked salmon. They ate in silence.

A few rocks away, Abilene noticed a scaly length of rope basking in the sunlight. It was dark green and coiled around itself in loose knots.

The Man of God saw it, too. He shivered in disgust. "Despicable creature," he spat.

She laughed. "I take it you don't like snakes?"

"I don't trust them," he said, glowering in its direction.

Abilene squinted at the sunbathing serpent. It seemed quite content with its life. "Why not?"

"Snakes are the emblem of sin." He sipped from his flask. "The scripture tells us that Man and Woman were first led into temptation by a snake's beguiling tongue."

Abilene glanced at the snake once more. It looked more benign than beguiling. "You believe that men and women should forgive each other for their mistakes, don't you?

"Of course. Forgiveness, after all, is the way of God."

"Is it then impermissible to forgive snakes for their mistakes?"

"I'm afraid so," he said with a grimace. "I don't think that was God's intention."

"Why wouldn't it be?"

"There isn't a single passage in the Bible that portrays snakes in a favorable light."

"What does that matter?" Abilene said. "You told me yourself that you don't agree with everything the Bible says."

"Even so," the Man of God said. "I have yet to meet a snake that's changed my mind." He offered her a drink from his flask. "Do you like snakes?"

She swallowed the warm wine thoughtfully. "Some of them," she said.

"Not all of them?"

"No, not all of them. But I'm willing to judge each one differently."

"Hm," the Man of God said.

"I wasn't always," Abilene confessed. "My people call Christians snakes, from time to time."

"Really? I don't blame you."

"But we always remember that our assumption could be wrong. Not all snakes are poisonous, as the old saying goes."

The Man of God tugged at his beard. "That's very insightful," he said. "But how do you know which snakes are poisonous?"

She shrugged. "It's only ever a matter of deciding the snake's true character."

He nodded toward the snake in the sun. "Any idea of his true character?"

"Lazy," she said after a pause. "And happily oblivious to our debate."

The Man of God took another swig of wine, then narrowed his eyes inquiringly. "So, Christians are known as snakes, eh?"

"Generally, yes."

"I'm fascinated to hear the story behind that."

"It's not a story, so much as it's a fact of life," Abilene said. "The Christians I've met are dishonest and sneaky. They slither into places where they don't belong and lash out when they're approached. They rename, retract, and rebuke with their forked tongues." She paused. "I hope I'm not offending you. You're not anything like them."

"Not at all," the Man of God said. "Although I know many people who speak with a forked tongue. Lost souls, all of them..." He trailed off, chuckling to himself.

"What is it?"

"I just find it ridiculous that we call your people savages," he said. "You should be violent and barbaric, but you're not. Ironically enough, I can only think of one occasion when your people fit that description."

"When was that?"

"On the sabbath day, many years ago. A Pax mob crossed the marsh, but we stopped them before they could reach the church. I remember it well."

Abilene remembered it, too. "We were going to ask if you would stop ringing the bells," she said.

He gaped at her. "You were there?"

She nodded. "The bells were keeping us from hunting. They scared the animals away."

"Those infernal bells are loud," the Man of God agreed. "But you could have just asked. There was no need to try to burn down the church."

Abilene frowned. That had never been their intention. "What are you talking about?" she said.

"The word was that you were coming to burn down the church." He looked perplexed. "You weren't?"

"No, of course not!" she said. "What would we have used to burn it down?"

"Someone said you had torches."

"Torches?" She laughed. "Why would we have needed torches in the morning?"

"Lord Almighty," the Man of God groaned, rubbing his forehead. "We thought we were repelling a raid..."

"We thought we were outrunning an army," Abilene said. "That's what it felt like, at least."

"You say that jokingly," he grimaced, "but some of us were armed—I threw rocks." He turned white. "Please tell me no one was injured."

She told him they had escaped the fray unharmed, and he sighed in relief. "Why do you ring those bells, anyway?" she asked.

"They call people to worship," the Man of God explained. "Although I agree with you: they are quite loud. Perhaps the sabbath day would feel more reverent if it commenced with silence instead."

"You don't ring them to spite us?" said Abilene, surprised.

He shook his head. "Of course not, sister. Certainly not intentionally."

She regarded his earnest eyes with pursed lips. "I admit," she said. "I expected you to be a snake just like the others."

The Man of God chuckled. "And I thought you'd be an ignorant heathen," he said with a wink. "It's always nice to be proven wrong." He raised his flask and made the sign of the cross. "We drink to your insight, Lord. To this unexpected friendship."

Abilene beamed. "To friendship."

As he drank, she noticed a dark object move by his feet. A mangy rat had emerged from a crack in the rock and was creeping toward the tendon in his heel. Its fur was matted, its worm-like tail was curled, and its scissor-like teeth were prepared to bite. She couldn't get the warning out quickly enough:

"RAT!"

There was a flash of black and a shrill squeak. The Man of God leapt up as though shocked by lightning, choking and sputtering on wine. Abilene winced, immediately straining her mind for rat bite remedies. Her silent search concluded as soon as she opened her eyes. She broke into a grin as the Man of God, collecting his wits and his breath, gawked in disbelief.

The rat was dead, firmly locked between the jaws of a particularly exultant serpent. Abilene looked to the sunlit rock. The coiled sunbather was gone. It stared up at them knowingly before tightening its grasp on the rat and slithering out of sight.

The Man of God massaged his unscathed ankle gratefully, looking after his serpentine savior. "Perhaps it's like you said," he said in hushed awe. "Perhaps not all snakes are poisonous after all..."

CHAPTER ELEVEN

They followed the trail as it switchbacked out of the ravine and broke above timberline, meandering on toward Spero. The relative absence of trees ensured an endless vista with every step. It was breathtaking: the trail, marked by quartz-topped cairns, was a ribbon draped over the back of a slumbering giant. It ambled to the base of the next mountain, a bald dome of a peak, and disappeared into the halo of clouds obscuring its summit. The wind wailed to the mountain, alerting it to their approaching presence, while the cairns tautly ushered them along.

"I have to say," the Man of God said, over the wind. "I'm still perplexed by our serpentine friend."

Abilene looked back at him over her shoulder. "What about him?"

"I suppose I expected him to be poisonous," he said. "It's nothing against him, it's just that some snakes have left a legacy of lashing out at the slightest advance."

Abilene chuckled. "That's why it's usually best to stay away."

"Without a doubt," the Man of God conceded. "But had I known his intention was not to bite me, I would have regarded him with more respect from the beginning."

They hiked on.

"Abilene," the Man of God said.

She looked back at him once more. "Yes?"

"Why do snakes bite?"

She scanned her memory and saw herself as a girl, stepping unknowingly on a scaly tail. The snake snapped at her foot; she yelped as it slithered away. "They bite when we wander too close to them," she said, cringing at the ghost of the bite wound.

"Maybe," the Man of God said. "Why else?"

She consulted the memory again, watching her younger self scour the woods for creatures to amuse her curiosity. "They bite because we're nosy."

"Possibly," he said. "Look again, more carefully."

For the third time, Abilene returned to the memory. *A bird cannot fly without both of its wings*, she thought, and instantly witnessed the incident from the snake's perspective. She saw the incoming foot and felt her serpentine heart seize up. "Fear," she said, finally understanding. "Snakes bite because they're afraid."

"Exactly!" cried the Man of God with a clap of his hands. "Afraid of what is different and afraid of what they don't understand. Afraid of a young Pax woman who knows her worth and speaks her truth with poise."

"That's why it's best to keep a distance," Abilene said. "We'll just provoke them."

"That's a risk we must be willing to take."

"What, being bitten?"

"Yes," he said. "But also, the chance that we could walk away from the encounter unharmed." He stopped mid-trail to catch his breath, bright blue eyes resting on Abilene. The trail had abandoned its level grades and had begun a winding ascent to the top of the Bald Dome. "Is it not, as your people say, better to plant a tree out of goodwill than to fell one out of spite?"

She sighed. "It would be near-impossible."

"But won't you at least try?"

"What are you suggesting?"

His gaze was sincere. "Peace," he said.

"Peace?" The word sounded foreign, like a name long neglected.

"Yes, peace."

"With the Christians?"

"I know it sounds impossible," he said, "but a new treaty must come to light. It is the will of God."

Abilene recalled the sneering faces of the Christians who had demeaned her. "You need two sides to sign a treaty," she said. "They would never agree to it."

"You'd be surprised," the Man of God said. "People are growing tired of the looming threat of war. They seek resolution, either by the pen or by the sword."

"I don't know..." Abilene exhaled. "There's just so much history, built up over years and years and years. I'm not so sure one person can mend that divide."

"I think you'll find it's not as difficult as you think," the Man of God said. "Besides, you won't be alone. I'll be with you."

She grimaced as she hiked, daunted by the sheer immensity of his proposal. "Where would we even begin?"

"At the same place where you and I began," he replied. "With a conversation. And through that conversation, understanding. Forgiveness. Peace."

"That's much easier said than done," she pointed out. "It's much easier to forgive a single mistake than a long list of them."

"As true as that may be, it is still necessary. There's little use in holding a grudge. God teaches us that much."

"A grudge develops over time," Abilene reminded him. "We forgave the first time, the second time, and maybe even the third. But after so many trampled apologies, forgiveness feels meaningless."

They trekked through wisps of cloud, which collected on their faces like iridescent gems. The Man of God's whiskers were soon bejeweled with atmospheric wealth, and he collected the twinkling droplets in his hand with a pensive pull of his beard. "Christ had much to say about the power of forgiveness," he said. "A man came to him one day, frustrated. 'Lord,' he sighed, 'how often shall my brother sin against me and I forgive him?' And do you know what Christ told him?"

Abilene shook her head.

"He told him to forgive unconditionally. No matter the severity or the frequency of the trespass, we should always find the will to forgive. Forgiveness is the strongest antidote against any snake's bite."

"I like that," said Abilene. "I like that a lot. But still..."

"You're doubtful."

"A little."

"Why?"

"It's never been done before," she said. "What makes you think we can do it?"

"What makes you think we can't?"

Again, Abilene shook her head. "It would never work. The sachem would need to see evidence of a Christian desire for peace."

"I'm not talking about the sachem," the Man of God said. "I'm talking about us. About you. You have something the sachem doesn't."

"What's that?"

"The truth," he said. "It's obvious that your bird has both of its wings and all of its feathers—all it lacks is the will to fly."

They stepped onto the summit, which lay within a pearly whirlwind of clouds. Before them, a massive cairn braved the gusting wind. A scant layer of coarse-grained soil had somehow found its way into the cracks of the bedrock and harbored a slim assortment of alpine vegetation. There were no trees in this blustery environment, and hardly any plants dared to grow higher than Abilene's ankles. A few patches of rust-colored sedge clung to the summit like the fleeting remnants of the mountain's thinning hairline.

They departed the summit relatively quickly at Abilene's suggestion that they find somewhere to camp before dark. It was a perilous descent through the fog. The sheer flank of the Bald Dome was creased and folded like elephant skin, and the two navigated the narrow ledges with breathless caution. The trail switchbacked down the crag, rounding a bend and pressing into the rock face. It left a vertical impression in the granite bluff where the light seemed to vanish. Abilene rubbed her eyes, but the mirage remained. It was a beautiful blemish, as nondescript as a pore in a giant's neck.

She inspected the cave eagerly, running her palm along the craggy walls and smiling in satisfaction. It was a shallow shelter with a drooping overhang for a ceiling and a smooth, damp floor. The Man of God peeked into the cave behind her. A quick sign of the cross signified his approval. She scavenged the barren ledges for firewood while he sank to his knees and prayed in silence. A lifeless clump of twisted shrubs was the only fuel to be found. She built the fire against the back wall of the cave, away from the wind, and lit it with some difficulty. The shadows rejoiced at her efforts, dancing in the flickering light.

The view from the cave was completely obscured by clouds, but Abilene knew full well that Spero lay just beyond. They would reach their final summit in the morning. She shook her head in quiet disbelief, letting it all sink in. A day from now, the hardest part of her Rambling would be over. It didn't feel real.

The Man of God stirred suddenly, raising his head from his prayers. With his eyes still tightly shut, he calmly notified Abilene of a man standing outside the cave.

She squinted through the gloom. "Where? I don't see anyone."

He opened his eyes. "What?"

"You just said there was a man."

His puzzled frown melted into a smile of understanding. "There's no man," he assured her. "I said 'amen.' That's how I conclude my prayers. It's an affirmation of my faith."

Abilene felt somewhat sheepish. "You pray a lot," she remarked.

"I do," he said. "I praise God for His wisdom and thank Him for all He has given me. I find comfort in His strength and ask for His guidance."

"Did you ask for guidance just now?"

The Man of God nodded. "I asked for deliverance to the top of the two highest peaks in the land."

"There are no mountains higher than Spero," Abilene pointed out.

"There is one," the Man of God said. "It's called Peace, and it's the tallest mountain of them all."

"I don't know of any defined trail leading to that summit."

"That hardly matters, sister. I have no doubt that you'll find your way."

Abilene tossed a twig into the fire. "We're bound to upset generations of expectations with our return," she mused. "We should wait to part ways until a group of fishermen comes into view, and then plant a tree right in front of them." She grinned at the thought of a speechless Captain Armand witnessing a handshake between her and the Man of God. It would be an unforgettable spectacle.

She waited for the Man of God to smile, but his gaze was concentrated on the flames. "What are you thinking?" she asked him.

"I'm thinking they would arrest us if we did that," he said quietly.

"What?"

"They would arrest us," he repeated. "They'd arrest me for being a heretic, and they'd arrest you for associating with one."

"But what about peace?"

"Heretics are obstacles to peace," the Man of God replied sadly. "And so are lunatics. I have no place in that wretched village."

The numb realization made its way to her lips. "You're not coming back."

He looked pained. "I'm sorry."

Abilene massaged her forehead, unable to conceive of the sadness she would feel if she finished her Rambling without a home to return to. She remembered her mother's embrace thankfully, then smiled at the Man of God.

"You could come back with me," she offered.

He patted her hand appreciatively. "You're too kind, sister."

"I mean it," she said. "You'll be safe among my people—I promise."

He shook his head. "I can't."

"Why not?"

"Because," the Man of God sighed, "when the priest learns that your people are sheltering a heretic, he'll have his garrison march on your village."

"Then we'll protect you," Abilene said immediately. "We'll fight back."

"And your bird will be silenced by the drums of war. All of this will have transpired for nothing."

"If that's the cost of peace, then—" His blue eyes blazed, and she fell silent.

"I won't forsake the progress we've made along this path," he said. "I'm not going back."

"Please," she begged him. "You'll be received as a wise man and a friend. Please."

"You're a kind soul," the Man of God said, "but my will is strong." He tried to pat her hand again, but she pulled away. "I'm sorry."

Abilene drew her knees to her chest and there rested her head. "I understand," she mumbled. The ensuing silence was punctuated by the crackling fire.

The Man of God inhaled slowly. "Sister?"

"Yes?"

"Will you promise me something?"

"What?"

"You don't have to forgive me—I realize that may be difficult. But promise me you'll make every effort to forgive the other Christians in my village. Forgiveness is the only way to peace. Promise me you'll forgive, and that you'll let your bird fly."

Abilene exhaled through her nostrils. "All of them?"

"Yes. Each and every label-obsessed soul."

She raised an eyebrow. "Even that horrible priest?"

"Even that horrible priest," he affirmed unflinchingly.

"I don't know..."

"You must."

"How can you say they deserve forgiveness if they won't even forgive you?"

The Man of God didn't say anything.

"I know it's important to forgive," she said. "But I don't know if I can. They *exiled* you. I'm sure that's something not even you can forgive."

"I can and I have," he said.

"I don't believe you."

"I forgive them," the Man of God repeated.

"*How?*" she demanded.

He stared into the fire contemplatively. "When someone makes an enemy of you, it's instinct to fight back. But what good is it to wage war if neither side is willing to apologize? If neither side is willing to understand the other? The only outcome is ruin. Yes, conflicts often result in spilt blood, but they end the same way—with compromise and peace. Sooner or later, forgiveness must prevail."

"So, you forgive them," Abilene said frustratedly, "but they don't forgive you. What difference does it make?"

"It makes *all* the difference!" the Man of God said. "Regardless of whether or not they welcome my ideas or forgive me for my heresy, I'm at ease knowing I've offered my contribution to peace. As your people say, it is better to plant a tree out of goodwill..."

"...than to fell one out of spite," Abilene finished begrudgingly. He was right. The old axiom held true.

"So," he said with a smile. "Do you promise to plant a tree, even in the name of my deplorable village?"

"I do," she said at last. "But I still wish you'd be there with me."

The Man of God tapped his temple and winked. "Remember your promise, and I will be."

CHAPTER TWELVE

Abilene awoke when the early morning darkness had begun to lose its inky potency, just before the arrival of the dawn. She sat huddled next to the fire's smoldering remains, looking out over the sprawling ridgeline. The mist had dissipated over the course of the night, leaving a full view of Spero behind. Soft streaks of orange and pink stretched across the slowly-brightening sky, standing out against fleeting traces of indigo. The horizon flashed with the first beams of sunlight, and the gray slopes of the highest peak were bathed in a fiery glow. At the base of the mountain, an alpine oasis glimmered gold.

Abilene closed her eyes as the sunrise graced her smiling face. The flute-like trills of wood thrushes drifted up to meet her ears from the trees below. Their ethereal songs coaxed her groggy mind awake. She opened her eyes, leveling them at Spero's rocky pinnacle. It was time. She roused the Man of God.

Breakfast was brief and light, as their food supply was steadily waning. The fire was extinguished and its smoking embers were scattered about the floor of the cave. Abilene held her scallop shell in her palm and kissed its sea-spawned grooves. She saw the Man of God make the sign of the cross over his chest. They departed for Spero in the morning light, hiking side-by-side.

Abilene led the way down from their craggy perch. The soil was scant and loose beneath their wary feet. She lost her footing more than once, but the Man of God was always there to brace her fall. She shuddered to think of the grim fate that otherwise would have awaited her. Below the Bald Dome, the trail meandered in and out of low-lying scrub. A cluster of squat evergreens bordered the trail, thwacking their legs reproachfully. Tottering cairns nodded stiffly at them as they passed.

Before long, the brush gave way to bare ridge. Beyond lay the glassiest surface Abilene had ever seen, a perfect reflection of the sky. It was a beautiful pond, framed by a rigid ring of pines. Jays darted from tree to tree, peering curiously down at the two ramblers. Abilene knelt at the shore, dipping her cupped hands into the icy water. Liquid sunlight, cooled by the dawn. It tasted divine. The Man of God knelt beside her. He had the quiet air of a man content with existence. She smiled at him fondly, savoring his presence. In time, he would be but a memory to her.

They left the pond behind, hiking in silence. As they neared Spero, the trail was transformed. The ridge looked fragmented and cracked, tossed about in heaps of sparkling slabs. Abilene imagined that the howling wind had once reached a pitch so shrill that the bedrock itself had shattered. It was shockingly magnificent. The wedges of rock wobbled and clinked beneath their feet.

She spared another glance at the Man of God. His decision to leave the seaside behind stung her conscience. She hated to see him so resolute.

He was an odd man, but a good man. A true learned man. A gentle and pensive soul, not like any other Christian she had ever met. She tried to imagine herself in conversation with other Christians, and her prior encounters with them on the trail came rushing back to her. Their condescending jeers echoed in her head:

Ignorance is hardly a choice for your kind!

You're practically an animal, anyway!

Trust a savage? Not a chance!

You're really not much of a woman, are you?

Forgive, Abilene reminded herself. *Forgive.* She wanted to end the tensions between her people and the Christians, but it felt impossible. She sucked in a deep breath, knowing the Man of God was right. She had to try. But if he would only just come along...

As she struggled up the trail, she saw the remainder of her Rambling stretched out before her. A short, steep scramble to a glinting granite ledge was the final test of her resolve. She filled her lungs with the strength of the shrieking wind and heaved herself up to the perilous precipice. The Man of God clambered up alongside her, and both of them witnessed the unmistakable curvature of the treeless zenith beyond. They had reached Spero at last.

Abilene's heart soared. She stepped forward breathlessly. The summit was beautifully barren—she could hardly discern the point where the sparkling bedrock ended and the pale blue heavens began. The wind bellowed a moan of triumph for all that they had endured. The force of the gale brought tears to Abilene's eager, unblinking gaze. She glanced at the Man of God. There were tears in his eyes, too.

She looked about dazedly. The view was unparalleled. The surrounding peaks, an innumerable alpine audience, looked to this prestigious perch for guidance. Spero was an all-purveying pinnacle of majesty, of wisdom, of strength, and of hope. Its mountainous kin bowed before them, festooned in cloud-spun coronae. She was humbled by their deference.

The panorama seemed to stretch on forever. Abilene's eyes settled on the horizon, on that hazy line that marked the beginning of the unknown. Somewhere out there, she swore she caught a glimmer of the sea. Home. She stared, in awe, toward her village. Vaguely, she realized that her mother had once stood where she stood now. Generations of her ancestors had visited this skyward sanctuary and today, she joined them. The feeling was numbing.

The Man of God sank to his knees beside her, his robe billowing about in the summit cyclone. "The Lord hath His way in this whirlwind," he observed. "The clouds are the dust of His feet…"

Abilene found herself at a loss for words. This was it. Their journey was at an end—and so was their time together. "How do you feel?" she asked him.

There was a pause, punctuated by the whipping wind.

"Blessed," he said finally. "Blessed to have made it this far and blessed to be so close to God. Most of all, blessed to be here with you."

Her heart twinged as he spoke. She tried to concentrate on the view, but found it difficult with tears in her eyes. She bit her trembling lip until the levee broke and the truth rushed forth.

"You're a good man," she said as the tears began to fall more freely. "I don't care that you're a Christian—you're the best friend I've ever known—"

The Man of God rose to his feet and wrapped her in an embrace. For a while, they said nothing.

She felt him stir. "Abilene?"

She grasped him tightly, holding her breath long enough for him to register her silent reply.

"Forgive me," he said.

Abilene heard herself tell him she would, but the meaning of the phrase was lost in the wind.

CHAPTER THIRTEEN

The wind grew increasingly fierce throughout the course of their descent. By the time they reached Spero's base, the ridge was engulfed in a miniature hurricane. Abilene looked to the sky, where the clouds were rushing together in bulbous congregations and blotting out the sun. There was a tension in the air, the sort of ubiquitous unease that usually preceded a storm.

They moved quickly through the moaning gale. The cairns stood incredibly still, preparing themselves to brave the impending storm. They paused at the pond. The wind had wracked the peace of its once glassy surface and the jays had long since departed for the shelter of their nests. Abilene set her eyes on the flank of the Bald Dome, which towered above them. She could barely make out the cave in the side of the hulking crag, and that worried her. Below the screaming wind, she discerned a low growl of thunder. The vibrations traveled up her heels from the quivering bedrock—the mounting storm resonated in her bones. They didn't have much time.

"Abilene..." the Man of God started anxiously. He was staring, wide-eyed, at the seething sky. The great black clouds were swelling and rearing above them in monstrous anvil shapes.

"Go!" she yelled. They stumbled into a sprint as the rain began to fall. There was a blinding white flash—lightening, like the crooked fingers of a godly hand, reached over them menacingly. Seconds later, a deafening clap of thunder rattled the ridge. They were at the total mercy of the raging sky.

There was another flash—a writhing splinter of lightening prodded the Bald Dome with an echoing crack. Far overhead, the resulting shower of sparks dissipated into the gusting rain.

Abilene's heart leaped. Shelter. They needed shelter—now. She grabbed the Man of God as lightening streaked once more across the sky; they dove into a nearby cluster of pines to escape its spindly reach. Stiff evergreen boughs tore at them as they crashed into the thicket and flattened themselves against the granite. The wind shook their hiding place with unrelenting ferocity. The pines, nevertheless, stood tall and aimed their pointed heads at the rampant clouds with bristling audacity.

"Thank God for your quick thinking," the Man of God panted.

"We have to get to the cave," Abilene said. "These trees won't protect us for long." She listened hard for the next blast of thunder as rain pelted their backs. It came in an instant, shaking her to the core. "We won't have much time. Get ready..."

"When?"

"Soon."

A few more moments passed. The Man of God inhaled sharply. "Now?"

A lingering rumble of thunder in the dark. "Wait..."

Silence. Abilene swallowed her fear. "Now!"

She launched herself from the thicket, yanking the Man of God behind her. The wind shrieked with laughter at their distress. They bolted toward the Bald Dome, reached the base of the cliff, and started their frenzied ascent of the steep trail. They scrambled up to the cave with precarious haste, slipping over the loose terrain and gripping each other with each staggering step. At last they collapsed beneath the overhang of the shallow cave, drenched and blinking in mild disbelief at the furious storm.

There was still some dry wood stacked against the wall, left over from the previous night. The two assembled a fire, fumbling with the logs in their numb hands. Before long, they were huddled around a meager flame.

The Man of God laid out his sopping food parcel, squeezing out a soggy piece of bread. "So, this is it," he said, rotating the bread over the heat. "The beginning of the end."

Abilene nodded vacantly. "I hope you're prepared to weather more storms like this," she said with a limp gesture toward the entrance of the cave.

He pursed his lips thoughtfully. "All storms, no matter how fierce, dissolve in time."

She said nothing.

"I'll make it through this one," he said, rubbing her back kindly. "And I know you will, too."

Abilene hugged him. He was so warm—in both body and soul. "I'll miss you," she said.

"I'll miss you, too," he murmured back. They drew apart. "Never forget to forgive, and remember to let your bird soar."

She swore that she'd never forget.

The Man of God tugged at his beard. "Do I have your word?"

Abilene nodded. "Of course." The prospect of pursuing peace still intimidated her, but she would persevere with their friendship in mind.

"Good," he said, satisfied. He lowered his head and retreated into prayer, leaving her to her melancholy thoughts.

She studied him sadly, taking in all that she could. His presence emanated peace amid surging seas. The worn surface of his little cross winked at her in the firelight. It was a curious relic that she would forever associate with his invaluable insight.

Her fingers wandered absentmindedly toward her own necklace, grasping at empty air. She clutched at her neck in growing alarm. Her scallop shell was gone.

"I lost my necklace," she lamented, feeling around for it on the cave floor.

The Man of God looked up from his prayers. "What? How?"

"I don't know," she said earnestly, straining her eyes in the scant firelight.

"Do you think it could have blown off?" the Man of God asked, helping her search.

Abilene considered the possibility, but she knew she hadn't felt it leave her neck. "I would have noticed," she said glumly. "It's not here."

Outside, the thunder grumbled cantankerously.

The Man of God furrowed his brow. "Do you remember having it on the hike to Spero?"

"I think so."

"What about on the hike down?"

Abilene combed through her memory furiously. "I'm not sure..."

How could she have lost it? She hadn't taken it off once since her mother gave it to her by the shore. She felt herself go cold and pale. It was as though the fire had stopped giving off heat. Somehow, a piece of her identity had been lost to the storm.

How could she have been so careless, so thoughtless, not to have noticed it was gone?

She carried very few possessions, and what she did carry, she carried out of a matter of necessity. Her dress kept her warm; her hook and line kept her fed; and her intellect kept her safe. Her necklace was the only thing she had brought along that offered no practical use—but it was easily worth more to her than all of her possessions combined. That shell kept her determined, reminded her of her roots and resolve, and symbolized her ambitions. Its purpose was to remind her of her purpose. And now, all of that was gone. All because of her own negligence.

The Man of God scratched his beard and looked down at his crucifix solemnly. "Where did you get it?" he asked.

"What?"

"Your necklace. Where did you get it? I made mine—whittled it from a piece of driftwood."

Abilene rubbed her eyes. "It was a gift from my mother. She gave it to me before I left for the mountains."

"I'm sorry," he said.

"I know it seems silly," she admitted. "It's just a shell, after all. The shore's lined with hundreds of them. But there's not a single shell out there like mine. It's been with me through everything."

The Man of God took his cross between his fingers, deep in contemplation. He drew in a deep breath, then paced to the entrance of the cave.

"Where are you going?" she asked him.

"To get your necklace," he replied matter-of-factly.

"In that storm? You're crazy!"

He nodded. "God will light my way."

"Don't," Abilene said. "It's not worth it—honestly."

"From what you just told me, it most certainly is."

"You really don't need to do this."

"I know." His blue eyes twinkled. "I'll be back before sunrise."

"We'll be back before sunrise," Abilene corrected him. "I'm coming with you." She grabbed a pair of readymade torches from the fire and handed one to him.

They stood at the edge of the cave, savoring the last of the fire's warmth. The Man of God made the sign of the cross, then stepped out into the rain. "Blessed are the pure of heart," he said, looking back at Abilene with a smile. "Do not fear, for I am with you."

She grinned, grateful for one last adventure with him. They sloshed down the trail, which had since become a slippery torrent of mud. The wind slapped them with sheets of rain, as though admonishing their every step. The route felt narrower, scarcely wide enough for a pair of feet. It skirted the precipitous ledge, which loomed above a sheer talus slope. Abilene, plastered against the dripping rock face, peered over the side. The tops of the trees below barely reached midway up the cliff.

A tremendous boom of thunder set the world into slow motion. She saw the Man of God stumble forward, struggling to regain his footing in a desperate quickstep. He fell soundlessly, tumbling from the ledge with his arms outstretched. The light of his torch disappeared in an instant. She heard him go crashing down the slope like a bear in a freefall, plummeting farther and farther away. Gradually, the din subsided and silence reigned.

Abilene swore the scream that pierced the mountain air did not belong to her. It fractured her soul and quieted the storm. She tore down the trail at so reckless a speed that she expected to fall as he had. She was a loping doe, a bounding wolf, a bird in flight. Her heart bulged in her throat. She had to find him.

She dimly recounted that the trail, in its numerous switchbacks, passed by the base of the slope. She abandoned the path and darted into the scrub, rain pelting her face in an icy barrage. She scoured the glade in a panic, squinting through the mist. Why, why had he suggested such a stupid endeavor? *Why?*

She approached the talus slope, picking through the scree fretfully. Her torch smoldered in the gloom. With a start, she discerned a robed heap lying motionless among the dark rocks. It was the Man of God.

He raised his head as she stepped closer. "Abilene?" he croaked.

"I'm here," she whispered, sinking to her knees beside him. "I'm right here." He lay sprawled atop the scattered fragments of a white birch, which had evidently splintered beneath his weight. Then she noticed several of the gleaming shards were streaked with red and realized, with a jolt, that she was staring at the remains of his legs. She didn't even bother to search for an herb to treat the injury. There was nothing she could do.

His eyes drifted about in the light of her torch, finally settling on her face. His left hand was twisted and tucked out of sight, so he reached up to feel her cheek with his right. His touch was as cold as the rain. "Your necklace," he managed. "I didn't—I'm sorry—"

Abilene shook her head, taking his hand in hers. "Why did you do it?" she said. "You stupid, stupid man..."

The Man of God suddenly seemed to become aware of his condition and craned his neck to glance down at his mangled legs. He winced in pain, then looked to Abilene for her verdict.

She choked on her words. "You're—going to be all right."

He smiled sadly. "We both will be." He groped at the neckline of his robe until his trembling fingers closed around his little wooden cross. "Here," he said, trying to jerk it from his neck.

Abilene demurred, but his gaze was firm. "Please," he breathed. "Take it as a reminder."

She nodded, gingerly looping the necklace over his head and slipping it on. He grasped her hand. "Remember your promise," he implored her. "Remember the bird..."

"I will," she whispered. "You have my word."

He smiled again. His gaze flickered and he seemed to ease back against the rocks. "My time here is dwindling," he said regretfully. "Soon I'll have to go..." His eyes clenched shut in a passing spell of pain. "Forgive me..."

Abilene squeezed his hand gently. "I do," she professed. "Of course, I do!"

She felt his grip slowly begin to slacken. "Thank you, sister," he breathed. "For everything..."

His chest rose and fell one last time, but his smile was unfading.

CHAPTER FOURTEEN

Abilene spent the night huddled beside the Man of God in bouts of restless sleep. She sat up at the first indication of morning light, half-expecting to see him breathing softly. He lay absolutely still, but he may as well have been sleeping. She stared emptily at his peaceful features. They were free of pain and unburdened by consequence. She kissed his cold forehead and bid him farewell. Then she returned to the trail with his little wooden crucifix dangling from her neck.

Abilene raised her puffy eyes to the sky. The bulging thunderclouds had mellowed into wispy gray smudges overnight. The world was muted and dull, but at least the rain had stopped. She longed for the sunlight, but knew that even it could not rid her of the chill in her heart.

She wandered listlessly along the trail. The ridge was hard and callous beneath her somber feet. Her mind was cloudy and her ambitions were stranded in the fog. Her necklace was lost, and so was the Man of God. She ambled onward. She didn't care if she reached Spero again. She just needed to walk.

She felt like a dead tree that was only standing because the wind had yet to blow her over. *He's gone,* she thought. *Gone, gone, gone.* The truth was an unremitting echo throughout her fraught mind. *He's dead. Gone. Gone, gone, gone.* She repeated it over and over, in a fruitless effort to convince herself.

Abilene shivered as the wind welcomed her back onto open ridge. Yesterday they had trekked this way, bound for the summit of Spero. All of that seemed so far away now. She passed a familiar thicket of pines, recalling the storm's ferocity with anguish. The trees tensed in her presence, brandishing their needles like miniscule spears. Abilene eyed them mildly. The scratches were still fresh on her arms.

She froze mid-step. There, snagged on an evergreen bough, was a strange ornament—a scallop shell, so far from its seaside home. She gawked at her necklace, freeing it from its ensnarement. Its sinew cord had been forced into two frayed ends. Abilene retied them and returned the shell to her neck, smiling as it settled beside the Man of God's cross.

She gathered immediately that it had been torn from her neck when she and the Man of God had plunged into the thicket to escape the lightening. She rubbed her forehead in disbelief. It was insane to think that both of them had ventured into a thunderstorm just to retrieve it. It was a brash decision that she should have discouraged from the start. She had known it was dangerous, but she hadn't stopped him.

It was her fault that he was dead.

The glassy surface of the pond winked at her through the trees. Abilene stooped down at the water's edge, washing her face with the previous night's rain. She splashed away the sorrow the best she could, threading her fingers through her hair.

Why had she let him go? Tears mingled with pondwater as she rubbed her cheeks and eyes. They could have easily waited until morning to go searching for her necklace. She had been so selfish. In that moment of panic, she had valued a shell more than the life of her best friend. How could she have been so shallow? Her necklace was valuable, but it was worthless in comparison to him. Why hadn't she realized that?

Abilene stood, breathing shakily. A dull ache in her stomach prompted her to unwind the length of fishing line from her waist and tie an end of it around her ankle. She tossed the hook, free of bait, into the pond and waited. Three wriggling minnows became her breakfast. She built a modest fire on the shore and prepared the fish in silence, mourning all who had given their lives for her happiness.

This was hardly how she expected to be feeling at the end of her Rambling. She always thought she'd be feeling fulfilled, having hiked to the summit of the highest peak in the land. But now, emptiness overshadowed her triumph. She had found herself, perhaps, but had lost a friend in the process. Her success felt irrelevant.

The minnows didn't take long to cook. She nibbled at them languidly, barely registering the taste, and stared across the pond in meditative melancholy. The fire sparked and popped, sending a column of smoke into her face. Abilene wiped the tears from her stinging eyes in frustration. They continued to flow as she bowed her head.

The Man of God was gone, and she would never see him again. The bleak reality weighed upon her, crushing her spirits. She wept unabashedly. There was no other way to express her grief, no use in suppressing what would at length emerge. Her tears hissed as they peppered the flames.

When she grew weary of crying, she looked up to find a small jay perched before her. It cocked its head curiously and hopped closer. Abilene silently offered it a palmful of fish. The jay lighted itself upon her outstretched hand and ate graciously, plucking up morsels with its short black beak. She regarded the bird with interest. It resembled a dove daubed with ash.

As Abilene observed the feeding jay, she couldn't help but feel impressed by its decision to venture so far from its flock.

She could easily have been a predator, but the bird seemed to know she meant it no harm. It had taken a risk by approaching her—did that make it wise or foolish? Abilene supposed it didn't matter. The jay's risk was clearly worth the reward.

Remember the bird, the Man of God had said. Her bird. Her dove, her multifaceted truth—the poised perspective with both of its wings and all of its feathers. She wondered what people would make of it. Some, without a doubt, would turn away as soon as her dove opened its beak to sing. But she predicted the majority would stay and listen. A dove's song, after all, is far too sweet a sound to spurn.

The jay, with a nudge from Abilene's finger, took flight. It soared off to rejoin its kin, leaving a smile in its wake.

CHAPTER FIFTEEN

The journey home felt empty without the Man of God by her side. Abilene had known all along that she would be making the trip back on her own, but there was an undeniable sadness in knowing he wasn't watching her from the mountains. She was reminded of his absence with every step she took.

The trail tormented her at every turn. She relived their rambling conversation atop the Bald Dome and strolled past their serpentine savior at the bottom of the ravine. The memories made her heart ache but she scarcely wept. In time, she came to recall their experiences with a smile. She missed him, but she was grateful for the time they had spent together.

On and on Abilene walked. Her departure from timberline meant a return to the everlasting pattern of uphill scrambles and downhill descents. She was comforted by the cycle—it kept her humble, exhausted, and moving forward. Some days were harder than others, but she always persevered. When the trail was particularly steep, her gaze dropped to the scallop shell and cross that hung side-by-side from her neck. She would stare at them, her spirit flickering, before her heart would pump like a bellows and reignite her determination. She had given her word to the Man of God, and she fully intended on keeping it.

In the beginning, she tried not to think of him. If she forgot about him, a part of her reasoned, then maybe she wouldn't hurt so much. But she soon realized that forgetting the Man of God, aside from being impossible, was hardly the solution to her grief. And so, Abilene thought of him often. She remembered his bright blue eyes, his introspective manner, and his tranquil presence. She extolled his many perspectives and his will to forgive. He was the first Christian who had truly treated her with respect—and she hoped that he wouldn't be the last.

It occurred to her that she had never learned his name. This saddened her at first, but she remembered his dogma: *We are who we are, regardless of what people choose to call us.* She supposed, then, that his name was of little importance. He had been a kind, pensive, and insightful man. That was how he would remain in her memory.

Sometimes she dreamt about the night he died—she would see him slipping off the ledge, over and over. They were torturous dreams, but they helped her weather her grief. He had been a beacon of altruism, and she realized there was nothing she could have done to have stopped him from going out to recover her necklace. There was no use in taking responsibility for his selflessness. He had been aware of the risk he was taking when he stepped out into the storm—and so had she.

The Man of God's fate, she came to understand, had been completely out of her hands. What had happened had happened. She could have her regrets, but they wouldn't bring him back.

Even with this realization, Abilene lamented the loss of her friend. She had never lost anybody except her father, who had died when she was an infant. She remembered asking her mother about him once, and could still see the pallid rue in those lunar eyes.

"He was a good man," her mother had said. It was a very simple statement, but Abilene could tell she meant every word. "He was as radiant as the sun."

"What was he like?"

Her mother smiled nostalgically. "He was one the best fishermen our village had ever seen, and he was loved by all—including the sea. The sea loved him so much that, one day, it decided to keep him. It was a sad day, but the waves offer us many gifts as an apology. Since he went away, our nets have swelled with more fish than we have ever known. To this day, the sea leaves shells upon the shore that shine with your father's humility."

"That's not a fair trade," Abilene grumbled.

"I know," her mother said, "but there's no use in staying angry at the sea. We must move on. It's what your father would have wanted."

"Do you miss him?" The question had left Abilene's lips before she understood how insensitive it sounded. She supposed she asked because of how little she knew about her father, and because of how seldom her mother mentioned him.

Abilene's mother stared off into the waves, watching the gulls tumble and rise above the water. "The ocean is cold," she remarked. "Sometimes, the waves catch us by surprise and pull us underwater. It's a terrible experience, but it is so important that we learn how to swim. It is better to paddle through the icy surf than to drown in a whirlpool of misery." Her mother's gray eyes glistened with tears. "Of course, I miss him," she said. "I miss him more than twinflower misses the sun in the wintertime. But I'm thankful for the years we spent together, and I confront my memories of him with the knowledge of how to swim."

Abilene had hugged her mother and glared at the ocean through a gap in the embrace. "The sea took him away too soon."

"Yes, it did," her mother sighed. "Remember your father, Abilene, but let go of your remorse. We cannot control when the waves will crash."

CHAPTER SIXTEEN

For many miles, Abilene walked alone. She estimated it had been about two weeks since she left the pond when she heard voices a short distance off-trail. It was mid-morning, and the river had since rejoined her side. She slowed her pace to investigate, scanning the bank for the source of the sound. A family of black grebes honked at her as the current swept them past. She followed the path of the birds, and her gaze soon fell upon a trio of fishermen casting their lines into the eddies.

Abilene decided to cast her line, too. She clambered down the to the riverside, setting her sights on a nearby lull in the swirling water. She felt a bite almost instantly and yanked back on the line. As she pulled it in, she caught sight of the dazzling pink salmon twisting about on her hook. Abilene beamed at her sparkling prize and set it on the bank beside her. She hooked a few more in quick succession and jumped as a chorus of whoops erupted from the fishermen downriver. She couldn't help but grin.

As she carefully removed another salmon from her line, one of the fishermen approached her. He was short, bearded, and barrel-chested. The wide brim of his straw hat was cocked to the side, and a tangled tuft of wiry chest hair protruded from the top of his unbuttoned shirt. He regarded Abilene with bright, jovial eyes.

"That's a beautiful catch!" he boomed. "We wondered if you'd have much luck without a rod, but you're clearly a capable angler. Well done!" He followed her line to its anchoring point around her ankle. "A fine technique, too. Ever used a rod?"

Abilene shook her head. "I trust my hook and line," she said. "Rods break too easily, and I'd rather not catch anything than lose a fish from a broken rod."

The fisherman grimaced through his whiskers. "I don't blame you," he said. "I've broken many a rod—in the end, it does all amount to the strength of your line. I wind mine up my rod so, if it snaps, I'll still have hold of the fish. But to each their own." He cleared his throat. "If you ever think of trying your luck with a rod again, I'd suggest a sturdy willow branch for your pole. It's a strong and supple wood, perfect for fishing."

"I'll definitely give it another try," Abilene said, a bit surprised by his good-naturedness. "Thanks."

The fisherman studied her as so many others had, but his gaze was far from condescending. "Are you alone out here?" he asked.

She felt a stab of grief. "I am," she said. "But it's peaceful."

"It is," the fisherman concurred. "A welcome escape from the weariness of the day-to-day." He tipped his wide-brimmed hat. "Andrew," he said.

"Abilene."

Andrew gestured over his shoulder toward his companions. "We've had a considerable streak of luck a little way downstream. Care to join us?"

Abilene thought of the jay by the pond, remembering the risk it had taken by eating from her hand. She shrugged. "Why not?"

He beckoned for her to follow him further down the riverbank, where two other men were flicking their willow poles into the eddies. They had evidently spent the previous night there.

Their knapsacks lay open atop a mass of disheveled woolen blankets that Abilene figured were unmade bedrolls. A colorful assortment of flies and hand-painted bobbers peeked out at her from the open hatch of their wicker creel. Nearby, within a ring of smooth river stones, the men had arranged a neat pyramid of logs over the last fire's embers.

Andrew's companions eyed her like a pair of wary dogs. She smiled at them hopefully.

"Lads," he said, "this is Abilene. Abilene, meet James and Peter."

James winced, shading his eyes from the sun. The legacy of his scowl was etched into the lines of his thin face. His gaunt cheekbones were angled downward, and his bushy eyebrows were eternally furrowed. He stared at Abilene in growing alarm. "You're a savage," he grunted.

"I'm Pax," she corrected him. "And you're a Christian."

"But we're *all* fishermen," Andrew interjected, clapping James on the shoulder. "And there's no reason why we can't cast our lines in unison."

James pursed his lips, regarding Abilene with sheepish deference. "That was an impressive catch," he said.

"Thanks," Abilene said coolly, gripping her salmon by its lower jaw. She nodded at their mound of fish. "You're clearly skilled with a rod."

James sniffed, rubbing his nose with a calloused thumb. "It's a necessary skill. Damned good fun, too."

"Why don't you start a fire, James," Andrew suggested. "That way, it'll be good and hot by the time the fish are ready."

James acquiesced without another word.

The man called Peter knitted his brow. He had piercing blue eyes like the Man of God. "You live across the marsh, don't you?" he said.

She nodded. "I do."

Peter smacked his forehead. "It's no wonder why you're such an angler! The Pax are some of the best fishermen I've seen. Taught me everything I know about tying a net. As a matter of fact..." He lumbered over to the wicker creel, seizing a handful of a massive net from within. "Recognize this?"

With a start, Abilene did. It was a Pax net, weaved from resilient marsh grasses. She admired her people's meticulous craftsmanship. A conical snail shell was tautly secured in the center of each knot for just the right ratio of weight and buoyancy.

"It was a gift," he said proudly. "Our hooks were, too." He tucked the net back into the creel with care, then scratched his chin. "They're good people, the Pax. Simple people, but good people. Pleasure to meet you, Abilene."

"They are indeed," said Andrew. He turned to James. "Any luck starting that fire?"

James was knelt over the heap of logs with two pieces of flint. "None," he puffed. "Damned thing won't light!"

"Well, keep at it," Andrew said, beginning to scale their fish alongside Peter.

Abilene retied her line around her waist and added her salmon to the pile. "Do you want me to try?"

Andrew grinned. "Even better, James, let Abilene have a try. No bad has ever come from asking the Pax for help."

James rose and handed the flint off to her. "Good luck," he chuckled, standing back and crossing his arms. She struck the flint together repeatedly. By the third strike, the logs were smoking.

Andrew winked at James, who gaped at the blaze in disbelief. "See?"

"Close your mouth, James," Peter added with a smirk. "You'll catch a fly."

James accepted the flint back from Abilene, impressed. "I'll be damned..."

"I'd like to see any of the women in our village do that," Andrew said.

"Ha!" laughed Peter. "You never will! They'd be too afraid of the spark!"

James pulled a log up beside the fire and offered Abilene a seat next to him. She accepted warily. "You seem...different than other savages I've met," he said, eying her curiously.

"Maybe I'm not," she said.

"I can't quite place it." His gaze drifted to her neck. "Ah," he said. "There it is. You're Christian, too, aren't you?"

Abilene took the Man of God's crucifix into her palm. "I'm not Christian," she said. "But I'm familiar with your faith."

"You don't believe?"

"I don't need to believe to understand."

James acknowledged her point with a tip of his hat. "Then why do you wear a cross?"

"This was a parting gift from a close friend," she explained. "I'm on my way back from a journey to the mountains. I hiked alongside a Man of God to the top of the highest peak."

James narrowed his eyes. "The highest peak?" he repeated incredulously. "Is that so? And how did you get there—on the back of an imaginary horse?"

"By foot, actually."

He glanced down at her muddied, trail-hardened feet. "Impossible," he said. "That would take days—*weeks!*"

"Months," Abilene said.

"I don't believe a word of it!"

"It's the truth," she insisted.

"I believe you, Abilene," Andrew said, looking up from the pile of fish.

"Like hell you do," James scoffed.

"I do," Andrew affirmed. "I've heard tell of an old footpath leading to the mountains. Blazed by the Pax, if my memory serves me right. That journey is something of a tradition, isn't it?"

Abilene nodded.

Again, Peter knitted his brow in thought. "Now that you say that," he said, "I think I remember an old Pax fisherman mentioning a hike to the highest peak. He called it the, ah, Ambling, I believe."

"The Rambling, yes!" said Abilene.

Peter snapped his fingers. "That's it!" he cried. "The Rambling. It's a remarkable feat of will." He laughed, looking at Andrew and James. "From here to the seaside took us how long, lads? Two days?"

Andrew nodded. "And two days back, too."

"And to think," said Peter, "that's hardly even a fraction of her journey!" He smiled. "Very impressive, indeed."

James studied Abilene some more. "I suppose so," he said, prodding the flames with a stick. "But what about your traveling companion, this 'Man of God?' I don't see him sitting here beside you."

"He didn't make it," she said solemnly.

"Oh." James coughed, then made the sign of the cross. "I see," he said. "May he rest in peace."

It was silent for a moment. Abilene stared vacantly into the fire. Most of the glowing coals had been reduced to papery white ash.

She heard James take a deep breath. He pointed at her neck again. "What about your other necklace—the scallop shell?"

"It was a gift from my mother. It reminds me where I'm from and calls me back home."

Andrew nodded curtly in James's direction. "Add some wood to that, would you?"

James went to fetch a log from the stack, then retracted his hand in an instant. His face was ashen. "Somebody hand me my hatchet," he hissed.

Peter craned his neck. "What is it?"

Abilene spotted the object of his terror coiled at the base of the wood pile in a watchful heap. "It's just a snake," she said.

"Stand back," Andrew told her. "We'll take care of it."

Peter passed the hatchet to James. "Aim for the neck," he advised grimly.

As James raised the blade over his head, Abilene considered the snake. It stared back at her unblinkingly, tasting the doom in the air with every flick of its tongue. *Not all snakes are poisonous,* a voice in her head reminded her sharply.

"Wait," she said.

James froze, mid-swing. "What?"

"This one doesn't bite."

He scowled. "How you can tell?"

Abilene said nothing. Instead, she took a step forward and stretched her hand toward the wood pile. The snake observed her with its cunning eyes. Calmly, she lifted three logs from the stack and handed them to Peter. Then, for good measure, she seized a handful of kindling. Her fingers grazed the scaly tail and she drew back slowly, holding the snake's gaze. It bobbed its head and slithered into the underbrush, out of sight.

The three Christians gawked at her as she set the kindling onto the dying fire with a small smile. The flames flickered back to life.

"Incredible..." Andrew muttered.

"I wouldn't have believed it if I hadn't just seen it with my own eyes," Peter agreed.

James was awestruck. "How?" he said. "How did you know it wouldn't bite?"

Abilene merely shrugged. She heard the Man of God laughing on the back of the breeze. "I didn't," she admitted with a grin. "But sometimes you have to risk being bitten to learn the truth."

CHAPTER SEVENTEEN

Abilene passed the remaining two days of her journey with the trio of Christian fishermen. When forest faded into marsh, they parted ways. With a shrill chorus of red-winged blackbirds as a backdrop, she bid them farewell.

"Hope we meet again," said James with a nod. "Preferably on the same side of the shore."

"It's always a pleasure to fish with a Pax," Peter added.

Andrew lowered his hat respectfully. "Godspeed, Abilene."

"I won't soon forget this," she said, addressing each of them separately. She watched them step off the trail and embark on their march through the sea of sallow grass, bound for the Man of God's former home.

Abilene followed the well-trodden path as it snaked on through the swaying marsh. The sun winked at her from the east, above the sea. A short distance off-trail, she observed a pair of egrets spearfishing with their beaks. Abilene waved to them as she rustled past. One of them bowed its elegant head in greeting. She inhaled the morning air, reveling in the mingling aromas of smoke and brine. The trail, she knew, was about to reach a long-awaited end. It would lead up the embankment ahead, leaving the marsh behind, and disappear among a familiar scattering of wigwams. Her Rambling was practically finished, and she was beaming at the thought, but there was something keeping her from sprinting up that final hill.

She paused, her fingers tracing the grooves of her scallop shell. The waves beckoned. Her village could wait. She sought solace by the sea.

She headed for the shore, smiling as the soil gradually gave way to sand beneath her tired feet. It was cool and damp—a stark but welcome contrast from the mountains' coarse terrain. At last, she emerged from the grass and gazed at the glimmering sea. The tide was receding in a reverent bow with sweeping flourishes of its watery robe. Abilene breathed deeply, savoring every ounce of ocean air. Each saline breath was soothing to her soul.

She felt circular, complete, and above all, fulfilled. Spero had granted her an elevated perspective, while the ocean had kept her grounded. She had explored and experienced, received and reciprocated, and had come to know wisdom as a close friend. Somewhere deep within her heart, a bird opened its beak to sing. Its song flowed through the tears gathering in the corners of her eyes. She was finally home.

The long strokes of the retreating tide had left the shore glassy and smooth, but Abilene vaguely distinguished a rambling series of tracks disrupting the surface. She took a few paces forward, following the footprints that nearly mirrored her own. At length, her eyes settled on a solitary woman wandering along the water's edge. She had hair like long, frayed ribbons of moonlight. Abilene called out to her with resounding delight.

The woman turned slowly, scanning the shore for the source of the sound. She squinted at her daughter, beaming in recognition and spreading her arms wide. Abilene dashed into them, clutching her mother tightly. They wept together, rejoicing through silent tears of strength and relief.

Her mother grasped her by the shoulders. "My girl," she murmured. "My brave, beautiful girl..." She looked her daughter up and down proudly. "Home at last," she continued. "You've rambled and returned. I can't even begin to imagine the trail you've blazed."

Abilene blinked, and her entire journey flashed through her mind. She saw it all, in a matter of seconds: jeering Christian faces; fireside conversations with a pensive Man of God; a singular serpentine savior; Spero's majestic monolith amid a plethora of peaks; rampant thunderclouds raging above the ridgeline; the jay at the pond; and a trio of fishermen who had accepted her as one of their own.

"It was a beautiful trail," she said. "Sometimes it was level and other times it was steep. I was slowed by adversity and sustained by friendship. I came across several agreeable snakes and a very shrewd owl who kept me focused on the path ahead. I learned to forgive, to have faith in myself, and realized that no storm lasts forever. I've seen the value in planting a tree out of goodwill instead of felling one out of spite."

"And through it all," her mother rejoined, "you've done your people proud. You've sowed the seeds of your legacy in the footsteps of your ancestors. You've become the woman you were always meant to be..."

She trailed off, beaming at her daughter's neck. She considered the pale scallop shell with fond reminiscence before realizing that a second necklace now hung beside it. Abilene's mother took the little wooden cross into her weathered palm, studying it with a bemused expression.

"What's this you've found?" she asked.

"It's a bird," Abilene said after a pause. "With both of its wings and all of its feathers."

CHAPTER EIGHTEEN

A lone seagull was gliding through a cloudless sky. Its wings caught a gust of the early autumn air and it soared higher, peering down at the sparkling oceanic expanse. Sand and surf mingled along the curving outline of the shore, and the trees of the encroaching forest were seared red and orange. Beyond the forest stretched a yellow marsh, whose estuary veins had since emptied into the sea. With a piercing *scree*, the bird observed a small group of people marching through the rippling grass.

Abilene was among them, walking beside her mother. They were bound for the summit of yet another mountain, one far taller than Spero. This mountain was seldom explored, formerly deemed too daunting to approach, and there was no established trail to the top. She supposed that didn't matter. They would blaze their own way, trekking into the unknown as a people. This was a different journey, but the feeling was the same. They were Pax. Ramblers. They would reach their destination even if they moved at a snail's pace. Abilene was sure of it.

Their group was eleven strong. Abilene and her mother paced alongside Soto, a scribe, and Lobelia, the village healer. Cephas, their sachem, led them silently. Three hunters and three fishermen took up the rear. Abilene surveyed their expressions. Their lips were pressed together in thin horizons of resolve, but she discerned a glimmer of optimism in their confident strides. Their eyes burned with hope.

She tightened her hold on the staff in her hands, unaccustomed to its weight, and considered it pensively. A buckskin banner was knotted to the top of it, fluttering in the wind like a white wing. She and her mother had prepared it during the celebration of her Rambling, bleaching it with the very same pigment used to blaze the path to Spero. She thought of her hike to the highest peak, of how she only carried objects of absolute necessity. Two of them still dangled from her neck, reminding her of a promise she had made to an old friend. This staff, too, was an object of necessity. She knew without a doubt that they couldn't reach the top of the next peak without it.

Cephas motioned for them to stop. Their line stood still, waiting, as the grasshoppers trilled intermittently. Abilene scoured the horizon, watching as a row of men emerged from the shifting grass. She counted them quickly. They were also eleven strong and—she realized with a start—had hoisted a white banner above their heads.

Her heart was pounding. The summit was in sight.

The Christians came to a halt before them. Abilene studied them. They mirrored her people with rigid backs and staid countenances. Her gaze drifted down the line of solemn-looking men, settling temporarily on a tall, well-groomed fellow with a feather in his cap. His arrowhead-shaped goatee pointed down at his frilled collar and dark blue tunic. She figured him to be the Christian sachem.

Her eyes moved further down the line, resting upon an old man clad in dazzling white robes. The silver cross hanging from his neck glittered with diamonds. Abilene stared at the priest, knowing full well that he had once threatened the Man of God with death. She heard a voice on the breeze, a whisper from the highlands. *Forgive*, it advised, and she grasped her dual necklaces placidly.

Pax looked upon Christian and Christian looked upon Pax. Both sides were motionless, holding their breath, as though seeing each other fully for the first time. Neither quite knew what to do next.

Abilene felt her mother squeeze her arm gently. She glanced at the sky, the brilliant cloudless sky—the same sky beneath which she and the Man of God had summitted the tallest mountain in the land.

She took a deep breath, then stepped forward.

Every pair of eyes snapped to her. Abilene raised her staff, regarding all of them. With the grace of bird spreading its wings, she brought it down into the dirt. Banner and shaft protruded from the rich black soil. Marsh soil was fertile soil, caressed daily by the tides and nurtured by its briny touch. Anything could grow here. It would take time, it would take effort, but Abilene had faith.

She stepped back into line. The Christian flagbearer stood across from her, eying her with interest. She perceived his gaze on her neck and displayed the scallop shell and crucifix in her steady palm.

His lips were parted in mild shock. They formed a smile. A score of heads watched him step forward and plant his staff beside hers.

The two white flags fluttered beside one another like long-separated kin, reunited at last. As banner and banner flapped side by side, Abilene witnessed a fabled bird take flight.

Pax and Christian looked on, unified in thought:

Long may it fly.

Long may it fly...

Michael Lajoie is an avid oceanside explorer, mountain climber, and wilderness lover. He lives in Seacoast New Hampshire with his family.

CPSIA information can be obtained
at www.ICGtesting.com
Printed in the USA
LVHW052228201220
674641LV00008B/292

Made in the USA
Middletown, DE
18 January 2020

83372273R00215

To my ... pal. Rice meeting

American
Canticle

you Lidia, Love

By

Robert Carroll

Robert

Metamorphic Press

This is an original publication of Metamorphic Press

Cover Art and photography by StrikingImages.com

ISBN-13: 978-1-951221-07-2

First Edition printing January 2020

Published by:
Metamorphic Press
PO Box 151
Tenafly, NJ 07670
metamorphicpress.com

Proudly printed in the United States of America

DEDICATON

To the legacy of great+ grandfather William "Wild Bill" Carroll and to the beloved memory of my cousin Norbert "Doc" Sander.

ACKNOWLEDGEMENTS

I want to give a shout out to my good friend Jon Koons, who mentored me in the craft of writing. Without him not a single word would have been written. He lit a fire in my mind to recreate with words the different landscapes that dwelt within me. He then guided me through terrain unknown to me—the actual technique of writing a book. Jon is not only a published author and editor but a fellow variety entertainer. He took me under his wing and patiently showed me the building blocks of constructing a novel, and for this I am forever indebted. Jon you are truly an artist and a mensch. Sincere thanks, most appreciated.

I would like to thank Mike Wilson for his support and how much he has nudged and inspired me to keep on writing. Good luck with your own projects my friend.

Thanks also for the discerning eye and frank nature of Pamela Friedman who, upon reading excerpts from my original manuscript commented, "It is most interesting when you write from a more personal viewpoint. This is not a single novel, more a series I think." Because of this sage advice I broke the original idea into five distinct novels, of which this is the first.

And, of course, my wife Kathryn for her patience and support.

If the doors of perception were cleansed everything would appear to man as it is, Infinite.

—William Blake

One

May 5, 1847

An Gorta Mor, The Great Hunger

Florence Rose O'Neill sneaks the hardened loaf of brown bread out of the folds of her tattered Kerry cloak. But she does not look at it for fear that she will forget herself and simply gulp it down.

She found it hidden in the bottom of the turf rick inside of her neighbor's two-room cottage that is just across the field from hers. A field that used to be filled with potatoes but now has grown fallow and is barren due to the ongoing blight. As many mothers have done, even though they were starving themselves, Florence's neighbor, Grace Malloy, must have intended to save the bread for her children to have later. But as she wasted away, delirious as she was, it seems that poor Grace forgot all about it.

Since Florence had not seen anyone about in her neighbor's cottage these past few days she found what she expected: All present were gone from this world, the three wee ones in the back room huddled together in death and in the front room lay Grace and her husband, separate but also dead. Gazing at the area around all five

of their mouths that is a light shade of green so desperate in the hunger that they had resorted to eating grass, Florence clutches the small loaf of bread onto her breast and flees the scene in a blind panic as visions of her own dead children Moira, Owen, and Dennis along with her departed husband Conner appear before her.

Half blind and weak as a newborn kitten, Florence O'Neill, stumbles away toward the remains of her own cottage. The whole time looking back at this house of death, half expecting to see an apparition like a pretty lady all dressed in black smiling at her. Something that she once saw, years ago, at a funeral outside of Dingle town when she was but a child.

Falling to her knees over and again, while navigating over stones and rotten patches of black potatoes here in the rugged terrain of County Kerry, Florence crosses herself over and over again.

The last time she fell the temptation to just stay there lying on the cold ground and wait for the end almost overcame her. But the image of her sole surviving offspring, her son Daniel Sean, made her push herself up and continue on.

As she gasped for air and haltingly walked, one searing foot in front of the other, she makes the decision to hold out for as long as she could with the bread, so she hid it inside of her cloak next to her racing heart that is pleading with her to eat it.

In agony she finally makes her way back to the wasteland that used to be her farm, realizing, along the

way, that for her, the end was near. This is not just a physical realization, for she could also feel the presence of darkness and lightness all around her. Presences that she knows are the vying spirits of this world and the next fighting one another for possession of her immortal soul. The light, with the help of free will, nudging her along to 'follow her spirit,' the darkness nudging her back into this world, tempting her to just eat the bread and the hell with Daniel Sean.

Now, back at the remains of her cottage, she lies down next to her son who has his eyes closed. As she listens to his shallow breathing, the thought and the urge to devour the bread overcomes her.

Without looking at it, she caresses the borderline sacred loaf, clasping it tightly to her sunken chest as if it were a precious gem. The whole time she keeps fading in and out of reality. One minute seeing Moira, her youngest, alive and laughing with her beautiful, dancing blue eyes that seemed to twinkle like diamonds. The next minute dead. Black as the rotting potatoes in the field. Her husband, Conner and her two sons Owen and Dennis appear, all three laid out just before they were buried. *It is just me and Daniel Sean, my Shaneen, left here in this world. The rest of the Kerry O'Neill's? All gone they are and lucky the lot of them are at that.*

As her mouth waters, the urge for the bread grows and the pangs come like a gigantic needle in her stomach, clutching and clawing. For there is nothing

there, only a ghostly, ever present gnawing that is an eternity of want and emptiness. Hugging her stomach, she thinks to herself, *food, glorious food, anything. A morsel, a universe dear sweet Lord. Hunger is the best sauce for it makes almost anything seem delicious. Bram brack, drisheen, colcannon, and rashers, good Lord, these visions of food dance before me.*

Her whole body, her shell needs to absorb. Her heart, her soul, her entire being is in her mouth and stomach. She places the loaf back underneath her cloak and breaks off a tiny portion of the bread, careful not to let her son see it. She silently pulls it out and turns her head away from him in order to eat the bread unseen.

Put the bread into your mouth now says the devil himself.

She is so close to putting it into her mouth. So close. Her hands stop inches from her lips. There is such a push, a drive to swallow this, to shove it into her mouth.

But in the middle of this overwhelming urge, instinctively she touches the Celtic cross that is around her neck, the cross that has been with the O'Neill family for generations, and the powerful, fierce hunger stops for just one second. She knows that whomever has this last bit of bread will have a slight chance to live, to maybe survive another day at most, but the one who doesn't, surely, will die. *Like all the others.*

She thinks of all the starving mothers who have snatched food from their own children's mouth. Letting

them die instead. *'Tis the work of the divil himself. But by God I want to swallow this right now.*

She looks at her son who has his eyes closed. *Sweet Jesus don't be letting me eat this morsel. Holy Immaculate Mother, give me the strength to pass it on to Daniel Sean. He must live and remember all that has happened here.*

I am so desperate. I cannot resist.

The bread is an inch away from her mouth when she again touches the Celtic cross that is around her neck. At that same moment her immortal soul wins out and plucks her hand away. Her lips silently intoning, *Holy Mary, Mother of God, Give me strength. Give me courage to proudly face my Lord. Make me brave, blessed Brigid, make me brave. Be with me Mary, Holy Mother of God, keep me steady. Pray for us sinners now and at the hour of our death. Amen.*

She clutches the Celtic cross once again, holding on tight when, in the twinkling of an eye, the miracle of Remembrance enters into her heart; she remembers who she is, where she came from and where she is going.

Weak salty tears fall from her eyes, tears of triumphant joy. *As it was in the beginning is now, and ever shall be, world without end. Amen.*

She takes a labored breath. *I am not worthy to receive but only say the word and my soul shall be healed.* Without hesitation she quickly breaks the loaf of bread into bite size chunks and slowly places the cherished portions one at a time on her son's tongue,

who gobbles it all up, sucking it down, smacking his lips together, as she lies and says to him, "don't worry, eat it, I've had me fill, this is all for you."

Then in defiance of the Saxon foe who is watching from afar, she says in Irish:

"A Thriana dean trocaire."

{Lord have mercy}.

"Go raibh an Tiarna libh."

{The Lord be with you.}

"Is beannaithe an te ata ag teacht in anim an Tiarna."{Blessed is he who comes in the name of the Lord.}

Bowing her head in reverence Florence O'Neill says to her son in a hushed feeble whisper. "The Eucharist is when life and death come together, Daniel Sean, tis a blending of the body and the spirit. Twill keep you until you get on your way to Cork, God willing. In the future whenever you take Communion, through the body and blood of Christ, you will remember this moment and me, your mother. You will also remember the Holy Mother herself, who is the mother of us all, always, for the truth is she is always waiting. As it was in the beginning is now, and ever shall be, world without end. Amen."

Ironically a sense of peace comes over her now that the bread is gone even as she starts to cough up phlegm with a bit of blood in it. She wipes her bloody mouth on her sleeve. Weak as she is, Florence cannot help herself, she cannot stop talking.

"Now, Daniel Sean, don't be showing your lamentations to the blood tipped Saxons." She points at the man in the distance, one of the English men who used a wagon with a team of horses that pulled and tumbled down their small thatched house just this morning.

Florence and Daniel Sean could not pay the last five months rent and were evicted from the home that has been with the O'Neill family for generations and generations. "You hear me now Shaneen? When it's himself with his crinkled and gaping earflaps, desperate he is to hear what we're saying. Who but for the grace of God we'd be cracking his skull with a mighty Hawthorn stick or running him through with a pike. The Son of God forgive me for saying it, but 'tis the Holy truth. Destroyed we are indeed, but divil if I'll be letting 'em know that. For we still have our immortal souls. And our pride as O'Neill's."

She gasps, takes a tortured, labored breath, but she continues."And by the glory of God I will have no shame meself, for I will stand a tiptoe in the presence of The Lord of Lords surrounded by the glory of all the Holy Angels themselves. Thanks be to Brigid, the Holy Mother, and the Truth that is in the Cross."

She says with desperation in her voice.

"You have to leave now and go with Seamus. He's the friend of your fathers and the Fenien your da told us about. He has promised to take you with him. In just a little bit he'll be at the fork in the road down the hill

there, next to the field where Donal Creagh shot his lame horse two years ago and drove him mad with the sorrow of it."

Looking her son in the eye Florence O'Neill says to him. "There's nothing here for you. Seamus has a cousin in Cork who will make sure that you get on the boat to America." She pauses and adds. "If, God willing, you do make it to Cork. But I know that you will. I have faith in the power of the Spirit and prayer. And I will be praying as long as I am still six feet above the duggened earth."

Then she lowers her voice conspiratorially saying. "Last night before the sliver of the moon rose over the 'cuddys,' the same mountaintop reeks that Turlough O'Carolan, the blind harpist himself, sang about. Well just last night, when surely it was as black as the eyes of one of those handsome Spanish gypsies or one of those lost tribe Hebrews who live even farther out and up in the wilds of the West Country, I heard a banshee on the wind come howling down the mountainside. Aye, 'twas whistling through Kirby Flynn's stone wall. Groaning through the same field where the ghost of the tinker woman has been seen, dead these thirty years, stabbed through the heart she was by her jealous husband. The same ghost that has been known to be seen by scores of Christians in the time of the Beltran, when the moon is full, walking barefoot over the frozen earth." She does the sign of the cross. "Rest her soul, restless as it is. Now last night, as I was

saying, just as the wind grew mightily, aslant the banshee wanders as it careens up and over the dark forest and into our church right up into the steeple. Clanging and clashing the bells were. Did you not hear them ringing in the silence of the night? Whist you were and lucky you are for you slept right through it. After leaving the church the banshee then whooshed across the long and lonesome bog to their church. Would you know not a sound come out from their steeple? False though it is. With that I'll be thinking now. This is a power of a sign. Of bad things to come. Of much blood and sorrow on top of the hunger. Can you see now that you must leave soon?"

She grabs his face in her hands. "You with your wild, desperate anger and the strength and fine savagery of more than one in your eyes. That being the way I know that you'll make it through and raise up a fine brood of O'Neill's yourself. The continuation."

He looks at her with a puzzled look on his face. "I don't understand mother."

She pauses to catch her breath, realizing that since her son is barely a man, only seventeen years old, that an explanation is in order. "The Circle of life, the continuation." She looks up to the misty sky with the rain falling in the west.

"See the rainbow, Daniel." *Strange to have these thoughts,* she thinks to herself, *strange. A gift from the Almighty. A slight respite.*

"The soft rains fall on the mountains and blends with the earth, till 'tis saturated and full, then enters into the streams and rivers. Like a song it flows down to the sea. After the long journey of sighing and breathing this same rain blends into and becomes at one with the vastness of the ocean. That once blessed, clean, and holy rain, now filled with the shite of this world, then rises up to the sky. Kisses heaven, becomes clean again and forms a cloud. The cloud drifts back to the mountains falling as rain, and there it is all over again. The Circle. No beginning and no end. 'Tis true that we all must die from our bodies. But Daniel, we can leave part of ourselves with those we leave behind. Like the rain that's left over. That's the earthly continuation. There is also the circle of the spirit. The circle that after all is done creates a glorious rainbow. Such will be my home, such will be my home."

"It's alright mother, you need to rest." He says to her, but she doesn't even hear him. She closes her eyes. He almost forgets that she sees and feels things that he does not. Essences she used to call them when he was young.

"Ah, the mysteries and shattered beauty of this world. There are spirits in everything. There are also the spirits of the dead that surround us. I can see them all, here, surely, right now. Your da, your brothers and your sister, they are all here. Always with us."

She snaps out of it. Grabs her son's hand and holds it to her face. "We are descended from one of the

oldest clans. The Ui Nhail. The great O'Neill's. No matter where you go, Daniel Sean, be a proud Irish man. Do your people well." She lets go of his hand and lies back down.

This whole time Daniel has said nothing. Just sat there and silently wept, too weak to produce tears.

"Here Daniel take this." She takes the Celtic cross off from around her neck. "Keep this cross with you and you'll never be far from me." She touches her heart. "Or your home." With a barely perceptible wave of her hands she indicates Ireland.

"But mother I don't need to be carrying this at all. You keep it with you now. It's worth nothing to me."

"That's the truth Daniel, 'tis worthless by way of money. But it's still ours, it has us in it. Sometimes that's all you have."

She holds the cross out for him to take. "Look at it, Daniel. She may not be much to look at anymore, but 'twas once the wonder of the West. From Donegal to the ring of Kerry. The glory of all the blessed martyrs themselves would pale to think of how even the power of the Almighty is woven into this by way of faith and love. Hold it to your heart Shaneen. Look at it. Even now you can see the circle and the outline of the cross. Forged by an O'Neill it was. There's much blood and spirit in it."

"Daniel Sean remember that you have flowing through your veins, from both your fathers and from my line, a wee remnant of the blood of the Tuatha da

Danaan, the people of the goddess Danaan who never completely disappeared into the earth as the stories go. You also have on your father's side going way back, the first Naith or great Chief of the five Kingdoms of the Celt, who were named the Milesians and came from the east across the sea. The Celts had conquered the Tuatha da Danaan but instead of totally destroying their way of life they adopted parts of it as their own, allowing the spirits of the Tuatha to mix with their Celtic ways. This blending of the two peoples gave birth to a unique warlike but also artistic way of life. A former slave of a druid priest, St. Patrick, then came later and introduced the truth and compassion that is in the way of the Cross. But even so."

She pauses to catch her breath as she is utterly shattered with exhaustion but she then continues.

"Though we believe in the resurrected Christ and the power of the blood, we also believe that all three of these blended together into a single unique culture, which is a meshing of the three—and that is who we are."

She places the Celtic cross into his hands.

Slowly, reverently, he places it around his neck. He then reaches down and grabs a handful of earth. Dirt from where his family has lived and died for countless generations. He places that in his pocket.

Florence then pulls out from the folds of her Kerry cloak a parchment, like a makeshift book, which

is a collection of varying sheaves of paper that are bound together with a thick string.

Despite the pain that she is in Florence smiles to herself and says "We love our stories. And language is truly the best way to be capturing the unruly meaning of this wild, untamed world that we live in because language is, like life, messy and beautiful in its imperfection which makes it dance in tune with the human heart."

She smiles faintly at her son while he feels the shadow of death all around her, and it is at this moment that his heart shatters into a thousand pieces. For he knows that he will never see her alive again. Ever.

Florence O'Neill raises her weary head and in a small voice starts to speak as she holds the bound journal up for Daniel Sean to see.

"This is the story of the O'Neill's. 'Tis a story that has been handed down from the oral tradition of your fathers ancestors. His father, your grandfather, James Patrick O'Neill himself, decided to write it all down in 1798 when the great Irish Rebellion failed in that same year."

Looking away into the distance she continues. "Right before your da left this world he made me promise to safeguard it and to give it to whomever survives An Gorta Mor. And Daniel Sean you are the last one left. Now I know 'tis true that you are not one for reading but you will learn to read better, that you will

survive and this will help you to understand who you are. And where you come from."

She takes the journal, that is already tightly wrapped in a waterproof covering of deer hide, and hands it to Daniel Sean. He takes it, rearranges everything, and buries it in the very bottom of his small pack.

"You must go now. Seamus is our last chance. He won't be waiting for much longer. You have to go. You must go and live. For me and your father. Daniel can you understand?" She then says in a whisper. "Go, my son, be brave and live."

The two of them struggle to their feet and stand their silently looking at one another, once again knowing that this is goodbye. His mother is desperate for him to leave. Desperate for him to abandon this place of death and sorrow. She looks up at the sky assessing the time, steels her heart, points into the distance, and says. "Go, go now, before it's to late. And don't worry about me I shall have my peace."

She kisses her son's hands. " 'Tis your duty to those who have passed on to remember so that they can live on through you."

He gets up and starts to leave, then stops and turns to his mother. "I'll never forget you."

They embrace one final time. She pushes him away. He walks away without looking back. She watches him as he walks away. His long shadow becoming

smaller and smaller, bending to the late morning sun, until he finally vanishes into thin air.

After hours of just lying there on the ground, hardly moving at all, right around the time that the sun starts to set, Florence's hunger pangs momentarily disappear, only to be replaced with a melodious fluid sound, a singing that fills her up. As she feels invisible hands gently touch her face, soothing her, like water being silently poured over her head, she protests against the ministrations of the Spirit. "Stop, stop, no please."

The agony of hunger returns and through the piercing pain Florence O'Neill says out loud. "No, no, I can do this, I can, on my soul, I want to, I want to have it and to endure it for you, all of it, all my wretchedness. I want to offer up all my pain to you, all of it, even the sorrow that I have had in this life. Do not take it away. Please I beg you, dear Lord God in heaven, please let me have it for it belongs to me. It is mine and no one else's. It is all that I have left in this world, and it is mine alone to endure to the end."

Florence O'Neill, proud woman that she is, looks up at the darkening sky and whispers. "Please. It is the only thing that I have left to offer to you in this world. Everything else is gone."

She gasps for air, her mouth is so dry that her lips stick together, making it hard to speak. But once again she feels compelled and speaks in a wavering but loud

voice. "My pain is an offering to you Almighty God, Holiest of Holies, Lord of Lords. "

A sharp shunt of piercing pain thrusts into her and takes away her breath, as if the devil himself is driving a knife into her chest, causing her to gulp for air that will not enter her lungs through the membrane of this torment. In a tortured whisper says. "This is my cross, thank you for letting me proudly carry it for it is mine. And now, I want to offer it back up to you dear God in heaven, and to you Holy Mary, you whose heart was pierced with sorrow and who brought into this world, the Son of the Most High."

She feels a feathery flutter around her as she touches her filthy, sun burnt, caved in face. In absolute agony she then moves her trembling hands downward touching her beautifully wretched, emaciated sheath of a body, the whole time smiling weakly to herself, for she knows that she is leaving herself. "I am yours, forgive me all of my sins."

The invisible part of her being detaches itself from her mortal self and she feels her soul tumble downward, falling, twisting, as she whispers to herself.

"Daniel Sean, my muchusla, May the road rise to meet you. May the wind be always at your back. And until we meet again may God hold you in the palm of His hand."

Two

Seamus Fitzgerald spins around and glares at his newfound companion for a couple of seconds, stopping them both in their tracks. He then relaxes and says in a soft voice. "Daniel Sean listen to me now me boyo. The only reason that I'm taking you with me is that your da was not only a friend of mine you see, but 'twas a good man who dearly loved Ireland. Sure but ya might not know but he secretly assisted the cause on a few occasions. So when your ma asked me to help you I couldn't say no."

After a slight pause he continues. "I know that your heart is heavy but we need to keep moving lad, we need 'to stay six feet above the duggened earth.' To do that now we have to not slow ourselves down and if the truth be told there, we need to travel off the beaten path to stay away from other people as much as is possible. 'Tis the way when things are as they are now. People are our greatest threat, therefore we have no choice but to go the way of Bantry Bay, following the coast where there is less traffic. 'Tis much longer than going directly to Cork over the Reeks but twill be safer you see. So let's get ya moving now."

Once they start up again he rambles on a bit. "You see lad, once we get out of Kerry and into county Cork I

hear that 'tis much more desperate there. There's men who'll cut you for the shirt on your back and do even more for a morsel of food. So we travel the longer but less populated route. I know the roads and layout of Ireland like the back of my hands, you see, especially down here in the Southwest of Ireland. It's always been my turf so to speak, so there isn't a town, a road, mountain, bog, beach, or a field that I don't know about around here."

As a true-blooded rebel, a Fenien, possessed with the desire to liberate Ireland from the yoke of the English, Seamus is schooled in the art of survival. He knows how to live off of the land, how to depend on his wits, relying on his instincts.

His plan is to travel and settle in America and attempt to convince the Irish Americans who reside there to give financial support to the Irish cause. He had been a member of the Young Ireland movement, but only on the periphery, and he eventually left because he thought that they were too opposed to the use of force, which he thought was inevitable. He was more aligned with the idea that to drive the English out of Ireland it was necessary to wage a 'holy war' against them.

Daniel Sean also has his conviction, which is devoid of any politics. He simply wants to survive. To live so that his mother, father, brothers, sister and all his ancestors could live on through him for he is the last of them all. God forgive him, but he feels that the death of his father, his two brothers and the little one Moira, plus

leaving his mother and Ireland, is a clean and total split from his native land. And the truth of it all is that he would never return, not ever.

It would be almost impossible to describe the pain of leaving his home, his soil, his earth, his heart, his Ireland. Only one of his own would ever understand.

But the pain of losing his family is a thing he will never share with any living person. It is his and his alone. He would forever cherish this pain in his heart, a pain that would help him remember that the souls of his family would always be with him cementing his resolve to carry on, to keep on moving for them, especially his mother. He must go and not look back. Ever.

"Now Danny if we can keep up we will still be in Kerry but not too far from county Cork by the time it's dark. Two days walk maybe. And a couple more to get there to Cork City itself. But we have to keep on moving there me boy."

Daniel Sean is weak from not having enough sustenance over time, but the bit of bread he got from his mother and the look on her face keeps him going. He's not sure when he will fill his belly again but he keeps his hand constantly clutched around his Celtic cross, the whole time issuing forth a steady stream of prayers, sending them up to the heavens.

"*Dear God in heaven, I am in your Hands. Christ in me, Christ above me, Christ below me, Christ beside me, I arise with the strength of the Trinity.*"

Step after step they walk on, to Daniel Sean it is like a blur, except that as the miles stretch on he feels weaker and weaker. He starts to stumble but Seamus eggs him on with gentle nudges and encouragement. Sometimes they stop but only for a few minutes at a time.

It is starting to go dark, the sun already set and the sky still with a bit of light in it when they skirt around a small unobtrusive village where they encounter four haggard rail thin bodies, just lying there. What belies the uncertainty of the seemingly posed posture of the dead is the stench. The foul, unmistakable smell of corruption when the flesh has started to go back into the earth, taken again to the source.

The two of them stop and throw some dirt over the corpses and say a decade of the rosary. They are not sure what else to do but they both figure that this is the best that can be done.

They keep walking heading south again, which is counter productive to getting to Cork city, but which Seamus insisted upon.

"I know what's what, Danny, trust me, if you want to stay six feet above the duggened earth, trust me."

That night, their first night on their voyage to America, they find a place to sleep in a stump filled field. With empty bellies they pull their jackets and worn out clothes over themselves and lie down to a restless night.

They arise the next morning to a grey rainy day not a heavy downpour but enough to put a bit of depression into their souls. With sharp pangs in their stomachs they slug through the morning, past the noon hour, hardly speaking a word lest they consume energy by doing so. On and on they go as they walk and walk, over bogs, around overgrown, neglected fields, heading south and east toward the sea stopping to drink from a stream or just to lie down.

After almost a full day of walking south and east they finally find themselves completely alone, walking along the southern banks of a bay that leads out and into the Atlantic Ocean. Around sunset they head toward the end of a jutting slice of land where Seamus signals Danny to hurry up so that they can make their way down a rocky ravine to the waters edge.

"There's not much light left, me boyo." When Daniel Sean starts to object, Seamus says forcefully. "Trust me."

Once there on the bottom of the ravine, Seamus steps down onto a crag of black rocks next to the crashing foaming sea that is filled with floating red and green seaweed. He points to some round shells that are attached to the black rocks, and with the help of a sharp rock that he picks up he knocks then scrapes off about a dozen or so of these small, helmet-shaped shelled objects. "Here we go now, this will be enough to keep us going for tonight. Limpets they are."

Daniel stares at them—he has never seen this before. "Can we eat them now?"

"Aye, we can, most Irish are too stubborn or ignorant to realize that you can eat these. I learned all this from a French lad that I met years ago over in Brittany. Those Frenchies will eat almost anything, I tell you."

Seamus pulls out a knife from his back pocket and scrapes the meat out of a couple of limpets handing them to Daniel who stares in disbelief at them. "Are ya sure we can eat this?"

"Eat or die Danny Boy. This is what is known as famine food and most Irish don't know about it, but the bleeding French do. Go on eat it."

Danny cautiously nibbles at a few limpets, at first holding back a gag reflex and then chewing them quickly and swallowing them, then another one, then another.

They spend the early part of the evening scraping up and eating all the limpets that they can find underneath the light of a full moon. Danny feels a warm golden glow spreading out through his blood as he absorbs the meat of the rubbery shellfish. His skin loosens up and a jolt of strength blasts through him, with a giddy flow of hope coursing through his veins. He feels his muscles literally bursting with joy, while his eyes and ears and mind start to actually breathe with life. Not death but life is his now! With this realization his

eyes fill up, brimming with tears, and even this is glorious, this fullness all around him and in him.

Daniel Sean says to himself, looking out into the distance.

"I coulda maybe save me ma with this knowledge. I should go back for her."

Seamus gently places his hand on top of Daniel's head, the ancient sign and acknowledgement of grief.

"She could not have lasted another day, believe me Daniel Sean. May she rest in peace, there is nothing that could be done Danny, nothing."

The two of them eat to bursting and then, with the light of the moon guiding them, they find a place to camp out a little ways from the crashing surf.

Daniel prays that night, a Pater Nostra for thanks, and an Ave for forgiveness that he left his mother, even if he knows that she is at peace. The reason that he believes this is because he had a dream where his ma appeared to him with a great big smile on her face, winked at him, waved to him and then walked away without looking back. To Daniel Sean it felt as if it was more than just a dream; he felt her presence all around him like it was not a dream but a visit.

And the fact that he saw her smile and walk away means, to him, that she is in a better place than here.

Three

The next morning when Daniel Sean wakes up to an unusually warm and clear Irish day, the first thing that he notices is that Seamus is gone. He frantically checks to make sure that the Celtic cross is still in his small parcel along with the five pounds which is buried in the very bottom and is the only money that he has there. Both are there intact. "Thank God."

Just then Seamus comes into view carrying a load of plants and flowers. Daniel Sean can only stare in amazement. *What in the hell is this?*

"Danny me boy, here is a breakfast made for the high King of Tara himself; the bitter but oh so lovely sorrel plant, roots and tubes of the thistle, and here you are, purple curly kale. We've gotten so used to our spuds that 'tis forgotten all around that we also have our own plants here. Dig in. Not as great as shanks and turnips, but 'twill do. Besides it will be tough soon to find anything once we get closer to Cork city and are back in the civilized world surrounded by other starving souls."

They suck the marrow out of the stalks of thistle, which is tasteless; they chew and swallow the sorrel, which leaves an aftertaste like rusty iron; and they suck down the purple curly kale, which is surprisingly sweet.

Before they leave the vicinity they find their way back to the cove and eat as many limpets as they can find, filling their bellies for the long march to Cork and the boat to America, not knowing when they would eat again or what would be their fate in the next couple of days.

"The limpets will not keep so, me boyo, we have to eat and then be on the run there," Seamus tells Daniel Sean.

All that day they walk with the strength that they drew out from their breakfast and nothing else, for all they encounter along the way is a wasteland; no trees, no berries, no plants, no roots. There is nothing to eat at all. The whole day they encounter no people either, as if they are the last inhabitants of planet earth.

That night they do come across a residual shadow of humanity as they sleep in the ruins of an abandoned thatch cottage that has five crudely but freshly dug graves to the side of it, with small wooden crosses on them. As they enter the cottage and set up for bed they see a proclamation written on the walls in charcoal.

This was once the home of Pat Caulfield and his wife, Kate, and our four children, as the Lord above took my whole brood and I am all alone now, therefore I, Patrick J. Caulfield, leave the blessed shores of Ireland for America. I am now in the hands of fate and words cannot begin to express the sorrow that dwells in this broken heart of mine, for it is a trick of the devil that I did not go with them.

The next day Seamus and Daniel Sean rouse themselves and ransack the cottage finding nothing to eat—but underneath a small pile of peat Daniel Sean discovers five unused sulfur matches. The large kind that strike against any rough surface.

When Seamus sees them he cries out, "Good God in heaven Danny this is a grand find, a jewel me lad, a jewel."

After filling up on water to staunch the pains of hunger they head out. They walk on through the abandoned fields and wastelands of eastern Kerry encountering no one, using up the fuel they derived from the limpets, but, after awhile, the pangs return unabated.

The next two days are simply repeats of each other as they continue on their trek to Cork City. At this point Seamus and Daniel Sean start to really feel the familiar sensations of hunger, and the weakness that stems from the lack of food, for they have not seen anything that could even remotely be edible. Nothing.

Later in the day, May 10th, a couple hours past midday, they enter into County Cork, keeping their distance from the vicinity of Bantry Bay. Sticking to the plan to avoid contact with anyone, at least as much as is possible.

Even though there is still light and more walking to do they find a place to sleep inside of a small makeshift hut. It was probably used by somebody or somebodies who had been in the same predicament as

the two of them in the past year or so. The two of them lie down and fall asleep out of sheer exhaustion even if their bellies are empty.

The following morning with growling stomachs and starving pessimism once again invades the consciousness of Daniel Sean, but not of Seamus. He keeps gently prodding his traveling companion on with encouraging words.

"Ah don't be worrying yourself now, Danny. We're well on our way and by God we will persevere. Ya have my word as an Irish gentleman."

This ridiculous unbridled optimism on the part of Seamus is slightly infectious, and Daniel Sean bucks up and keeps moving one step in front of another.

Just north of a town named Skibbereen, they stop to rest underneath a rock escarpment that juts out from a slightly wooded area. As they lie there Seamus signals Daniel Sean to be quiet. They both watch as a rabbit darts out from the foot of a tree only to disappear under a rock near to where they are lying.

Seamus puts his finger to his lips for silence and then slowly gets up and walks over to where the rabbit vanished. He stands there staring at the rabbit hole for a long three minutes or so, then makes his way back to Daniel Sean beckoning him to follow him away from the rabbit's hutch. Once they are on the other side of the escarpment, out of earshot of the rabbit, he whispers.

"We may just be able to have some meat tonight for our potage, me boyo, God willing. Luck be with us

Daniel, luck and the will of God, be with us. But first we need to gather some branches to make a snare and we'll be needing your laces that you have on your brogues there. Now, off wid them because they'll be of use to us. Now let's get cracking lad."

Even though both of them are so weak that they have trouble even moving about, they both come to life and head out on a sortie to find materials. After an hour or so they find three pieces of wood, branches from an oak tree that are about two feet each in length. Two of the pieces of wood have a two-pronged fork on one end that will be used as the bottom for stability.

With his knife Seamus digs a groove into the top of those two sticks. He then places the sticks, forked ends in the ground and grooved ends upright, to the side of the rabbit hole. He then whittles the third branch so that its two ends are thin enough to fit into the grooves of the two standing ones. He now has a sturdy frame that stands by itself.

With this done he takes the two shoe laces that Daniel Sean has given him, both old and striated with wear and tear, ties them both together for length, and then weaves it together with a bit of strong ivy that he has found, creating a strong but flexible rope. The whole time they are both working as quietly as is possible, so that they do not alarm the rabbits down below in their hutch.

With the 'rope' Seamus makes a small circle at one end and slides the other end of the rope through this

circle creating a noose that is large enough for a small to medium rabbit to step into and, hopefully, tighten in on itself. That is, of course, if a rabbit does make an appearance.

With his hand he rubs the grease, grime and filth off of Daniel Sean's and his own hair, face, and arms to lubricate the rope and the inside of the noose. Explaining to Daniel Sean in a whisper, "Aye but 'twill help the snare to move smoothly."

Seamus finally fastens one end of the snare onto the top of the frame, tying it tight so that it will be secure and not break. He then digs a small hole right in front of the entrance to the hutch and places the lasso/noose on top of a few leaves so that it cannot be seen.

After checking that all is steadfast, and assuring himself that if a rabbit does come out of it's hutch it will, hopefully, step into the noose and as it falls through the hole the noose tightens around and onto one of its limbs.

Seamus grabs Daniel Sean's arm silently pulling him back, slinking away from the snare to wait.

After lying there waiting, right around sunset, a medium sized rabbit with brown fur pokes its head out of the top of the hole. It looks around, hops out of it's hutch, steps into the hole, and right into the noose. It closes in on itself, catching the end of the rabbits right hind foot. The rabbit cries out which wakes up Seamus and Daniel Sean from their reverie. They both jump up

and Seamus quickly grabs the rabbit, shaking it and breaking its neck.

"Sweet Jesus, holy angels from the throne of light, Danny boy we did it, oh dear God in heaven, thank you, thank you."

While Daniel Sean searches for some kindling and dry shrubs to start a fire, Seamus skins, guts, and cleans the rabbit. He saves the frame that they used for the snare so that they have a means to cook their dinner.

Within a short while, using the matches that Seamus found in the Caulfield cottage, they have a small fire going. Seamus hangs the rabbit over the fire loosely trussed so that they can turn it while it is roasting inches away from the flame.

They both stare at the rabbit as it cooks, turning it as it grills away. Both of them chomp at the bit to devour it, but Seamus says to Daniel Sean,

"We have to make sure that it's cooked all the way now. We are in a weak state and we don't want to get the stomach ailing. Hold on a wee bit longer now, just a smidgen now."

Finally, Seamus gives the decree that it's time. He takes it off the fire, burning his hands just a little. They let it rest to cool, then with his knife Seamus cuts the rabbit in two, handing one half to Daniel Sean but stopping him before he starts to eat it.

"First we need to let it cool off and we must also give thanks to Almighty God, you hear me now Danny."

They both bow their heads as Seamus says out loud:

"Whatever happens dear Lord thy will be done. Our fate is in your hands Almighty Father, but for now, dear God, thank you for this poor little rabbit which we are about to receive. From thy bounty through Christ our Lord." They finish with the sign of the cross and say, "Amen."

In silence they devour the meat of the rabbit, chewing the cartilage, breaking the small limbs and sucking out the marrow from the bones. At the end of their meal there is literally nothing left but a few shards of sucked clean bone.

Glorious, glorious sustenance flows through the two of them. A golden liquid light fills them up, billowing through the smallest most minute cells and layers of their corporeal existence. The life force of the sacrificial rabbit imbues them with energy, hope, and simply an outward push up through the dregs of decay. Both knowing, of course, that this will not last for long.

They lay there watching the fire until it dies down, the sun having set an hour ago, and an almost full moon rises over the mountains in the distance.

"We will find my cousin and be on a boat to America in a few days, God willing," Seamus says.

Four

They trudge on and on the next day through a cold lashing rain, pulling their raggedy coats tight around themselves, and attempting to staunch their shared misery. As they walk on they start to encounter more and more people, nobody uttering a word in the pouring rain.

It is a sight that breaks the proud heart of Seamus, who keeps saying over and over. "We are no longer Irish, for that race of poets, dreamers, and warriors has been knocked down to the ground by fate. Now we are a nation of ghosts, hobgoblins, and shadows that are no longer of this world. We are restless spirits who dwell in the midst of the land between life and death."

The road thickens with thin emaciated skeletal beings, bones pushing back against the surrounding skin, as they all trudge on. Sallying forth to God only knows what. It is the ageless diaspora of humanity. Like the Jews driven out of Egypt, or countless other times that this has been enacted time and again, where multitudes have been displaced and forced to flee.

After walking for miles, late afternoon, after the rain has subsided and a weak sun has appeared in the sky, Seamus stops in his tracks, squints into the distance, nudges Daniel Sean and says, "Follow me."

Seamus then walks against the tide, away from the flow of people, looking over his shoulder so that he will notice if any one is following them. At the same time the two of them are acting as it they are giving up and just leaving. When they get a little distance from the throng, he urges Daniel Sean onward.

They make their way down through green stunted shrubs until they come to an area that is adjacent to a small stream. The stream empties into a small, light green pond that is surrounded by large willow brushes. Seamus tiptoes down to the edge of this small pond, where he squats on the very edge of the water.

He motions for Daniel Sean to do the same. They stay in position for a minute or two until there is a slight movement in the surface of the water. A small head pops up and then it leaps out of the water onto the grass that circles the small pond. It is a frog.

Seamus grabs a medium size rock that is lying on the side of the pond. He then stays motionless, staring at the frog until the frog jumps a little bit closer to where he is, and then Seamus smacks the frog across the head, killing it. He freezes and then waits until another frog appears and kills that one in the same fashion.

He repeats this over again for a short while, until there is a total of eight dead frogs. Seamus then scoops them up, places them in a dirty shirt that is in his pack and with Daniel following behind together they walk across a treeless terrain to a wooded area that appears to

be totally deserted. Seamus motions for Daniel Sean to sit.

"I saw that pond in the distance and was thinking that we'd find some frogs moving about there after the rain, and by God we did." He smiles at Daniel. "We should be safe here. This is the remains of a lumperers field where spuds, the big ones, are grown and harvested. That is…" He pauses and looks away into the distance. "Until the blight came and took away our glorious potatoes."

With a shrug Seamus continues. "We'll start a fire and eat, but first I am going to look around here for something to go wid it."

Seamus wanders off as Daniel Sean sits there in astonishment.

"How in the Holy name of God Himself did this man come into my world? This is the work of divinity, this is a blessing from above and I am hardly worthy of this."

Daniel Sean rouses himself and starts to collect anything that will burn. But he finds only dried grass and a few small twigs from a small bush nearby. By and by Seamus returns holding a small bundle in his arms. He has a huge smile on his face.

"I found some wild turnips and weeds that we can add to our potage, and a bit of fungi, mushrooms me lad, that will flavor the froggies a bit. Not exactly Sunday dinner on a veranda overlooking St. Stevens Green but it will keep us on our way."

"Seamus, tell me if you don't mind, how do you know all of this, how do you know where to get these things, I mean people are starving all over Ireland and you come up with…" Daniel Sean points to the pile of food stuff. "This?"

" 'Tis part of the training now me boyo. As one of the 'lads' of the Irish cause, we decided to partake of all that is Irish. Not just the history, or the music or the legends but also what nature herself has to offer us. The bloody English have taken to keeping for themselves what is ours so much so that we, in our own ignorance, have forgotten who we are as a people. The spirits of Ireland, the land itself will never betray us. It is us who have taken ourselves down the road to perdition because we allowed the damned English to control us. But with the grace of God that will end someday and we as a people will rise up, throw the Saxons off of our land and become a nation once again."

The whole time that he has been talking Seamus has been cleaning the frogs by cutting off the heads, hands, and feet. Then gutting the poor little bastards. When done cleaning the frogs he chops up the other things that he found.

They succeed in getting a little fire going with the small amount of twigs and dried grass using the last of the matches. Seamus places the small frog carcasses on top of the mushrooms, the chopped up wild turnip roots and then lays the weeds on top of them to steam the lot, letting them all cook together.

When Seamus decrees that it is done, they both chew and swallow the whole lot—the frogs, the mushed up turnip roots, and the mushrooms. The two of them crunching down on the rubbery bones, the whole mess sliding down their throats with the consistency of slimy seaweed. And even though it has a disgusting texture to it, the taste is not so bad. Daniel Sean smiles to himself and thinks of the saying. *Hunger is the best sauce.*

They lie there holding their stomachs, which are feeling a bit peculiar from the strange food.

"Soon, I figure in two days time at the most," Seamus says, "we will be in Cork City and find my cousin and set our course. I reckon that this will be our last meal until we find the boyo. Aye, but we should be all right, just a wee stomach hungry, but not starving."

He lowers his voice to a whisper. "We'll see even more poor souls tomorrow, starving sods who will break our hearts, but, God forgive us, we have to keep on moving. There is nothing that we can do for them, so we both need to buck up and not pause."

They sleep right there, where they had devoured the froggies garnished with mushrooms, and actually get a good nights sleep.

Five

They stay off the main road, crossing over fields and stone fences that are both barren and unattended, coming to a small stream, at which Seamus speaks to Daniel Sean.

" 'Tis a tributary of the River Lee which will lead us into Cork City proper."

Walking next to green, treeless hills, they trudge silently past abandoned cottages that seem to cry out in anguish to the beautiful rained out clear Irish sky. A sky so blue that it shimmers in contrast to the green rolling hills in the distance, creating a slice of pastoral heaven right in front of their eyes.

It is so lovely that it gives them both a small bit of hope for the future. A feeling that will last only as long as they do not run into anyone who is simply fighting to stay alive and attempting to stave off the process of physical dissolution.

Not being able to help himself, and knowing that Daniel Sean is probably thinking the same thing Seamus stops in his walking, puts his hand out to also stop Daniel Sean, and looks him in the eye saying.

" 'Tis beautiful my lad, but you can't eat beauty."

They keep moving all day long until they come to a desolate area that is bereft of people. Seamus decides that this is where they will stay the night.

That night they sleep underneath a small stone bridge that crosses over the River Lee. It is at a lonely bend in its meandering course, with a hard rain once again buffeting the landscape.

Later that night the rain stops but a blowing wind comes in from the south churning up from the Atlantic Ocean which is dead south of where they are camping.

The wind sounds as if it is a screeching baleful keening, like a mournful cry in the distance. Around midnight the wind picks up in strength, trembling the very air around Daniel Sean and Seamus. They both wake with a start. The sound intensifies taking on almost human attributes, crying and bellowing with a high-pitched shrieking wail.

Seamus whispers to Daniel Sean while crossing himself. "'Tis a banshee riding on the wind, she is foreshadowing the death of someone out there this very night. God have mercy on whoever it is, and deliver that persons soul to the realm of light in the name of the Father, the Son, and the Holy Spirit."

Sleep does not come easy for the two of them. The little bit that they do get is not gentle or complete but rather tempest tossed.

The two of them lay awake as the night air stays wind blown and the shrill shrieking wails on into the early morning. It's as if an entire legion of banshees are

out doing their duties as oracles of death during this time of famine and disease.

The rising of the sun finds them both moving at a brisk pace at first light, as the sun melts the dew and starts to dry the rain-splattered ground.

They continue to follow and stay on course with the River Lee as their guide, heading east towards Cork proper. After an hour or so they start to run into people who are also following the River Lee.

At first it is a scant few, but the closer that they get to Cork City the pathway along the banks of the river begins to fill up with people walking to their uncertain future.

The air itself reeks with desperation, as the quick furtive looks of the starving souls who are helplessly beseeching everywhere and everyone for anything to eat. This is coupled with the ones who have gone mad, crazed with the hunger, as they talk to themselves with their eyes fixed on a spot some place in the distance.

The most heart wrenching for Seamus and Daniel Sean are the sole survivors, the last shattered remnants of once intact whole families. These are individuals who are so alone, so weak, and so despondent that some of them have simply given up the fight. They stop where they are, lie down on the side of the road, and do nothing but clutch onto their meager earthly possessions and wait for the end. Sometimes among them are mere children, some barely nine or ten years old, who are alone and

have no family. These desperate pathetic kids look as if they are old men or women with drawn out haggard faces and with heads that are almost hairless due to the privations that come with starvation and disease.

The most desperate of these are the 'grass eaters.' Those walking skeletons whose faces are green around their mouths from eating grass to stem the hunger, which only makes them more sick and weak, and which just quickens the passing over.

Surrounded by this sea of misery Seamus and Daniel Sean walk with their eyes averted, their heads bowed, looking down at the ground so as to avoid any visual contact.

They cannot be moved, they cannot tarry, they cannot be side tracked. And even though this is very arduous and taxing on their souls to be in the midst of all this suffering and do nothing, Seamus knows that it would be much worse if they attempted to help anyone, for they have no resources to give.

He also knows that it would be even more of a nightmare if they were traveling on one of the other roads, for they would be jam packed with the absolute lowest, forlorn, and most desperate of those who have nothing to lose.

Here on the pathway along the River Lee it is desperate, but not so much so as on the main routes to Cork. Seamus knows this to be true because he knows all the highways and byways of Southern Ireland, Kerry and Cork counties in particular.

All day long the throngs move as one. Like a giant accumulation of seaweed gathered and taken along by an undulating, pulling, gently pushing, slow moving current. The ones who can barely move are herded towards the far edges of the mob so as not to impede the slow but steady progress of those in the middle.

Late afternoon, with the sun low in the horizon, they come to a bend in the road at an unusually high spot where Cork City is visible way in the distance. Daniel Sean stops in his tracks and stares open mouthed at the sight. He has never seen anything so big and he is slightly taken back.

Seamus clasps him on the shoulder saying, "This is nothing to what you'll be seeing in America."

Unbeknownst to the two of them they have stopped the flow of traffic. The collective force of the people behind them, who have been mindlessly walking without pause for hours, ram into them, knocking them both violently forward. This mob does not stop but keeps surging forward and onward piling one against the other.

Within seconds the gathering becomes a frenzied whirlwind with Seamus and Daniel Sean at the very center, the eye of the storm. Panic sets in and already exhausted starved bodies start to fall as those behind push forward and over those fallen with the horrific specter of fear urging them on.

This is when Seamus bends down, headfirst, and with all his strength tackles Daniel Sean pushing him out of this throbbing mass of humanity. They both tumble

over a small rise and down into the River Lee where a slight current carries them away.

As they float on they look up and see a full on stampede, with people being trampled under as the wave of desperate men and women behind them crushes over them.

The mob keeps moving forward as if it is a tidal wave overtaking those in its path, the ones ahead of them oblivious until it is too late, falling like dominoes, and then crushed underfoot by a herd of out of control human cattle.

Blood curdling screams pierce the still air as dreadful chaos rules the day.

Seamus and Daniel Sean silently look away, unable to witness any more of this sickening sight.

Securing a large branch that floats near him, Seamus hooks his arms around Daniel Sean, who is in shock, and places him on it. Together they paddle into the middle of the river where an even stronger current takes them on toward Cork City.

After a short distance the path along the river disappears as it veers up hill, away from where they are cruising along, taking the crowd of people with it, so that they now are pretty much alone.

All is silent except for the distant muffled cries of pandemonium, the sound diminishing the farther away the two of them drift along on the River Lee.

The current seems to slacken its pace so that they travel at a slower pace than before, which is a relief to Seamus.

"It can be an unpredictable lady, I've heard, the River Lee. Dead calm at one spot and then foaming angry at others."

After a few minutes of silence Seamus shakes his head.

"There is nothing that we could have done for those people, ya hear me now Danny? Nothing, nothing at all," he says.

Six

With the sun getting lower and lower on the horizon, with about an hour and half of light left, Daniel Sean and Seamus float on, not uttering a word until they come to a spot that is in close proximity to the city limits. Seamus speaks up.

"She splits into two parts right before we hit Cork City. I'll be letting you know when we'll have to paddle like the divil and stay to the left."

The two of them furiously paddle as they come to where the River Lee splits into two separate tributaries, and as planned they keep to the left one.

"Jaysus Danny, but this is the way to enter Cork, holy Mother of God." Seamus laughs out loud, which is the first time that Daniel Sean has heard laughter in a long, long time.

Floating down the river with the island center of Cork City to the right of them, they travel for a short while until Seamus points to a spot that doesn't look too difficult to land on. On Seamus's direction they point themselves toward that area.

The closer that they get to the shore a whole bunch of foul smelling trash, sewage, and all sorts of human refuse surrounds them, causing them to swim through this disgusting floating garbage dump.

They kick like mules and paddle like a couple of dogs until they get to a small sandy area below a stone wall that is about ten to twelve feet high.

It is late, late afternoon, the 14th of May, when Seamus and Daniel Sean enter the confines of Cork City.

Breathless, tired, filthy, and hungry, Seamus still manages a tight smile.

"We may smell like shite but this is the right side of the city where me cousin lives. We have to climb up to the street there so that I can get my bearings, then we'll go find him."

After they rest for a minute or two, Daniel Sean climbs up onto Seamus's shoulders, gets his balance, then literally jumps up and grabs the ledge above his head, holding on for a second to rest. He then pulls himself up, all the way to his feet, stands there, turns and looks down at Seamus.

"Find something that I can stand on and throw it down to me," Seamus says.

Daniel Sean turns around only to see a crowd of men and women across the cobble stone streets, just lying there on the pavement, showing absolutely no interest in him at all, as if a man rising out of the river is an everyday occurrence.

But then suddenly a small pack of them stand up, break away from the crowd and start to cross the street towards him. Rags for clothes, no shoes, filthy, and with bleak desperation in their eyes.

As the pack converges on Daniel Sean with absolute assured menace he wastes not a minute leaping back up onto the wall, pivots himself around, swings down with his hands on the ledge, and then quickly lowers himself down to where Seamus is standing.

The pack stares down at them until one throws a brick, barely missing the two of them. Enraged Seamus quickly picks up the brick and in one motion, tosses it underhand back up at one of the heads that is peeking over the ledge. Seamus receives his just reward with a muffled thud and a cry as the brick finds its mark.

The two of them, Seamus and Daniel Sean, start running down the shore of the River Lee yelling obscenities back at the pack. Exhausted and weak both of them stop running after a short distance knowing that no one will chase after them, for they will also be weakened by the hunger.

As the shadows start to lengthen and the sunlight begins to grow fainter, they keep walking and walking along the riverbank, crossing over and under a number of wooden fences, finally stopping at a small sloping hill that is heading upwards into the city itself.

"Daniel Sean, we have only a little more light left so we need to find a weapon of sorts before night settles in and we head up and into the city. Gotta be ready to fight, me boyo, there's desperation in the air."

They scour the banks of the River Lee and come up with a sharp rock for Daniel Sean and a hard wooden stick, which Seamus brandishes.

"Right you are, this will do. It's shillelagh law now. Let's go, and bad luck to any lad or lads that tries the likes of me."

The two of them cautiously tread up the incline into Cork, practically tip toeing one step at a time so as to be as non-existent as possible. When they get halfway up the street Seamus silently pulls Daniel Sean over to the side of the street, signals for quiet, and then whispers. "Do ya hear that?"

"I don't hear a thing," Daniel Sean whispers back.

"That's the point. All is silent. There should be movement about."

Suddenly they hear lightening strike in the distance.

"A storm is coming Danny. 'Tis a good thing, for if needed it will give us some coverage to add with the coming night. And if it really lashes rain then it will wash off some of the shite that is all over us from the river," Seamus says as he rubs his chin, thinking. "We must be near the northern section of the city and I reckon that there is a curfew in place, that's why there are no people about. Dear God we don't want to be caught out and about breaking the curfew. It would be the cane for the two of us, or worse. We have to become invisible."

With the sun just starting to melt below the horizon, Daniel Sean mimics Seamus as they both press their backs against the wall, blending in with the coming night, and slowly inch their way up the hill.

Coming to the top of the hill, in the last vestiges of the receding light, Daniel Sean sees that Cork City is a collection of hills with streets meandering this way and that way. He has never seen so many houses in his life. The largest town that he has ever been in is Dingle out in the farthest west peninsula of his county Kerry, and there is no comparing of it to the size of Cork.

Seamus squints his eyes to see better in the vanishing light and then points to a church steeple that is barely visible a short distance away. He leans over to Daniel Sean.

"This is grand, sure it is," he whispers. "I have me bearings now, even though 'tis been a couple of years since I've been here, I know where we are. Stay close and not another word."

Continuing on, the encroaching black night now shrouding their movement amongst the shadows, the two of them silently make their way down the other side of the hill until Seamus pulls them both back into the recesses of a dark alleyway.

Two English soldiers stroll by, casually glancing into the alley but not seeing anything, and then go on about their nightly patrol rounds.

Seamus waits for a full minute until he is sure that all is clear before they proceed on, sticking to the dark crevasses of the city, traveling down dark, deserted streets until the widths of the pavements start getting smaller and smaller.

The whole time Seamus moves effortlessly through one tight blackened labyrinth after another, pulling Daniel Sean with him into the hidden corners of the streets whenever a patrol happens by.

Silently they walk on turning right, then left, and then sharp right passing between row after row of tight-laced stone buildings. They move on over cobble stone streets, transversing across old rickety wooden sidewalks, and sliding down garbage strewn dirt alleys twisting one way then another. To Daniel Sean it doesn't seem possible that Seamus could be anything but lost.

After what seems like an eternity, but is really only about 20 minutes, they round a corner and Seamus leads them back into what looks like a dead end.

Barely visible in the far back of this closed in, dead end alley, off of the side of a nondescript building is a small door. It looks like it is a door that leads to an abandoned shed of sorts. A place that is now derelict but maybe was once an entrance to a horse stall or something along those lines.

It appears to be totally defunct and vacant. This is in contrast to the four to five story Georgian style houses and buildings that surround it, which are clean, orderly and seem fairly well to do. Unless you knew exactly where you were going it would be near impossible to know that there was anything back here.

They make their way down the deserted alley to the door.

Seven

Seamus knocks five times, pauses, knocks twice, pauses, and finally kicks once on the bottom of the door whispering to Daniel Sean, " 'Tis the secret passwords knock."

After a minute or so the door opens all the way and a hand reaches out and gently grabs Seamus around the neck, quickly pulling him inside, then waves Daniel Sean in also. In the glow of candle light Daniel Sean finds himself looking at a mirror image of Seamus.

Like Seamus he has all the attributes of the Normans who came here from western France centuries ago and completely embraced the Irish culture. In contrast to Daniel Sean, who has all the physical attributes of the ancient Irish—thick, jet black hair, blue eyes, stocky build and short bandy legs—Seamus and his cousin are both slightly built, medium height, with thinning, fair, sandy-brown hair, and welcoming green eyes. And, like Seamus, the cousin is about thirty years old. He has an eel-like almost manic energy emanating from him, that is identical to Seamus, as if either one of them could strike out at you without warning.

But any sense of danger is down played by an easy, casual, smiling charm that makes Daniel Sean immediately trust him.

"Jaysus now there Seamus, ya still remember the knock. Well look at ya now, what the hell has happened to the likes of you? First of all, did anyone follow ya?"

"No not a soul, I have not forgotten how to be as smoke around the bloody English and the Irish Garda. Not to worry, me boyo."

"Good man." They both smile at each other as Daniel Sean stands there gawking and taking in the remarkable similarities of the two of them.

"Daniel Sean O'Neill, this is my cousin, Francis Xavier Fitzgerald. But ya can call him Frankie."

Daniel Sean shakes his hand, then Frankie wipes his hand on his pants as if he is avoiding the plague.

"Let's get moving boys," he says, "this way to the back of the house. When we get outside ya both need to take off all of your things. It's about ready to lash rain out there and we have to get the two of you rinsed off. You are both as filthy as a tinker on Sunday morning before he cleans up for church, and we have had bouts of cholera the last couple of months. And we can't be taking any chances here, we have to throw away those rags that you are wrapped in."

When Seamus starts to object Frankie says. "Off wid ya now, shh, whist with the both of ya, we can't take no chances here with typhus, cholera, and the shadow of death that is all around. Here out the back."

They walk from the front foyer down a hallway through three small rooms that are lit with soft candlelight and completely devoid of any furniture. In

fact it looks as if there is nothing in the whole house. There are also no windows, and strangest of all are the walls, which are of a smooth grey limestone and have absolutely nothing on them: no pictures, no cabinets, no shelves, nothing but blank space.

The room farthest from the front of the house, is furnished with a small bed, a small wardrobe, a wash basin, and a large map of Ireland that is pinned to one of the walls.

Frankie goes to the very back of the room and opens the back door.

"We have to get you clean before ya even touch anything. Give me your clothes after you get good and wet. I don't want to touch them as filthy as they are."

The back yard is a small, totally secluded, enclosed rectangle, about twelve feet in length and about six feet wide, with a cement floor that ever so slightly tilts on a slope downward toward the back. Four walls that stretch about twelve to fifteen feet upwards, with a view of the night sky, and nothing else. It is as if they are completely encased, alone, and invisible, even though they are in the middle of a fairly populated city.

Just as they step out into the courtyard, Frankie reaches down into the washbasin and pulls out a bar of lye soap, handing it to Seamus.

Daniel Sean and Seamus both strip down to nothing, throwing the grimy, tattered rags that have been plastered to their skin to the side and lather up. Using

just his thumb and index finger, Frankie gingerly takes up the filthy clothes to throw them away as trash, he then closes the door to give his two guests an air of privacy.

In a matter of seconds the sky opens up and it starts to pour down rain. The two lads spread out their arms and receive this glorious gift of cleansing rain, causing them both to gasp with unmitigated pleasure.

An indescribable feeling of unfettered freedom wells up in the bosom of both Seamus and Daniel Sean. It is as if they have left the earth bound torments of this world and found themselves dwelling, albeit for a short temporary stay, in the fields of Elysium, as the lashing rain pours down, unabated, over their emaciated bodies, cleansing them both to the marrow.

They breathe in life once again as they receive this gift from above. As the rain continues Seamus and Daniel Sean take the opportunity to relieve themselves in the far corner of the courtyard where a small aperture in the bottom of the wall acts as a drain.

Due to the lack of food it has been a long, long time since either have had a decent bowel movement, and they both know that the powerful deluge combined with the lye soap will throughly cleanse the two of them. It is a wonderful sensation to feel clean once again. They both take turns squatting against the wall, groaning, pushing, and defecating.

Done with that they both scrub and rinse every single nook, cranny, and orifice on their bodies.

Standing under the falling rain both Daniel Sean and Seamus start to laugh giddily, exclaiming over and over again.

"Good God, oh my God, brilliant, never thought anything could be so wonderful, oh, oh brilliant, magnificent. Life again."

All in all they stay for a good half an hour under this glorious cleansing torrent of water until Frankie decides that the rite of purification is over and calls them both in, handing them both towels to dry off with.

Teeth chattering with cold, Seamus and Daniel Sean make their way inside of the house and finish drying off. Then they put on some old, slightly tattered, ill fitting but clean clothes from a pile, that is on top of the bed, which includes undergarments, shirt, pants, a sweater for each of them, socks, and shoes.

Frankie then leads them both to the small wardrobe that stands in the corner of the otherwise barren room. He pushes it aside revealing a small door that is hidden behind it. He bends down and opens the door and crawls through it into another room. Daniel Sean and Seamus follow suit and enter the hidden room.

It is a large open room that is spacious and generously furnished. There is a sleeping area with four small beds on the farthest left side of the room. In the very middle of the room is a table that can seat up to six people. On the back wall, behind the table, stands a large two door wooden cupboard.

Against the wall that borders the back of the building facing the courtyard is a small well, complete with a bucket on a rope to lower into the water below. Next to the well is a small table with a pitcher and a wash basin on it, with a couple of towels hanging on hooks.

On the opposite end of the wall from the well, sits a small fireplace.

Frankie goes directly to the fireplace and places a couple briquettes of turf on top of a pile of wood kindling, strikes a match and touches it to some crumpled paper that is under the kindling. The paper flames up immediately, catching the kindling on fire, and after a few minutes a soothing turf fire is blazing away.

"I set this up while the two of ya were washing up, figured you'd be needing to warm yourselves."

There is a clay pipe that ventilates up from the hearth, which connects farther up onto a flue that is a part of a huge chimney that serves the big grand house that abuts Frankie's structure. Frankie explains this to the two of them as they watch the fire and smell the turf.

"Of I course I only light up here when the companion house has smoke coming out of their chimney. That way the smoke coming from here is not seen and my abode remains invisible and my presence undetectable."

On the table Frankie has put out two small bowls of thick "stir about" soup, which is a combination of Indian corn meal and rice, both donated from America.

Also for the two of them are a couple slices of buttered brown bread next to the bowls. He gestures for them to sit and eat. Frankie waits for them to sit and then he makes the sign of the cross, praying, as Daniel Sean and Seamus join in.

"Bless us oh Lord and these our gifts which we are about to receive from thy bounty through Christ our Lord, amen."

Ravenously hungry they slurp down their stir about and chomp on the bread washing it down with mugs of fresh milk, which is the single most satisfying drink either one of them has ever had in all their days.

"I have not had a drop of milk in years now. Frankie me dear cousin, how in the hell did ya get this?"

"I have me ways Seamus. I know a couple of good decent Protestants out there who love Ireland and hate the English as much as we do." He looks hard at them and says. "There is a new movement underway to drive the Brits off of our shores, and it ain't just us Papists, by God."

As the two of them eat in silence, relishing every single morsel of this simple dinner, Frankie knocks the top of the table to get their attention.

"Listen the two of ya. While the workhouses flourish, while women and children starve to death, while we, the Irish, spend all our time fighting to stay alive, the cursed English take food right from our mouths. That's right, I seen it meself. Large boats larded down with grain and cattle sending off from our shores,

right here in Cork, stealing food meant for us, sending it out to London and Liverpool to feed the fat English while we starve like scarecrows."

He slams his fist down on the table. "We have enough resources to stave off An Gorta Mor and while it's true that the blight of the potato is an act of nature and the work of Almighty God, it is also true that it is the English who created the famine by not seeing us as full on human beings but rather as brutish animals. That's all we are to them, not human but more like animals."

He stops and shakes his head.

"But the world is watching, and there will be a reckoning someday."

Frankie stops and looks at the two of them, who are both still eating.

"Yes the world is watching and the truth will out. You see, this dinner that you are eating, as simple as it is, well…" He stops and smiles. "Have the two of ya ever heard of the Choctaw Indian Nation in America?"

They shake their heads no.

"Sixteen years ago," Frankie continues, "in 1831, that bleeding bastard Andrew Jackson, whose family were Antrim born by the way, commenced to pack up the Choctaw Nation, plus some members of the Cherokee Nation, and send them on their merry way so that he and his associates, whoever the bleeding hell that might be, could take their lands."

His voice rises up in indignation. "Prime grazing land that belonged to the Choctaw and the Cherokee.

These bastards took the Indians land to graze on and cultivate, using it as they damn well pleased."

He shakes his head in disbelief.

"The Red men did put up a fight but were outnumbered and out matched by the Jacksonians, so they didn't stand a chance from the get go. After being defeated, subjugated and losing their land, the real authentic Native Americans were forced to march on a 500-mile exodus from the eastern part of America, near Mississippi I believe, out west to Oklahoma. It ended up being called The Trail of Tears."

Stopping to collect himself while the dual elements of anger and sorrow rise up in his chest he looks up at the ceiling and continues.

"Well, despite the efforts to enact genocide over a race of people considered to be inferior by that Scotch Irish bastard, President Jackson, the Choctaw Indians did make it all the way to Oklahoma and survived."

Frankie pauses once again, fierce hot tears clouding his eyes.

"The only problem is that over half of them died of starvation and disease along the way. Fifty percent of them, half of the population of the Choctaw bleeding nation, laid down on the side of the road and gave up the spirit along that blackened accursed Trail of Tears. But by God the ones who did make it, despite the loss and misery, did not harbor hatred but instead got the revenge of survival."

"And you know what the Choctaw Nation did after all those years?" Frankie laughs out loud and then goes down to a whisper.

"This past year upon hearing about the plight of us Irish, and as poor as they are but with hearts as big as the blue sky hanging over Oklahoma itself, just a few short months ago they took up a collection from the members of their tribe who reached down deep and collected one hundred and seventy eight dollars. Then they used those precious dollars to buy corn meal and, because they wanted it to go to those most desperate, they had it sent here to Cork City."

He shrugs and points at their empty plates.

"Which is where this stir about that you just ate came from—the cornmeal was sent from the beautiful hearts of the Choctaw Nation."

With a resolute wink at Daniel Sean and Seamus he continues.

"They said that they felt a collective connection with us because they too had been purposely persecuted, they were considered inferior as a people and also faced forced migration, loss of property, exile, disease, and starvation.

"But what has hit a cord with the Choctaws is exactly what the English are trying to do to us now, which is the complete denial of our culture, our religion, and our language. Just like they tried to do to the Choctaw Nation but against all odds they did not let that happen. Those were the precise sentiments expressed by

their chief, so help me God. So you see, cousin Seamus, and Daniel Sean O'Neill, we are not alone."

For a good five minutes not a word is spoken and as this revelation of the generosity of the Choctaw Indians sinks into the hearts of the three of them.

Finally Frankie makes a proclamation.

"So one of the two of you, God willing if you survive, has to, after you get settled and start to prosper in America, well one of you has to make a trip to Oklahoma and give thanks to whoever is the Chief of the Choctaws for saving your life. I beg of you to do that for the people of Ireland. This cannot be forgotten, how they reached out to us in our darkest hour. This has everything to do with how we, as a race of people, end up as a result of this famine. Will we be magnanimous and do noble spirited acts, or will we look the other way when others are downtrodden as we are now? That will be the pivotal point in our history to show who we are as a people when we emerge from the ravages of this famine. We will either survive like our altruistic Choctaw brothers and sisters with our hearts and souls aflame with compassion and pride, or will we forget and no longer be Irish."

Frankie stands up goes over to the cupboard, opens it, reaches into it, closes it, and then comes back with a couple more slices of bread and spreads them with the last of the butter that he has.

"This is the last of the bread. All I have is a bit of oats for the morning, and that will be the last of the food

for now. But we will be all right. I do have my connections around here you see."

Frankie stands up and looks at Daniel Sean and Seamus. "Listen the two of ya. I'll be back in bit."

Then he commences to put on his rain jacket, crawls through the 'secret' door into the other part of his abode, and heads out into the night.

Eight

Seamus and Daniel Sean sit there in silence wondering what the hell is going on. Sure enough, after only about fifteen minutes, they hear the key in the door and both crawl under the hidden door to the main area of the house to meet Frankie. He comes in carrying two buckets of stout with him.

"We might be starving to death these days but by God we don't have to die of the thirst." He motions for them to follow him as he bends down and crawls back into the larger more secluded room.

They bring the stout into this room by sliding it under the small door where Frankie picks it up.

After Daniel Sean and Seamus get seated at the table again Frankie sets the buckets down in front of them and a wee bit spills over onto the tabletop. Daniel Sean immediately, without thinking, reflexively passes his finger over the spill and places it in his mouth.

Frankie laughs, walks on over to the cupboard reaches way into the back, pulls out three pint glasses and carries them to the table. He then fetches three short tea cups out of the cupboard and places them on the table. He smiles and waggles his finger at Daniel Sean to relax and wait. Finally he pulls out of the bottom of the

cupboard a small bottle of clear liquid. He sits at the table with the two of them.

"This is the last of the poteen that I have been saving for a special occasion, and seeing my cousin Seamus is just that special occasion."

Seamus is all smiles now. "Where did you get the Guinness from? I thought that there is a curfew about."

"Aye there is, but that hardly applies to the Protestants now does it? And the ones that I know want the same thing as us. A free and democratic Ireland for all Catholics, Protestants, Jews, and whoever the hell calls themselves Irish. A nation once again. Anyway there is a shebeen around the corner that is blacked out, but even so everyone knows me and that I am no enemy to them, only to the English. But we keep all that very quiet, don't we now?" Frankie looks at Daniel Sean,.

"You probably don't know but Cork is called the Rebel City, behind closed doors of course." He winks and places his index finger over his lips to signify secrecy. "But enough of the jabbering let's have us a drink."

He pours two inch shots of the fiery poteen into three teacups, and then pours each of them a full pint of Guinness. He leaves just a small amount of poteen and another pint of stout in the bucket for the three of them.

They raise their teacups and toast in unison:

"Slainte, God bless all here."They clink glasses and drink the poteen first, then follow that with a

swallow of the Guinness, licking their lips as the heavenly stout slides down their throats.

This is something that is inconceivable to Seamus and Daniel Sean just a few hours ago. To go from absolute starvation to having dinner followed by a pint of stout was not even remotely in the realm of possibilities to either one of them. It gives them an otherworldly feeling of possibilities that could exist in an alternate universe. *How is this possible? It makes no sense whatsoever.*

They take their time with the rest of their first pint of Guinness as a level of contentment settles into their bones.

After a while Frankie breaks the silence. "You see now, ya have to realize that as for us being Irish, well now, it has nothing to do with who we are as a people, it is the land itself. It is Ireland. It is a mystical place, full of spirits and magic. Once this place gets a hold of ya, then you become part and parcel of it. Unless of course you're English, who already know everything and have no sense of wonder."

Frankie sits back and pours the three of them the last of the stout. And on the side, he pours another small smack of poteen, finishing that off also.

As they delve into their libations Frankie becomes quite serious, leaning forward so that he is about a foot from Daniel Sean's face, which surprises him because it is something that the Irish people consider impolite to do unless there is a point is to be made. You do not get into

another persons face like this, you simply don't do that unless it is very important.

In a low soft voice Frankie says, "What I am about to tell ya boyo is something that on pain of death can never be repeated again, do you follow me?"

Daniel Sean nods his head.

"Good on ya lad. Now this place where ya are now, well it is what we call a 'safe house,' all right? I tole ya before that Cork is the Rebel city and this place here where you are now is one the many secret cubbyholes that we have scattered around the city. Any Irishman or Irishwoman who longs for freedom and is willing to fight for it is welcome here. This is a refuge for the likes of them, and some day Ireland and the Irish people will stand up with the rest of the world as a nation all its own without the yoke of the English around our necks." Frankie raises his pint glass and they all drink.

As a typical loquacious man of Cork, once he gets started talking it is hard to stop. Frankie continues.

"But these are rough times now, because of the hunger. And the likes of you are leaving our shores and spreading out into the world. There is no other choice. But Daniel Sean ya must always remember where ya come from and not forget your people back here. You best show the Yanks who we are as a people or the spirits of your still suffering departed ones will never let you rest in peace. Never." He smiles a sad smile at Daniel Sean and Seamus.

"We are an ancient people going back to the mists of time, but as nation we are a just ready to be born. And that is why we, the true Irish rebels, have taken up the cause for freedom. And soon, sooner than you think, we will rise up to ride upon the wind that shakes the barley, and by God there will be a grave reckoning for the Saxons. And as the souls of our wretched starved mothers, fathers, brothers, sisters, wives, and children watch with bated breath from above, this new Irish Nation, will be brought forth into this half breathing world." He stops and smiles at Seamus and Daniel Sean. "But enough of this, let's have a us a toast."

Frankie raises his pint glass.

"Here's to giving Ireland back to the Irish. And may God have mercy on us in this time of need. Slainte."

With the rain still lashing outside and the wind wailing as if the banshees are riding on its currents, once again foreshadowing someone's death, they all drink and then settle back into a melancholic stupor, into their own thoughts of lost loved ones and the life that they had lived before the Great Hunger came.

Eventually Frankie gets the two of them settled in on the small cots in the large secluded room, but not before Daniel Sean strips down once again and takes himself out into the pouring rain to vomit and defecate— for his shrunken, gaunt, malnourished body is not used at all to the drink.

After cleaning up he comes in, dries off, puts on his newly acquired undergarments and lies down on his small cot with heart broken dreams of his family haunting him as he begins to nod off. But after this night of cleansing, nourishment, and the stout there is also a small hint of light for the future.

As the storm rages outside, Daniel Sean settles into a thick dreamless slumber as his besieged body gives over to utter exhaustion, thankfully, at long last, 'knitting up the raveled sleeves of care.'

His last thought before he is dead to the world in sleep is of his mother and one word: *Remember.*

Nine

The next morning they each have a small bowl of cooked oats, along with a cup of tea to help curb the bit of hangover that they have. Daniel Sean has never had tea before.

"What is this?" he asks Frankie.

Frankie is incredulous that Daniel Sean's lips have not had the pleasure of tasting tea, but rather than making a big deal of it he only replies.

"'Tis the only good thing that the English ever brought to Ireland. It's tea, smuggled in from London. Drink it up lad, it will get ya going. I forgot that you're from West Kerry where a lot of different things can't be had. Especially during these dark days that we're having."

After they have consumed the meager breakfast Frankie opens the back door and the three of them carry the last of the tea out into the small courtyard beneath a glorious, clear blue, Irish morning, with clouds racing by at a clippers pace.

There is a slight chill in the air after the storm from the night before, and everything feels so clean and fresh that, just for a minute, it is inconceivable that people are starving to death a mere stones throw from the confines of this walled in 'safe house.'

Frankie speaks to the two of them.

"I have no more food, but I may be able to go out on a sortie and get a few odd items. Things are scarce even here in Cork. Last night at the shebeen, a couple of the lads were talking about a band of desperados who on the brink of utter starvation broke into one of the ships out in the harbor down there looking for food. They were shot on the spot. Now the patrols are coming down hard on the locals so ya have to watch out as to what you're doing here and there. Fact is we have to get the two of you on a ship out of here as soon as we can."

The whole time Frankie is looking at the ground avoiding his cousin Seamus's eyes. He shrugs his shoulders.

"I best go see what I can find in the way of food, and also see about transport for the two of ya."

With that he finishes his tea, puts on his hat and heads out the door. "Be back in a mo."

Seamus and Daniel Sean use the time alone to go through the contents of their belongings and to get organized for the voyage to America. This takes the better part of five minutes, seeing as how they both have next to nothing.

They spend the next couple of hours lounging about in the courtyard, whiling away the time until Frankie finally turns up. When he does turn up he is all smiles and has a small bundle under his arms.

After locking the door behind him, Frankie takes off his hat with a dash of theatrics and bows.

"We have steerage for the two of ya for tomorrow, your passage to America. And, on top of that, included in the deal, will be some foodstuff that the ships men will supply for ya. It's not much but 'twill do for what you're needing, and its part of the deal. What they have is oats, hard tack biscuits, dried bacon, some Indian corn meal from the Choctaw Nation, along with rice, molasses, and that's about it.

"Now what they supply should be enough to make it over there to New York City, for that's where the ship is going. You'll have to be sharing the stove that is on the lower deck with the rest of the passengers. That way ya can cook your meals. They let you out of the downstairs cabins twice a day for an hour or so. It will be a hard voyage, death will be everywhere, as I've heard tell, but by the grace of God you'll make it. Here, here's your certificates. It's all done up and paid for and by God Seamus hold your stammering, for I'll not take any money from the likes of either of ya. This is courtesy of the Young Ireland. For even though the two of us, that being you and me cousin Seamus, don't necessarily agree with the overall policies of those lads, well Seamus, I have to tell you they do sometimes get things done."

He smiles at the two of them continuing on.

"But there is one thing. A catch so to speak. And that is this, that was stipulated to me by Captain Major O'Brien of the Young Ireland in Cork, the man who delved into the funds to pay for both of your passages.

Capt. O'Brien said this to me: 'Tell the two of them to, first, remember who ya are and where ya come from and second, after ya get settled in over there in America, you must go find the chief of the Choctaw Nation and shake his bloody red hand."

Standing up regally, puffing up his chest, and slamming his fist on the table Francis Xavier Fitzgerald says in quiet but authoritative voice. "It is time now to come to terms as to who we, the three of us, truly are as men of Eire. We come from a proud race of warriors, not just the men but also the women, a race that does not look lightly on one who does not keep his word."

He looks from Daniel Sean and back to his brother Seamus. "I know me brother will keep his but Daniel Sean do you think that you'd be willing to keep yours?"

Daniel Sean becomes introspective for a wee bit then starts to speak.

"When the first Celts came to these shores, two thousand years ago, when they first spotted our Emerald Isle while on their boats from a distance they made an oath that the first man to touch the ground would be the first High King of Ireland. Well as it goes my ancestor, the head of the Ui Nhail clan, or the future O'Neill's was the first one to touch the shore. He was slightly behind and about to lose the race so he cut off his left hand and with all his might he threw his severed hand ahead of the other ship that was just coming ashore and as it goes, his bloody hand landed first on these shores, making him the

first to touch these shores and making him the first High King of Ireland."

Frankie laughs heartily at this and then tells them both to open their hands palm up. He then pulls out a knife and in a flash cuts the three of them in the middle of their upturned hands and clasps all three palms together so that their blood mingles. The oath is that if either Daniel Sean or Seamus outlives their voyage and gets settled in America that person must go and shake the hand of the Chief of the Choctaw Nation.

"There ya have it, a blood oath, something that I don't reckon neither of ya want to break for the divil himself would be chasing ya down after all is said and done. Bad cess to anyone who does not live up to a blood oath and fulfill it all the way through."

He washes his bloodied hand in the basin and then dries it with a towel.

"And speaking of luck itself, she is with us right now. For this ship does not leave from Cobh like most of the ships that do be leaving for the Americas but from right here in Cork City itself."

Frankie finally opens up the small bundle that he brought in with him which contains a few articles of food that he procured along St. Patrick Street in Cork proper.

"This is what we'll be having for our dinner tonight, not much but it is all that I could find. Things are getting more and more desperate out on the streets

there, everyday there is more and more people and less and less food.

That night they have a bit of hard tack biscuits with some dried bacon, washed down with a bit of porter that Frankie goes out around the corner to the shebeen and buys.

"I know that it is not exactly right to be indulging like this with the great hunger out there," he tells the two of them, "but when you two are gone I will have no reason to have a pint for I will have no one to do it with. So we'll wet our whistles here together one last time. Not much but just enough for the two of ya to get a good nights sleep. For who knows what tomorrow will bring?"

After finishing their meal they talk for a while and try to keep the gab going, but as it's been a long day, and with a lot to do tomorrow, it eventually comes to an end. They fall into a deep but troubled sleep early in the evening, with no one saying hardly a word at bedtime, for all three of them know that the next couple of days are sure to be wrought with uncertainty.

The last words from Frankie before they retire say it all. "We are at the mercy of God above, me here in the Rebel City holding down the fort, and the two of ya on the winds of fate itself, fleeing this God forsaken island just a step ahead of famine and pestilence. All I can say boys is this, "Dia's Muire dhuit. May God and Mary be with us."

Ten

They wake up the next day with thoughts full of promise mixed in with trepidation, knowing that all will not be well these next couple of days. But this is also mixed in with a slight sense of hope that only movement can bring when things are so desperate.

Leaving their homeland and An Gorta Mor fills both Seamus and Daniel Sean with a bitter touch of melancholy but also with a hopeful notion that it could be possible to run away from the wretched desperation that is now Ireland and somehow, someway, find another life that is not surrounded by death and despair.

Seamus and Daniel Sean say their goodbyes to Frankie, who gives them directions to the boat, and then surprises them with an extra change of clothes and a small chunk of bread for each of them, which they both slowly eat to let it last a bit longer, not knowing when they'll taste bread again.

"The last of all the food now you two. This is it. But I will manage and survive; it is you lads that I am worried about."

He pauses for a second then says. "You will be at the dock in less than fifteen minutes, but move swiftly and stay together."

Frankie embraces the two of them, opens the door, and peeks outside to make sure that no one is watching or waiting. Seeing that all is clear, he again quickly embraces the two of them, pushes them outside onto the street, and quickly closes the door, leaving both Seamus and Daniel Sean alone in the secluded alley and on their own again.

Seamus motions for Daniel Sean to move, and the two of them leave the womb-like world of Francis Fitzgerald's safe house, thrust out into a less than auspicious future without even so much as a look backwards.

Daniel Sean holds the O'Neill Celtic cross tightly in his right hand, which is in the pocket of the frayed jacket that Frankie gave him, and clenches his left fist into a ball lest he comes to blows with anyone. Seamus whispers to him.

"Here we go now me boyo, this is it, we have to do whatever we have to do to get on that boat."

The street savvy Seamus leads the way, darting in and out of the crowds that seem to have appeared overnight. They slide past the slowly moving masses of humanity who are shoulder to shoulder, beard to beard, all reeking of desperation. They not just fill the sidewalks but also the cobbled streets, which are peopled with the absolute dregs of the Irish populace.

All this is as a blur to Daniel Sean as he follows Seamus north and east as they make their way, once again, to the banks of the River Lee.

As they approach the ship that will take them to America, which is the only ship on the small dock lining the river, Daniel Sean notices that there are Irish police, or Garda, Irish patrols, and English soldiers everywhere. Shoulder to shoulder, standing together brandishing clubs, herding the people away from the boat unless they have a ticket.

"Danny, now carefully take out your ticket, but hold on to it with your life and stay close to me."

They move as quickly as is possible while being jostled and pushed this way and that. But Seamus is on top of it all, and when Daniel Sean feels a nudge and then whirls around to confront a waif of a man who tried to grab his hand, Seamus intervenes and collars the man before anything can transpire.

Daniel Sean pulls out the Celtic cross and shows it to the shell of a man standing there in rags who looks to be just a day or so away from the call of the reaper. The man looks at the Celtic cross and then collapses to the ground and starts to weep saying to Daniel Sean. "Lookit what I become, it is the divils own invention, to ferget our very souls itself. Be off widja now and good luck to ya young man. For I am ashamed of meself for what I did indeed intend to do."

Seamus roughly pulls Daniel Sean away from the man, moving him through the throngs surrounding them. They come face to face with a Garda, who checks their ticket certificates and shoves them both down a wooden pier. This leads them through a gauntlet of English

soldiers who line the sides of this walkway. The one that will take them to the ship, and the voyage to America.

Daniel Sean and Seamus, along with a crowd of fellow travelers, walk down the planked walkway that leads to the ship. They pass by sour and disdainful English soldiers. One of them laughs at the sight of the poor wretches.

"So much for the luck of the Irish," he bellows, which elicits a hearty laugh from his fellow guard.

Seamus stops for just a second and feels his fist itching and begging to strike this man, but instead he only smiles at him, raises his left hand in the air and sends a curse to him in Irish, which, of course, the English man does not understand.

"Go ndeana an diabhal dreimre do chnamh do dhrona."

He then repeats it in English, whispering to the man.

"May the devil himself make a ladder out of your spine."

The soldier is stunned into silence, and is unable to move or say anything.

As Seamus and Daniel Sean move on, the English soldier starts to feel a wave of heat suddenly move up his back, and he has to sit down to ease the pain.

Daniel Sean looks at Seamus saying, "Didn't know that you know the old curses. Me ma was good at them too."

"It's all nonsense," Seamus replies, "but the English are scared to death of us when we speak in our Irish tongue. They are the ones who believe that it's true, but to me, it's all nonsense."

Nine days after leaving his small meager farm in the West of County Kerry, on the 16th of May in the year of our Lord 1847, Daniel Sean, along with his magnificent companion Seamus Fitzgerald, boards the ship, the *Athlone*, to make his way to America.

Both of them keep to one side of the ship, trying to stay as much out of the way as possible, contentment shining from their faces as they watch the English soldier contort in pain.

It is not an overly large vessel, not half as big as the ones that, according to Frankie, have acquired the notorious moniker of 'the coffin ships'—due to the staggering number of deaths that have occurred on the larger ships that generally sail out of Cobh.

The two of them are herded together with a motley group of thoroughly forlorn looking individuals, all weak and gaunt from the lack of food.

After a short fifteen minute wait, a large thick bell that is on the front of the ship begins to clang, which as it turns out, is the signal for the ships departure. Once it stops ringing the captain of the ship materializes from the inner bowels of the fore deck and stands center stage on a platform overlooking the rest of the ship.

He is an imposing figure; a stocky, thickly muscled man, topped with a curly mane of hair, piercing green eyes, and a jutting chin that seems to telegraph pugnaciousness. Physically he commands immediate respect and garners about himself a sense of wariness from all who come into his presence.

There is also another dimension to this fairly simple yet complex individual. He appears to have a modicum of calm reassurance that he now conveys to his passengers. Speaking with a heavy Cornish accent, which is surprisingly pleasant with its flat vowels and elongated consonants, he smiles as he addresses the crew and his passengers in a most measured tone.

"I am your Captain, Captain Thomas Newton, and one thing and everything that I say will be obeyed if we are all to get along. This is the *Athlone* and she is a most seaworthy ship. And she is not what is being called these days, a coffin ship, for we are duty bound, and you are in the best of hands. I have made this journey a multitude of times and so has this crew. So by the grace of God and the competence of the crew we will land in New York harbor unscathed and healthy."

He stares out to sea and continues. "There will be no fighting on board, no hoarding of the ships supplies and no physical displays of Papist proclivities on deck. Down below decks do as you please. There will be one hour of fresh air up on deck in the morning and two hours in the late afternoon and early evening. The rest of the time you shall be sequestered down below. If any of

these rules are violated there shall be dire consequences, which include flogging, at the least, and hanging at the worst. At this point we will supply hard tack with water for tonight and nothing else, tomorrow you shall receive the first of your daily allowances of food and water. They shall be doled out first thing tomorrow morning. You will take turns using the stoves for cooking your meals, if indeed cooking is at all required, and you will also take turns using the wooden bucket latrines that have been set up in each quarter cubicles down below decks. These will be your responsibility to keep clean and sanitary. I ask that the men respect the privacy of the women. If not there will hell to pay from me or some other member of the crew. This is one thing that will not be overlooked."

He glances at the men on board and also to the crew to make sure that this is understood. He looks intently at the sight of the passengers whose lives are basically in his hands. Lives that are already only a half a step away from death.

Unlike some of the English captains, who are disgusted simply at the prospect of being in charge of these ships that shuttle back and forth with their Irish chattel, Captain Newton's heart goes out to these poor wretched souls. After all, he is a Cornish man, and like the Irish he is of Celtic descent.

He hitches up his pants, gazes out into the distance at the low hung sun, dangling like a ripe peach

on the horizon, shrugs his shoulders, smiles at no one in particular.

"This evening we will bend the rules a bit and you may all stay on deck to eat, which I have decreed will also include a small portion of molasses. You can then have a bit of fellowship with one another, and say goodbye to your homeland before the night falls."

He then waves his hands in a circle to signal the crew to get moving. The boatswain blows his high-pitched whistle to augment the order for "All hands on deck."

The crew of the ship springs into action and the passengers are taken aback by the sudden movement that seems to occur spontaneously but has, of course, been done over and over by the crew members of the *Athlone*.

Eleven

Ever so slowly the *Athlone* sails on, tacking to and fro, back and forth, the crew quickly and methodically scrambles across the ship, some moving like monkeys up and down the masts.

Sliding from one shore of this section of the River Lee to the other, the ship carefully makes its way though the tight channel that meanders along the northern shore of the island that is the center of Cork City.

While it is labor intensive it is also fairly smooth, for the crew on the *Athlone* is, as Captain Newton said in so many words, very competent and reliable. So the ship sets out on its journey at a good and solid pace.

The haggard, phantom-like specters who happen to be the passengers, clinging to the side rails of the ship, or sitting, or stumbling blindly from one side of the crowded ship to the other, trying to make their way around the deck, watch the crew doing their duties in complete and total awe.

And at the same time these same passengers struggle to make some kind of logical sense of what exactly is transpiring right in front of them. After all, the majority are in a state of absolute physical and cultural shock, for most have never even left the confines of their

village or farm, and now to be on a voyage that will take them out onto the ocean blue heading for America is almost inconceivable.

After a short while, by and by, another section of the crew takes the lead and methodically herds the bewildered passengers into twelve separate lines. These are designated by different numbers that are on each individual boarding ticket to determine which cabin quarters they will be located in for the entire voyage. The below deck or passage area, is divided up into twelve separate cabins.

Of course Seamus and Daniel Sean have corresponding numbers, which means that they will be in the same quarters.

It takes a little maneuvering to get one and all into their correct lines. This is because there is a huge language barrier between the English crew and some of the passengers, for some of the Irish speak little or no English at all.

It is a bit chaotic at first, and some of the English crew are frustrated and start to roughly push the Irish about. Man that he is, Seamus takes the lead and instructs his fellow countrymen in Irish on what needs to be done, smoothing things over.

After this is done the passengers are taken below deck, and then led down a small wooden ladder into the hold of the ship, where they will spend most of the voyage.

As Daniel Sean makes his way down into the dark and gloomy interior of the belly of the Athlone with Seamus right in front of him, he is immediately struck with the physical discomfort of overbearing claustrophobia. The ceiling is so low that anyone over medium height has to duck in order not to bang their head. This feeling of closeness is intensified for it is packed from top to bottom with people and their meager possessions.

There are numerous types of beds across the length and width of the room consisting of large, raised flat beds for entire families to sleep on, accommodating up to six individuals, triple decker bunk beds that sleep two per bed, and then there are single cots against a wall which are for single men to share, usually taking turns sleeping.

Daniel Sean and Seamus are to share one of the cots, which is an area separate but in close proximity to where the families will reside. They both look down at the small cot.

"We'll be alright now. Like they said, we can take turns sleeping in it, the other can sleep on the floor underneath it, that's all." Seamus pauses. "We'll just have to keep an eye out for the mice and rats who are sure to be about."

It takes only about ten minutes for everyone to get settled in, as no one has much in the way of material possessions. People take to sitting on the sides of their beds looking dumbfounded at their new surroundings.

Everyone looks around at one another, realizing that they will be together in this space for a good while, and that they must get along or it will be a most difficult voyage.

Once again, being the somewhat worldly man that he is, Seamus makes the most of the circumstances. He walks around introducing himself, shaking hands with the men and women, winking at the little ones, acting as if all will be well soon. This creates a sense of cohesiveness with his fellow travelers, especially the children, who seem to be in a state of numbing shock.

His initiative seems to work because brief but weary smiles come up from the darkness within and each lights up the room for just an instant.

One young woman, barely a girl of sixteen or seventeen years of age, thin—of course, from the hunger, which makes her look younger than her age—starts to cry. For her it is an embarrassing display of giving over to the situation, but she can't help herself and starts to simply let go of her inhibitions, practically howling in pain.

Seamus is startled yet quite moved by this, so he steps over to her side and puts his hand on the top of her head, letting her know that he understands her sadness. He speaks softly to her.

"It's alright now me darling. We are all here together, and as God is my witness we shall get through this. Besides, someone as lovely as you will be the belle

of the ball over there in America. The name here is Seamus Fitzgerald."

She sniffles, and with more than a little bit of pride in her voice, bucks up, straightens her shoulders, and looks him in the eye, almost defiantly challenging him to mock her.

"My name is Molly Ryan and there's just me and me Mam left in this world. Me Da and all of my brothers are all gone. The youngest, Michael went over to the other side only just two days ago. We couldn't afford to give him a proper send off, no wake, no coffin, no priest, we put him in the cold ground and said a few Ave's over his body."

Not being able to help herself, she starts up crying again so that a few of the women present surround her and comfort her. She points over to a corner bed where a woman of about forty years of age is sitting and gazing out into space, seemingly unaware of her surroundings.

"Me Ma is going daft with the sorrow, and keeps droning on and on wondering where Michael is now."

"Well let's do something about your ma. Now Molly, ya come with me."

Seamus leads her over to where her mother is sitting while everyone else watches in silence. He goes right up to her mother, puts his hand under her chin and lifts up her head so that she is looking into his eyes.

"Mrs. Ryan, the name is Seamus, Seamus Fitzgerald, there is something that I have to tell you. Are you listening?"

She looks at him with a dumbfounded stricken look and says nothing, so he repeats himself. She finally shakes herself out of her trance like state and nods her head. He continues.

"I have a brother who is a priest and he told me a little secret. You see when we die there is no time limit to when our immortal soul takes flight to meet all the angels, the Holy Mother, and Christ himself up in there in the everlasting throne of Light. So if we say the rosary together right now for the eternal soul of your son Michael, our Almighty God, who, believe it or not, likes to be reminded of things that have past, He will hear us and in the twinkling of your lovely blue eyes He, along with His Son, and blessed Mary, the Golden Rose, will take Michael up into their arms, away from all the pain of this world. I promise you that this is true."

She clasps Seamus's hand with a vice like grip and starts to shake it up and down holding it to her chest.

"Oh my poor Michael, my wee darling, not quite six he was and so tiny, so small. But, I swear my other sons all got the proper burial, we had a coffin, and a priest with holy water, but not for Michael, not for Michael." She starts to wail and keen at the memory. Seamus shakes her and speaks to her in a strong, commanding voice.

"Whist with ya now, for I tell you woman that if we do a full decade of the beads then all will be well with your Michael. Are you willing?"

"Oh yes, yes, will ya start now Mister Fitzgerald? I have my rosary right here."

They both fall to their knees and start the rosary. To which most of the people in the steerage area join in so that there is a soothing hum of sacred intonations filling the air around them.

Molly puts her arms around her mother joining in the recitation of the rosary.

As she kneels there next to her mother, Daniel Sean looks at Molly and her mother, both with jet-black hair and ethereal sky blue eyes, and sees an image of his own family in her. She is not Viking, not Norman—she is Celtic, and just like himself, she has all the signs of having some of the lineage of the Tuathan da Danaan on top of the Celt that is inside of her. Like his family, she is a descendant of the ancient ones, and probably a distant relative of his from way, way back.

Looking at this girl, Molly, this heart broken angel, and then at the other men and women and their offspring who are kneeling, praying, and methodically moving past one bead after another on the rosary, Daniel Sean has a sudden revelation. He realizes that all the hardship and loss that he has endured is nothing compared to the overall blow that An Gorta Mor has had on the collective soul of his people.

Strangely enough, though he feels the pangs of heart wrenching sorrow it is also mixed in with a powerful sense of pride. Pride in his people for their strength of spirit and persistence. Pride that even while

they are suffering an undue amount of pain, despair, and borderline hopelessness, there is still a glint of rebellion in their eyes. Pride that there is still an unbending sense of optimism springing forth from their unwavering faith. A sort of devil may care attitude about the gravity of the situation for, miraculously, they have not totally abandoned hope.

Truly there is a feeling of fierce pride welling up inside of him at the uniqueness that is instilled here and now because of their ancient ties to Ireland. And this sense of pride gives them an anchor and an ironclad feeling of assurance in their collective fate as Irish men and women even if they now have no home.

As Daniel Sean experiences this epiphany, the room seems to glow for a second or two.

Twelve

After finishing a decade of the rosary and finally getting settled in, the bell for dinner rings, and they all go back onto the deck to receive their evening allotment of hard tack, molasses, and water.

Time ticks by as they eat, leaning over the edge of the ship and watching the ship tumble and tack its way through the watery confines of Cork city.

The mizzen sails, the main topsails, the topgallants, the foresails, and even the different jibs all working together in communion with one another to sail down the River Lee on its way to the ocean.

The river is getting bigger and bigger until the ship opens up into one harbor, then straight along the shore of green fields toward the bay. They pass the Cove, or Cobh harbor as it's called, which is packed with larger vessels that are waiting to fill up with their human cargo and sail west to Canada and America, east to England, or maybe south and west all the way to Australia.

They glide past other small islands and inlets with rolling hills sloping down toward the water. After a long straight run in the bay the *Athlone* sails smoothly through an opening in a rock walled jetty, slicing

through the breakwater. Gaining momentum and anticipating its release, while at the same time being surrounded by the shores of Ireland on either side of it, like a prisoner shedding shackles from around her wrists and ankles, the *Athlone* bursts out and into the open sea.

They immediately catch a favorable wind and the sails unfurl even further, filling and bulging out as if the spirits of famine ravaged Ireland have relinquished their gravitational hold on the ship, and she is responding with a full throttled dash to freedom.

Heading south-to-south-west, roiling and rollicking on the crest of the briny brine, the *Athlone* glides speedily along on the surface of the Atlantic Ocean. With full masts both fore and aft open, the ship and those on board become as one with the wind.

Getting pushed and at other times being pulled by the force of the wind, the chilled salty air stings the skeletal faces of the children as they gasp to catch their breaths, or shyly look at the other children around them.

The excitement of being on the open sea is contagious, and the freedom of movement along the surface of the Atlantic Ocean gives them pause, and as one they all seem to momentarily forget all the misery that has befallen them these past few years. But it is only a temporary reprieve from reality, and the undeniable fact is that they are refugees fleeing a most horrific situation. Homeless refugees, at deaths door, going into the land of the unknown.

Right before the setting of the sun, as they round the tip of Dunamore at the most southern end of Ireland, the people on board spot on the starboard side of the ship the ever vanishing rolling green hills of their mother's and father's land going back through time to thousands of years of mother's and father's.

And on the port side nothing but the frothy rolling watery expanse of the Atlantic Ocean, which right now is the single most frightening vision that anyone of them has ever beheld in all their days on Gods green earth.

Stoned silence envelopes the deck of the ship as everyone convenes on the starboard side of the *Athlone* and intently turns their eyes homeward to their quickly receding beloved Isle. Nobody speaks a word lest the vision of Ireland would disappear. They gaze and stare unblinking, each one knowing that this would be the last time that they would ever lay eyes on her again. They stand en masse, stock still, until darkness and distance erases the island from their sight.

They are ordered to go down below, where they settle in on their new "home turf."

Only a few minutes pass before the shattered Irish men and women are unable to stop themselves, and the keening and wailing and strange balladry starts. Lone voices too heart broken to be consoled, lamentations reaching out to the sky. Vocal tears mixing with the sweat and blood of their loss, with only blurred memories of green fields, majestic mountains with rising

moons, setting suns and the rivers, valleys and hearths of their childhoods.

Even the children join in.

Oh dear sweet Jesus what am I to do, how will this heart ever be mended?

Eventually things settle down, and that night most of the children cry themselves to sleep. But Daniel Sean notices that Molly is not crying, she just lies there intoning, over and over again, a Glory Be and then a Hail Mary, which is joined in by other people who hear her praying.

Soon most of the adults and some of the children reflexively but also fervently cross themselves in the time tested ritual of touching their foreheads, then the heart following with left shoulder and finishing with the right shoulder, while pulling out worn out rosaries, and dropping to their knees. As the the ship rings with Ave Maria's, Our Father's, Creeds, and other prayers, all give themselves over willingly to the power and majesty of the Lord of Lords, the Light of Light, while the *Athlone* sails silently over and through the watery troughs of the Atlantic Ocean.

After close to an hour of praying they finish with, *"Hail holy Queen, Mother of Mercy, our life, our sweetness and our hope. To thee do we cry, poor banished children of Eve. To thee do we send up our sighs, mourning and weeping in this vale of tears..."*

At this point in the prayer most of the people are unabashedly weeping. This is so, for they all know what it means to be ensconced in a "vale of tears," as most of Ireland has now become a valley of tears, and everyone has been touched by the hand of death in one way or another.

Next comes, *"Turn then, most gracious Advocate, thine eyes of mercy toward us. And after this our exile, show onto us the blessed fruit of thy womb Jesus…"*

When this prayer ends a semblance of silence returns. Molly turns and smiles at Daniel Sean, then rolls over next to her Mam and goes to sleep.

The next morning, they receive their rations and wait in line to cook their meager meals. The small stove is in an area right below the one small shaft of a window. Boiled oats with a bit of molasses in it. And a cup of fresh water. Everyone gets the same amount. There would be no more food until around sunset.

This becomes the routine: Wake up, cook, eat, walk on deck, go back down to steerage, come back up on deck for a bit, cook, eat, and then go to sleep. The less movement and activity the better, for the food is barely enough to allow them to simply survive at a subsistence level.

Whenever someone uses the chamber bucket to relieve themselves everyone goes to the other side of the

room to give them privacy while someone else holds one of the tattered blankets up to help hide the person.

The waste is immediately taken out and thrown over board and then washed out with seawater from a barrel that is on deck. This would be the only time anyone is allowed on deck aside from the designated slots in the morning and late afternoon.

Even though they are all weak from not having enough food they are all fairly optimistic about their fate because, for the first week or so, the weather is calm, and apart from a few downpours, it is dry and fairly manageable.

Of course all good things come to an end in this world, as they soon find out.

Thirteen

Two and a half weeks into the voyage, while the passengers are on their early evening break, up and about on deck, the sky turns black. A few minutes later an angry wind suddenly kicks up from the west. It gathers in strength, fluffing the sails and shaking the masts with a violence that causes the crew and passengers alike to scatter for shelter.

Captain Newton appears on deck.

"Move it you rapscallions, move it, down, down into your quarters, this is nothing to play with, go, now."

Everyone scurries down into the belly of the ship while the crew battens down the hatches all around the *Athlone*. This includes the one small window above the stove.

As the wind howls across the surface of the Atlantic Ocean, everyone sits in total silence, completely aware of the uncertainty of the moment, and the power of nature.

There is crack of thunder and lightening that cleaves the air, lights up the blackened sky, roils the sea, and shakes the ship, causing everyone below deck to shriek with fear.

And then silence.

A minute passes and no noise at all, except for Molly whispering a Hail Mary. Then there are a series of lightening strikes above and around the ship. A grouping of ear splitting thunder claps follow.

Then the rain comes, and pelts down with a vengeance. In Ireland they have all been witness to "lashing rain" numerous times, but nothing with the power of this.

One man says it quite succinctly when he states.
"It is a deluge as such that only someone in the Bible could understand the likes of."

While nowhere near the forty days and forty nights that Noah went through, it ends up raining non-stop for the entire evening, into the day, and through the next night, while the ship bucks and rolls to the violent whims of the never-ending sea.

Because of the violent unpredictable bucking up, down, and sideways of the *Athlone*, seasickness is rampant.

Most of the passengers are retching and it is absolutely horrific and disgusting but also unavoidable.

One cannot help it if afflicted, as it is something that one has no control over and here on the *Athlone*, unfortunately, it is most of the crew and passengers that are beset with the seasickness bug.

This includes Daniel Sean and Seamus but, strangely enough, not Molly. She is completely unaffected, with not even a trace of nausea, and ends up assisting those who are sick.

With a sweet smile on her gaunt but lovely face Molly is everywhere and in a strange way she is happy in her role. She feels needed and confident as she soothes the younger children, and with an offbeat sense of humor comforts one and all of the adults.

"Ah sure but you didn't really want to eat that hard tack anyways now didja? 'Tis a good thing that ya got rid of it there."

It is ghastly all through the first night and into the next day, and the second night down below deck. The smell alone would be bad enough, but the floors are also quite slippery and even though Molly is right in the middle of it, surprisingly she is physically untouched by the nightmarish scenario and strangely upbeat about the whole scenario and seems to waltz around as if it is all a lark to her.

It is astonishing to both Seamus and Daniel Sean to watch her scamper back and forth from one retching person to the next retching, holding their hands or placing a bucket underneath one or another of them as they vomit. Daniel Sean and Seamus are both powerless to do anything but lie there, totally helpless, for they are both incapacitated by the rolling and rocking of the ship.

Right before dawn the next day, the storm dies out and the rain ends. Bedraggled men, women, and children rouse themselves slowly, start to shake limbs and move cautiously about their now sordid below deck home.

After everyone is up and about Seamus gathers himself together, and quietly walks up the stairs. He gets permission from Captain Newton, and organizes a work crew to bring down some rainwater that was caught in a barrel.

While some clean the inside of the various quarters, Seamus takes the ones who were sick up and onto the deck where they are all doused with a combination of fresh and sea water to get the mess off of them. Any clothing or bedding is also rinsed off.

Captain Newton says in his loud booming voice.

"Now it will be a bit itchy with the salt but it's the best that could be done. Next rain you can all come on deck."

The next couple of hours is spent cleaning up, and ridding the below deck area of the smell and presence of vomit and bile that permeates the entire interior of the ship. But it does get done as the people all work together, even if they are not exactly robust or vigorous in the body. It does get done.

With most of the smell gone but the interior of the hull wet everywhere the passengers can only do one thing and that is to make light of the whole situation.

"Sure but being Irish we're used to the mist and the rain with the moist dew each and every morning wetting our faces and clothes. So now tell me, what's the difference here?" One woman says with a shrug.

It is two days before it rains again and Captain Newton lets everyone out to rinse off, but he keeps a

wary eye on the sky. He lets them stay out there on deck for an hour or so, making sure that everyone gets properly rinsed off.

Because of this little act of kindness, the respect of the passengers for this Cornish man goes up a notch, for everyone on board has heard horrific tales of the brutish behavior of the "coffin ship" captains. And whenever anyone crosses paths with him it always with a curtsey from the women, or a tip of the hat from the men, and all the children are told to smile or wink at him when they are in his presence.

Fourteen

The storm becomes a kind of bonding event for the three of them, as Molly, Seamus, and Daniel Sean become fast friends. Malnourishment has stunted Molly's physical development, as it has done to most of the children, so she is a thin ragamuffin of a lady. But underneath all that is a beauty that, even with her urchin like appearance, cannot be ignored.

This is something that is not lost on Daniel Sean. He finds himself discreetly looking at her whenever she is at a distance.

With Daniel Sean being 17 years old, Seamus 30 years old, and Molly also at 17 years of age, the three of them make up an unusual alliance. Daniel Sean is delighted to be a part of this little trinity, as he has no one at all left in this world. Seamus is like an older brother, and Molly is like a little sister. In fact there is an uncanny resemblance that Molly has to his dead sister Moira.

The three of them have their meals together, sometimes with Molly's mother, but not always, because she is deeply depressed most of the time, and is hardly even aware of her surroundings. Molly says that sometimes her Mam doesn't even know where she is,

and she keeps looking for her dead husband and her three sons who, of course, are all gone from this world.

In the presence of Seamus and Daniel Sean, Molly finds a feeling of belonging while on this voyage. They spend their time talking about what they will do when they get settled over in America and how, as they've heard, anything is possible in the land of opportunity.

Every once in awhile someone on board ship will break out in song, usually a tune about going to Amerika, as it is pronounced. This includes verses about "streets paved in gold," and money flowing like water. Everyone has his or her dreams, but most know that those dreams are just that; dreams and their fate will not be like that. There will be hardships and disappointments galore.

Molly turns out to be smart as a whip and can read at a level way beyond anything the two of them, Seamus and Daniel Sean, have ever seen. She explains to them why this is so.

"My aunt was trained as a teacher when she was young, before the English gentry went out of their way to prevent us from learning and attending school. They thought, rightfully so, that it would give us ideas, such as freedom and self reliance and other such high brow things."

She spits onto the deck of the *Athlone*, as is the Irish custom when addressing all things English.

"Well low and behold, me boyos, my aunt became a nanny for the children of a rich Protestant who lived on an estate that me Da worked at as a caretaker. My aunt could read, write, and speak both English and Irish, so she was in demand with the Anglo-Irish aristocracy because she could help the Protestants communicate with us Irish." Molly smiles at the two of them.

"She taught me how to read and write in Irish and in English, and also how to speak English correctly. Like the way an Englishwoman would speak. But," she whispers, "I will never be anything but Irish, and so I will speak, act, and think like an Irishwoman to the day that I die. And I shall always be Catholic to boot."

Daniel Sean looks at her with deep affection but does his part to hide it. Taking a bit of a chance he taps Molly on the shoulders smiles shyly and asks her to read from the O'Neill archives.

"I can't read much myself but I'd love to hear what is written about my family."

She agrees.

"I will, but you have to let me try and teach you the basics of reading at the same time. Do we have a deal?"

They shake hands and make the deal: Molly will show Daniel Sean the basics of reading and writing, and she will read aloud from the O'Neill archives.

This is the first time that Daniel Sean has had physical contact with Molly and, to him, it is a most pleasant sensation.

Throughout the next day Molly silently reads the entire manuscript by herself starting with a long ago distant ancestor of Daniel Sean, a women monk named Niamh, and the sack of her monastery. Since all of the oral stories were transcribed by Daniel Sean's grandfather, James Patrick O'Neill, the final section is on the failed Irish Rebellion of 1798. That's because James Patrick served under Theobald Wolfe Tone and as the story goes, after being captured by the English, Theobald slit his own throat while in prison thus depriving his Saxon captors the pleasure of hanging the great Wolfe Tone. James Patrick claims that he was the one who sneaked in the knife that allowed Wolfe Tone to slit his own throat. Was this the truth or was it a touch of the "blarney?" Doesn't matter, it is a good story.

After reading the archives Molly declares that she will read only the first section of the archives out loud because she believes that it is the most interesting story in the O'Neill saga. It is the longest part of the manuscript, the very beginning of Daniel Sean's family archives and Molly insists on reading this fairly long tale.

"Your ancestor, Niamh, was a true Irish woman. She had the soul of Kathleen Ni Houlihan. The other stories are fairly common Irish stories and I could tell them to you, but the one about the abbess monk Niamh is the gem of the whole manuscript."

Daniel Sean agrees but then says to Molly. "I never heard of Kathleen Ni Houlihan, who is she?"

"Ah sure and I will now start to educate you Daniel Sean, my friend from the wilds of Kerry." Molly scrunches up her face thinking to herself then says. "Kathleen Ni Houlihan is the mythical personification of Ireland. She is said to be an old crippled woman who turns into a beautiful lady when someone dies fighting for Ireland. She is unblemished, as pure as the driven snow. And shows her true self when someone is a martyr for Ireland, for she loves courage, not just in a man, but also in a woman."

On the first night of the story telling, as they start, it is just Molly, Seamus, and Daniel Sean. But as Molly gets to the second page of the story the word gets out, and before she even starts reading the first sentence on the second page, others eagerly gather around her as she reads. The truth is that they, meaning almost all on board the *Athlone*, are desperate in their longing to hear an old fashioned story. This is a tradition that they all come from: The love of the spoken, written, or sung word. For the Irish a good story is sometimes the only escape or entertainment that they have ever known. It is part of who they are as a people. For them it is a throw back to all those present. It takes them back to their childhoods when a traveling Seanchai would show up and stay for a spell. Night after night, at least as long as the one telling the stories would be in their village, they would be regaled with some of the familiar, and not so familiar,

stories and legends of Ireland. The Seanchai would not only tell the story but would act out and assume all the mannerisms and voices of the different characters in the story.

Even though they were really quite impoverished so grateful were those who lived in these remote places, that they shared all that they had to give in the way of food, drink, and lodgings with the Seanchai.

This very night Molly Ryan would become the esteemed Seanchai aboard the *Athlone* and, with the power of story telling, let slip into their quarters a small respite from the hellish reality that every soul on the ship has been put through for years now.

Molly decides to start over from the beginning of the story of Niamh so that the "newcomers" can glean the story in its entirety. Reading by the glow of candlelight, Molly becomes the Storyteller or Seanchai of the *Athlone*.

Fifteen

For three nights straight Molly reads from James Patrick O'Neill's manuscript. It is hand-written almost entirely in archaic and uncertain English, but also peppered through with Irish words. Daniel Sean and the others are instantly mesmerized by the story and the quality of Molly's voice, which she modulates to make the story as interesting as possible. The story centers around the making of the O'Neill family Celtic cross by a woman named Niamh who is a descendant of Daniel Sean and who is of the Ui Nhail clan, one of the oldest clans in Ireland. It is the very same cross that Daniel Sean has with him right now aboard the *Athlone*.

The story takes place in an all female monastery in the part of Eire that was known back then as Cairrai but which is now called County Kerry. It is in the far southwestern portion of Ireland.

Daniel Sean watches Molly with absolute awe as she waits for her audience to calm down and for a semblance of quietude to settle in amongst them before she begins to read. It does, and she begins.

Thee monastery stoode near healing welles by the banks of a river that flowed to thee ocean. Thee ancient

ones knew it to be a mystical place, 'twere thee spirits of land and sea dance.

Of raven haire ande blue eyes Niamh, of thee clan Ui Nhail, sat bye a fierce blazing fyre. A grand metalsmith, and head abbess at thee monastery of St. Brigid, patroness of thee Emerald Isle, she smiled at the tools of her trade. Thee anvil, thee bellows, thee different hammers for shaping of thee metal.

Niamh helde a crystal and chanted, as 'twas thee ancient tradition, to readie her heart and her hand to the worke that she was soon to undertake.

Let me dip thee, thou beautiful gem of power. In water of purest wave, in thee name of the Apostles twelv, in the name of Mary, the Virgin of virtues. Ande in thee name of thee High Trinity and all thee shining angels.

Molly raises her eyes from the book, and looks around at her audience, who are rapt and gazing at her with their full attention. Pleased, she continues.

Daniel Sean can barely contain himself at the joy that he is experiencing while watching Molly read the story about *his* family. He feels as if he is falling into her soul as she reads. Molly describes the hearth inside of the forge where Niamh makes the sacred cross and he is there, next to Niamh as she melds and shapes it.

Thee forge was found anext Thee Great Hall, where thee monks didst gather. On this day, methodicly writing and drawing. Theye record the stories of thee life

of Christ, and use their artistry to illustrate them with beautiful smalle paintings.

Molly rests her hand on the manuscript and looks out over her audience. "I've a dear friend who has *actually seen* the great Book of Kells," she reveals with wonder. "She says that it is a glorious, miraculous book and is filled with these beautiful little paintings. They are called eluminures."

She stares off picturing the sight for just a moment, then lowers her head to the manuscript once again.

Niamh sette thee new minted crosse unto thee fierce coles beside the strap of metal 'twould soon be thee circle round thee crosse. She felte thee rhythm of her own hart, thee spirits that dwelt in thee natural worlde. She tasted salt of thee sea, smelled earth, felt rivers and waterfalls flowing through her. She believed 'twere sharing this Isle of Eire with thee spirits, ande here thee land, thee sea, ande thee people 'twere as one.

Bye and bye, alike everything that lives, her owne place in this worlde would be nay more. All, including thee music, 'twould be gone. All 'twould remain woulde be her essence.

Almost everyone, including Daniel Sean, has their eyes closed as they see images in their minds. Molly continues to read, describing the process of chiseling the red hot malleable cross with the desired Celtic whorl-like patterns and spirals that symbolize the connection that they have with the resurrected Christ. A feeling of prideful reverence settles in on the audience as they begin to see their own connection to life, death, and their belief in an afterlife through the words in the story.

Niamh sette gently thee crosse unto thee anvil. She, with breath abated, attached thee red hot circle to complete thee crosse. She baptized it in water clear. Now 'twas naught to do butte wait, for 'twould soon cool ande sette in place.

She didst feel a presence ande it spake thusly to her. Thee light shalle always o'er come thee darkness. For in't light 'tis no darkness. Walke in thee light. Niamh spake those samme wordes out loud. In't light 'tis no darkness, ande her mother and grandmother, deceased tho they be, appeared to her, smiling.

Her mother said, Ye must follow thee light. Whiche is everywhere. But ye must find it yersel'. 'Twere I you I'd putte thee light unto thee fire ande thee metal.

Her grandmother looked then at her. Remember this mine child. There is a grate Light brought to us by Patrick. Looke to it. 'Tis no greater light than that of thee Holy Spirit. Ande fear evil not, for if it existes then rejoice in thy knowledge, fore it means also that good

ande therefore God too existe. Remember that love is thee light.

Mother ande grandmother then suddenly disappeared into thin aire.

She reads on, but Daniel Sean hardly even hears what she is saying, for to him it is as if watching Molly read is a dream. He barely follows the story he knows so well, for he is so enamored with her. He has never seen anything so lovely as Molly reading, the soft candle light reflecting off of her lovely face as he watches her lips move.

This strange sensation recurs the next two nights also. He has never had feelings like this before and he realizes that he is experiencing something totally alien. As far as Daniel Sean is concerned she could be reading anything and it would be magnificent.

Molly starts off the second night by rereading the last paragraph from last night as a refresher, and then continues on with the story.

Niamh grasped thee Celtic crosse from the water took from Bridget's ancient welle of Remembrance. Stared at it, she did, near bewitched, thinking to herself. Remember, remember. I am a daughter of a priestess of thee Tuatha da Danaan. I am of thee Clan Ui Nhail. Ande I am a child of Almighty God through the blood of Christ.

Niamh studied her labor's result. Thee crosse had four red stones at corners, fore thee four winds, North, South, East, ande West, ande of thee four woundes of the Redeemer.

At bottom half of't crosse are thee finished Druidic inscriptions. No beginning no ende. Thee circle at top of't crosse 'tis circle of life, ande also eternal life that comes from resurrected Christ. Niamh aloud softly said, It is imbued with all 'tis from here. If bye its power one person only will see thee spirits of't earth, thee sea, thee sky, thee Tuatha da Danaan, thee Celts, thee power of the Trinity, thenne my duty I will truly have done.

Niamh chanted with thee monks. I summon today these powers between us ande those evils that may oppose my very soul. I arise today through thee strength of heaven, ande thee might of the Trinity. Light of sun. Radiance of moon. Speed of lightening. Splendor of fyre. Swiftness of wind ande depth of sea. Stability of earth. Firmness of rock.

She placed hand to heart. Christ within me. Christ abov me. Christ below me. Christ in every eye that sees me. Christ in every ear that hears me. As t'was in the beginning is now ande ever shalle be. World without end, Amen.

She had the knowing of it that thee Celtic crosse was not yet complete. Niamh knew that more was required. Show it to those who came afore. Thee warmth of't newly forged Celtic crosse in her palm, she walked

alone out of thee Great Hall ande unto thee bright autumn sunlight chill air.

Thee monastery stoode in rolling green hills ande mountains. Niamh walked to thee river to her favorite spot, amongst thee white ash, oak, juniper, and holly. Wearing naught but thee Celtic crosse round her neck she swam to where thee waters ran warmer, where river ande sea become as one. Niamh felte as a mythical selkie, a female seal that could change twixt human and seal. Niamh felte right at home in thee water.

Out of thee river she climbed and pulled on her robe. She walked backe uphill through thee trees ande peat bog to thee small cemetery by thee monastery. Passing through thee small wooden gate she called out to show respect for the hovering spirits, Dia leir anseo. God bless all here.

She walked amongst thee gravestones ande said to each, Dia is Muire dhuit. God ande Mary be withe you.

Towards the end of the second night, and through the third night, the story of Niamh takes a number of dramatic turns as Vikings attack and pillage the monastery. While dying Niamh hands the Celtic cross to her brother. As she lay dying he realizes that Niamh has found her own truth, and that he now would find his own.

Molly concludes the tale for her rapt audience. She is aware that this is a very dramatic ending, so reads the story with the skill of an actor. She frequently makes

eye contact with her audience, and is obviously enjoying her role as Seanchai of the *Athlone*.

Niamh handed Cathal the Celtic crosse. Do nay forget I love ye forever, brother. There is much beauty in this world, if ye but walke in thee Light. She gasped ande clutched her chest and neck, as thee lifeblood pour'd out of her. Withe her last breath she didst say to her brother, And now I will dwell in thee house of the Lord forever. Cathal did watche as thee light faded from his sisters eye, ande thence he did see her spirit.

Cathal clasped thee Celtic crosse, covered in thee blood of his kin, ande tightly helde it to his heart. He made a pledge to his sister. Bye my soul I will watch over ande protect this relic. This Celtic crosse. To remind myself ande all those who come after, through themme, thee memory of thee dear departed live on. Even hence the body leaves this mortal worlde.

At the end of the tale, Molly added "And may all our memories live on in those who come after us." She closes the book with a stunning smile and turns her head in mild embarrassment when she gets applause.

On this last night everyone present is moved to the core, for they all believe that this not just *a* story but *their* story. Despite everyone's protests, once the tale of Niamh and the birth of the family Celtic cross comes to an end she refuses to read any of the other stories. Even

though everyone wants to hear more of the O'Neill family saga Molly steadfastly holds her ground.

"No. Sorry there now, but you see the other stories just aren't as interesting as this one," she says with a hint of mischief. "Besides, if I were to keep this up I might get a sore throat." She couldn't contain her grin. "So no, that's it. Now off with ya, go and use your own imaginations and remember who you are and where you came from. Even when we get to New York. And when we become Americans we still have to remember that we come from a place—Ireland, *our* Ireland, that is full of wonder and joy but also full of heartache and sorrow. It's who we are. We are a joyful people, and yet a sad people. That is why we have our songs, and our stories. And no one can take those away from us. Not even the bloody English."

Sixteen

Halfway through the voyage, on June 15th, in the middle of the Atlantic Ocean, a young man in one of the other quarters starts screaming bloody murder. For the past two days he has been having shattering headaches that pulsate from the inside out. On top of all that pain in his head he is also feverish and keeps shaking violently, and cannot stop twitching and convulsing.

Upon lifting up his shirt he is found to have yellowish skin with red spots on his chest and stomach. That night he is in absolute hell as a rash develops around the spots, and he cannot stop scratching it.

The word gets out and the whispering starts up and circulates. " 'Tis the 'ship fever.' "

All through the night the man tosses and turns. An hour or so after the sun finally rises he is dead.

Before he is brought up on deck, a number of people surround him and without coming into contact with him, say the rosary. Then a woman pulls out a small vial of blessed holy water and pours a small amount on her hand and slowly shakes it over the man as he lies there. All the while people take turns praying different prayers over his body because they know that no Catholic rites will be allowed on deck, only Protestant ones.

After he is brought up onto the deck and slid into the ocean for his burial at sea, Seamus and Daniel Sean leave with Molly to go back to their below deck area.

"God forgive me but I am relieved that it is another one and not our cabin that is affected," she says.

The whole ship is now under a blanket of intense scrutiny and fear, for the fever is not something to be trifling with. No one is immune from the arms of this possible epidemic; it is impossible to predict where or when it will strike, or who will find him or herself in its embrace.

Even with the heightened awareness, every two or three days someone comes down with a new case of the ship fever, and the screaming starts up again. Then after two or three days, with a cloth wrapped around his mouth, the ship's doctor goes below. Then the body is brought up from within, covered with a coarse shroud of tattered wool. And just like the first man who died, the body is slid over the side of the ship and into the sea, with no eulogy or prayers delivered.

To the Irish it is inconceivable that no prayers are said over the corpses. To remedy this there is a constant stream of praying, down below in all of the cabins, not only when someone catches the ship fever but constantly.

A week later, and five weeks into the voyage, an event of epic sorrow occurs that touches every single person on board, including the crew and Captain Newton.

Megan Murphy is an extremely well liked and precocious but frail girl, with pale blue eyes, who is about seven years of age. She always has a shy smile for everyone on board, which has endeared her to one and all.

She catches the ship fever and, though the prayers are said non-stop, she dies very quickly, lasting less than two days from the first symptom to her last breath.

The whole ship is inconsolable over her death, as a black shadow seems to descend upon the deck of the ship, for Megan had that elusive but recognizable intrinsic childish charm where, even in misery, she could melt the hardest heart with just the smile in her eyes.

When she is brought up on deck every single passenger is up and on board to say goodbye to her. The hearts of all present, and the air itself, seem to be cleaved with sorrow.

Immediately after she receives her watery burial and starts to sink into the depths of the Atlantic Ocean, her heart broken mother jumps in to join her. Clutching onto her child's body they both bob up and down for a bit, but then, with the seawater soaking into the mothers heavy garments, the two of them are weighed down.

She ignores the flotation device that is thrown out to her, and keeps saying in a hoarse but loud and pleading voice. "Mucushla, my dear mucushla." This is a term of universal endearment in Irish, that literally translates to "my pulse" or "my heart," but can also

mean "my darling" or "sweetheart." Then both of them sink like a stone, the mother clasping on to her daughter.

All on deck are frantic and leap into action desperate to do something with their arms and heads shaking and gyrating toward the water in utter frustration. But it is obvious that nothing can actually be done, for the two of them, mother and daughter, descend too quickly under the great mass of water, absorbed into the roiling froth of the Atlantic Ocean, disappearing into the depths of the watery abyss. They leave not a trace behind on the surface.

Every single man, woman, and child on deck are frozen in grief. No one present is able to move or utter a syllable in the passing twilight, with the fading sun barely reflecting off of the now calm surface of the ocean. This peaceful void that they now see down below them is one of the saddest sights that one and all has ever seen, collectively shattering the lot of them.

There is no movement whatsoever until one man begins to sing in Irish.

> *"My love, more dear than this life you are to me*
> *Your eyes clearer than the crystal of the sea*
> *Please save me I'm fallen here*
> *We are lost and alone*
> *An angel weeps*
> *I hear her cry*
> *A lonely prayer*
> *A voice so near*

Dry all your tears
Come what may
And in the end the sun will rise
On one more day"

When he finishes there is once again a silence that is deafening in its totality. Then the strangest thing happens: All—not just some—but all of the passengers on deck, in unison, turn and face back east toward Ireland, bow their heads, and against Captain Newton's orders, drop to their knees and all make the sign of the cross, touching their foreheads, then there chests, left shoulders and right shoulders as they all start to quietly weep. After a long minute or two, they stand up and then they all depart, and without a sound, walk down the stairs to their respective quarters.

Later, all alone on deck, Captain Newton gazes out to sea at the spot where little Megan and her mother went under the cold green Atlantic and, despite himself, a lone tear trails down his cheek.

He thinks to himself, *No one does death like the Irish, no one. It never ceases to amaze me but these people seem to understand the bloody inevitable end game. It's as if they have a relationship with the reaper himself.* He looks out to sea. *While they can be a messy lot with their strange habits and traditions they also have something that not many people have, a gift of sorts: They are not afraid of the specter of death as any sane normal person would be. In truth they are mad,*

crazed, for they care more about how you leave this world than being in it. And I cannot help myself from feeling slightly envious of them.

****

The closer that they get to America the weaker the passengers get, and a quiet gloom descends upon the ship. This is because a good portion of the food supply has gone bad due to rot, and the voyage is taken longer than expected. There has been an unusual amount of rain during the passage so far, and water has seeped through and into the area where the supplies are kept. All of the rice and most of the hard tack biscuits are destroyed. Leaving only the Indian corn meal, molasses, and a small amount of dried bacon. There is enough water to make it because of all the rain that they have had on the voyage but hardly enough food.

Every day the food rationed out to the passengers gets more and more meager, but it cannot be helped. While everyone knows that this is true, and make do with what they get, their spirits are quickly waning, and hope is pretty much gone. Most are simply worrying about surviving the passage.

Six weeks into the voyage and getting closer and closer to New York, as the sun sets in front of them in the western sky, Captain Newton stands gazing toward the setting sun thinking about the journey so far.

It's taking longer than I thought it would take because of the bit of damage that we took on, due to that storm we had. And the times when there was hardly any wind. At this point it will be a few days short of two months before we land in New York Harbor, when I had figured six or at most seven weeks. While only about a sixth of the passengers have died, and this is a wrenching shame, it is much better than some of the trips that I have been on. I wish that I did not have to ration the food, but I have no choice. Time is of the essence now. I just pray that this fever does not get worse, for it can accelerate quite quickly because of the hunger. Most of the passengers are on the brink of starvation and weak, and this makes it easier for them to get sick and catch any fever. Be it cholera, typhus, or any other of the devils fevers.

He looks up at the now darkening sky. He then turns and looks at the few people who even bother to come up on deck, and who are lumbering around on shaky legs. The ones still down below are so weak that they can barely walk. *Dear merciful God in heaven please watch over these wretches under my care here on the Athlone.*

Unlike the majority of the people on the *Athlone* Daniel Sean and Molly aren't all that sickly or suffering from any drastic physical disability, even if they are both thin as rails and weak from malnutrition. Neither one of them are suffering from being constantly exhausted, or

feeling all the time like they are weak or depressed, nor are they losing hair like some of the others.

It is true that they are not themselves as they once knew themselves to be before An Gorta Mor, but the actual physical and emotional comfort that they glean from being around one another appears to be keeping both of them in a state of stasis, rather than sliding downward like so many of the other passengers. Not only do they have one another to lean on, and Seamus too, but they also have the magic of youth. This makes all the difference in combatting the specter of death that seems to be omnipresent here on the *Athlone*.

While leaning on the outward rail of the ship Molly whispers to Daniel Sean.

"I'm worried about Seamus. It's not like him to miss time up here in the open air."

Daniel Sean nods.

"Aye, 'tis the first time that he has not come up on deck during our allowed time."

Molly slides her right hand down into Daniel Sean's left hand and they both squeeze tight, something that they have been doing for a couple of days now. Neither one of them acknowledging the intent, but both knowing and loving the fact that they are simply doing it. And deep down the two of them realize that there will be a reckoning later on. At least they both hope and pray for that.

As Molly repeats the observation that Seamus has not appeared on deck, they both look at one another with

fear in their eyes. Daniel Sean finally breaks their silence.

"But Molly, he has the strongest spirit of any man that I have ever met. He is a fighter. He would scare the devil himself if they were to meet."

"But like us all, he can't cheat death Daniel Sean. You know that. It's out there always waiting for us, doesn't matter if you are a beggar or a king, your time will come. It could be a beautiful woman all dressed in black, or an old hag, but the angel of death will tap us all with a bloody kiss if she wants to—or with a sweet one. It doesn't matter. For the angel of death will do what she must do. We have to pray that the Holy Mother is there at the hour of death for all of us if that be said. With faith, she will help to ease the crossing."

She gently squeezes Daniel Sean's hand.

"I am pretty sure that he has the ships fever. I heard him moaning in the middle of the night, and doing the Act of Contrition over and over." She looks at Daniel Sean. "The Act of Contrition, Daniel Sean. You know what that means." She crosses herself, touches the Celtic cross around Daniel Sean's neck, and then turns to look out at the sea.

"He's getting ready, I'm sure of it."

They both stand there in silence until Molly whispers.

"I wonder what happens when we leave this world? I mean I do have my faith and it is all intact, if you know what I'm saying. But I sometimes wonder

what happens to our immortal souls when we leave this
life? I know that there is something, and that it has to do
with how you behaved in this life, you know like a test
or something, but nobody knows what it is, now do
they?"

Daniel Sean smiles at her.

"I believe that we all become a part of the earth
and sky, that heaven itself is the blending of the two and
that it is gloriously beautiful."His eyes narrow
dramatically. "But if you have led a wicked, selfish life,
then you don't get to see all that beauty and so you have
nothing. And that is hell."

Molly punches him and laughs.

"Mister O'Neil you are indeed stark raving mad.
But you do have a touch of the dreamer in you." She
looks at him with great affection.

"Well Molly Ryan, if it makes you laugh then I
reckon that I would rather be crazy than sane. Because
the sound of your laughter is one of the most beautiful
things that I've heard in all me life."

His smile broadens. Molly squeezes Daniel Sean's
hand then they both laugh out loud, which causes a few
of the people on deck to stop and look at them as if they
are both crazy. Which makes them both laugh again.

This is the moment when Molly Ryan and Daniel
Sean O'Neill both realize that there is something going
on between the two of them that they have absolutely no
control over.

Seventeen

Seven weeks into the voyage and only four days before they make land fall in New York City, on a moonless, bountifully starlit night, in the deep and endless expanse of the wild and wasteful Atlantic Ocean, Seamus Fitzgerald disappears from the face of the earth. He said nothing to anyone including Daniel Sean or Molly.

Like an elfin sprite, silent and with no noticeable physical presence, he places a small bag with three English pounds in it and an old rosary on the pillow next to Molly's head while she is sound asleep.

On Daniel Sean's pillow, he leaves the last of his money, five pounds in all, and a note that simply says, "Choctaw Nation." The few articles of clothing that he had are also gone, as is his one blanket. Wordlessly and without making a sound he makes his way up onto the deck with the night watchman not seeing a thing, and simply vanishes.

No one in the below deck area saw him at all either. It's as if he was smoke and not a man. Of course that is who he could be as an Irish rebel who was used to being under the yoke of an oppressor: Invisible and undetected.

The watchman on deck saw nothing, however he did say that he thought that he heard a loud splash on the port side of the ship after the changing of the third watch. He thought that it was just a large fish, or something like that, jumping up and out of the water and then splashing back down into it.

Molly shrugs her shoulders for she already figured it out.

"He jumped ship is what he did."

"Christ Almighty! That's a mortal sin, you know Molly."

"What is?"

"Taking your own life is a bleeding mortal sin."

"Who said that he killed himself?"

"He jumped into the ocean laden down with his garments knowing that he would drown himself. That's suicide if ever I did see it."

"Daniel my dear, do ya really think that the Holy Mother herself would allow that to happen? That she, whose heart was pierced with sorrow, would let a man like Seamus do something as grievous as committing a mortal sin? No, no Daniel Sean, that's not the way things are with the spirit. A second before his earthly body sank down into the abyss, and before his eternal soul passed over the river of death and on to his reckoning, the Holy Mother took him into her arms while the Son of God forgave him and Seamus, of course repented, changed his mind and opened his heart. I know this Daniel Sean, for there is forgiveness."

She looks into the swells of the Atlantic Ocean and smiles.

"Well now, the way that I see it is that Seamus went out for a bit of a walk, and himself being a slight bit chilly, throws on all his clothes. Then while walking and thinking he slips, on account of the fact that he's weakly because of the hunger, and falls out and over into the deep churning ocean. The extra clothes, that being the second sweater with our man Seamus, is what drags him down under and into the vastness of the sea. Just like what happened to that woman when she jumped in after her daughter, little Megan, those long weeks ago. Or some such thing…"

She stops and cannot say another word, until she finally crosses herself, touches the Celtic cross that is around Daniel Sean's neck and whispers. "God rest their souls. The three of them."

After Seamus is gone, Molly and Daniel Sean become inseparable. Spending practically all of their time together, even with Daniel Sean sometimes sleeping underneath the small cot that she and her mother share, with him holding Molly's hand all through the night.

One day, while out on deck after the morning meal, Daniel Sean catches her looking at him from a distance. Daniel Sean winks at her, and walks over to where she is standing.

"What are ya thinking now Molly Ryan?" he says playfully. "Ya look as if you are in the land of the fairies, all to yourself you are now."

"Just having a bit of a day dream, that's all."

She smiles at him and Daniel Sean thinks to himself, *She is the light of my life. My Mucushla.*

They stand there looking at one another, not wanting to look away. Finally Molly breaks the silence.

"Did you know that Molly is another name for Mary? As is Moira, Mara, Marie, Muira, and Maureen, which means Little Mary. We have many names for the Holy Mother."

Daniel Sean is at a loss for words about what to say but just stands there mutely looking into Molly's eyes.

"Aye we do Mary, I mean Molly."

"I don't mind, you can call me Mary if you like."

"Nah I like Molly, but on special occasions I'll call you Mary."

As the *Athlone* sails closer to New York City the people onboard become more anxious about what lies ahead for them. This is not to say that they are depressed, which is not the case. This is more a deep-rooted sadness that belongs to them and them alone.

In the past even when they faced insurmountable odds, whether it be the era of the different invasions such as the Vikings, the Normans, and now the English, they still had Ireland. Even through the failed rebellions that

occurred, and a number of short-lived famines, they still had their island home, their Ireland. It has always been something that they could look to with pride and hope, because she was theirs, and they belonged to her. They were willing to fight and if necessary die for her. They all assumed that they would live their lives there, die, and be buried in the precious Irish soil like so many of their ancestors over the years.

But because of the Great Hunger this was not to be, and they now have no choice but to leave her shores to live and die in a foreign land. They no longer have their homeland, have nothing to cling to, and as a people they feel lost, betrayed, and empty in spirit. In essence they are, as a people, a ship lost at sea, rudderless and with no compass to guide them.

The last night at sea and onto the morning there is a subdued air on the *Athlone* as it glides on toward New York harbor. The weather is fairly mild, with a slight wind coming forth from the west, that pulls the ship onward. The sky is blue and the cumulus clouds are so clear and distinct it seems as if you could almost touch them.

On their break the passengers are up on the deck because the word is out that the *Athlone* is getting nearer and nearer to its destination: New York Harbor!

It is July 13th, 1847, in the middle of the day. The passengers are still out and about on deck, for Captain

Newton has eased the rules, and wants everyone to be on deck when they first sight New York City.

Suddenly a man up in the crow's nest yells down for all to hear.

"Land Ho!! Land Ho!!" As he yells it out he points westward into the distance.

The ship breaks out into a series of whoops and hollers as the crew gets busy, and the passengers crowd the front of the ship to get their first glimpse of America.

Molly and Daniel Sean embrace for the first time and they cling to one another like spent swimmers, fighting against the currents of life.

Even though she knows that she is dressed in rags, and that she does not have the womanly figure that she once had before the Great Hunger, and that she is not all together cleaned up, Molly tightens her arms around Daniel Sean's chest pulling him closer to her.

While she has a great emotional affection for Daniel Sean she also has a strong lustful desire within her to make him want her, and Daniel Sean feels it too.

With their thin bodies pressed against each other, melding, commingling, their hearts rapidly beating together as one, their eyes lock onto one another, and, with the Celtic cross crushed between the two of them, a feeling of incalculable longing and heated passion enters into the two of them.

This desire is also a result of their shared experience on board the *Athlone,* and only adds to the deep but not so understood feelings that they both have

for one another. It is a yearning of the heart and soul of two young lovers borne out of unbearable loss. It is love, lust, blood, and the spirit all together.

They press their bony bodies against one another as they both let out a sigh, and kiss one another's cheeks and lips over and over again in absolute surrendered desperation.

It is at this moment that Daniel knows that he is in love with her even if they are both only 17 years old. He desires only to protect her and to be with her.

Molly also feels this way and looks at him with her sky blue eyes, sending out an SOS of sorts to him, attempting to let him know that she is his and that this moment is theirs.

She whispers to him. "I'm frightened Daniel Sean."

"Me too, Molly. But I think 'tis the weakness caused by the hunger."

"Yeah I reckon you're right. But I have other thoughts and emotions, for I am also hungry for you, my darling Daniel Sean. Not just in the body but in my soul. I would be shattered to lose you."

They look into each other's eyes, almost ready to give in and acknowledge each other's love, when an old bedraggled man breaks out into a jig, even though he can barely move, obliterating the moment between Molly and Daniel Sean. They both know that the moment has passed. The rest of the weak, skeletal passengers settle

into muted conversations, or silently watch as the horizon gets larger and larger.

The closer they get to New York City the more ships they encounter. Everyone looks in awe as the *Athlone* sails from the Atlantic Ocean and into New York Harbor. Even more ships are floating in from the other direction, from the mouth of the Hudson River, around the tip of Manhattan Island, and the beginning of the East River.

Molly and Daniel Sean stare in disbelief at the sheer number, and the frantic rush to and fro, of the people on shore.

"They look like ants scattering about on a dried up bog, don't they now Daniel Sean?"

Eighteen

When they land in New York Harbor, at a small quay, they find out that they have to spend the night there due to such a long line to get processed before disembarking. There is also the routine of receiving an inspection by a doctor to make sure no one has any diseases. So that night they bed down and listen to the city noises coming forth from New York City.

Molly and Daniel Sean huddle together, with him once again lying under her cot, holding hands, and sweetly caressing each other as much as they can get away with in such a crowded, closed in room. Molly keeps on stroking his hands and up onto his arms, while he lays his hands any place he can touch until Molly finally stops and peers down at him. She cannot help herself speaking to Daniel Sean in a light quick whisper so that she is sure to get it out before she changes her mind.

"Some day, God willing, we'll be lovers and make desperate love together. And maybe, if it is in the stars, we'll have our own children and have a family to care for."

She squeezes his hand hard. "But first tell me that you are in love with me."

Daniel Sean feels his heart skip a beat as he replies in a hoarse whisper.

"I love you Molly Ryan."

Molly scrunches up her face, shakes her head.

"No Daniel Sean I don't want to know if you love me, I want to know if you are *in love* with me. There's a bit of a difference you know."

Daniel Sean thinks for a minute then breaks out into a big smile as if a light has gone on in his head.

"Ah, Molly, I am so much in love with you that I have trouble sleeping at night just thinking of you, and wishing that we were arm to arm walking the streets of New York."

Molly smiles and blows Daniel Sean a kiss and squeezes his hand, while at the same time he kisses hers. Molly laughs.

"Aren't you the brazen forward one there, my darling Daniel Sean."

Bright and early the next morning with everyone assembled on deck, and immediately after their morning meal, the gangway is brought up to the *Athlone* and put in place. Captain Newton goes ashore to talk to the clerk in charge while everyone else on board starts to blindly stumble around the deck of the *Athlone* as if in a daze.

After about twenty minutes Captain Newton comes back on board with a stern look on his face and addresses the crew and passengers.

"Gather round. It seems that there is a logistical problem here in New York. While the women and children are allowed to come ashore, only men who have a family to care for are allowed to disembark. The single men are not allowed to leave the confines of the *Athlone*. Let me read you a missive that was handed out to me."

He reads from a sheet of paper.

"No Irish need apply. The streets of New York City are already packed with Micks, Paddys, bloody Papists, who come uninvited from that God forsaken hell hole, Ireland, especially the men, who are nothing but trouble. Hell and damnation they bring disease, crime, immorality and fornication. They are lazy, drunk, and fight all the time. They contribute nothing and will obviously amount to nothing. While the women can be loose and free of any restraints they are not the primary problem, it is the single unattached men who are the real problem. It is crucial that we do not let them into New York City but rather send them upriver."

He looks up from the missive.

"We have been ordered to sail on northwards up the Hudson River to Albany, which is a two to three-day trip. I am truly sorry but there is nothing that can be done, we have to follow orders. And I have to collect more supplies for the trip so every single man on board is obligated to pay one more pound for this detour, that is the law. I also have a crew to pay so this inconvenience will be levied in the way of a payment against you, the passengers, which will be another ten shillings per man."

There is a collective outcry as the passengers realize that they are being barred from their longed for destination of New York City. The crew leaps into action to stem the situation from getting out of control. Reluctantly they push and punch the male passengers into submission as the women and children and the few intact families are quickly herded down below to get their belongings, and then brought back on deck to depart.

As they stand on opposite sides of the ship Daniel Sean and Molly stare at one another until Molly yells out to him.

"I love you Daniel Sean."

Daniel Sean yells back.

"I love you too Molly. My mucushla, my Mary."

As they hustle the women, children, and the few fathers down the gangplank, Molly yells back to Daniel Sean.

"Find me, I will wait for you."

He tries to yell but is so choked up that he only manages a whispered, "I will, I will."

As soon as the exodus is complete Captain Newton orders the ship to immediately get ready to leave the quay here in New York Harbor and start the voyage up the Hudson to Albany. After collecting the extra pound and ten shillings from the single men who are now on board, Captain Newton sends a sortie out to gather some more dried bacon, molasses, and maybe some rice.

"Or whatever the hell is available, just go and hurry back before the situation gets out of hand."

An hour later the men return laden down with the supplies, and Captain Newton gives the order to heave ho and start the, "Bloody voyage up the damned Hudson to Albany."

He is in a foul mood due to the detour, for he had many people to visit here in New York City. But the law is the law and cannot be circumvented.

Daniel Sean stands looking across the bow of the ship at the shore of the city as they slip north toward Albany. Watching the landscape slowly change from city to small towns to thick woodland he thinks to himself. *How could this be happening?*

Adding to this predicament is that he has almost no energy, for he is so exhausted from the lack of food, and was looking forward to finding something in New York City to eat. He is desperate in his longing for Molly and deeply frustrated that he is not going where she is going. But there is nothing to be done, nothing at all.

Daniel Sean makes a decision as the Athlone slices through the Hudson River creating eddies that he stares at while thinking to himself. *I can't be leaving Molly, no that cannot happen, that won't be happening, I will make damn sure of that. In the name of God I'll not be going to this Albany. And that's it. New York and with Molly is where I'm meant to be and by God that's where I'll be staying, fair enough.*

The ship sails on until she comes to the very top of Manhattan Island, where the Harlem and Hudson Rivers converge. Desperation sets in and the choice is made by Daniel Sean to take immediate action.

Daniel Sean O'Neill, aged 17, looks to his right at a rounded, rocky, wooded hillock that seems to be beckoning him. He gathers up his meager possessions that are in his pack, shoving the manuscript that is in there all the way to the bottom. Checking to make sure that the other remaining vestige of the clan O'Neill, the family Celtic cross, is snugly around his neck, he clasps onto it and jumps ship.

All on board the ship gather at the starboard side of the deck and start yelling at Daniel Sean, while one of the crew throws a rope. Daniel Sean waves it off and yells back to him.

"I'm not coming back, leave me and go on your way. I'll be all right now. Go now, off with you."

As he starts swimming toward the shore the man at the wheel starts to turn the ship in the direction of Daniel Sean. Captain Newton signals the man to leave it be.

"It's his decision as a man. He is now at the whim of fate and is none of our concern. This is a doing of his God given free will so the lad is on his own."

He salutes Daniel Sean, waves goodbye to him, wishes him "God speed," and blows his whistle to get the ship heading back upriver.

Nineteen

The *Athlone* slips away around the bend in the Hudson River at the point where Manhattan Island ends, disappearing like a ghost ship into the steamy mist. Daniel Sean treads water as he watches it sail away, a deep-rooted uneasiness settling in on his bones.

He turns and faces the shore and attempts to swim, something that he has very little experience at doing. Though he comes from an island nation, Daniel Sean never learned how to swim all that well, which is not uncommon back in Ireland.

But now weak from the hunger and all alone in an unknown land, Daniel Sean swims frantically on toward the shore.

A minute passes by, then two minutes, five and then ten minutes, and it seems as if he is not making any headway. After fifteen minutes he is completely exhausted. But he swims on. With all his will he marshals up what little strength he has, and with all his might he swims on toward the shore, mimicking what he has seen while watching people swim back home.

Gulping, over and over for air, as his sapped body begins to fail him, Daniel Sean slowly begins to panic and swallows water instead of air. His lungs begin to fill

with the muddy Hudson River water, making him start to retch.

Knowing that he is losing this battle the fear factor begins to overwhelm him, taking with it all of his hope.

After another five minutes or so, there is no strength in his arms or legs, none. They are as jelly, and his arms, legs, and in fact his whole body is practically useless.

Not going to make it.

With nothing else to do Daniel Sean holds on tight to the Celtic cross, and prays like he has never done before. It is a fervent, desperate, passionate attempt for God Himself to see him, Daniel Sean, in his desperate hour.

Please reach out your hand to me dear Lord above.

As exhausted as he is, he refuses to give up the fight, flailing onward with his arms and kicking his feet. After another several minutes of this, he knows that his time is up. As simple as that. Yes, his time is up, of that he is sure. It is too far to the shore.

I have it in me mind that drowning is not so bad, not so painful, you just kind of go to sleep like. But what will become of my Molly? Dear God in heaven look after her.

With visions of Molly wrapped in his arms Daniel Sean gives it one more desperate shot, flailing madly as he gazes at the shores of America, but not getting any

closer, for the current is too strong to allow him to gain any leeway.

The irony of being this close but yet so far away is not lost on him, as he accepts the inevitable. He relaxes his body, not even bothering to make an attempt to swim, just going limp, with his right hand holding onto the Celtic cross that is around his neck.

Readying himself to die, Daniel Sean says a Hail Mary.

"Hail Mary full of Grace the Lord is with thee….."

Holding onto the cross, holding it high up in the air, Daniel Sean hears his mother's voice, from somewhere below him, right underneath the murky Hudson River.

"Now and at the hour of our death, Amen. "

****

Jubal watches the drowning man from his spot behind the tree thinking it would be better to just let him go under.

Do nothing. After all he doesn't really trust white people.

Why should I? Also by the looks of it, I might be looking at one of those famine people. Irishers or something like that. What I done heard and seen about them, and some of my dealings with them, well I reckon

*they may be a little bit hard to understand,
unpredictable. So it's best to just do nothing.*

Jubal watches listlessly. Uninvolved. The man
goes down under the water. Then comes back up
speaking in tongues or something *cuz it sure enough
ain't English.* The man is struggling, that is plain to see.

*That's nothing when you think what my people
done went through. The death ships that some people
didn't even make it across on. Died along the way. Of
course I didn't do that, the crossing, but my grandmother
and grandfather did. Just like my mother and father I
was born here. I'm a true American not that that means
anything since I'm an African. I ain't probably never
gonna be nothing to these people. But some people say
that, at least that's what I done heard, that, that there's a
time a coming. Some people says that there is a time a
coming when we, as free men of color, will take our
place side by side as men with the white man. Equal. But
I know it ain't never gonna happen. Because we hate
each other. So that's it, it's settled. I ain't gonna do
nothing.*

As he stands there, completely still and unmoving,
watching the white man drown, Jubal remembers what
his grandfather taught him. Who, like himself, was a
believer in Syncretism, the blend of Christianity and the
old Orabu religions. He told him about the Griots and
their stories about the righteous spirits that exist in the
natural world. How they always give signs to the ones
under their care. That "someday when you don't know

and where you can't be sure, you gonna be tested. You better be ready."

But then Jubal thinks to himself. *No this is a white man. Ain't none of my business.*

In the back of Jubal's mind, an echo of sorts reverberates into his consciousness.

Remember, remember.

Suddenly he recalls hearing a white man, an English man, taunting his father up on the pier upriver in Dobbs Ferry where, the two of them were working as horse wranglers.

"You bleeding sods! You're worse than those Irish bastards. Yes, you black bastards are even worse than those animals, those damned papists, devil worshipping white apes, who are slaves and whore mongers, just like you. They were niggers before you niggers were niggers, but you're worse because you're a black nigger bastard."

But Jubal's father only laughed at the English man.

"This is New York and I am a free man, as is my son here who was also born a free man. You can call me any name you want to, but I am a free man. I desire no ill feeling toward any man, white or colored."

Jubal's father stared the man down until the man looks away with a touch of fear in his eyes.

This memory makes Jubal think to himself as he watches the white man continuing to struggle. *Irish nigger bastards, who are these white people who are called niggers?*

As he continues to watch the white man get weaker and weaker, he shrugs his shoulders and speaks aloud under his breath.

"Ain't none of my concern whether he lives or dies. He's white and I'm black."

Then like a clap of thunder he hears his mother's voice.

"Through the blood of Jesus we are all the color of water. Just the way it is. Don't matter white, black, Christian, Jew or nothing at all. We all the same. The color of water, so that the Lord can see through us."

He doesn't budge. As he debates with himself a flash of light shines from around the neck of the drowning white man, the sun reflecting off of something on his chest, blinding Jubal for a second. Jubal blinks. *Is this a sign?* Again, a bright beacon of light shines from around the neck of this man.

He doesn't know why he does it, but he jumps into the water and swims out to this white man, hooking him around the neck. Swimming with long, strong strokes, bringing him to the shore, dragging him up out of the water. He then pounds him on the chest, holding his nose because he has heard, "that white people smell funny." Working up the courage, he takes a breath and breathes into the white man's mouth. Something his father taught him to do if anyone was ever drowning around him up north along the Hudson where they work sometimes. He does it numerous times.

Daniel Sean contorts violently and his body springs up as he coughs up water. And he keeps on coughing until he falls back down onto the ground. Then he starts to greedily drink in the sweet air. Filling his lungs to capacity.

He opens his eyes and looks up at the blackest face he has ever seen. In fact the first black face he has ever seen. The man is smiling at him and looks to be about the same age that he is, around 17 or 18 years old.

But then that's not possible. I just died. Yes this is the other side, this is a saint. Yes it's a black saint sent from the vault of heaven. Blessed Mother! That's the only way it could be. No, by Jesus, not a saint that's not right, it's an angel. A beautiful, bleeding black angel sent down from the throne of light. Why do they always look white in the stories? And who cares what color they are?

Jubal smiles again at the white man.

"Welcome to the Isle of Manhattan."

"I'm… I'm alive?" he croaks out. "And you're not an angel?"

"My name is Jubal. You must be one of them Irishers. And no I ain't no angel."

Twenty

Jubal gets Daniel Sean settled in to rest on the shores of the Hudson River, hiding him behind the shade of a huge oak tree. In case someone comes around who doesn't belong here.

Before he leaves he says to Daniel Sean.

"Boy you are so weak that I got to get me some help to bring you on up to our camp. You stay here, I'll be back in a bit."

After Jubal leaves him, Daniel Sean lies on the ground feeling the earth underneath him, thinking to himself.

I am alive, I am not going to die, and I am in America. All praise to God for this, as it has nothing to do with my doing, it is a gift from above.

Feeling the soft ground below him and the scattered leaves that are his first bed in his new homeland Daniel Sean remembers the bit of Irish soil that he had put into his pocket. He digs into his pocket but the soil is now long gone, it was left it in his old clothes back at Frankie's safe house. He shrugs his shoulders and says out loud, "Ah that's alright now for this is my new home, my new land."

Opening his eyes wide and looking around, the first thing that is noticeable is how hot and humid it is

here in America. Never has he experienced such searing heat.

Back home in Ireland the wind was always blowing— down from the mountains, across the sea, over the bogs, there was always a steady stiff breeze. It was usually cool, damp, and windy.

Lying there sweating, his mind retraces what he just thought. *Back home is no more. Ireland is no more. America is now my home.*

Above him is an endless canopy of huge green leaves hanging underneath the largest trees that he has ever seen.

I've heard of trees this big up in and around Glendalough or even farther north into and around Dublin, but nothing as such back in Kerry. Nothing this big. And so many trees, so many.

Along the outstretched limbs of these oak, maple, and elm trees a coterie of furry travelers, mostly squirrels and chipmunks scurry back and forth. Above the trees and flying overhead, underneath a clear blue sky, are thick cumulus clouds that slowly drift by as if this is all just a dream. A lone eagle flies underneath the clouds.

As if on cue Daniel Sean is suddenly aware of noise and he hears the constant buzz and clicking of insects. It seems as if the heat is stirring the insects up and it's like they are plaintively crying out for rain.

It is all so new to him, these sensations. No wind, the heat and humidity. The sights and sounds of this new

country are so different from the ones that he's used to, there is a different feel here. It does not have the settled almost sacred feel of Ireland with its mist and quietude juxtaposed against the constant wind and sometimes lashing rain. Here the air is completely still, but strangely it feels as if there is movement, energy, and vibrations everywhere.

As the volume echoing in the still air increases with the chirping of the squirrels, birds, and insects, Daniel Sean realizes that he is so tired, so exhausted that it is difficult to keep his eyes open, but he is also energized with fear of the unknown.

Who in the bleeding hell knows what the hell is going on with this black fellow?

Is he a good decent man who is truly looking to help me out? Or else is he something else? A thief? Or worse? Maybe a murderer? Wait now, is he a cannibal coming back to gather the evening meal?

I've heard tell of the lust of human flesh that some cultures have, for it is said to empower the lot with the soul of the departed. There are all kinds of tales of African tribes not only partaking of the flesh but also the mutilations that have occurred, not to mention the shrinking of heads and worse.

This has been reported not only in Africa and Asia but also along the steppes of eastern Russia, the bloody Cossacks themselves. Of course none of these have been proven true, but ya never know, now do you?"

His mind rambles on with weird thoughts and conjecture for in Ireland the worst thing imaginable is the eating of human flesh, and even those in the last stages of starvation died first before partaking of the flesh. For the Irish it has always been thought to be the work of demonic spirits, top of whom is the Demonah, who is the highest personification of evil. This evil spirit believes that he gets his greatest strength by the eating of the flesh of the most pure, of which the ideal target is newborn children.

Daniel Sean resolves himself not to take any chances but to flee. He starts to stand but only gets to his knees before falling back down. Lying there for a minute or two, he then takes a breath and pushes back the weakness and the hunger, rolling over onto his knees and attempting to push up onto a standing position.

After three attempts he succeeds in rising up into a standing position. But as he balances on his legs for a second, he is surprised because the ground is not moving. For close to two months the surface that he's been standing on has been in a constant state of rolling, bucking, and undulating while he walked or stood. The movement of the Atlantic Ocean under his feet forced him to adapt and find his "sea legs," and now he has to find his "ground legs."

Swaying this way and that way, totally disoriented, and unable to move he becomes completely light headed, causing him to falter. Then, with stars in his eyes, he falls backward onto the bed of leaves,

landing on his pack, just missing a huge rock that would have split his skull.

Daniel Sean lies there, his breathing not only labored but fast and furious as he tries to get enough oxygen into his lungs to gain some sense of stability.

Just then, with a loud crash through the thick bushes along the side of the Hudson River, Jubal comes down a steep hill and shows up with three other men who look to be in their early twenties or maybe even younger, 18 or 19.

For Daniel Sean panic sets in and he tries to get up and hide, for he is convinced that he will be this evening's main course for Jubal and his obviously cannibalistic cohorts.

"No, no please don't eat me, I'll go away and never come back."

The African men look at him, and two of them start to laugh at the ludicrousness of Daniel Sean's reaction to them, while at the same time they all take pity on him, for he is a pitiful sight to behold. One man sighs, and shakes his head.

"Look at this boy, he's crazed and one step away from the grave. He done look like a skeleton. Like the ones I done heard about getting off of the ships from Africa back in Maryland. Who they say were a step away from starvation, with crazy notions and had the same look of fear around the eyes that this boy done has."

Jubal pulls out a canteen with water in it and hands it over. Daniel Sean's parched lips, mouth, and throat can't stop drinking it. Finally Jubal takes it away from him, wiping the top just in case and then saying "Slow down now boy you gonna get sick."

With Daniel Sean lying there the four Africans have a spirited discussion on what exactly to do with him.

At first the other men say that they do not want him to stay, but Jubal insists on it, saying that the spirits that dwell in the river gave him a sign through the cross around his neck and that there was nothing they could do but follow the spirits.

"The blood of the Lamb ordered those spirits to obey His command. And they did. So we gotta do the same."

After a while they come to an agreement.

Reluctantly the other three men agree with Jubal that they have no choice but to take Daniel Sean back to their camp until he regains his strength and is ready to move on. But they are not happy about this, one man summoning it up.

"Don't really want no white man with us, it could cause some trouble for us not only where we are staying but also on the job. If the boss man finds out about it we gonna lose our jobs, you know that for a fact."

Jubal agrees also. "Yeah you right, could definitely be a problem. Okay how about this then." He

looks right at Daniel Sean and says. "We take him for a couple days to satisfy the spirits, then he be on his own."

They go back and forth with their different options as to what to do with Daniel Sean right in front of them, as if he is invisible.

The funny thing is that Daniel Sean can't understand a word of what they are saying. He's never heard people speak like this, even if it is English, which is his second language and which he understands fluently.

While they are discussing all this in front of Daniel Sean, in his weakened hallucinating state, he thinks that they are going over the best way to cook him for dinner, or murder him or mutilate him. He's sure that it is something like that.

So while it is agreed that Daniel Sean will come back with them to their encampment to recuperate for a few days, he starts to struggle and makes a pathetic attempt to bolt away, but only falls flat on his face.

Taking pity on him once again, the four men speak very slowly and deliberately, all four of them taking turns reassuring Daniel Sean that they are not going to devour him, nor are they going to kill or mutilate him.

The kind looks on their faces are what finally convince Daniel Sean that everything is going to be all right.

Twenty-One

After he calms down they help him to his feet, and with a man on each side of him they start to climb upwards away from the river. They trudge uphill, struggling on up the side of the steep wooded hill, away from the river, until they reach the knolls peak where it flattens out on the crest of the hill.

From there Daniel Sean looks the opposite direction from the river, down below at a heavily forested area that ends at an open field of closely cropped small bushes and trees.

The area of smaller trees looks as if the trees are not all that old, meaning that the original ones were cut down to make room for some planting but then abandoned. Beyond the open area it is flat, but again heavily forested all the way to a small meandering river.

As he looks to his left, behind where they just climbed, he sees that this smaller river empties into the river that he just sailed up on, the larger Hudson River.

In the distance to his right, which is at a north easterly direction, there is what looks like a farm of some sorts, but it is a ways away from where they are standing. Other than that it looks fairly deserted.

On the banks of the smaller river upstream, about a half mile away, is the biggest tree that Daniel Sean has

ever seen. He points to it and the man who pulled him out of the river, Jubal, speaks very slowly so that the white boy will understand just what he is saying.

"Right here we are at the spot where the Hudson and the Harlem River meet, with the Harlem River emptying into the Hudson River." He points to his left towards the Hudson River, where the two rivers meet.

Jubal then points to his right, upstream of the Harlem River toward the gigantic tree.

"That's a tulip tree, and the very spot where the Injuns who done lived here sold away the Isle of Manhattan. The chief went and gave it to one of the first white man that they ever did see, some Dutch fellow named Minuet or some such name as that. The chief sold Manhattan for some trinkets and twenty dollars or so. And so the Dutch folks decided to plant a tulip tree to mark the occasion. That was about two hundred years ago."

They stop for a couple of minutes to let Daniel Sean catch his breath.

When he is rested, they walk about ten minutes along the ridge of the hill, passing steep promontories and cliffs until they come to a spot that looks navigable.

After determining that Daniel Sean will be okay in making it down this section of the ridge, they start heading down the other side of the hill. They hike downward along a small almost perfectly symmetrical and well-trodden path.

Jubal explains to Daniel Sean, once again speaking very slowly and deliberately.

"This here is an old Lenape trail, which is the name of the first native Injuns who lived here. This path was already here even before the Europeans or us Africans were here, and even before the present day Injuns were here too. The animals used it before the Lenapes, so that's why they call it a deer trail cuz it was here before any of us people were."

As the terrain starts to level off, a little ways from the very bottom of the hill, they come to what looks to be a series of caves. When Daniel Sean asks about them Jubal explains.

"They is what's called the Injuns caves. We stay outta them since they are said to be cursed by the Lenape Injuns who, like I said, lived there a long time ago. The word is if you spend any time in there you might lose your mind. Go crazy with the curse. Some people don't believe in all that stuff, the juju, the curses, the supernatural, and the seen and the unseen world. They say it's all superstition. Hell some don't believe in the devil. But I done seen the devil himself." Jubal nods his head and continues. "Face to face. People who don't believe in the devil got themselves an easy life, ain't been around hard times. He don't show hisself to them, I mean, why would the devil waste his time with them? It's the salt of the earth that Satan is afraid of, cuz he knows that the salt of the earth know what he's all about.

As the Lord said, 'You are the salt of the earth. You are the light of the world.' "

"Now don't get me wrong. 'Course we got some Injuns around here we see by and by. But even so, the Lenape Injuns ain't been around for a hundred years or so. And they say that them caves is where their spirits reside."

Daniel Sean is having a hard time even remotely comprehending what Jubal is saying. He just keeps smiling and nodding his head yes.

After walking down the sloped hill for another ten minutes or so they come to a flattened out area that Daniel Sean spotted before, where all the trees are new growth. It is mostly scrubby bushes and not many trees like there are on top of the hill.

They keep walking until they come to an area that appears to be a wall of green bushes, an impregnable thicket. After stopping for a minute and looking around, Jubal pulls back one of the branches, and then another one and then another one. Holding them back he creates an opening in the thicket, and they enter an enclosed, flat, totally secluded area that is surrounded by a surfeit of brambles and thorny bushes.

It is a completely hidden encampment with a tamped down dirt floor in the middle of a grove of trees and bushes. And it is much larger than it looks like from the outside of the copse.

There are four makeshift canvas tents that are set apart from one another and laid out in a semicircle. Each

tent is tautly enclosed and has a flap around the opening to ward off mosquitos and any other unwanted creatures, and to keep out the rain when it lashes down.

"You ain't got to worry," Jubal tells him, "these old tents will keep you dry as a tick's stomach when the rain come down."

All the tents are tied off to separate trees that not only secure the tent but also act as a clothesline to hang stuff on. In the open end area of the semicircle of tents is a small fire pit. The openings of all four tents point toward the fire. Out the back of the right side of the encampment, facing a small river that is about thirty yards away, is an enclosed area made of homemade planks, with a raised seat with a cover that acts as a commode where the men relieve themselves.

But usually they just use a bush a ways from the tents or the river. The commode is used only when it is necessary such as at nighttime or during a storm. The river is the Harlem River, and water from it is brought up using a large bucket and then boiled for drinking, or used for washing, cleaning, and keeping the commode sanitary.

The four men lead Daniel Sean into one of the tents and help him get his stuff settled in on one side of the bedding that is in there. Before they allow him to fall asleep, Jubal and another man, make him strip down so that his clothes can dry out on the clothesline.

Then the two of them help Daniel Sean to stand up and walk him back out to the front of the tent, where

Jubal helps him to wash off all the grime and filth, using water from a barrel that they fill with the bucket carried up from the river. One of the man, who is taller and thinner than the other three, then brings out some clothes from his tent: Shirt, pants, shoes, socks and a light sweater if needed.

"Here we go boy, these are some extra g a r m e n t s for you to wear, them other ones are gonna take awhile to dry. The other fellows clothes would be too big for you, these should be all right."

After Daniel Sean dresses in the clean but old, used dry clothes, two of the men, lead him back behind the tent area where there is a small table with four chairs set up around it. They slowly sit Daniel Sean in one of the chairs.

One of the biggest individuals that Daniel Sean has ever seen goes over to a pot that is hanging over the small fire in the middle of the copse and spoons out a portion of something from it into a small wooden bowl.

He then brings it over to Daniel Sean, handing it to him with a flourish and a smile. It is a bowl of squirrel stew that also has potatoes, lima beans, and corn in it. As the man does this one of the other men, the tall and skinny guy, says a blessing.

"Blessed be the earth for this food, blessed be the spirits of the river for this mans life, and blessed be God for the gift of His Son, Christ Jesus."

Tears of joy and gratitude come to Daniel Sean's eyes as he is handed the bowel of thick soup. He looks at

the four men and speaks in a broken voice that is barely audible.

"Words cannot express what I am feeling right now, I, I…" He goes silent and starts to weep.

Jubal replies softly.

"It's alright now. Go ahead and eat, you have been delivered. Emmanuel, God is with you and us right now."

Daniel Sean raises his bloodshot, tear filled eyes and says, "Thank you." Then he eats, at first slowly because he is not used to so much food, and then he speeds up, chomping the squirrel stew with a vengeance and passion that only those suffering from starvation can know. At the end he can't stop licking the bowel, the spoon, and his fingers.

The giant but gentle man who gave him the soup then places a chunk of bread in front of Daniel Sean who wipes it on the bowel and eats it.

The whole time all four of the men have been watching him with intense curiosity, small smiles on their faces, as Daniel Sean eats his first full meal since he was at Frankie Fitzgerald's safe house.

When the meal is done Daniel Sean starts immediately to fall asleep, his eyes closing even as he fights to stay awake.

Jubal inquires of him before he passes out, speaking in a loud voice and slowly annunciating each word in an exaggerated pattern.

"What's your name boy? We didn't catch that one yet. And speak slow cuz we having trouble understanding what you saying cuz you speak so damn fast with that accent of yours."

"Daniel Sean O'Neill. Sorry about the brogue there, but English is my second language."

A short stocky fellow with a stern look on his face says in a no nonsense tone.

"Well now let's get to the point here, Daniel Sean. You done met Jubal, my name is Nicodemus, that tall string bean over dere is Joseph, and right there sitting on that log in front of the fire is Nathaniel."

Daniel Sean looks over at the fire and sees the mountain of a man who gave him dinner and who has a boyish face smiling up at him.

The four of them seem to all be about the same age as Daniel Sean, around 18 to 20 years old.

With the formalities done, Joseph sets Daniel Sean up in a tent, on makeshift bedding made of old rags on top of some leaves off to one side. This tent is slightly larger than the other three, so it acts as a guest room for any infrequent visitors. Daniel Sean falls dead asleep as soon as his head the bed of leaves that are his pillow, even though the sun has not yet set.

Twenty-Two

The next day Daniel Sean wakes up early in the morning, the sun is still low on the horizon, but the whole encampment is empty. There is not a soul in sight. He sees a note on top of a bowl that is placed upside down on the table. The note is crudely written and says "Lok heer, fer U."

He lifts the overturned bowl to reveal a huge slab of bread with some butter and jam on it with a small handful of some type of wild berries to the side of the bread. Next to the bowl is a canteen of water.

After eating the food and drinking from the canteen, he takes out of his pack the manuscript that chronicles the O'Neill family history. A portion of it is ruined from being submerged in the Hudson River.

He carefully goes through the contents, salvaging as much as he can. He lays those pages that have not dissolved onto the bark of a fallen tree in the far corner, away from the tents. The idea is that this will allow as much of the manuscript as possible to dry out in the sun. He places small rocks on top so that the papers will not blow away.

As he counts the pages that are salvageable he figures that well over a quarter of the manuscript is useless and unreadable. But he also figures that he will

save what he can. Maybe later Molly can tell what other stories were in the manuscript and that are now lost.

He also has to go over and practice what she taught him about reading and writing during those days on the *Athlone* that they had together. Before he forgets.

For the whole day Daniel Sean is all alone at the encampment wondering where the hell the guys went to and when they will be back home. And a million other thoughts keep floating up into his brain, such as what he will do and which direction he will head in to find Molly.

He checks up on the papers, but some of them are still a little damp, so he leaves them where they are and eventually forgets all about them and goes on to other interests. He walks all around the encampment inspecting the tents and the grounds in and outside of the thicket.

The whole set up of the encampment is astonishing to Daniel Sean. It is secluded, wind resistant, fairly cool compared to the outside late July weather, and comfortable. And looks as if it could be defended fairly well if need be.

Kinda like a country version of the Fitzgerald safe house.

At one point he decides to do a bit more extended exploring. Even though he is still a little bit weak, the bread and the berries have given him enough sustenance to at least warrant an attempt to check out the surroundings.

He walks through the scrubby bushes into the forested area and then all the way up the hillock past the caves to the very top of the knoll where he came in from yesterday. Across the Hudson River, in the distance, is what he'll later learn is called New Jersey.

After that he walks on down the hillock back to the encampment and straight ahead to the marshy banks of the Harlem River. He sits on a rock on the shores of the river, spending a couple of minutes looking at the fish swimming around the undercurrents and eddies, and at the snakes sunning on the rocks.

Glancing up to his left and westward, is a wooden bridge that connects the northern tip of Manhattan Island with a place later learned to be called Spuyten Duyvil. It appears to be brand new and looks to be a railroad bridge.

To his right, in the distance, is the huge tulip tree that appears to be even more massive this close up, and farther along, barely visible, is a huge house that appears to be a working farm. Up behind this mammoth house is another large house, or else a barn or something like that. It is some type of large structure.

He did not know that there were any people around, but apparently even with these two farms the area is scarcely populated.

Gazing across the Harlem river he sees two men watching him, both with shawls around them and one with a feather sticking out of his hair. Daniel Sean waves to the two of them, but they just keep staring at him with

total indifference. The two of them look away from Daniel Sean and go back to what they were doing before being distracted, which is spear fishing.

Daniel Sean thinks to himself. *Are these what Jubal called Injuns?*

After a couple of minutes watching the two men fishing, and trying to figure out their technique in case he needs to do some fishing in the future, Daniel Sean suddenly realizes that he is completely exhausted.

The heat has sapped him of all the strength that he might have had, and he has trouble standing up. But his legs seem to be slowly adapting to Mother Earth as he slowly starts to lose his sea legs.

He heads back to the encampment, walking slowly to preserve his strength, caution in every step. Along the way he stumbles a few times as his legs struggle to hold him up. Getting back to the camp, he finds his way to his makeshift bed and falls instantly asleep.

A couple of hours later Daniel Sean is awoken by the return of the 'fellows' as they push their way through the thorny barrier and into the encampment. Peeking out of the tent he sees that they are carrying a couple of fish with them, and some more wood for the fire. Jubal sees him and motions for him to come out and join them.

Daniel Sean joins them in the center of the encampment.

Joseph starts up the fire, while Nicodemus starts to gut and clean the two fish on a large flat rock next to

the fire. The large slate-like rock acts as small table to help prepare the different meals that they make.

Jubal and Nathaniel go around to the back of Jubal's tent and pull out a couple of yams that are in a closed wooden bin that is buried in a small hole, and covered with a pallet that has leaves on top of it.

Jubal explains to him that everything has to be hidden and covered because of all the different animals that would "jest love to get their paws on what we got here."

"Sit down now Daniel Sean," he adds, "and listen up." He waits for Daniel Sean to get settled then continues.

"Ya see now boy, I'm gonna explain to you just what's going on around here." Jubal pauses for a second to gather his thoughts "What we doing around here is this: we build bridges."

He talks real slow-like and then pauses to allow Daniel Sean to let that sink in.

"Right now we's working on a bridge, called the Aqueduct Bridge or what some people have nicknamed as the High Bridge, which is gonna be used to bring water across the Harlem River into Manhattan. It's a big job my man, and it's about one and a half miles thataway." He points eastward.

Jubal squints his eyes toward Daniel Sean, hoping that Daniel Sean is following just exactly what in the hell he is talking about because there is a bit of a language problem with the four fellows and Daniel Sean.

They don't always understand one another ,because of their different ways of speaking, even though it is technically the same language. Jubal goes on.

"Now we just finished this past year working on a bridge which is called the Spuyten Duyvil Bridge. It's a railroad bridge. Spuyten Duyvil is a Dutch word that means, in English, the Devil's Whirlpool."

He takes a moment to let it all sink in for Daniel Sean. Speaking with a bit of pride, he tilts his body west and points toward the Hudson River to the Spuyten Duyvil Bridge.

"We are done working on that one right there, so now we on the High Bridge, and every morning we walk to work, which done takes a little less than an hour or so. We do all the laboring work on these bridges cuz the white boss man don't think that we's smart enough to do the building on account that we are colored. And even though all four of us can do carpentry and concrete work, well, that's just the way things be. So we do the digging, the carrying, the demolition, and whatever else the boss man wants cuz, like I said, that's just the way things be. But that don't mean that we like it. You hear me boy?"

Daniel Sean nods his head, and smiles.

"Yeah, I saw that bridge earlier today, a helluva bridge there too, lads."

They all stare at him because they don't know what the hell he just said. But they kind of got the drift

of it. At least they think that they did. Jubal shakes his head and continues with his monologue.

"Now if you look at me you'll see that I ain't colored, instead I am blacker than coal, which is why when I was young some people used to call me Midnight. My blood is all African. Now Nicodemus and Nathaniel are mostly African, but there is a bit of white in him as are most black people here in New York. Joseph is about half and half so he is what's called colored."

He looks at Daniel Sean to see if he is following all of this. Daniel Sean nods his head up and down to show that he understands what Jubal is saying—well most of what he said.

Jubal starts up again. "Now us four don't give a damn about any of this stuff of what color you is or what color you ain't, we just trying to survive and get some kind of life of our own. Some day we gonna have enough money to move downtown someplace, or else go some other place where we accepted. None of us got no family no more so we's the only family we got, so we take care of one another, you see?"

He stops for a few seconds and then finishes, speaking even more slowly and enunciating very carefully each and every word.

"That's why we can only allow you to stay here for a couple of days or so, we can't be taking no chances. Some white folks wouldn't take too kindly to us taking in a white man. Hell some black folk wouldn't

much like it either. Now don't take this too badly but because of our circumstances we don't really like or trust white people. Too many bad times ya see?"

With the speech done and the food ready to cook they all go their separate ways. Resting up, relieving themselves in private behind a secluded bush, washing up at the river, getting their clothes ready for work the next day, or just being alone by themselves, until finally they are ready to cook the meal and eat.

The yams are chopped and put in a small pail filled with water from the river, and with diced wild onions that grow all around over the place this time of the year. The fish is cooked in a skillet that Joseph lathers up with a little bacon fat, to which he adds pepper, a little salt, and a couple of small tomatoes that Jubal picked up on the way home from a vegetable stand that they always buy from.

After the yams and wild onions have softened Nicodemus adds them to the fish concoction and there it is, dinner is ready. A very simple, inexpensive, and healthy meal.

They say grace, as they usually do, and then eat the meal with a bit of stale bread to sop up the liquid that, to Daniel Sean, is one of the most delicious treat that he has ever had. They wash it down with water. Of course it is true that "hunger makes the best sauce," but to him it is still deliriously delicious.

Twenty-Three

After eating and cleaning the wooden bowls and spoons, they sit around the table talking about the day, mostly complaining about the bossman.

That is until Nathaniel comes up to Daniel Sean with a couple pages of the O'Neill archives that had been laid out to dry and asks Daniel Sean in a hushed whisper which sounds a little strange because he is so big."Can you read and write?"

"A wee bit, but I am learning."

All four of them stand stock still, staring at Daniel Sean, who looks at Nathaniel.

"Can you?" he asks.

"No, we never had the chance to learn. We weren't allowed, none of us can read or write, even though I was free born, there just wasn't any place to go and learn." Joseph answers for Nathaniel.

For a few moments nobody says a word.

"Can you teach us a bit, of how to read and write maybe, just a little bit?" Joseph asks Daniel Sean.

Daniel Sean starts to laugh, and can't stop laughing, probably because this is the first time he has laughed since he did a few times with Molly, and it feels good to actually laugh.

He notices the fellows glaring at him thinking that he's laughing at them.

"Sorry lads, sorry," he says quickly. "No disrespect, not laughing at you. Well you see, it's just that I can barely read meself, I'm just starting out with it ya see, so for anyone to ask me to teach them is well, kinda funny. But why not?" He dives right in. "Well now me buckoos," he says to no one in particular, speaking with his Irish brogue, "I'll show you what I know. I had me a good teacher who started me on it. In fact she is the love of my life you see. We'll learn together."

Joseph speaks up in a clear loud voice, as if speaking to someone who barely speaks English.

"We'll not learn a thing if you don't slow down and speak more clearly. We can't understand but every third or fourth word that you be saying. Use your mouth and your lips—you're talking without hardly moving your lips at all—plus you talk too fast and too much, and please, please, get them damned rocks out of your mouth."

Daniel Sean is a little taken back but he did follow what Joseph said and replies very slowly to Joseph.

"I can follow when you talk because you speak better than the other lads, so you gonna be the one that I will turn to if I don't understand just what in the hell someone says. Now can you understand me Joseph?"

Joseph smiles and nods his head. "That's the first time that I done got every word that you said on account that you slowed down, so yeah, we good."

Daniel Sean starts to laugh and Joseph joins in and the two of them find themselves unable to stop. All the while Jubal, Nathaniel, and Nicodemus just stand there with impatient scowls on their faces.

After awhile Joseph and Daniel Sean collect themselves and stop laughing.

"The truth is," Daniel Sean says to Joseph, "I can't follow hardly anything that he says," pointing at Jubal. "I just shake my head or smile and pretend that I understand, like I'm some kind of bloody idiot."

This sets off the two of them laughing again and the other three fellows can't help themselves and join in too.

Nicodemus finally breaks the ice.

"Well I reckon we gonna have to work on this communication thing, but please let's get on with the reading and writing thing. But white boy, you gots to slow down, way down."

Daniel Sean collects all the dried papers together, and puts them on one of the cleared tables. Surprising Daniel Sean, Nicodemus goes into his tent and pulls out an old beat up bible that he keeps hidden under his bed.

"I have always dreamed of being able to actually read the Word," he says. "Can we use this?"

Daniel Sean is a little surprised, but he smiles, making sure to speak slowly and as clearly as he possibly can.

"I am a wee bit surprised that you have a bible since you can't read, but what the bloody hell? Ah sure

now, I guess that even if I butcher the scripture I reckon that the good Lord will laugh with us. Now did you fellows follow what I just said?"

The four of them nod their heads yes with a look of grateful thanks that they could finally understand what the Irisher is saying.

They begin the lessons, and Daniel Sean starts to teach them the same way that Molly did. Beginning with the alphabet, going over every single letter, vocalizing each one. This takes less than an hour or so. Then, moving along, he shows them two letter words: *of, by, to, up,* and so on. Following Molly's tutelage, he then presses on to the usage of everyday common three letter words like *the, and, yes*, and other similar three letter words. He then, very, very slowly, reads a few paragraphs from the archives, which completely amazes them, as if he is doing a magic trick.

After this he picks up Nicodemus's bible, but before he can start on the first page, which is the very beginning of the bible, the Book of Genesis, Nicodemus objects.

"No, not there. But if you can, could you read this part, right where I done got the page folded down? If you don't mind teacher, how about we start right chere?" He points to the marked place in the bible, the Gospel of John. "Start there."

With everyone hunkered down and looking at the bible over Daniel Sean's shoulder, he starts carefully, and with total concentration, to read the Gospel of John.

He does this very, very slowly with his right index finger stopping at each and every word.

"In the beginning was the Word." He slides his finger to the next sentence, pausing at each word. "And the Word was with God." He repeats the sequence, sliding his finger, then reading. "And the Word was God." In the same manner he moves down the page. "The same was in the beginning with God." And on. "All things were made by him and without him was not anything that was made was made."

He pauses a moment so that he can concentrate, as this is not easy for him. He starts up again at the next section. Lo and behold, like a gift from above, he surprises himself as he reads straight through the next section.

"In him was life, and the life was the light of men. And the light shineth in the dark. And the darkness, compree...comprehe...*comprehend* it not." He keeps reading without stopping, struggling over certain words. "There was a man sent from God whose name was John to bear wit...wit...to bear *witness* of the Light, that all men through him might believe. He was not the Light but came to bear witness of that Light. The true Light that lighteth every man that cometh into this world."

Daniel Sean is in shock and overcome with a feeling of pride that he actually just read all that, more than he has read at one time in his whole life.

He looks up to see the four rough hewn, strong men smiling like kids, with tears of joy shining in their

eyes. Even though they try to hide it, the evidence is overwhelming that all four of them are filled with joy and contentment at the possibility of learning to read. Especially important to the four of them is the chance to actually read the scriptures. Which is something that has been denied to them their whole life.

After two hours or so, and with the night starting to collect all around them, Daniel Sean does a quick overview of what they went over and declares, "That's enough for one day."

The next day, when the fellows return home from working on the High Bridge, the four of them sit Daniel Sean down and inform him that he is welcome to stay for as long as he needs, since he is contributing to their learning to read and maybe write too. But he will also have to help prepare meals, keep the encampment clean and tidy, and do sorties for firewood and berries.

Daniel Sean, thanks them gratefully, and readily agrees to these rules of his upkeep and habitation.

Every night they add more and more words to their repertoire. Then sentences, and paragraphs, and finally they find themselves slowly reading whole sections of the bible. Even though this process is terribly laborious they keep at it. They would do this even on nights when the rains came where they would crowd into one of the tents and do their lessons.

After finishing the Gospel of John, on the sixth straight day of stumbling, halting, but still reading, they decide to go with Acts of the Apostles.

After only two weeks progress starts to take hold. The joy the five of them derive from learning together and actually reading is a small miracle.

On the fifteenth night after finishing the lessons, while getting ready to go to bed, Daniel Sean hears Joseph and Nicodemus talking while also getting ready to retire for the night.

"Never thought I'd be reading the good book by myself. It's the hand of God that brought that Irisher to us," said Joseph.

"I reckon it's a good thing that we decided to let him stay with us for a spell and didn't throw him out the door after only a couple of days like we said that we was gonna do," agreed Nicodemus. "At least I'm glad that we let him stay on."

"Yeah you right, I'm glad too. It's a good trade off all around. God is good."

Twenty-Four

Day after day Daniel Sean finds himself getting better and better due to the good hearty food, the outdoor exercise and the nightly lessons. All three of these have contributed to his recovery. His strength is returning, he feels his muscles start to fill out, and his body is beginning to return to his pre-famine stature, when he had a thickly muscled body on his bandy-legged Irish body. A physique that was made for physical activity.

When Daniel Sean was not quite ten years old, he found himself to be blessed with a gift from above. He was a natural acrobat. One day after experimenting, he found that he could walk on his hands with the greatest of ease. Almost as easily as walking. Flipping up onto and then walking on his hands became as natural to him as breathing. Doing dive handsprings over stonewalls and hedges was a daily routine.

It was a natural high that he reveled in, and which gave him so much pleasure because it made him unique and different from anyone else in the vicinity of the small West Kerry village of Killeenleagh. The village was near where his family's half-acre farm was located.

On his tenth birthday he walked forty-seven steps on his hands. It was a huge event, stemming from a

challenge from an older kid who was sick of seeing Daniel Sean walking on his hands all the time.

"Okay now there me buck ," the older boy taunted, "let's see how many steps you can actually walk on your hands. I'll give you a penny for every step that you take over twenty."

So on the day of his tenth birthday, Daniel Sean walked on his hands for forty-seven steps, *forty-seven*, and while it took a gargantuan effort on his part, he did it.

For Daniel Sean walking forty-seven steps on his hands on the morning of his tenth birthday was a great accomplishment. It gave him a feeling of invincibility, which only bolstered his confidence as a boy and lifted him up in this world.

This was all gone now of course. For the last two and a half years, because of the Great Hunger, his skill as a budding acrobat has virtually dissolved into a thing of the past, a memory at best. In his weakened state, he could only dream of doing something like that again.

But now, because of his life with his African cohorts, it seemed possible that he was maybe, just maybe, recapturing his former life. And that maybe, someday, that specific acrobatic skill of walking on his hands, that trick of his that God had given to him, might return. A gift that through the machinations of the devil himself had been depleted.

This possibility filled him with an incalculable degree of hope that anything like this could even

remotely occur, for he had missed this ability so very, very much.

His convalescence at the encampment continues unabated under the watchful eyes of his four hosts for almost three weeks until he is feeling strong again. In fact, he feels so good as he knows that he has a second lease on life. Like he is reborn.

One night he makes an announcement to the fellows.

"Lads, I want to go to work with you. I could work for a while and pay you back for all that you've done for the likes of me and then take my leave. Do you think that it is possible for me to get some work on the bridge there?"

Daniel Sean is greeted with total silence. The four of them look at one another until Joseph speaks up.

"Looky here now Daniel, you been a lot of help here, keeping the place clean, helping cooking dinner, and helping us to learn to read every night. "But we can't be bringing a white man on down to the bridge. The boss man wouldn't be happy to see us mingling together, no suh!"

The other three nod their heads and voice their agreement.

"Wouldn't set right with none of them," Joseph continues. "We keep our mouths shut and do the work, don't even socialize at all with them white boys on the job. We the only colored folk on the bridge."

Daniel Sean thinks for a bit.

"What if I just show up looking for a job, pretending that I don't know you lads? You think that might work?"

Jubal thinks for a minute.

"I heard the boss man saying to another higher up that they be needing a couple more laborers. But I also heard him say that he didn't want to be hiring any more Coloreds or any of you Irish. He don't like you Irishers, especially if you be one of them Catholics. That's what I heard him tell another of the foreman's out there on the job."

Two days later, in the middle of the afternoon, Daniel Sean follows the directions that Jubal gave him and shows up at the site of the High Bridge construction site and asks to see the 'boss man.' He tries his best to not sound Irish but it is not easy to do so he decides to imitate a Scottish burr, which he heard from one of the crew members on the *Athlone*. When the foreman shows up he says, "Ach now, the names Daniel Angus Macdonald and I'm looking for a wee job, you know what I'm talking aboat?"

The boss man looks him over, and says with a touch of disdain in his voice, "Sorry Paddy but we're already filled up."

"Christ now laddy but I'm no Paddy, I'm from Scotland and I'm a Protestant."

"Oh, well sorry but I thought that you was a bloody Mick and a papist." He looks Daniel Sean up and down. "Scottish eh? All right then, come back tomorrow and we'll give you a go. Be ready to work. Bright and early."

That night, after eating dinner, cleaning up, and before doing their lessons, they all sit around the table and take turns telling Daniel Sean the different tasks that he may have to do on the job. Also how much money he will make, which is $1.30 a day, six days a week, 10 hours a day.

It will be hard physical work and they wonder if he is up to it.

"I am so desperate and I have seen so much misery on my path here to America that I have no choice but to buck up and do whatever it is that I have to do." Daniel Sean tells them. "I will survive."

After doing their lessons Nathaniel hustles everyone up to hit the sack.

"Going to be a hot one tomorrow, I can feel it in my bones so we got to get some rest so that our Irisher boy, Daniel Sean there, is up to the task on the job. Ya hear me fellows?"

Later that night Daniel Sean wakes up and thinks of Molly, and wonders where she is and when he will see her. But he knows that he will. He just knows that he will be reunited with her. He has faith in that, so he says a quick Ave, and right before he falls back asleep again,

he sees her face and promises her that he will see her soon. *Soon, muschusla. Real soon.*

They wake up the next morning, August 12th, before the sun is even up and it is already hot. The five of them get moving, and as soon as they begin the walk, following the shore of the Harlem River, heading east and a little south, they all start sweating like crazy from the heat.

A short distance from the location Daniel Sean stays back, hides in the bushes, and waits for about ten minutes before he heads out so that he will arrive at a different time, but not late.

When the workday begins at the job site they are put to work immediately. The work is hard physical labor with no need for any type of skills or training. It is also very taxing on Daniel Sean, at first mainly because of the heat, but he does it, and through the course of that first day it gets easier on his body. He feels as if he is adapting, and his body is expanding because of all the lifting, breaking, pulling, and pushing that he has to do.

This happens the next day and the day after that. In the morning it is a tough go on him but by the middle of the day he finds himself in a rhythm of sorts and finds himself reveling in the return of his strength.

In fact he finds himself getting stronger and stronger every day, which is a great feeling for him. Before An Gorta Mor Daniel Sean was known for his physical strength, not just because he could walk on his

hands, but also because he was a stocky, muscular lad strengthened by a steady diet of potatoes and buttermilk and hard work out in the fields. His nickname was the "Baby Bull," and he could out work men years older than him. He had immense pride in his strength, and from an early age was also known to put up a good fight when the need arose.

So he is ecstatic to be slowly returning to his pre-famine stature. And he can't wait to show his newly recovering physique to his Molly.

Day after day for the next couple of weeks Daniel Sean gets up before the sun and then, along with Jubal, Joseph, Nathaniel and Nicodemus, he walks to the site of what some have begun to call the High Bridge, even though the real name is the Aqueduct Bridge.

They are in the last stages of the construction of this bridge, whose sole purpose is to carry water into Manhattan from Croton, New York, which is close to 41 miles away. The bridge is designed so that the water travels by the force of gravity from Croton on Hudson all the way down to the isle of Manhattan. It is an immense project that is, at this point in time, considered to be an engineering marvel.

A week after Daniel Sean started working on the project the Aqueduct Bridge is completed and most of the crew is sent on their way. As fortune would have it, the five of them are picked to stay on the job site to finish all the touch up work.

Mainly their job is to do the final cleanup all around the site, but also a little touch up which includes some painting here and there and, last but not least, removal of all the remaining debris. It is tough, hard, and dirty work, not for the faint of heart.

So just like the back breaking work that they did on the Spuytin Duyvil bridge, the fellows are scraping, chipping, digging, and hauling debris out of the construction site, mostly burying it on the outside perimeter of the site. Anything that is deemed of value or reusable is being hauled away by horse driven carts to be used later at some other construction site.

There is a building boom that is starting in Manhattan. There is even talk of building a bridge that will span the East River from Manhattan to Brooklyn.

A bridge to Brooklyn, the Brooklyn Bridge. Which, of course, most people think is simply not possible.

Twenty-Five

One day after a small detonation is used during some demolition work the noise spooks one of the horses, and he starts to kick and head butt anything and everything around him. The driver lashes him with a whip, which only further enrages the horse.

Jubal sprints over to the horse, which is pulling a cart that is laden with debris, where he jumps up and onto the side of the horses rigging and gently pulls the horse by the neck to his chest and caresses him all the while whistling softly into his ear and saying, "I got you boy, I got you."

The horse kicks the ground, once, twice, and then calms down, nudging Jubal's chest, as if asking for Jubal to keep petting him, which he does. The horse whinnies and rubs up against Jubal as if they are the best of friends. Everyone present, boss man, driver, and the five lads, are all silently staring at Jubal.

Suddenly there is a tumultuous round of applause from a small crowd of civilian spectators who are watching the crew and are standing on the Manhattan side of the bridge.

The crew crowds around Jubal, slapping his back and smiling at him.

"I done worked with horses in the past, with my father afore he left this world, and he taught me how to talk to them."

Boss man speaks up.

"Well I'll be damned, never knew a black man could do that with horses. You can help out when needed with the driver."

Looking up at the driver Jubal realizes that the man is relieved to have the assistance, for he grins and nods his head.

Unlike other handlers or wranglers Jubal does not beat, strike, or whip the two horses. Instead he pets, combs, and cajoles them while speaking softly to get the two of them to cooperate whenever the driver has trouble with them. He is strong and stern with the horses, but this is also tinged with a streak of kindness which seems to enamor the horses to him, soothing the savage beast within, so to speak. This creates a bond, a friendship between man and animal that amazes anyone who sees them together.

Jubal even gives both of the work horses names— Balthazar and Gasper, the names of two of the Magi, the wise men from the bible.

Already a few people have started to congregate at different spots on both sides of the Harlem River, in Manhattan and the Bronx, to view this engineering marvel. And to watch the four colored men and the one white man scurry around doing the final touch up work

on the Aqueduct Bridge site. Some yell encouragement at them, while some yell obscenities and slurs at them.

Daniel Sean works side by side with his four friends, but he has to pretend that he does not really know them because that is simply the way things are on the job site, and in huge swaths of society in general. He eats lunch by himself, shows up at the job alone, and leaves the site without them. But they always catch up with one another at a given spot on the way back to their camp. All the way home they spend the time figuring out how to get dinner.

They fish when they can, and sometimes they are lucky enough to buy from a few local hunters that they know; squirrel meat, rabbit, and whatever else is available. Most of the time, however, they have to do with dried meats like bacon, or smoked fish. That's if those items are available, if not, which is usually the case, the menu is beans, yams, and whatever else they can find.

On their day off, which is Sunday, they spend the day fishing along the Hudson or Harlem Rivers. Some Sundays this past summer when the Harlem River is at low tide, they swim across to the other side and pick blackberries and wild strawberries. Joseph then makes jam out of them; a skill he learned in his youth.

Along the way on the walk back to the camp from High Bridge, on the banks of the Harlem River, there is a colored area, a little enclave, where they buy most of

their supplies. Occasionally, once a month or so, on a Saturday evening this includes a couple buckets of homemade beer that they drink out on the dirt road in front of the makeshift bar. Daniel Sean goes with them one Saturday evening to have a beer or two. He is the only white person around but he does not feel that uncomfortable because of his friends, who make sure that everyone knows that he is with them.

Here is where Joseph, Nicodemus, Nathaniel, and Jubal feel the most comfortable, and here is where they spend almost every first Saturday night of the month in the Summer time and into Autumn. Relaxing, chatting, having a couple of beers, maybe something a little stronger, and cut loose just a little bit.

One this Saturday night, his second week on the job, and the first time that Daniel Sean has gotten paid, they all drink an extra bucket of beer. He is feeling good, and after a while Daniel Sean finds himself doing a little step dancing to a fiddle and a washboard that two black men are playing. Jubal joins in and shows him some torso movements to go along with his Irish step dancing.

Right around sunset Daniel Sean goes back to the camp by himself because Jubal and Nathaniel have both decided to spend some time at the "House;" a place where ladies of the night are available. Joseph and Nicodemus never partake for the two of them are both, as they say, "God fearing and devout." However they are staying to drink a few more beers, Joseph saying "The

Lord did turn water into wine at Cana, so I do believe that it's alright to have another round."

Daniel Sean is invited but he begs off, for not only does he not want to spend the money, but as he tells his pals, "My heart and mind are elsewhere."

This makes one of the girls who is with Jubal laugh.

"That ain't got nothing to do with what's down there," she says to Daniel Sean, which makes everyone laugh and causes Daniel Sean to blush.

The girl that Nathaniel has picked, whose name is Sugar, shakes her head.

"Hush up now," she says. "I think it's a sweet thing that this boy is holding out for his girl. Wish I done had me someone waiting for me."

To which Nathaniel replies, "Sugar I will wait for you and even write you a love letter."

"You can't write, so why you saying sumpin as crazy as that?" Sugar laughs.

"Oh yes I can, I'm learning real good, all of us are gonna be reading real soon. And writing too."

Sugar is dumbfounded.

"Is that true?" She whispers.

Joseph puffs up his chest.

"As God is my witness we are learning right quick, ain't easy but Glory be we are, all of us, learning to read and write."

Sugar squeezes Nathaniel.

"It's a new day adawning. I only knows one or two people can read or write around here. But now we got you boys, God amighty but a new day is acoming. Some day, some day." She pauses and smiles at Nathaniel. "You gonna get the special treatment tonight Nathan baby, gonna give you all of my honeysuckle rose, an you gonna find out why they call me Sugar."

Nathaniel's knees buckle and tremble in response to Sugar's sweet sounding voice, and the tenderness oozing from her eyes.

Daniel Sean walks back to the encampment, taking his time in the fading light with thoughts of Molly going through his mind and a numb empty feeling in his heart. *I have to find her, I am so worried about her, and all that I can think about is having her in my arms. Is she healthy? Is she in good spirits?*

"Does she still love me?" he questions softly aloud. He pauses and looks up to the stars.

Oh dear God in heaven look after her, watch over her, and help me find her.

Right before he falls asleep Daniel Sean thinks about his four friends, and how much they've gone through together.

When they first met Daniel Sean kind of heaped them all together. They are his black friends that he worked with and lived with but now he sees each one of them not as a group but as individuals.

Jubal is medium height and build but with a powerful wiry strength. He has amazing skills and

stamina and can do most any job. What sets him apart is that he is a man with a complete and utter non negotiable sense of loyalty. It is something that he lives and breathes by, and something that he would never back track on. He is also one of the smartest men that I've known with an uncanny gift of sensing another's feelings and thoughts. Reckon that's why he's so good with horses.

Plus he has an inner strength that makes him a natural leader of men. Everyone here, including me, look up to him.

Joseph is tall, over 6 feet, and thin, but not weak, he can labor all day long doing hard, heavy work in the hot sun. He is a deep thinker, kind, and his faith is the most important part of his life. I feel as if he is full of the Holy Spirit, you can feel it in him.

He can recite whole sections of the Bible with no hesitation, it's just there on the tip of his tongue.

Physically, Nicodemus is medium height but compactly built, stocky and strong. He is a no nonsense man with an unwavering sense of right and wrong but he is also an individual who is logical and down to earth, Like Joseph, his faith in Christ is possibly the most important element to him.

I think that both Joseph and Nicodemus would be great priests or ministers.

Nathaniel is a giant of a man with a soft heart but something happened to him in his past, he seems wounded and vulnerable at times. While he can

sometimes be gentle and caring there are times when he seems to be so sad and alone.

All in all, I have the fondest affection for all four of these lads. And since every man that I have ever known growing up, including my father and two brothers, are gone from this world well the truth is; I feel closer to these lads, my African brothers, than to any other men that I know in this world.

Twenty-Six

Almost four weeks after Daniel Sean started work with the crew, on September 8th, the job at the High Bridge Aqueduct Bridge is completely done.

Now it seems as if there is nothing in the way of opportunity for the lads; no job, no work, no hustle, nothing in the way of immediate employment.

But luck is with the fellows, because another opportunity arises on that very last day of work. When they are finished for the day, a man, who is visiting New York City and who spotted them working on the bridge a few days ago, approaches them. Apparently he is very impressed with their work ethic, and the energized way that they did their jobs.

He follows and then approaches them as they start to walk away from the job site stopping them just before they travel onto the little path that leads them into the woods and back to their encampment.

A little out of breath but, with a smile on his face, he presents the five of them with an offer. Which is an invitation for the five of them to come north to work on the Black River Canal, which is an extension of the Erie Canal way up north in upstate New York.

It turns out that it would be a lot of the same type of work that they did on the Aqueduct Bridge but, more as well.

"You'd be doing more than just cleaning up. I see that you fellows can work and it's a good opportunity for you," the man explains. "I have a good eye for talent, and I think that you men could do more than just the demolition and clean up. I have been observing the five of you for the last three days and I'm quite impressed by your work ethic. And your ability to work together as a team." He pauses and looks directly at Daniel Sean while saying this.

Glancing at Jubal the man smiles and says. "And you are a wizard with those horses. It is a pleasure to watch you with them."

Then he looks at the other men. "I know that your time is up here, so if you have nothing else going on you could come up north and work for me. There's also a whole community of Colored folks living up there, has been for a while, since 1825," he explains. "It's different up there for your people now, not as hostile. Even got black Quakers up there, living and working side by side with white Quakers. You see my wife was raised as a Quaker and she said I should do what I can to hire those who are shunned by society. And I believe that she is right, so here I am."

He pauses to let it all sink in.

"I'll be back next week, on September 16, and if you decide to come on up, I will set up transportation for

the five of you. We also have housing for you—cabins, rustic but comfortable. Even when there is bad weather you'll be dry. The work will stop when the permanent freeze sets in, probably just right before Christmas, so it will be a little more than three months of work for you boys. That's when we go on a skeleton crew, because we have to wait until the thaw sets in around early spring. So all in all it would be a good three months work for the five of you, or however many wish to join my outfit."

Looking from one man to the next he continues.

"You will be obligated to work only for this next session, which ends, as I said a little bit before Christmas. But if it all works out you can come back for the spring, summer, and fall season next year. We'll see how it all goes. The pay is $1.35 a day of which we take out twenty cents a day for food and housing. Think about it. Oh my name is Johnson, by the way, Charles Johnson."

Later that night, after stopping at their enclave and sharing a couple buckets of beer, the five of them make their way home, clean up, cook dinner, and then sit around the campfire to discuss their options. Jubal starts the discussion.

"I done heard that upstate is more open to us. You see, someone once told me that in certain areas up north they got more of the righteous type ideas floating around. Including now, they say, that upstate they also be

having meetings for equal rights for women called suffergates or sumpin like that. Can you imagine that? Equal rights for women and us? It may sound crazy but I'm all for it. Before she passed away, the time that I spent with my momma was the best times of my whole life. She was the most spirited and smartest person that I ever did meet. She was my best friend." Jubal's eyes start to light up at the memory of his mother.

"She encouraged me to do as many things as I could do with myself and my life. And she shoulda had the same rights as any man. My father thought that way too. So I reckon that upstate they may be believing and acting in a more different way in this world than what we be used to. If that's the truth then we might be alright up there, but I don't know, whatchu fellas think?"

Joseph, Nathaniel, and Nicodemus, all three say yes, with no hesitation.

"I'm crazy about that Sugar," Nathaniel adds. "In fact I would like to marry her and take her away from this life she leads and hates, but I ain't got no chance without money because she has a sickly little girl who she has to take care of. I want a family of my own no matter what I got to do. And this is a good opportunity for me to make some money. I grew up with nothing but hard times until I met up with you fellows. Never knew my mother or my father, they were owned by somebody else. After I run away from that plantation down in Virginia I went straight up the Railroad, through the

mountains of West Virginia following the North Star like I was told to do."

Everyone is stock still, this is the first time that Nathaniel has ever spoken of his past. Jubal, Joseph, and Nicodemus were all three free born and know nothing about being 'owned' by anybody. Nathaniel shrugs his shoulders, slightly embarrassed and continues. "Plus up there with nothing to do but work, I can get on even more with my lessons. I can see the light at the end of the tunnel. I'm gonna be educated. Maybe even run for president just like Fredrick Douglass done did last summer."

They all laugh, imagining Nathaniel as president. Jubal concedes that he thinks that it is the right thing to do, going on upstate to work on the Black River Canal. But Daniel Sean shakes his head.

"I have to see if I can find my Molly, so tomorrow I head south down into Manhattan and look around for a couple of days. I may be back before you leave, but if I don't then that means that I found her." He shrugs his shoulders. "Sure and it's all up to fate now. But you know Jubal, my Ma was my best friend also. She was smarter than any man that I ever knew, so yeah I agree with you about that equal rights for women thing. Throughout history in Ireland the women did not sit by and watch the men folk do everything, they even would go into battle side by side with the men."

The men take all that in, and in silence they sit around the fire until it dies out and then all retire to bed.

The next morning after a little breakfast and the other morning rituals, Daniel Sean packs up his small knapsack for the trip down into lower Manhattan. While saying his goodbyes to the fellows, he hands a packet with half of his wages over to Jubal, with the other three men standing next to him. The amount is exactly $20.85. Jubal takes it, removes ten dollars from it and returns the rest to Daniel Sean.

"We good. The three of us decided that you might need more than half so here you are. And if you can't find your angel, you come back and we will make some more money up there in Black River."

"But I owe you more, and someday I will repay you," Daniel Sean says as he takes the money.

"Yes we know that, but for now, we're good."

"You know since we've been doing those lessons I do believe that our speech has gotten better," he says to Jubal. "You don't have as much trouble understanding me, and I have an easier time understanding you."

Nicodemus does what Daniel Sean does a lot, he winks at him, then smiles and says. "Ain't that the truth!"

"See you in six days, or not, depends on which way that it goes," Daniel Sean says to the lot of them.

Twenty-Seven

After saying his goodbyes, Daniel Sean walks along a path that Jubal told him is named the Wickquasgek Trail. It is an old Indian trail that traverses the entire length of Manhattan. The Dutch also used it and renamed it breg wede or in English, the broad way.

For the first two hours he sees hardly any people, just a few farmsteads, a few huts, and a lot of wildlife. Even with the dearth of human habitation he feels as if he is being watched, as if there are forces or movements all around him, it is just a feeling but he cannot shake it. He keeps looking over his shoulder and around trees but sees nothing. It's as if the granite hills, the trees, and the ground itself is shaking with its own unique energy. What Daniel Sean decides to call Manhattan energy.

Unbeknownst to Daniel Sean is that while it appears as if he is in a place where there aren't all that many people, this same trail will eventually end at one of the single most populated places on planet earth: Five Points, at the very bottom of Manhattan Island, about 13 miles away from where he is now.

The Broadway is a well used trail that takes him up and down over granite rocks, past ponds, streams, and through diverse, thick foliage that is sometimes surrounded by huge oak, elm, and maple trees. The

farther he walks the more signs of humanity he encounters; an abandoned fire pit, tamped down leaves, and on occasion a working homestead, but not much in the way of farm animals. Most of the habitation seems to be temporary where individuals or groups of individuals stay for a night or a week and then head out. It's as if a kind of nomadic lifestyle appears to be the norm.

After walking for three hours Daniel Sean emerges from a secluded area that is mostly pine trees with needles on the forest floor, creating a cushion that absorbs all sound around him.

He pushes through a morass of thorny brambles, and out of nowhere he finds himself on the outskirts of a fairly large village. Upon inspection he sees that the inhabitants are mostly African and colored, but with a small smattering of whites, who upon further inspection definitely look to be Irish. It is mostly families.

All eyes are warily watching him as he walks into the village and then traverses a very crowded area of tents, homemade shacks and, surprisingly, well tended, lovely two story wooden houses.

"God bless all here," Daniel Sean says to no one in particular.

A man steps right in front of him, shakes his head and says to Daniel Sean. "The *Athlone*. Am I right me boyo?"

"Holy Mother of God, I know your face! You were on the *Athlone*, Sweet Jesus! You had a wife and a small son as I recall." Daniel Sean hesitates before

asking the man. "Are you all right with it all now? The family I mean."

"Aye, aye, ta, all are accounted for. Not to say of course that we haven't, by God, had it rough, but got to count our blessings—after all we are six feet above the duggened earth. 'Tis a problem here in New York City, mind you, because it seems that no one wants us here. Except for these people, God bless them. My son here plays with the black boys like they are blood, and nobody here calls any of us 'dirty Paddys.'"

Just then a boy about twelve years old, with a smile on his face and a bit of the devil in his eyes, walks on up to the two of them. "This here's my boy, Willy."

"Well my name is Daniel Sean O'Neill, and 'tis a great pleasure to be meeting the likes of you."

Daniel Sean and Willy shake hands.

"And my name is William, William Nolan." The father says. "I believe that you and we have a bond that no man can break: the crossing, and the fact that we made it. God rest those who did not." His face clouds over as he speaks to Daniel Sean.

"To the day that I die I will never forget that look of desperate devotion on the face of that shattered woman." He stops and looks away, then continues. "The mother who choose to go down into the bottomless cold foam of the Atlantic Ocean with her daughter, Megan Murphy, that little one who was touched by the angels herself. May Christ Himself keep her and her daughter,

and may the Holy Mother hold them both in her loving arms."

"Nor shall I forget, nor shall I. It is seared into my soul."

They look away at the memory, slightly embarrassed, but also knowing that each of them have a fierce determination to never forget mother and daughter sinking down into the watery abyss clasped together. William quickly changes the subject.

"So Daniel Sean what brings you here to Seneca Village?"

"Looking for a girl, my mucushla."

"Would that be the one that you were with day and night, the one with the eyes of blue and hair the color of a blackbird?"

"Aye, one and the same. We were separated and I jumped ship up north. Have ya seen her? I'm shattered to find her, desperate so to speak."

"She's not here, that's all I know. For your own sake I hope that she is not down there in that hell hole, Five Points. The devil himself would feign to stay away from there and then show up in all his black glory to tempt even the most pure hearted of men or women to do his bidding."

"All the more reason to find her."

"Well Daniel Sean if ya like you can stay here for a bit whilst you look for her. We all watch out for one another so that it's safe, which certainly is not the case down in Five Points. They'll cut ya for the shirt on your

back down there. Oh, by the way, you have to change those English pounds you got over to American dollars."

"Will do, will do. Much obliged my friend."

"Come inside now Daniel Sean and we'll have us a jar."

Daniel Sean spends the next few days searching for Molly and his nights sleeping on a pallet with straw in an area between two wooden shacks as a guest of William Nolan, who is a caretaker, not an owner, of the two shacks. The shacks belong to a cousin of his, originally from Ireland, who has been in New York City for close to ten years now. He is usually away at sea working as a seaman, a kind of merchant marine, and comes home only on occasion, so William keeps an eye on his little abode.

One night it rains so Daniel Sean sleeps on the floor inside one of the Nolan's modest shacks. This is the shack that the Nolan family stays in when the cousin is back in town. The outside is just a wooden structure, but the interior is surrounded by memories of Ireland; homemade lace curtains and a Celtic cross that hangs above a small iron cast stove used a source of heat and also to cook on. There is a giant quilt that depicts four green fields symbolizing the four counties of Ireland, a giant bed for the couple, and a small cot in the corner for Willy.

Even with these mementos to remind him of Ireland, to Daniel Sean the most Irish keepsake of all is

Fiona Nolan herself, Williams's wife, and the center of all that transpires in the Nolan household.

Fiona Nolan is from a small village in County Clare, and while she is a devout Catholic she is also bound to the "old ways," not just a belief in the existence of fairies, leprechauns, and Banshees, but also pooka, selkies, mer people, and sprites, which she believes exist only in Ireland and nowhere else on earth.

Omens, curses, and blessings are her specialty, obligating her to send forth a steady stream of intonations and prayers usually culminating in a plea to the Holy Mother of God.

On top of this knowledge that she has, she is also a redhead, which she claims causes a bit of confusion.

"Most people get it in their heads and think that I am bad luck to them. Ah sure their all daft, for I am only the carrier of the sight, and some can't handle what they don't understand. I've seen things that most people don't see. For I was born the same night that lightening struck the giant Hawthorne tree sitting outside of our house in Clare—a sure sign, as anyone should know, that the fairies gave me their blessing at my birth."

"Me mother had the sight too." Daniel Sean says to Fiona. "I would catch her talking to certain trees or just the sky itself. Once she went out into a raging storm and stood under the falling rain with the wind whipping all around; scared to death me and me two brothers and me sister were that night I tell you. When these things would happen my father would just laugh and shake his

head or shrug his shoulders as if saying, 'just the way it is with her.' "

"Ah sure, Daniel Sean, but she was only having a bit of a talk with Lugh, who is always around and about in a storm, at least back in Ireland, or maybe she was chasing away a banshee, which one should never do. For banshees never forget. You have to look to and invoke the power of the Trinity with you at all times when dealing with some wayward spirits. 'Tis the only thing that works to send them on their way."

While there are a lot of hardscrabble homes in Seneca Village, ones that have been thrown together so that they appear to be somewhat shabby, none of them are haphazard. There is an order about the place that trickles on down to every single shack, hut, house, and tent that gives the village a feeling of "Home."

On down the road in the middle of the village are some modest but nicely built and impeccably clean homes, with small parcels or yards that are staked out and used in the summer as vegetable gardens. Most of these homes are owned by native New Yorkers of African descent who moved here before the Irish, and a smattering of German Catholics who arrived sometimes afterwards.

The Irish and Germans are not welcome with open arms by the nativist New Yorkers, mainly because of their ties to Catholicism, but they are welcomed into

their fold by the African New Yorkers, who by and large refer to themselves as "coloreds."

Surprisingly there is very little friction between the three groups, mainly because the majority of the residents are independent, family oriented and have strong traditional values. They have made a commitment to "work things out" if there are disagreements between factions of any of the three groups.

But even more than that there is a level of tolerance from the African/colored majority. So much so that on any given Sunday one could see white and black people attending the same service at All Angels Church in the heart of Seneca Village.

One thing that impresses Daniel Sean more than anything else is how friendly and open most of the people who live here are to him. Everyone says hello or simply wave at him from their front porch.

It is a living, breathing, unique, town that even has it's own cemetery, and one midwife who resides in the Seneca community so that this diverse population of approximately 250 souls have a shared experience from birth to death.

Twenty-Eight

For five days Daniel Sean wakes up at dawn and, with a small parcel of food from Fiona, he rambles all over the southern portion of lower Manhattan.

The first day Daniel Sean is astonished at the jostling crowds that bump and push him as he walks on downtown toward Five Points. When he finally gets there he is accosted by gangs of Irish hooligans who can tell that he is just "off the boat" and naive to the ways of lower New York City.

But most of this is just giving him a hard time, making fun of him as a fellow Irishman here in America, and not creating any real trouble for him. That is until, just outside of Five Points, he runs into a couple of hard cases—the locals, the Nativists, the ones who hate all things Irish and all "papists."

It happens while Daniel Sean is walking south on the Bowery. Two guys both dressed identically, wearing tight fitting pantaloons, loose black coats, even though it is hot as hell out, and each sporting a big idiotic looking black top hat, step in his way and block him from walking on down the sidewalk.

"A stupid bastard of a Mick, cousin to the apes and monkeys," growls the bigger of the two and giving Daniel Sean a shove. "Only those who are really and

truly from New York get to walk here on the Bowery. You Irish pig, whose mother was probably a whore, has to walk on the other…"

The ruffian doesn't get to finish his sentence, for Daniel Sean rises up fully on the balls of his feet for leverage and, with lightening fast speed, knocks him backward with one shattering punch, a right handed straight on wallop right between the eyes. With barely a seconds pause Daniel Sean lunges forward onto his left foot and follows through with a left cross that slams into the right side of the mans face. Immediately stepping forward and shifting his weight to his right foot Daniel Sean swings from his waist on upward, with a tightly clenched fist, connecting with a vicious right uppercut underneath the bottom of the mans chin. He follows through with his fist upward toward the sky, lifting the guy up and off of his feet. Sending the man into dreamland as he stumbles backward like a felled tree, landing on and crushing his hat in the process.

Daniel Sean then jumps on him and starts wailing on him punching him on his head and face over and over again, all the while saying to the guy. "I'll kill you for saying that about me mother."

The other guy hesitates for a minute, in shock at the ferocity coming out of Daniel Sean but then comes to and pulls out a wooden truncheon from under his coat. Which is the reason that these nativists wear these heavy coats even in the summer; to hide the clubs or knives or

whatever other weapons that they carry with them all the time.

The guy nervously swings at Daniel Sean's head but misses and Daniel Sean instead is hit on the shoulder in a glancing blow. Wincing in pain for just a second but running on manic hate-filled adrenalin he stands to his full height, wheels back and using the element of surprise, rather than punching, he kicks the second guy in his left knee.

As he starts to stagger a bit Daniel Sean rears the same foot back and with all his might, then kicks him in his right knee. As the guy sways to and fro, Daniel Sean slugs him, with a straight on jab, square in the face probably breaking something in the guys nose because he starts gushing blood.

Daniel Sean doesn't give a damn because, as the guy continues to stagger around, Daniel Sean punches him one, two, one, two, like a piston, left, right, left, right, left, right, until the punk is bloody and unconscious and slides down next to his fellow nativist where they both lie not moving.

Daniel Sean kicks them both in the ribs to make sure that they are both down and out. Then kicks them both again for good measure and spits on the two of them just for the hell of it.

He looks up to see that a small crowd has gathered on the spot.

In the back of the growing crowd of spectators, about a half a block away, Daniel Sean spots four of the

same tall black hats and realizes that these guys are probably coming after him, since he just beat the hell out of two of their pals.

Looking to his side he asks one of the spectators. "Which way is to that street they call Broadway?"

The man smiles and points west.

"Seven blocks that away. When you get there take a right and head north cross Canal Street and you should be okay. But get the hell out of here on the quick. And thanks for the beat down, we hate these guys."

Daniel Sean winks at the man and takes off running, feeling not at all afraid but more of a carefree jubilant sensation as he thinks to himself, *Me boyo but that felt great. Good God but I am on my way back, these eejits can't catch me, I am on my way back. And sure but it is a lovely feeling.*

Making it to Broadway in ten minutes or so, Daniel Sean takes a right and heads up north, not even bothering to look backwards to see if he is being followed. He just keeps on moving, with the strength of more than one in him, his legs gleefully pumping him on. This movement is accompanied, in his minds eye, by the look of his mothers face smiling down at him.

Nobody says that about me mother, nobody. If I see that lowlife of a man again I'll give him another beat down, ah sure and if I won't. Who in the bleeding hell were those guys with those black coats and big black hats?

After he crosses Canal Street he slows down a bit and speaks aloud to himself. "Why the hell is everyone staring at me?" Daniel Sean glances down at his right hand and sees that it is covered in blood, which is the reason that people have been staring at him and scurrying away from him. *I have to cover up my hand; don't want to draw attention to myself.*

He hears a whistle and figures that can't be a good thing, so he starts running again. Figuring that he has to get off of Broadway he takes a right on Grand Street and then a quick left on Crosby and keeps running north.

The whole time that he is moving along, darting in between the people on the crowded sidewalks, he hears that same damned whistle. At the intersection of Crosby and Prince Street he comes face to face with a young fellow who is about the same age that he is, around eighteen years old.

He has curly, almost orange colored hair, freckles on every visible portion of his body, including his entire face all the way up to his ears. His front teeth are chipped and his nose looks as if it has been broken recently. He is medium height, stocky, thickly muscled but with the same bandy-legged lower body as Daniel Sean, which makes him appear as if he is in a fighting stance and ready to rumble. In a word he looks pugnacious, as if he would love to dive into the middle of a fray.

Daniel Sean likes the guy immediately.

"Jesus, Mary, and Joseph, what in the hell is going on with youse?" the kid says, with a fast paced Dublinesque Irish accent. "Come with me boyo before you get into trouble. Don't worry now, for around here we take care of our own kind, that's the way 'tis. Move it now."

Daniel Sean figures *what the hell?* and follows the guy all the way back into an alley where the kid pushes through a retractable part of a wooden fence. After they get through he rearranges the fence so that it looks whole again.

He then leads Daniel Sean down another alley until they come to a boarded up wall which the young man then simply lifts up off of its hinges. After rearranging the wall, they crawl through a small window, which the guy closes behind him, and enter into a dingy dark room.

It takes Daniel Sean a minute for his eyes to adjust. He sees that it is a basement apartment that is sparsely furnished with what looks like handmade furniture that includes a table, a chair, and a bed. There is nobody else in the room.

"Well now I can see that you are Irish, it's all over your face. Now tell me how didja get your bleeding hand so bloody?"

Daniel Sean proceeds to tell him what happened back there in The Bowery, including a description of what the two guys were wearing. When he is finished the kid, who has been holding his breath throughout the

whole monologue, lets out a big "Pshew," shakes his head and then starts to laugh.

"They have many names ya see; The Bowery Boys, the B'hoys, to name a few, and they hate anyone and everyone who is not a "free born American." So if you are Irish or even German you are not in favor with these lads. But for some ungodly reason, more than anything, they hate us Irish. And you have the map of Ireland all over that mug of yours. So now you have to know there, me lad, you gotta watch yourself, ya hear me?"

Daniel Sean shrugs his shoulders and shakes his head with a slight "yeah, yeah, okay" nod.

"The names Jack Brosnahan, now what's yours there?"

"Daniel Sean O'Neill, you sound like you are Dublin born, or, well at least you don't sound Cork or Kerry. Where's your family from?"

"Aye good ear. I come from a seaside town that is a bit south of Dublin. Bray 'tis called. 'Tis a lovely town...but not lovely enough to keep the famine away. Lost my whole family, just me left, but that was well over a year ago and nothing to be done about it. Here I am now in New York and damned alive. How 'bout youse?"

"Same here, same here. I come from a farm, I do, near a small wee town in West Kerry. But my family? Like you, all gone but me, so I left Ireland just this past

May. I've been working up in the northern stretches of Manhattan on a bridge doing laboring work."

Jack brings out a washbasin with water in it and Daniel Sean proceeds to clean himself up, washing all the blood off his hands, arms, and his face. The whole time Jack explains to him what life in and around the downtown area, in the vicinity of Five Points, is like.

"Well now Daniel Sean you see…while this is not Five Points, that notorious area is just a bit south of us. The fact is you have to follow the politics and maneuvering of that area, which is where the devil himself lives. Yes me boyo, the rules of Five Points extends all the way up to here, north of Canal Street, like a bloody cancer." Jack pauses to get his thoughts together.

"It takes a while to be getting used to all the shenanigans going on around here, and since I've been here longer than you, a whole year longer in fact, well I know what the hells what. You see, ya gotta make the criminals, the punks, and the gangsters think that you've been in New York for some time and belong, then they'll leave you be. It's all a matter of fakin' it. First ya gotta swagger like you own the joint, then make look like your bloody pissed and ready for a fight, and lastly make 'em think that you're crazy as hell and got nutting to lose. And walk fast and don't look directly at nobody. Course that's just the Irish gangs, it's the nativists, the Bowery Boys that you really have to avoid. As, by now, you well know. They are right vicious. Malicious they are, with

no sense of fair play at all when it comes to us Irish. So the thing is you gotta avoid the shites at all costs, cuz there is no dealing with the lot of them. Which means ya havta stay away from certain streets. Mainly The Bowery. That's where they rule, with an iron fist they do, and it's also where they congregate, the right rancorous bastards."

Daniel Sean looks around and sees, for the first time, how dirty the room is to the naked eye. The beat up mattress has a threadbare throw blanket over it and nothing else, and seems to be almost covering a dark stain. The table is an assemblage of assorted materials that were probably found in a trash pile, including four different colors of wood and a hammered down piece of tin, thrown together in hodgepodge mishmash to slightly resemble a table.

"I have many roommates here as 'tis, Daniel Sean, all young and trying to just get by here in New York, doing whatever it takes to just stay alive. So, as ya can right well imagine, I can't be inviting ya to stay, but I would like to offer ya a drink for doing your duty with the B'hoys there. I would surely love to have seen that. And ya have to stay until it gets dark, and then ya have to move fast up Broadway and stay in the shadows if ya want to make it in one piece, ya hear me now?"

Daniel Sean stays for a little while at Jack's abode until the sun starts to set and night begins to fall. The

whole time boys, white and black, come in and out, some bringing bits of food, which they share with one another. Others bring scraps of cloth, which they all put in a huge basket that hangs from a hook in the far corner of the room on account of the rodents who cohabit with these urchin boys.

They all eat and gossip a bit and then receive a small portion of poteen from Jack, which they call a "thumbful," and then head back out into the streets to God only knows what activities.

The cloth, it turns out, is sold to a rag picker over on Mulberry Street. Who stitches them together to make affordable clothes and raggedy blankets or curtains, all for sale to the downtrodden masses who live in and around the downtown area of Manhattan.

Daniel Sean asks about the different boys that appear and then disappear like phantoms in the dying light of day.

"Well Daniel Sean, they got nobody and nothing to themselves, for most are throw aways you see."

Jack stops for a second, realizing that he has been rambling, which he is sometimes wont to do, and then continues.

"You see there is an industry for these types which is this," he explains to Daniel Sean, "they become foster kids and are adopted by families a little ways upstate. You may be thinking to yourself that that would be a better life, you know, being part of a family and all. But the truth is most of them basically become low rent

slaves and are worked to death, beaten, and some even raped by their new 'family.' You can't believe the stories and what some of these lads have gone through, and it's not just the men who are mean to the boys. The women can be just as vicious—bloody sadists some of them are. They enjoy beating and humiliating the lads. Not to mention the twelve to fourteen hour work days that they have to do, seven days a bloody week. It seems to make some of the women happy to watch the boys slowly die of hard, brutal work." He looks away into the distance.

"A few years back, one couple would beat this poor lad, an eleven-year-old black boy named Joe, I believe that you met him earlier today. Well they would torment the poor lad and then call him a lazy nigger when he just could not do all of the work. And when this happened, when he could not do another thing, tired as he was, they would whip him 'til he passed out."

Jack clenches his fists and shakes his head in disgust.

"Like to get my bleeding hands on the two of them, but Joe can't remember where they lived, exactly…a farm upstate, someplace around a town called Monticello or something like that. Nor could Joe even remember what the hell their names are. But if I ever find out where and who they are there will be a reckoning, I promise you that."

Jack looks at Daniel Sean, once again realizing that he has been rambling on.

"You see Daniel Sean, I was one of these kids for exactly three days, that's it, three bleeding days. There I was, living upstate on some shite of a farm, working like a mule, not getting enough to eat, and the occasional beating from the missus there. But, on the third day, when the father tried to crawl into my bed, which was the hayloft, I thrashed him good and ran away that very night. Ran as far away as I could in the blackness of the night, didn't give a tinkers damn either about the cold or being alone and hungry, because the anger inside of me fueled me along. And I just kept on running until I could run no more. It took me six days to get back here to New York. I stayed alive by stealing fruit and vegetables from orchards and gardens that I came across along the way."

Downing another nip of poteen Jack suddenly remembers something.

"One day a kind old lady who caught me in her garden, took me into her house and fed me with the best buttered bread and mutton stew that I ever ate. I cried when I said goodbye to her, for this lovely woman was the first bit of kindness that I experienced here in America. I would have liked to stay with her for a while, for she reminded me of me mother, but she didn't ask me to stay so I came back here straight away and haven't looked back once." Looking at the floor Jack shakes his head ruefully.

"Joe had it worse though and finally ran away after being bloody tortured for close to two weeks," he tells Daniel Sean with a sad sigh. "God bless the lad, it

took courage to do that I tell you. Being a black boy and running away like he did, for he stuck out like a bloody sore thumb, you see, and could have been found and returned and got a helluva beating. But my pal Joe did it and I'm proud of him for it." Jack smiles at Daniel Sean and continues. "He walked and walked for a couple of days and nights, mostly in the forests and away from any towns or farmhouses. He traveled by getting his bearings from the North Star at night and then heading away from that direction walking southbound. Just like the runaway slaves do who leave the Southland and come north. But in reverse.

"On the fourth day he traveled with a group of fellows that he met the night before who found him in the woods, where he was lying on a bed of leaves. And let me tell you, Joe was cold, hungry, and alone. These guys were itinerant workers who were coming back from apple picking at different apple orchards upstate and they took pity on Joe, taking him under their wing. In fact Joe said that there was two black fellows and two white fellows, and all four of them were friends. They described themselves as "traveling workers" or what's starting to be called hobos. The four of them fed him and looked after him and pretty much came to the lad's rescue. Joe traveled with them for the next two days until they got him onto a steamer up along the Hudson in Haverstraw which took him back here to Manhattan.

"Well it took him, all in all, seven days to make it back here to New York City. So, while 'tis not exactly

paradise staying here with me, at least 'tis safe, at least right in here, in this room, 'tis safe. Every night the boys roll out their bedrolls, which we keep over there in that closet in the corner, and they sleep all in a row. At least until a mouse or a roach runs around and over them, and the boy gets up yelling, which, of course, wakes up everyone." Jack laughs at this and shakes his head. "But that does not happen every night, only on cold, cold nights."

As if on cue a calico cat comes sashaying into the room.

"And we have cats, two of them. This here is Nicky, she is a girl and a fierce hunter. The other cat is her brother from the same litter and his name is Natty, and he is a bit of a lazy one. But they do keep the mice on their toes."

Before Daniel Sean leaves he tells Jack about the crossing and Molly and how he has to find her or else he will go mad with the worrying. Jack assures him that he and the boys will be like detectives and search high and low for this Molly.

"The sun is just setting so ya better get moving there now me lad, and come back anytime ya like."

As he starts to leave and go back up to Seneca Village, Daniel Sean tucks a dollar into Jack's hand.

"I'll be back bright and early tomorrow if that suits you," he says with a wink.

Jack looks at the dollar, which to him is a lot of money.

"This isn't really necessary Danny, but it will help with the feeding of the lads. God bless ya for this."

Daniel Sean leaves and heads out into the night memorizing every street, store front, and face that he encounters along the way. He walks quickly over to Broadway with every cell in his body on high alert. As he treks north he clutches onto the Celtic cross that is around his neck, the hackles rise on the back of his neck standing up as if they were ready to alert him if any trouble should arise.

Once, in the distance around 14th Street, to the east of where he is walking, he could swear that he spots a group of men with tall hats, but he just keeps on moving, following the remembered route that he took this very morning. He doesn't stop until he gets to the safety of Seneca Village and the Nolan household.

When he enters the house Daniel Sean utters the customary, "God bless all here."

Fiona is beside herself with worry, and William is also upset and reprimands Daniel Sean.

"Daniel Sean you had the three of us worried to death there. But I see that you're alright, so come in and have a seat and a jar wid me and tell us where you been."

"God and Mary be with you," Fiona exclaims to no one in particular.

As Willy and William Nolan sit with Fiona, get comfortable, and give their total attention to him, Daniel Sean proceeds to drink his jar and tell them the goings on of his day.

Twenty-Nine

The next morning, after William insists that his son, Willy, goes with Daniel Sean to help keep on eye on things, the two of them, Willy and Daniel Sean, trek out for the day. They head west and, after walking a bit, head south, swinging a left on Broadway, and with a determined pace walk downtown towards Jack's place.

Dodging horse drawn carriages, and stepping over and around the mounds of horse manure they encounter, they chat as they walk. Willy talks away, telling him all about his travels in and around Manhattan. What Willy mostly ends up talking about is how lucky his family is to be able to live in Seneca Village.

After about an hour of walking down the crowded streets, along the dirt roads mixed in with the cobblestone streets, they show up at Jack's and rouse him to start the day's meandering.

The first thing that they do, Jack, Daniel Sean, and Willy, is to make some coffee. This a beverage that Daniel Sean and Willy have never had, and while they find it somewhat bitter they both love the effect, which is being wide-awake and energized.

While drinking their mugs of coffee, they pore over an old, worn out, tattered, homemade map of

Manhattan that Jack has pulled out of a wooden box that he has hidden under his bed.

While Willy and Daniel Sean peer over his shoulders at the map, with pen and paper Jack draws a crude but methodical pattern of where they will search for Molly. This is coupled with a schedule of when they will do each section of the City.

Jack decides that looking north of 10th Street would be a waste of time because almost all of the new Irish arrivals would be exclusively downtown.

"They don't want us uptown, lads, believe you me. We get chased out of the neighborhoods up north of 10th Street; even if we are allowed to do the work up there we can't live there. Just got to pass on through, that's all."

Jack starts the sketching while Daniel Sean explains that they only have four days to complete the search.

"If I can't find her in those four days I have a job opportunity that I can't be letting slip by, you see?"

And so Jack sketches out the daily schedule from there, figuring in the four-day time allotment. The overall goal is canvassing the area from 10th Street and on down to the bottom of Manhattan Island, and west from the Hudson River to the East River. He figures that they should be able to cover around fifteen to twenty blocks or so a day. "The lower part of Manhattan is extremely crowded, ya see, and to be thorough it will take some time covering the territory."

The map is broken up into four quadrants, one for each day. Jack figures that they will skip any area that is not "Irish" because he believes that Molly would stay with her own kind for a sense of security.

"She would not be allowed to be around the Protestants, who are mostly of English descent or the new ones here who are Scotch-Irish, and not Irish at all but really English," states Jack with a glare. "At least most of them, and they hate us as much as the English do. So we won't bother with them because from what you told me about your colleen, Molly, she wouldn't tarry with the lot of them. Agreed?"

Daniel Sean nods his head in agreement. "Aye, agreed."

"So we better get cracking lads," Jack continues, "for the day is not getting any younger. That's if we want to do a mighty thorough job of it all. So from river to river we'll work our way up from the bottom of the Isle of Manhattan to 10th Street. We have four days to do it. So let's get going now. And we stay together, for there is more safety in numbers."

They hail a horse drawn carriage that takes the three of them to the very bottom of Manhattan, just north of The Battery and work from East to West spreading out and slowly making their way north, not missing a single street unless it is fairly well to do—which means no Irish at all. Jack ascertains yeah or nay with a cursory glance at the street, the houses, and who is or isn't out and

about. The less crowded streets and empty sidewalks are passed over immediately.

"Can't be wasting any time here lads," Jack states often. "Let's move on."

Daniel Sean and Willy are amazed at the perceptible gift that Jack possesses as they move through the darkened bowels of lower Manhattan.

When they meet fellow Irish men or women, it is with great concern that most of the people that they encounter have for the whereabouts of one Molly Ryan. For they have all been in the same situation; the loss of someone that they love, either through the loss of life due to the ravages of An Gorta Mor or simply being separated because of the unpredictable nature of this wrenching exile from their homeland that has struck the Irish immigrants now living in America.

But there is also the Africans, who have suffered undue amount of anguish and loss because of their own personal travails. Even more than the Irish. So on the occasions that they cross paths with workingmen or women who have some of Africa in them, they inquire about Molly figuring that they may have crossed paths with her and could, maybe, relate to the situation.

"Ya never know, anyone may have seen her. And believe you me no one has suffered more than these people, no one, not even us Irish," Jack says to Daniel Sean and Willie.

The three of them move quickly and stop anyone they see who fits the right pattern, black or white, then

describe Molly, and ask if that person has seen the likes of her before. But even with Daniel Sean giving a vivid description, nobody knows anything about Molly, and the amount of people out and about on the streets that they talk to is staggering to them.

They come up with nothing on that first day, even after going at it for a little over ten hours, heading back home only when the light starts to fade and night begins to encroach.

The first day of searching has taken them from the bottom tip of Manhattan, back and forth, east to west and south to north, all the way to East Broadway, which cuts diagonally to Grand Street and the East River. Westward they make it to the Hudson River along Pearl Street which connects with Duane Street, ending up just south of Five Points and, at the same time, west and away from The Bowery, which, from reputation and experience, they wish to avoid at all costs.

The second day the next quadrant is north of East Broadway straight up to 10th Street, which will complete the area west of The Bowery but maintain a precautionary three-block distance from the B'hoys territory.

As happened on the search the day before, they get no leads whatsoever concerning the whereabouts of Molly Ryan.

Near the end of the second day of the search for Molly, with the same lack of results as the day before, Daniel Sean whispers to Willy.

"This is like a needle in a haystack finding her. Or maybe she has gone someplace else outside of New York City." He pounds his hands against his chest in frustration.

By the end of that day, Jack decides that first thing tomorrow they will scour the area in and around The Bowery first, two blocks east and two blocks west all the way from Chatham Street north to 10th Street.

"Most of the goons in the gangs never wake up until early afternoon," Jack assures them, "and if we cover those areas around where they stink up the streets early enough we'll not run into the dirty bastards. Agreed?"

Daniel Sean and Willy nod their heads in unison and say. "Aye, agreed."

"Then we hit Five Points right after that. Get it over with," responds Jack with determination. He looks directly at Daniel Sean and says, "I don't know what we will find out about your Molly if she is in that den of the devil. But I know some people there, and we'll be okay."

With that said and done for the day, and with all the maneuverings set for tomorrow, they head back to Jack's and have a thumbful of poteen, which is actually moonshine—the American version of poteen.

After twenty minutes or so Willy and Daniel Sean head back uptown along Broadway all the way to Seneca

Village. Daniel Sean having given Jack another dollar for his help before they leave.

The next day, on the third day of the search, as planned, bright and early the three of them work the area around the eastern part of The Bowery, going from 10th Street heading south to Chatham Street but never actually walking on Bowery Street. They are on high alert, looking over their shoulders for any black top hats coming their way. After they finish canvasing that area they cross over Bowery Street where it turns into Chatham Street, walking very quickly to avoid any nativists. They quickly make their way north up the western side of the dreaded area all the way to 10th Street and coming up with nothing, about which the three of them are greatly relieved.

They then go west on 10th Street for two blocks turn left and southward on Broadway heading down to the infamous Five Points, which borders the western edge of the lower portion of The Bowery.

Upon entering the vicinity of Five Points, Daniel Sean and Willy are shocked at the volume of people who are out and about, but, at this point it doesn't seem as bleak or as nightmarish as they have been led to believe. That is until they get closer to the epicenter of this section of New York City, which is where "five points" converge at the intersection of four different streets; Anthony Street, Orange Street, Cross Street, and Little

Water Street, which all come together to form a five pointed juncture on Cross Street.

The closer that they get to this urban crossroad the more the wind is knocked out of Willy and Daniel Sean. Jack has been here on numerous occasions and so is unnerved but stays cool and collected about the whole experience. He's been through it before so he is still on his guard. Anyone with a brain would be completely leery while here in Five Points.

Daniel Sean stops in his tracks and comes to a standstill for he is simply thunderstruck, for, coming from his simple Irish Catholic background, he has never seen such a tangible, tactile display of wanton degradation that is right before his very eyes. Never has he seen such filth and squalor, which are also coupled with the most disgusting displays of sexual and bestial actions and posturing that he has ever beheld. Coarse painted women, some barely in their teens, obviously Irish, smiling fake smiles at him, while behind them unwashed demonic looking men leer at anyone, male or female, who crosses their field of vision. There are makeshift bars that, it seems, pop up everywhere. The streets are all dirt, and mostly muddy now due to the heavy rain showers from the storm that blew through New York City two nights ago.

They get to the famed intersection.

"If ya have anything in your pockets keep your hands on it, for it will be nicked in a heartbeat, for the pickpockets here are the best in the world they say. And

watch for any flashing blades, it's many a man been cut down here."

Jack lowers his voice and continues.

"But it's still early, so we'll be alright for now, as the really devilish bad fellows are probably still sleeping it off, you know. But as you can see the whores, pickpockets, and other assorted citizens of this Sodom and Gomorrah are up and about. We gotta act quick and make our inquiries and get out just as quick."

The three of them make their way to the edge of the street onto a wooden sidewalk. Here they mingle and start asking the women who are not prostitutes and the men who aren't drunk yet if they've spotted Molly in Five Points at any time in the past couple of months.

Daniel Sean starts to acclimate himself and is not so much in shock at what surrounds him. He starts to observe exactly what Five Points is all about. First he notices that there are pigs running to and fro, which seems strange to him. On one corner there are three different fistfights going on simultaneously, with some men and women, who are already drunk, cheering them on.

He also observes that, while some of the people here are of African descent, it's quite obvious that the majority here are originally from Ireland. But they look changed, as if life here in Five Points has taken a heavy toll on them.

They are mean looking, with desperate eyes peering out of bloated faces, and twitchy hands, looking

as if ready to strike or steal something. All in all they no longer appear entirely human to him.

The very air itself smells sour, just like the people, and everywhere unbridled filth and debris cover the uneven dirt street and wooden sidewalks. The houses are packed together like a filthy beehive, with dilapidated wood shacks stacked together in a ramshackle jumble of lumbered chaos.

Daniel Sean wonders to himself. *I wonder what the hell goes on inside of these blasted structures that these people call home. God only knows what life here is like behind those bleeding walls. The devil himself is taking front center on this forlorn stage.*

Looking about, Daniel Sean, however, does notice one little thing that brings a small smile to his face. Across the way on a side street he sees a white boy around twelve years old, definitely Irish, and a black boy around the same age, who is as black as night like Jubal, therefor almost all African. And the two of them are exchanging dance routines. First, the Irish kid kicks his feet up doing a lightening fast step dance, and then the African kid follows this with a series of torso movements, and then he adds in the Irish step dance, much to the delight of the Irish kid who breaks out laughing.

This is followed by the Irish boy mimicking the African kids upper body steps. And then they both do the improvised routine together in a rollicking duet.

It is the only thing that he finds of any sort of delight down here in Five Points.

They move quickly and very efficiently, talking only to those who seem not quite as viciously predisposed as most of the men and women down here seem to be.

After three hours they come up with nothing. One ancient woman who, even though old in years, looks to be semi-reliable, gives them a bit of Five Points sage advice.

"If I was you I'd let it go, she ain't here I tell ya. If she was, I, Mary Margaret Brady herself, would know all about her. I've been in Five Points for a long time, and I don't miss nothing around here. This place may be crowded as hell is itself, but I'd a known all about your Molly with eyes of blue and black hair."

That's when Jack decides that she is most likely not here in Five Points after all, which is a huge relief for the three of them. Especially after seeing what they did this day.

"This is during the daytime," Jack says to Willy and Daniel Sean. "Just think what it is like here after the sun goes down. It's been said that there are murders every single night here in this god forsaken place. I mean every single bleeding night someone's throat is slit or bludgeoned to death or strangled or whatever the hell way one's life can be taken. I tell you lads, it's the devils playground here."

It's still before noon, so the three of them head back east to search the area east and north of The Bowery, inquiring all the way to the East River and north up to East Broadway.

"This days quadrant is not easy, seeing as how we had to break it up to avoid the B'hoys and their mischief," Jack tells them. "But we're getting there lads."

When they are finished with that area they move on to the next part that they need to cover, but first they buy a bucket of beer at a small makeshift tavern to split, and have a small roasted potato each from the bar keep. She is a woman with the saddest face that they have ever seen and she has a little fire pit grill set up in the back of the bar. As she brings their beer and food to them she sniffles and sighs the whole time. Jack takes her hand and whispers to her, "I know how you feel darling, I lost all of my own too. I'll say an Ave for you and your broken heart. Is that okay with ya?"

She gives him a shrug and then smiles at him while she touches his face with her other hand.

The next and final part of the days search is the area below Canal Street and West of the Bowery, north of Five Points all the way to the Hudson River. They start with heavily populated Anthony Street with its narrow streets then make their way to Leonard heading west to the Hudson River and north to Canal Street.

Below Canal Street and west to the Hudson River goes smoothly as they cover all of that area, because most of that area does not look or feel Irish, or even African, at all. It is almost exclusively Anglo and Protestant. And not nearly as unpredictable as Five Points or the area around The Bowery. They fly through it because it is obviously mostly well to do, there are almost no signs of Micks or Paddys, and the only Africans are coach drivers or domestics. So they pass over a whole bunch of the streets that they encounter.

Tomorrow, the fourth and last day of their search, they will return and finish the last and final quadrant: North of Canal Street and west to the Hudson River, all the way to 10th Street.

The next day, after the morning coffee, they head out into the fourth day of their search for the elusive Molly Ryan.

It is a jaw dropping sight for both Willy and Daniel Sean as they round the corner at West 4th Street right off of Broadway. The opulence that they encounter in and around an area that is on the edge of a tree-lined square shaped park is a wonder to behold for the two of them.

Daniel Sean asks Jack. "How many families live in each of these houses?"

"Ah sure," Jack laughs, "but these are for just one family, some with only one or two kids in their brood. Danny, this here is Washington Square Park, and is

where the rich live. No Irish around here me boy, none atall."

West of McDougal Street and north of Canal the layout of that particular area seems to have no logical rhyme or reason about it, but the search goes quickly because, like the area around Washington Square Park, there does not seem to be many people who fit the description that they have established of anyone who could help find Molly.

But still they soldier on and do a thorough search of the entire area that is in this final quad. They finish up the entire quadrant just a little bit before the setting sun fades into the western sky over the Hudson River. Daniel Sean's hope of finding Molly dissolves along with the setting of the sun.

They are exhausted after completing the whole in-depth but blind search routine for four days in a row, almost 10 hours a day, walking back and forth across downtown Manhattan.

After methodically canvassing every designated area of the city, block by block, questioning anyone and everyone that they deemed appropriate, it is hard to believe that they have come up with nothing.

It's not too much of a surprise then, that the three of them are totally crestfallen. And the realization that Molly is not here in New York settles in onto Daniel Sean's soul.

Leaving Jack Brosnahan is not easy, but Daniel Sean and Willy promise to come back again in the

foreseeable future to visit. They shake hands and Daniel
Sean gives him another dollar, which is greatly
appreciated by Jack.

That night, Daniel Sean and Willy sit with Mister
and Missus Nolan around the small stove, as Fiona
intones in Irish and then English, while throwing sprigs
of some sort of herbs into the fire. She says that this is an
attempt to protect Molly. "Solas Mhic De ar a a n-anam.
The Light of the Son of God light on her soul and protect
her until she is found."

After a few minutes silence William speaks up.

"Your Molly must have left New York, you would
have found her, and most people know who and where
the newcomers are because they stick out so much. She
must be elsewhere."

"Yeah, reckon so, must be," Daniel Sean
whispers.

He looks up at the Nolan's, and finds Fiona gazing
at him with tears in her eyes.

"I can't possibly tell you how much I appreciate
what you have done for me but I have to head north and
on to this job that I have. I will be back in the spring
though," Daniel Sean says to the three of them.

The next morning, with a heavy heart, Daniel
Sean bids goodbye to the Nolan family, but before he
leaves he insists on giving a few dollars to Willy and the
last of his English pounds to William and Fiona.

At first William tries to refuse, but Daniel Sean will have none of that. Willy quickly pockets his two dollars before anyone can take it back from him.

Daniel Sean heads out of Seneca Village walking north and back to the encampment retracing his steps that got him here five days ago. He figures that he will get on board with his four African pals for the trek to work up at the Black River Canal, make some money and then head back in a few months to find Molly wherever she may be.

I can still feel her all around. I'll find her. I have to find her. My mucushla.

That night Daniel Sean regales his four pals with stories about downtown Manhattan and also about the people who live in Seneca Village. They are astounded by what he tells them about Seneca Village.

"White and Black folk living together as friends?" Jubal asks with disbelief. "I ain't never heard anything like that before. Almost as crazy as that suffrage thing they got going on upstate there. Well, well, well…wish that my mother was around to see this, yes indeed, my Momma would love to see this."

Thirty

On the morning of September 16, Jubal, Nathaniel, Joseph, Nicodemus, and Daniel Sean begin the trip together that will take them all the way to Booneville, in upstate New York. They are traveling with their new boss man, Mr. Charles Johnson.

First they travel on a steamer all the way north, past Albany to Waterford New York. They eat simple food that Mister Johnson brought with him, which includes some fresh fruit, beef jerky, and lots of bread.

Mister Johnson travels first class on the steamer and the five fellows travel third class steerage the entire way up the Hudson. While it is somewhat rustic the five lads love it. At first Daniel Sean is a bit wistful, for being on the water reminds him of being with Molly since the whole time that he knew her he was on a boat.

One moonless black night while standing on the deck of the steamer there is a meteor shower that lasts a good ten minutes and completely astonishes everyone present. When it is done Joseph falls to his knees in "humble adoration."

"And there is some out there that do not believe in God. All you gotta do is see the wondrous spectacle that we just saw and you will believe."

When they switch over to the barge that travels along the path of the Erie Canal, the accommodations are even more rustic, but that does not dampen the gusto of Mr. Johnson and his crew.

The barge is equipped with a small sleeping area on the very backend of it that is perfect for the five lads . It is open but covered and has an area adjoined to it that is outside so that they can sleep under the stars when the weather permits or inside when it rains. It is furnished with a small commode that is just a seat that has a hole in the bottom of it that empties the waste into the river.

In the interior of the barge there is a separate room for Mister Johnson, also with his own toilet. They travel on the barge for two days and land just south of Rome New York, where they disembark. They eat dried meats and some local produce that they procure along the way. That and whatever else they can find.

They travel the rest of the way from Rome to Booneville, about 45 miles, following the portion of the Black River Canal that is already completed, but not in operation, by way of a plank road. This is done by horse driven coach and it is a very slow, bumpy, and not so comfortable trip that takes a little more than a day and a half.

On this leg of the journey, Jubal befriends the coach driver, and they talk about horses all the way to Booneville; the driver even giving the reins to Jubal for a spell.

The one night that they have to sleep and let the horses rest, they camp out on the banks of the Black River, light a fire, and have their usual simple meal of jerky and bread. But this time with a little whiskey that Mister Johnson supplies. Just a small amount of spirits for each man.

For all five of these young men, the trip gives them a feeling of unfettered freedom the whole way. While they have come into contact with a few white folks, it does seem that most people that they encounter done't really care much about race. In fact, even though most of the people do give them a quick look over, they hardly pay them any mind at all. And this is something that they all are extremely happy about.

When they mention this to Mister Johnson he agrees.

"That is true. It's because during the construction of the Erie Canal there were groups of men of all different walks of life and races working on it. After awhile the locals got used to seeing, and even rubbing elbows with, the different groups of men. Besides the whites and blacks on the job, they even had Chinese fellows and some Mohawks working there on that Erie Canal."

The entire voyage takes a total of five days, placing them at the job site on September 21. The trip has been an easy enough trek for the lads. In fact they really enjoy the whole experience of traveling out of

New York City, on their own, and being in the countryside.

After getting settled in their cabin at the work site outside of Booneville, on the banks of the Black River, they fall into the day-to-day rhythm of work. While the work is hard they are actually very happy with the living arrangements. They find that all they have to do is work and everyone stays out of their way, leaving them to their own devices.

The five of them are their own crew, they work in an area that has only enough room for small crews such as they. The project, when completed, will be used as a flood runoff for the actual Black River Canal.

They are here to make some money, expand their reading and writing horizons and figure out what to do next in their lives. For them this is the perfect opportunity to try and accomplish all three of those objectives.

The main crew, which contains over twenty men, is working down below them about a half a mile away. These men are doing the demolition, and the concrete work using wooden molds to form the sides and foundation of the main section of the canal. They use the wooden molds to pour the concrete into it, let it set to shape the huge canal structure. One large block section at a time.

That crew has their own living area, and some of that crew are, in fact, local hires who sleep at home.

The "Manhattan crew," which is what the lads have been dubbed by Mister Johnson, will be doing some excavating and removal of debris. But they also will be doing hands-on concrete work, which entails laying bricks, block for the side walls, and finally, pouring cement on the floor and then smoothing it flat and even, but it is crucial that the floor is at a slight downward slant in order for the water to run off properly. This is so that in times of heavy rains the canal does not overflow.

This type of job, this project, as it turns out, is something that the five of them become quite good at doing. The reason for this is, is that to be good at concrete and brick work you need to work together as a cohesive team. That is something the five of them excel at—teamwork—because they have spent a lot of time together as a team, living in close proximity and working together on the High Bridge project back in New York City.

While Joseph, Nicodemus, and Nathaniel have put some time into doing jobs with concrete and bricks, Jubal has the most experience doing this type of work; two years ago he had worked as an apprentice for a bricklayer on a couple of buildings in the upcoming Chelsea section of Manhattan, and in the process became a fairly accomplished mason. Therefore, with a fair bit of expertise, he does an in-depth seminar with the other four guys the first day that they arrive, which was a Sunday and okayed by the boss.

In the seminar Jubal teaches them all how to work with brick, stone, block, concrete, and cement. Jubal then assigns different jobs to each man depending on the individuals' skills so that everyone has his own niche in the crew. As a result of this insight from Jubal, the work goes very smoothly from day one. It is hard physical work, but they are all blessed with the gift of youth, and as it goes with this type of skilled craft, day by day the work gets easier.

Very quickly the five of them develop into a fine tuned machine, anticipating each other's action before it happens. Daniel Sean and Joseph mix the cement or the concrete, working in tandem with one another; burly Nathaniel carries the mixed cement from where it is mixed to where it will be used; Nicodemus and Jubal are like two artists with their trowels, plumb lines, and strings.

Monday through Saturday they wake up before the sun has risen and have a quick breakfast of buckwheat pancakes. These are already cooked and kept in a larder in the corner of the cabin, and replenished every two days by Mister Johnson.

With that done they move out into the dimly lit sky, with roosters crowing in the distance, and walk the quarter mile to where the upper portion of the Black River Canal is located. Once there they start their workday.

Each day starts the same: The first hour they go over, with Mister Johnson, the plans for the day and how far along on the project they plan on reaching that day.

This is done with mugs of coffee inside of the "office," which is where Mister Johnson lives for the duration of the project. At least when he is on site and not on the road inspecting other projects of his.

After the coffee, the five of them head to the work area. First they have to get rid of any residual cement left over from the day before that is left in the mixing pan. This has to be finished before they can do any mixing at all. They take turns knocking and chipping away with hammers until the pan is clean and ready to use.

Finding their individual places in the work force the five of them get to it: First, start to mix up some cement which is called mud, second, prepare the area where they will work that day and finally do some concrete work.

By ten o'clock, with the late Summer, early Autumn sun shining down on them, they have broken into a rhythm of movement. Like the Egyptians building the pyramids, it is the ancient rhythm of work.

Mix, shovel, carry, pour. Trowel, measure, spread, level, repeat. Again, again, and yet again. Go, go, go, go. *Don't keep us waiting now brother, move it, yeah man that's it. You got it going now.*

When they have to haul debris away with a horse that pulls a flat wagon, Jubal is utilized for the task,

which greatly lightens his mood, for he simply loves being with horses.

"They understand me better than people."

Lunchtime comes around one o'clock, and by that time they are starving. They stop working where they are, laying down their tools wherever they may be. The five of them stretch, sit on the top of one of the walls finished yesterday, and have their lunch.

Everyday Mister Johnson brings lunch in a large basket to where they are working. That way he can ascertain how much progress that the lads are making.

For lunch it is pretty much the same thing every day: A huge loaf of homemade bread accompanied with fresh churned butter, apple butter, or blackberry jam. To drink they get leftover coffee, water from the well, and, since it is apple picking season, homemade apple cider.

Included with all of this is a small portion of some sort of cured meat, fresh cheese or fish that has been smoked.

They work non-stop through the afternoon until the sun is low in the sky and then one and all, they clean everything up. They make sure that the trowels, shovels, wooden buckets, and the mixing pan are all fairly clean even though tomorrow morning they will have to start the day with the ritual "knock and chip" of the residual cement in the pan that had set before they quit work.

This is the basic routine that they go through every day, Monday through Saturday. Even when it rains they do the same thing, but under cover of a humongous

canvas tarp, which keeps them semi-dry and doesn't muddle up the "mud."

Sundays are usually spent relaxing, but sometimes on "The Lords Day," Joseph and Nicodemus go to church at the AME, African Methodist Episcopal church, that is located down in a colored area outside of Booneville, New York, a little more than two miles away. The rest of the fellows usually pass on attending service, spending most Sundays relaxing at the cabin.

However just this past year, the fourth Thursday of November has been decreed by the governor of New York State as a day to be put aside for giving thanks to God. A day to count ones blessings as a New Yorker and an American.

Because of this, semi-reluctantly, Daniel Sean, Jubal, and Nathaniel join Joseph and Nicodemus in attending service at their church for this new holiday called Thanksgiving Day. A holiday that recalls the first Thanksgiving the Pilgrims celebrated with the local Indians in Massachusetts.

Attending church on this day is something that Mister Johnson insists that all five of them do. They all get dressed up as much as they possibly can, making themselves as presentable as is possible and head to the AME church in Booneville.

Daniel Sean is the only white person in the church and, at first, it is a little bit strange for him. But Joseph puts him at ease by introducing him directly to the head pastor.

"Reverend Grey I want to introduce you to some friends of Nicodemus and me."

Joseph introduces Jubal, Nathaniel, and finishes with Daniel Sean.

"Now this boy may have a different color of skin from me and my friends here," he tells Reverend Grey earnestly, "but he is a brother to all four of us, and by the blood of Jesus that's the truth."

The minister smiles a big broad smile, shakes Daniel Sean's hand.

"All are welcome here in the house of God," he says in a loud, clear voice. "In His eyes we are all the same color."

Jubal can't help himself so he says what his mother used to say. "We all the color of water so that the Lord can see right through us. That's what my momma used to say to me, when she was alive."

Jubal's eyes brim up at the thought of his mother, and the minister's wife steps forward and folds him into her arms to sooth him.

"Amen, amen."

The lads are marshaled in to sit in the very front row with the ministers family, as their personal guests, while at the same time everyone, not just a few but practically everyone, smiles at Daniel Sean as if he is in for a wonderful treat. A few of the men even stand up and say to him, "Welcome brother in Christ. Welcome."

While Daniel Sean is a Roman Catholic he still has the Irish in him, and because of that he truly believes

in the emotions and mysticism that occur when different beliefs, such as Christianity and Celticism, blend into and transform the ancient ways into the Light. But only if it is done without negating that which came before but instead coalescing them together. So it is no surprise that this particular service, that is a fusion of African and American traditions, with calls to the spirit, the power of the blood, the battle of light over darkness, a fierce connection with the earth, and an overall sensation of the supernatural presence of a divine nature, would affect Daniel Sean in a most deep and profound way.

The sermon, the music, the singing, and the unrehearsed participation of the congregation is something that he has never seen before in a church, but also something that he finds so genuine that he feels his heart opening up with a heightened sense of emotion starting to swell up within his chest.

Near the very end of the service, when a woman with the most stirring voice that he has ever heard, sings a newly minted hymn titled "Amazing Grace," Daniel Sean is moved to the core. He has never heard this song before, but the words coupled with the melody remind him of Ireland, his family, and his Molly.

Daniel Sean breaks down and starts to do something that he has not really done yet since he left his mother and his Ireland, but is something that he really needs to do. He starts to weep uncontrollably, and it becomes a soul cleansing ritual, as crystal clear images of the green rolling hills of Ireland, and of his family

appear in his minds eye; his two brothers, his sister, his father, and the most powerful image of all, his mother. His whole family are in his minds eye; just standing there, smiling at him and alive.

Then he sees and feels Molly in his arms, with her holding him tight to herself. The last image that he envisions is the smiling face of Seamus Fitzgerald winking goodbye. The whole time the tears freely flow down his face, embarrassing him immensely as he struggles to hide them.

At this the minister's daughter, who is sitting next to him, and probably around nine years old, pats him on the hand and smiles the most beatific smile that he has ever seen. She hands him a little handkerchief.

"You sure are the lucky one, because that be the Holy Spirit descending down into your soul and opening up the eyes of your heart. Ain't it beautiful?"

She pats his hand again and whispers, "My name is Sarah, what's yours?"

Thirty-One

Every night without fail, Daniel Sean, Jubal, Nathaniel, Joseph, and Nicodemus, continue to do their lessons at the only piece of furniture in the cabin besides their sleeping pallets, a small table that also doubles as their kitchen table. Five small, rudely made wooden chairs stand beside it.

That is all there is in the cabin. There is an outhouse behind the cabin and a well for water on the side, and nothing else. But they don't really need anything else. They consider themselves lucky and blessed to have the table with the chairs. It becomes the center of all activity for them in the whole work cycle here at the Black River.

For close to three months they live this very structured life, centered on the building of the Black River/Erie Canal extension project. Even more important to them is their determination to conquer the craft of reading and writing.

They have no distractions and no reason to spend any money, therefore they save almost all their earnings. Mr. Johnson turns out to be a fair, no nonsense man who is on the cutting edge of hiring people that most bosses would think twice before considering. And this is why

they put out an extra effort each and every day on the job.

Upon discovering that they are learning to read, Mister Johnson, on occasion, presents them with books and manuscripts from his own personal collection. This includes a few novels by James Fenimore Cooper, and because some of the stories are set in upstate New York near where they are now, everyone of the lads love to read them. Even though, at first, they did struggle over the language a bit. But after they got used to Cooper's style of writing they enjoy the stories immensely. In fact, they become so enamored with the different characters in the Leatherstocking Tales that they have all started to call Nathaniel "Natty Bumpo" after the title character in all of the books of the series.

Included in their collection of reading material on loan from Mister Johnson are also some of the short stories of Edgar Allen Poe. Once again they struggled with the writing at first, but eventually, when they start to get the language, with the exception of Joseph, they find themselves enjoying his work.

"He knows the darkness, he done seen it himself, can't write like that without seeing it," says Joseph, sounding dark himself.

But the most read book in their possession is Nicodemus's well-thumbed bible, and Joseph finds himself memorizing whole sections of it.

One night Mister Johnson drops off the complete works of Shakespeare. They play around with it for a

while but don't much care for it until they come across Othello. They take turns reading from it and while they find themselves slightly befuddled and end up laughing at the language, they are glad to see that there was a play named after a black African. They all jokingly start calling Jubal "The Moor," which is a compliment of sorts to him.

The hard physical work, laboring in the sunlight or even in the rain, the local home grown food, and the isolation from the civilized world contribute to the five of them becoming very strong in body and in spirit. They find themselves reveling in their lessons as they grow in skill at both reading and writing. And they also revel in the strength that the five of them feel in their muscles and bones, a strength that is flowing from the top of their heads to the tips of their toes.

Daniel Sean still has not attempted to walk on his hands yet. When he tells the lads that he used to be able to walk on his hands they simply don't believe him. When he tells them that he once walked on his hands for forty-seven steps, they still don't believe him. With shouts and hollers they tell him to get off his lazy ass, and prove it.

With this challenge from his pals Daniel Sean attempts to walk on his hands again. The first couple of times he tries it he just cannot do it. He feels as if he has completely lost it and will never get it back again. This

goes on for a whole week—he tries and tries and then throws up his hands.

" 'Tis gone, gone, just like Niamh in the O'Neill archives said. ' 'Tis gone like the foam on the sea comes and goes.' "

Then one morning while waking up he leans over the side of his bed, kicks his feet up into the air and walks three wobbly steps on his hands. Jubal is the only one awake to see it.

"Damn boy that is right good."

This compliment from Jubal means a lot to Daniel Sean, for he has always admired the man who saved his life.

After working up from three to five to seven, Daniel Sean finally gets up to ten steps on his hands without keeling over, and it seems that he is on his way. After awhile, however, three or four days straight, he comes to the conclusion that he is stuck at ten steps on his hands and will go further. Which is fine with him, because he was sure that he would never be able to walk even one step at all in the upside down position. *Ah sure, but it might not be forty-seven steps, but ten is grand.*

The work continues unabated until the middle of December when the weather turns frigidly cold, and the temperatures drop into the twenties—and then finally, on one day, all the way down into the teens. The ground starts to freeze up and they have to quickly close

everything up on the job site, and make it secure for the winter and the long wait until the Spring thaw sets in.

After they do all of that they have a little powwow with Boss Man Johnson who, categorically and with no hesitation at all, offers them continued work. They have the choice of returning to work the first or second week of March.

"I have never had better workers than you five," Johnson tells the team, "and so if you wish to return I would love to have any or all of you boys back here on the job. It will probably last the better part of the year from March until this time again. So think about it and let me know. Here is my address, and since the lot of you can now read and write a bit I will expect a letter from each and everyone of you in the near future."

They all look at Mister Johnson who has been like a second father to them. A man who has been fair to them in a world where that rarely happens to any of them.

Jubal cannot help himself, and asks the boss man what the rest of them are all thinking.

"Mister Johnson, Boss, why have you been so kind to us? I mean no disrespect but we just ain't all that used to be treated so fairly by a white man. Even the Irisher here is kind of wondering why you been good to him too, and he's white. So, if you don't mind tellin', how come?"

Mister Johnson takes a minute to answer and when he speaks slowly and thoughtfully while looking from one man to the next.

"That's because I am not, completely, by definition, altogether speaking, a white man," he reveals in a calm and clear voice. "I am part African on my mother's side. She was an Octoroon, meaning one-eighth African, and came from New Orleans. My father was a white man from New York City, and they met and fell in love. Therefore, technically, I am colored. And I am proud of it, even if this world of ours thinks I should be ashamed. My father was a white man, a wonderful man and a great father, who fell deeply in love with my mother the moment that they met. It was on a train, a week after Christmas, that was traveling from Baltimore to New York City where the two of them both lived. Mama had relocated to New York from New Orleans the summer before and was returning back to the city after visiting her family in New Orleans." Mister Johnson smiles at the memory of the treasured family story.

"They courted for a while, and then one night, after a night out dancing, she told him that she was colored. At first he didn't believe her, but after she convinced him that indeed she was part black, he got down on his knees and said that he didn't give a damn, that he loved her and asked right there on the spot, 'Violet, would you be my wife, hell or high water? Because I can't imagine life without you.'" He laughs.

"My mother said yes, and they ended up getting married that very day. They hid it from their friends, family, everybody, so that puts me walking in between two worlds, white but colored. I tell very few people because I do pass for white wherever I go. In fact I rarely even mention race, because I like to be able to work, do business, and make money. My wife knows but she doesn't care because she is also a mix of two cultures. Yes, my friends, she is a lovely, beautiful mix of French and Iroquois, who has born me five wonderful children. As a family we are a genuine all American cornucopia of upstate New York."

He laughs again, heartily.

"And that is why I look after the ones who this idiotic society of ours thinks are less equal than them because of something as superficial as skin color or ethnicity. I say to hell with those ignorant fools, because I know better."

Pulling out a flask he takes out the only cups in the cabin, five chipped coffee mugs, and pours a little snort into each one, handing them out. He then raises his flask and makes a toast.

"To your health and prosperity." He pauses, then adds, "And to true love."

After they finish drinking the whiskey down, Mister Johnson reaches into a traveling bag that he carries all the time, pulls out five envelopes, and hands them one at a time to each of the lads, which they accept graciously.

"I put in a little bit extra for Christmas."

The time has now come for the lads to decide what to do and where to go. Nathaniel is dead set on heading back to New York City and rescuing Sugar from her predicament, as is Daniel Sean set on also heading back there to find Molly. Since learning to read and poring over the different pamphlets that Mister Johnson has given them, Joseph and Nicodemus are looking to "try out" a town called Rhinebeck, New York that they read about which has a large free African community. And to Joseph, most importantly, there is a vibrant African Methodist Episcopal community in Rhinebeck. He has decided that he has a calling, and that he wants to be a minister and spread the AME's message of belief in, "God the Father, Christ the Redeemer, Holy Spirit as comforter, and Humankind as family."

This message is all-important to him because he believes deeply in the inherent goodness of people.

"We are all children of God, but the ignorant ones have the loudest voices, so we have to send out the Word to all people, regardless of color. Even got me a couple white friends out there."

He says this while looking at Daniel Sean, and winks at him—an inside joke, because he once asked Daniel Sean why his people, the Irish, wink so much. At the time Daniel Sean just winked at him and said, " 'Tis an Irish thing ya wouldn't understand."

Jubal wants to be closer to New York City.

"Danny, after you told us about that Seneca Village I may want to go and check it out. Also want to check out a place I read about just north of Manhattan called the Hills up in Harrison New York. It is a thriving community of Africans that is in need of young men with skills to work the mills that are popping up all around the Hudson River. So those are my two options."

If none of this works out for them there is still an insurance plan in place; they will all go back to Black River by March 10 when work on the Erie Canal Extension Project will resume in earnest. Otherwise they will all continue on with their individual plans.

On December 15th, Daniel Sean, Jubal, and Nathaniel say their goodbyes to Joseph and Nicodemus, and reverse the route they took to get to Booneville. They take the plank road to Rome New York, where they grab a barge on the Erie Canal back to Waterford New York, and board a Steamer for the trip south down the Hudson River to New York City. It is a cold voyage on the barge, so they spend most of the time wrapped up in their bedding underneath the small over hang that is really their only protection from the wind and snow. The whole time they tell stories about their pasts, with Daniel Sean even telling them the story of the Choctaw Nation, which amazes both Jubal and Nathaniel.

"You got to make that trip out there to see them Choctaw people," Jubal exclaims.

"A blood oath is a blood oath after all,"   adds Nathaniel.

At the quay in New York Harbor, Daniel Sean and Jubal say their goodbyes to "Natty Bumpo," with him bidding "The Irisher" and "The Moor" adieu before heading out to find and extricate his Sugar from her present predicament. All in the name of love.

Thirty-Two

Daniel Sean and Jubal begin their journey north on foot, heading up towards Seneca Village. They, of course, avoid The Bowery, to steer clear of the nativists. They decide that anytime they come even close to a group of people, they will quickly cross the street and move on before anyone notices the two of them. A black man and a man with the map of Ireland all over his face is not something that those bastards would miss, not at all.

As it turns out they hardly run into a living soul because it is so cold out. The horse manure that lines the streets is frozen, the coal-blackened snow lining the wooden sidewalks is more icy than flaky, and is as hard and stiff as settled concrete. The arctic weather has brought the city to a standstill, and the streets are basically deserted. Therefore, the nightly gatherings of young hoodlums are nonexistent because the knifelike, piercing wind has kept most people indoors.

Happily they tighten their coats and wool hats and continue to stride up Broadway like phantasmal invisible specters that have all of Manhattan to themselves. The few individuals that they do encounter are scurrying, to get back indoors wherever that may be.

It is a long walk back to Seneca Village but they do it at a brisk and determined pace, actually feeling an uplifted sense of purpose in every step. It's as if the deep silence all around them, the cold wind blowing into their faces, and the flowing of blood through their bodies, are all three in tune with one another. It is like a symbiosis with the natural world, causing them both to feel so joyful at the simple act of being alive.

Once they are at the front door of the Nolan's little house Daniel Sean knocks and Fiona answers the door. She pulls them both inside without saying a word, closing the door behind her.

William and Willy are both sitting at the fire as Daniel Sean enters and the two of them jump up to greet him.

Daniel Sean clasps the two of them in a bear hug, laughing, and smiling broadly.

"God bless all here," Daniel Sean says quickly, almost forgetting his manners. "This my friend and the man who saved my life, Jubal."

The Nolan family have a plethora of questions for Daniel Sean but figure that it will come out in due time so they all just smile and hug one another.

After a short while a bottle appears along with five glasses. Everyone, including Willy, is given a small tumbler of whiskey.

Fiona, William, Willy, and Daniel Sean raise their glasses with the traditional toast "Slainte." Jubal, with

glass held high, adds "Down the hatch," then they all drink.

After the toast, Daniel Sean explains to them that he is looking for a place to rent out, that he has money, and that he is looking for some type of work.

"And so is my friend Jubal," he makes sure to include.

He does not mention Molly.

"You'll stay here until you find another place," the patriarch, William, says with a big smile on his face, "and if you find your woman, well then she is welcome here also. But I think that you should hear what my son, Willy, has to say first."

Daniel Sean looks at Willy.

"I think that I may have found your Molly."

Willy had returned with Jack, a number of times to the same places that he and Daniel Sean had been to before, inquiring about Molly and describing her as best as he could. After about a month of searching he got similar responses from two different women that could possibly be a lead. One of the women was Mary Margaret Brady, whom Daniel Sean, Jack Brosnahan, and Willy had talked to a while ago in Five Points.

Molly had allegedly just recently been seen down off of Mulberry Bend, in front of a "questionable house," meaning possibly a place of prostitution. Willy went down there, found a place to look about, a little cubbyhole in an alley way that was not too obvious, and

after a wait of an hour or so he spied a young woman who did fit the description of Molly. It was the black hair that first gave him a clue.

He found a way to get close to her and while walking past her he saw that she had the most beautiful sky blue eyes that he had ever seen. And that's when he recognized her from the *Athlone*.

Willy watched her disappear into the house with a well-dressed man. One thing that he did notice was that she was no longer the skinny, starving waif that he remembered, or that Daniel Sean had described. She was now a fully blossomed woman.

Daniel Sean insists that, first thing the next morning, he and Willy go down to where Willy has seen her. This agreed on, Daniel Sean and Jubal bunk up next door in the little annex house, sleeping fully clothed, covered in Fiona's quilts to fend off the cold.

The next morning over a pot of tea and some brown bread with butter Daniel Sean makes his plans.

Jubal decides that he should not come along with them, as it is a fairly delicate situation. So the next morning he heads north to Harrison to look around. But promises to return in a couple of weeks if he can.

"I got to get me some kind of work, but I do want to meet the people here in Seneca Village. From what Danny tells me it sure is worth seeing."

Daniel Sean and Willy head out the same time as Jubal, and while he heads north they head south to

Mulberry Bend. Along the way they see very few people because of the frigid weather.

They station themselves discreetly across the street from where Willy last saw Molly and wait for her appearance. For close to five hours they see no living soul come or go, up or down Mulberry Bend.

After a frozen day of standing around, taking turns watching for any sight of Molly, they decide to head home. They do this for two days, then on the third day the weather warms up and changes for the better. On this day Will wakes up vomiting with a slightly high temperature so Daniel Sean decides to go anyways by himself.

Miraculously in less than an hour he sees her. The image of her standing in the sunlight suddenly brings to mind what he had read in Booneville from Shakespeare's Romeo and Juliet, "Oh she doth teach the torches to burn bright!" For even in the piercing winter light she seems to glow brighter than the sun itself. As he watches her, he is unable to move, has a sudden intake of breath, and his beating heart speeds up in it's rhythmic cadence. He is suddenly light headed and he then he feels a bolt of energy in his forehead that travels downward and settles in on his chest. A sense memory enters into his heart and it's as if the mists of time have melted away as he feels her in his arms once again while standing on the deck of the ATHLONE. She is pressing against him and crying on his shoulder while they both pledge an unending love for one another.

Barely able to even move he comes to and simply stares at her in muted disbelief as the rest of the world simply disappears.

All that he sees is her, his Molly, but she is transformed.

She has filled out from her skeletal famine physique, Molly is now a beautiful, full blossomed woman.

Dressed in a clinging red dress that shows her attributes, a dress that he would never have imagined her wearing, unsettles him until he sees the familiar sadness in her sky blue eyes.

As he starts to walk toward her a well-dressed man, who it seems is familiar to her, approaches Molly. Daniel Sean runs in a desperate sprint across the street, practically leaping up the stairs, and he blocks the door before they even open it which stops them from entering the house. He looks at the man menacingly and raises his huge fist and shakes it at him.

"My good man, please break off from this rash behavior," the fellow says to Daniel Sean.

"Piss off me bucko, or it's your jaw I'll be breaking," Daniel Sean replies.

The man starts to object, looks at the ham hock of a fist in his face, thinks better of it and scurries away.

Daniel Sean grabs Molly by the hand and leads her into the nearest alley. Molly gives no resistance at all. He gently maneuvers her so she is standing up against the alley wall and stares at her not saying a word.

She finally breaks the silence.

"I know that you hate me now, I'm disgusting, I know. But I have been shattered with desperation. Go ahead hit me, slap me, do what you will, I don't care. I also hate myself. But I refuse to apologize, for I did not want to starve again; I did what I had to do. My mother, rest her soul, died two months ago and I had no means, nothing." She slumps down onto the ground.

"When we first arrived here in New York, the second day here in fact, we connected with a fairly well to do second generation Irish American family who had a thriving business of their own. They grow vegetables and raise sheep, so they hired us on, took us both on up to their farm. There we were living up in a place called West Farms in what's called the Bronx. It worked out for a while, at least we weren't starving, and the woman was kindly. Me Ma and mines job was taking care of the sheep. But after a bit the man's son kept at me, and the more weight that I gained the more he kept at me. He couldn't keep his hands off of me, so I stayed away from him as much as I could. Even slapped him once while I was tending the sheep. My mother took sick and after she died everything went to hell. I ran away because of the aggression of the oldest son. I came south all the way here to Mulberry Bend, a little over five weeks ago. I slept on the floor of a horrible flophouse with no running water. Bugs and mice everywhere. I tried and tried to find work, anything—and I looked everywhere for you, but come up with nothing. I tried to wait for you but you

never came, figured that you were gone, with another. So I started working here."

Daniel Sean slumps to the ground next to Molly.

"I have to know, tell me now. Did you have feelings, I mean did you well, you know? Did they mean anything to you? Molly please tell me, I have to know."

Enraged Molly stands up, leans over, and slaps Daniel Sean across the face as hard as she can, then slaps him again and again.

"You pig, you shite faced lousy pig, how dare you say something like that? You may as well cut out my heart. Yes I had feelings. There were three of them, just three, because I am what is considered exotic due to me eyes and hair. And I did have feelings for them." She starts to shake uncontrollably, then says in a whisper:

"With all my heart I hated every single one of them. And I hated myself most of all."

She raises her eyes and laughs a heartbreaking, jaded laugh.

"So there you go—you see it was mutual. Get out of my sight; you are no better than the lot of them."

She starts to walk away but Daniel Sean jumps up and takes her into his arms. She hits his chest with both hands, crying hysterically, "My heart can't take it any longer, I don't know what to do, I have nothing in this world, everyone is gone and I am so sad and alone. I'm broken Daniel Sean, shattered I am. And now…"

She stops and in a frightened, almost childlike voice says. "What you think that you can have me like

the others now that I am soiled? Is that it?" She sneers at him but then looks away. She says mostly to herself, almost forgetting that Daniel Sean is there. "I would have jumped into the ocean with my muchusla and gone under the black timeless waters with him, just like Megan Murphy and her Ma."

They sit in total silence, Molly barely breathing and seeming not to even notice that Daniel Sean is there.

"Would you have done that?" He croaks out in a desperate hopeful whisper.

Molly looks up and stares at Daniel Sean for a whole minute until she whispers. "Aye, I would have, and gladly."

She starts to quietly weep, withdrawing into herself and seeming to disappear right before his eyes.

Daniel Sean starts to also weep, great spasms of tears sliding down his cheeks, as he whispers to her in a choking pain filled voice."And I would do it for you right now, as I see you drowning here on the streets of Mulberry Bend, I want only to drown with you."

The world stops in its rotation around the sun as Molly turns and stares at Daniel Sean, their eyes lacing together like a fountain as the tears gush forth.

"Daniel Sean do you mean that, truly. Do you mean you could, that you would, do that?"

"Aye, I do, and gladly."

Frozen they both stare at one another neither one able to move. Finally Molly shakes her head and speaks, softly, sadly, the pain evident in her voice.

"You deserve better than someone who's done what I have done." She lowers her head and just stares at the filthy ground, resigned to her fate.

"Muchusla, you'll not be saying that again," he reprimands softly, "for by the Holy Mother herself you will be clean anew. As for you doing what you did, I know now that you had no choice—shattered you were with desperation, and just come from the gates of Hell itself. You have to try and forget those three men, who I'd like only to put six feet under the duggened earth. That life is over now, for you are my life and my soul."

Molly raises her head and grabs his arm fiercely, with a strength that surprises him.

"Surely you can't be forgiving me for what I've done."

"Yes, yes, oh yes I can. In the name of the Holy Mother I will, I do, now and always my love. My own Mary, for that is what I will forever call you. Not Molly but Mary. You said to me once that the names mean the same so Mary you are now to me. If you will have me. Please, you are…be *my* Mary." He pauses for a moment, looking deeply into her eyes, then says in a whisper. "Mary, my muchusla, we can start anew."

"I have some things upstairs that I should…"

"No, no please, don't go back there, I'm begging ya." He pleads with his eyes. "Molly, I mean Mary, do you have Seamus's rosary with ya?"

"Aye, I keep it with me always."

"Then that is all that you need, for I have some money and we will buy what you need, and don't be worrying. I have some skills and the strength of an ox in me. I have some jobs lined up for me already, and if needed, I'll get two jobs or three. Don't you be worrying now."

He pauses for a second and looks away. He then speaks quickly in a slow whisper, so that she hears exactly what he has to say.

" 'Tis all my fault ya see? I should have been here widja, but God forgive me I was not. So please, I'm begging ya, stay from going up there. For I don't want you to be reminded of what I made you do by not finding you sooner. If ya can find it in your heart to forgive and forget then, by God that is all that I want and pray for. Remember what we felt when we last saw one another, the light and love that we had for one another, while all around us the air itself smelled of death? If ya can do that then we might just have ourselves a chance at this. If you can't do that, and ya find that you can't take my feelings for ya to heart, then I will leave now and never shadow your door again. I only want to hear ya tell me whether you do or do not love me."

"Ah my muchusla," she says through her tears, "I only want to spend my life with you, drowning in happiness and in sorrow. With all my soul I love you. No…I don't love you, I am *in* love with you."

She smiles at Daniel Sean as he gently wipes the tears from her eyes, then she looks away into the distance, and continues.

"By the truth that is in the Holy Mother of God, I promise to jump into the churning seas of this new life in America with you, and hold on even if we both sink down into a bottomless watery grave for, like Irish ivy, our souls will be woven together and be as one forever."

They fall into each other's arms, and Daniel Sean despite the tears rolling down his cheeks, laughs.

"And, Mary I am in love with you, completely."

They kiss, at first gently and with a slight bit of hesitation, but then as they melt into one another their lips find their own sensuous rhythm and they drink each other up all the while pressing, grasping, and squeezing their bodies against one another. Not being able to help himself, Daniel Sean's hands are all over her body, amazed at her magnificent womanly curves and as she grinds her pelvis against him, the two of them, in unison, moan in ecstatic bliss.

Mary pushes him away from her body and they both look at one another like two wild animals, then they suddenly embrace again, pressing even harder against each other. She then stops and gently pushes him again.

"We can't my love, this is not the place or time."

She takes a step backwards and grabs his hand.

" Jesus, Daniel Sean, you're so big and strong, 'tis a bit like being with a kicking stallion."

Looking at him with more than just love in her eyes, Mary whispers knowingly. "But don't you worry about that honey boy, for I will tame my stallion whom I love. And while we may at times gallop wildly together, I will be your mare some of those times. And with you riding me I will canter, like one of those proud Connemara ponies, backwards, forward, and sideways. That's when you shall see the beauty inside of me, which is the love that I have for you, gush forth and bring a tear of joy to both of our eyes. Other times I will be astride you and sweetly, gently we will saunter as one, slowly without a care, as if we had all the time in the world, that is until I spur you on with my heels, then you will become my bucking stallion so much so that we will make the devil himself blush. Daniel Sean, I know this for I have hungered for you more than you could ever know. You are my love, my heart, my muchusla."

"And Mary my love, my eyes have never beheld anything as beautiful and desirable as you. I've never wanted anything as much as I want you. I want every single inch of you, my love."

"Yes, yes you shall have all of me, and I shall have every single inch of you, for you are all mine and I am all yours."

They smile and then both start to laugh, embracing again with a familiarity that surprises them both, as if it is something that they have been doing every day.

"Will you be my wife, tell me quickly, for I don't think that I can wait too much longer to have you?"

Mary kisses his hands gently. "Daniel Sean O'Neill, God Himself put us both on the ATHLONE so that all the Angels, Archangels, and the Holy Mother herself could be looking down from the Throne of Light and see with delight the two of us giving ourselves to each other as we are right now. I wouldn't dare go against His wishes."

She smiles at him and whispers. "Yes.'

Daniel Sean smiles broadly and also gets a little choked up. "We've come a long ways together my love, but we're just getting started."

He kisses her all over her face, taking his time as they both start to cry softly. They separate and stare at one another with absolute adoration.

"Then it is all said and done," he says, "and we need never mention this past life of yours again. We shall find a priest, Mary my love, and make the sacred oath before God Himself!"

Daniel Sean leads Mary west and away from her past life. After they cross over to Broadway, Daniel Sean splurges and they jump into a carriage, riding it all the way up Broadway to a short distance from where Seneca Village is located. The whole time they sit in silence holding hands as if the two of them are afraid to let go.

As they walk back into the vicinity of Seneca Village, arm in arm, the unusually warm weather settles in on the two of them. Suddenly Daniel Sean feels a tide

of giddiness flowing through him, and an impulse takes hold of him.

He lets go of Mary's hand, puts his hands on the ground, kicks his legs up and into the air, and then proceeds to walk on his hands. Ten steps and still walking, his heart pumping and his hands moving, he makes it to twenty then twenty-five, thirty, thirty-five, forty, forty-five, surpasses his forty-seven, and at forty-eight steps he collapses onto the ground right in front of the Nolan abode, banging the top of his head in the process. The now renamed Mary giggles and claps like crazy.

Unable to stop herself she throws herself down on top of Daniel Sean, pressing her body against his, kissing him all over his face, and clasping on to him as if he was a flotation ring thrown to her in a tempest tossed sea.

"Muchusla, my muchusla, my dearest Daniel Sean, my Shaneen, my love, my love, we have one another, and nobody can touch us or hurt us now," she cries, with a radiant smile on her face and tears in her eyes.

Thirty-Three

The next two days they sleep apart from one another. Mary stays under the watchful eye of Fiona, and Daniel Sean sleeps in the little hut next door. But every chance that they get they are all over one another; kissing, hugging, laughing, crying, and touching, with Fiona always smiling at both at them.

"Something needs to be done with the two of you before you do something rash," Fiona finally comments. "There is a special Mass that is going to be celebrated up in Yonkers New York, just north of Manhattan, on Christmas day. By way of the Irish grapevine I heard that, following the Mass, the priest will perform the Sacrament of Matrimony for anyone who is interested in getting married. Are the two of you ready to be joined together as one, or what? You look as one already to the likes of me."

Fiona has loaned some of her clothes to Mary but it is decided that they have to go buy some clothes for Mary. There happens to be a woman in the Village who makes dresses, gowns, and other apparel for women. She is a godsend to the people of Seneca Village, and in heavy demand, so there is a bit of a wait for her services. Fiona, however, has a way about her that can be quite persuasive. She works out a deal with the woman, who is

originally from Germany, so that Mary will help her children to learn how to read and write in English in exchange for some clothes—including a simple but lovely wedding dress.

The day before the before the wedding, while the men are out of the house, Fiona finds Mary all by herself crying in the back room. She runs to her and collects her up into her arms stroking her hair at the same time.

"What ever is the matter there, Mary my dear? What troubles your heart now?"

Mary looks up at Fiona through her tears

"I am afraid that something will happen to me. That God will not forgive me for what I have done. And that He will not let me have children with my Daniel Sean."

"Let us go and get some air where we can talk freely," Fiona offers.

She helps Mary to stand, wipes her tear stained face dry, and then leads her outside. They go for a walk around the block.

After they get away from any people who may be about they have a bit of a heart to heart talk, with Fiona taking the lead.

"Listen to me now Mary, you're 18 years old there, only a few months shy of 19, so you're a woman —but you're also still a girl." She stops walking, so Mary also halts.

"I know that you don't remember me from the ATHLONE, but I do remember you. Even if me and my

brood were in a different cabin, I do remember you. And I will just say this to you my dear. When that storm hit, and everyone was looking out over the abyss, not just the sickness you see, but the void itself was staring up at the whole lot of us. At least that's the way it felt to a score of us there, for we were all afeared of not only the vast wasteland of the eternal sea but also the presence of the hand of death in the way of the 'ships fever.' "

They start to walk again in silence until Fiona speaks.

"Well, you see, we all thought that the devil himself had come down upon us with a vengeance. But not you, no. And the word got out that there was this waif of an angel out there with the spirit and strength of Queen Maeve herself, just smiling and caring for one and all with not so much as a care in this world." Fiona smiles at Mary. Then the smile turns sad.

"I know what kind of life that you were forced to live for a wee bit while you and Daniel Sean were separated, but don't you dwell on all that. 'Tis nothing to linger over my dear. I know how it is, for us women have to survive, and you are a survivalist. As am I. For I have my own stories to tell which would curdle your toes if I told you." She lowers her voice to a whisper.

"I stabbed a black hearted man in the chest with a rusty knife that I kept with me during those times of An Gorta Mor back in Ireland. This was outside of a tavern in Mullingar a little over a year ago. He was a devil of a man who tried to not only rob me, but grabbed me and

tried to slap me about and force me to do God only knows what, while my William and little Willy were looking for food less than a block away. I stabbed him with all the strength that I had in my weakened body, aiming right for his heart."

She looks away into the distance.

"Never told the two of them about it, and I never intend to. I'm not sure if the man lived or died and I don't really care. But I know that God in heaven has forgiven me, for I did all the necessary prayers and incantations including a novena, nine days straight of prayers begging for forgiveness. So there you are. Believe me, you have nothing to be ashamed of, for you are here and you have the rest of your life to live. Like I said before, us women have to survive. But when all is said and done, thank God we are here in America. For this is our country now."

On Christmas day, 1847, Daniel Sean and Mary get married at St. Mary's Immaculate Conception Church in Yonkers New York. Mary, Daniel Sean, Fiona, William, and Willy, travel together, all the way up and back on the Hudson River in a passenger sloop along with a huge group of other Catholics. When they dock the whole lot of them walk together from the banks of the Hudson River to the church. It is about a half a mile walk filled with chatter, laughter, and singing.

This is the opening day of the Church, and following this celebratory Mass the priest, Father John

Ryan, performs a group wedding ceremony for close to one hundred couples. Daniel Sean and Mary are one. "Molly" is no more, as she has decided to tell the skies and the whole world that she is now and forever more to be called "Mary."

"Because my life is a small little miracle, and only the Holy Mother would understand how happy I am."

Since they are both being smart with their money, after the wedding Mr. and Mrs. Daniel Sean and Mary O'Neill along with the Nolan family make their way back to Seneca Village where the Nolans beg away saying that they have to meet a friend on the other end of the Village.

When Mary and Daniel Sean come to the front door of the house, they discover a note tacked to the door of the house. It reads: *Congratulations. The Nolan castle is yours for the night. See you tomorrow around half three in the afternoon. Nollaig shona dhuit. Merry Christmas.*

Daniel Sean carries Mary across the threshold and into the house as they laugh and smother one another with kisses. The interior is awash with mistletoe and holly which cover the ceiling and the walls. Mary finds a note from Fiona that instructs to light all the candles that she has set up in the room, which she does obediently.

On the stove is a lamb and potato stew, while on the one table in the room there is an Irish whiskey cake, a loaf of brown bread, fresh churned butter, a few bottles of porter, and a bottle of red wine from the Brotherhood

Winery in the Hudson Valley. Daniel Sean lifts Mary up and places her on the bed.

"How in the bloody hell did they get this whole thing together without us knowing about it? It looks like a real Irish New Yorker night for the two of us, my darling dearest love."

That night as they consummate their eternal love numerous times, An Gorta Mor, the voyage across the Atlantic Ocean, little Megan Murphy's death, the memories of their long lost family members, what Mary had to do to stay alive, all, all of their tribulations crystalize and solidify their passion for one another. They make desperate, fierce passionate love all through the night, with Mary urging Daniel Sean on. For the two of them it is earth shattering. And magnificent.

The intense heated passion is tempered by the knowing maneuverings of Fiona Nolan who has placed all the candles strategically around the little house in order to accentuate Mary and Daniel Sean's lovemaking. The mellow glow of candlelight throws off lovely shadows of Mary's curves and womanliness while smoothing out Daniel Seans innate outward masculinity allowing the two of them to melt together and become as one making the night a hallowed one that is not only lustful but also almost sacrosanct. They feel secure, protected and complete.

And after all is said and done, at long last, it becomes sweet and tender until, around sunrise, Mister

and Missus O'Neill fall into a dead sleep, their two hearts beating together as one.

Two days after their wedding night, Daniel Sean and Mary settle into their own small two-room shack behind a house that two German families live in. It has its own basin for bathing, a bed, a table and two chairs. They share a toilet with the other residents of the main house that has no running water. The shack is two streets away from the Nolan's abode in Seneca Village.

They pay rent with the money that Daniel Sean has stored up from his past jobs and the money he has been getting from working with William as a day laborer in and around the City.

Mary fixes up the room and adds some mistletoe and holly that is given to her by Fiona, so there is a holiday spirit about their space. They cherish it, and make love in their little nest anytime of the day or night. It is their honeymoon, and they make the most of it.

One thing that they do enjoy doing, besides the physical pleasures that they can't get enough of, is to lie together and talk about their future. One night, after the New Year comes and goes, Daniel Sean tells her about the Choctaw Nation and the blood oath that he made. Right then and there it is decided by Mary that, when the weather warms up, they will both make the trek to Oklahoma together.

Daniel Sean tries to dissuade her from joining him, feeling that it would be too great of a journey for a

woman. This turns out to be their first argument for Mary is greatly distressed by his attitude.

"Ah sure, 'twould be a wrong headed notion for a mere weak woman like myself to be joining her husband on a journey, when she has already breathed in the fires of hell, and buried not only a brother, a sister, a father, and a mother but also seen the devil himself up close—even forced to dance with the bastard himself—before being rescued by my muchusla." She pokes him in the chest with her forefinger. "And now for you to talk like this, which only breaks the words of other men, including Seamus Fitzgerald himself, who cut themselves to make the blood oath, 'tis wrong and ya know it. Tell me Daniel Sean O'Neill, now what kind of man would question his own flesh, his wife, when he did make that promise? You may as well call me Molly again instead of Mary."

"You'll not be saying the likes of this to me, there woman," Daniel Sean says, pointing at, but not poking her with, his own index finger. "Love of my life you are, I'll grant ya that, but there's great danger out there in the wilds of America, and I am responsible for you now, you being my wife after all."

"To hell with that, you hear me? You'll not be going anywhere in this world without me to look after you, and since ya did made the oath and cut yourself, you have no choice but to go. But as it stands we are one together now, and so we both have our own sacred blood oath to boot, you and I, the one that we made up in front

of God Himself. Therefore I also have no choice but to go with you. And my darling. I wouldn't have it any other way."

"*No!*"

"Daniel Sean, I am your wife and *I. Am. Going!* We vowed to jump into the ocean together, and this is just a little trip—not even near any ocean, I hear tell—so that's the end of it, and I'll not hear another word."

And because Daniel Sean was learning what it means to be a husband, and could fathom what was good for him, she didn't hear another word.

Mary, after doing some research, finds that on this "bank and shoal of time," as Shakespeare wrote, in the year of our Lord 1848, there is no way to travel to any part of Oklahoma. The newly devised railroads go nowhere near there, and the only viable route is the old Santa Fe Trail, which skirts Oklahoma by hundreds of miles due north. This inaccessibility to the region is a matter of logistics and politics.

Oklahoma is a name that comes from the Choctaw language and translates in English to the "land of the red man." It is where the "Indian Territory" begins. A closed and mostly prohibited area to anyone who is not from there. It is isolated and inaccessible.

While Daniel is somewhat relieved that they will not be making this journey, Mary is not mollified in the least.

"A blood oath is a blood oath," she insists.

They put the matter on the back burner for now, figuring that it will be dealt with later on in their lives when the traveling arrangements can be met.

On a cold blustery afternoon, March 2nd, 1848, Jubal appears back in Seneca Village, showing up at the door to the O'Neill abode. Fiona smiles and directs him to where Daniel Sean and Mary now live, two houses down the street from where they are.

It is a warm reunion, with Daniel Sean showering Jubal with many questions, mostly about where in the hell has he been for the last two and a half months.

"Been working a bit up in Hills in Harrison," Jubal explains, "but, as it turns out, the mills won't be fully up and going for close to another year they say. Came back here to see if you were interested in going back to Black River for the season and maybe even longer. Been in touch with Mister Johnson by mail. The boss man wants me to be a foreman of sorts, in charge of all the different horses up there. Good opportunity for me. Well, he wants to know if you're up to coming up there again." He runs his hand over his short, curly hair. "Looks like Nathaniel is on board, and so is Nicodemus, but Joseph is doing his preaching. He's in the process of getting ordained as a minister and is some place upstate. I figure on looking him up when I'm up there in Booneville."

Jubal looks at Daniel Sean expectantly. Daniel Sean smiles just as Mary comes through the front door carrying a loaf of brown bread and some butter.

"Jubal this is my wife Mary O'Neill. Mary this is my friend Jubal. The man I told you about."

Mary's eyes light up at the sight of Jubal.

"Sure but I've heard all about you there Jubal. Welcome to our humble abode."

Jubal ends up staying for the entire day and sleeps over in the Nolan's extra hut.

During the next day Mary, Daniel Sean, Fiona, and Willy take Jubal on a tour of Seneca Village.

Fiona Introduces Jubal to everyone that they come across as they stroll around the Village. As Jubal meets the different people he is taken back by not only the friendliness and diversity of the people he meets but also how clean and tidy everything is here. There is very little in the way of trash or debris.

"Nice feel to it Danny. Be a good place for a man to live," Jubal says to Daniel Sean on the way back to the Nolan's house. "But tomorrow I'm heading back to Hills and the following day I'm traveling on up to Booneville with Mister Johnson and the fellows."

That night after dinner, Daniel Sean and Jubal have a little chat.

"So whatchu think Danny, you up for going back up there to Black River and make some money?" asks Jubal.

"I do need the money," admits Daniel Sean, "but you see, Mary is with child." A wide grin spreads across his face. "We just found out yesterday. Fiona noticed something going on with Mary and she said she is dead sure that Mary is gonna be a mother."

"That's wonderful Danny," Jubal replies after pausing for a beat. He slaps Daniel Sean on the back. "Congratulations my man. Couldn't be happier for you." He shrugs his shoulders. "Just that me and the fellows are gonna miss you up there in Booneville. Sorry you can't come. But family is more important than anything, as I know too well.

The next morning Daniel Sean and Jubal bid each other adieu, not knowing when or if they will ever see each other again.

It will be fifteen years until they cross paths again, and it is under very different circumstances when they do. At this point in time neither one of them could have possibly foreseen how much their world would be turned upside down. But the bonds that tie the two of them together as friends would, fortunately, just keep on getting stronger with the passage of time.

Thirty-Four

On October 10, 1848 Mary gives birth to their first child, nine and a half months after she and Daniel Sean were married. Fiona and Mary have been lighting candles and saying prayers every day to St. Rita, St. Philomena, the Holy Mother, and, most powerful of all, to St. Gerard, who is the patron saint for women who are pregnant. They never miss a single day lighting a candle.

Mary is blessed with a boy who has, like the two of them, blue eyes and black hair. They christen him Daniel William O'Neill. The middle name refers to the chosen godfather, William Nolan. The godmother, Fiona, is ecstatic with the arrival of "Danny" and tells Mary that she will always be available to sit with him. She is constantly singing and sending out streams of blessings on him and whoever else is around at the time.

Less than a year later, eleven months from the birth of Daniel William, on September 20th 1849, Mary gives birth to a second child, a girl, which makes the two of them "Irish twins," which is when the mother gives birth twice in a year.

The little girl is named Mary Fiona. This gives great pleasure to Fiona who is finally pregnant with another child, something that she has been praying to

happen for a long time. She is due in two months time and delivers on November 29th giving birth to a baby girl. Following tradition, she names the child Fiona after herself, and takes Mary as the middle name, because, of course, Mary is the godmother. So there you have, thrust into this world two adopted cousins: Fiona Mary Nolan and Mary Fiona O'Neill.

Mary becomes pregnant with their third child and on the10th of November 1850, a girl, Moira Grace, enters into this world.

While the living arrangements are slightly claustrophobic, the O'Neill family manages to soldier through it all with the support of their neighbors and friends in Seneca Village.

For the last two years Daniel Sean and a few of the other men have been working at various jobs as day laborers. Mostly concrete work but also laying cobblestones for the different roads that are starting to be erected all around the New York City area.

The eclectic mix of mostly African, a few German, and a score of Irish families live in close proximity with little friction. This is in sharp contrast to the rest of society in general. The people who live here are a hard working, thriving, self reliant, fairly educated, God fearing, and forward looking group of men and women with the African New Yorkers as the core driving identity of the whole village.

****

Mary is out taking a walk with her three children. Strolling next to her are three year old Daniel, two year old Mary Fiona, and eighteen month old Moira Grace. She stops in front of the house of one of her closest friends, a woman named Nicole Francis who, like Jubal, is black as a starless night and is also very out spoken about many different issues.

Nicole gets up and out of the wooden rocking chair that is sitting in and walks over to Mary.

"Hey there Mary how you doing now girl?"

"Grand just grand Nicole, and yourself?"

"Could be better, could be worse. Been reading this gazette here about us you see. Didn't know that we were 'simple minded' and 'slow to understand,' or that Seneca Village is officially   called 'Nigger Village.' " Nicole slaps the paper that she holds. "No this is all news to me. Even mentions those lazy, dirty, ape-like Celts who live here too, along with the niggers. 'Squatters' is what we're called. Not 'home owners' but 'squatters.' No Mary, I didn't know any of this."

Mary is stunned into silence and stands stock still for a full minute or so while Nicole Francis shakes her head in disgust. Feeling the bile rise up in her throat and a line of red inching upward from her chest to her forehead, the Irish in her cannot be contained, and Mary lets loose a torrent of curses that causes Nicole to drop the newspaper that she is reading.

"Whoa there now Mary, calm down now." Nicole smiles at her friend. "But I gotta say there you wild Irish

rose, exactly, I feel exactly the same way as you. It's just that I never heard you talk like that before."

"Ah Christ, Nicole, sorry. Lies, lies, lies that's what it is, lies. I am damned mad about the lying press and about all of this blather. Calling you, my dear friend, a 'nigger.' You can bet that I am shaking, trembling angry, I won't be standing for the likes of it, not for a second."

"Well they called you and your family 'lazy and dirty and ape-like' which stirs me up too."

It's a mild spring evening, early May, in 1852. Mary O'Neill and Nicole Francis are standing in the front of Nicole's two-story house, which is in sharp contrast to Mary's three-room shotgun shack.

Here there is very little in the way of "haves and have nots. Mostly free born people of African descent, who bought plots of land so that the men would have the means to vote, because blacks are not allowed to vote in New York proper if they do not own land, these are the men and women that founded Seneca Village.

As is the law women of any race do not have the right to vote. This is something that rankles Nicole and a lot of the women here, including Mary.

The poorest residents are the Irish, but they are not treated as low class here and this is what truly endears Mary O'Neill to her friend Nicole, who lives in a castle compared to Mary's modest home. They are friends because the two of them have children who play together on a daily basis with no regard for skin

pigmentation or religion. In fact, on some occasions the O'Neill's attend All Angels Church, a Protestant church with Black American roots, as guests of the Francis family. This openness stemming from the African community is something that the O'Neill's will never forget, and is something that Daniel Sean and Mary hold dear to their hearts, as do the Nolan's.

Fiona Nolan, who is also quite fond of Nicole, regularly babysits for the Francis family, becoming almost an honorary aunt to her four kids. And while Nicole has many friends in the neighborhood she still manages to spend some time with her two Irish "cousins."

The attacks coming from the media concerning the moral fiber and character of the residents here continue unabated over the next couple of years. They are described as lazy, indolent, filthy, dangerous, and degenerate; and sometimes even as pigs and apes.

In the spring of 1854 articles in various newspapers say that the land that these people own, and where they had worked and sweated and had built a community on, is much coveted by the people who run New York City.

At a town meeting hastily called at All Angels Church, Nicole Francis and her husband Lionel take center stage.

"I knew it all along," Nicole belts out to the gathered audience. "All those stories that those gazette

and newspapers have been concocting were about getting us out of here! The big shots here in Manhattan want to demolish our homes, run us out of here, and make all of us disappear into thin air!"

Other speakers take to the podium and the general consensus is to stay and fight it out.

A year passes and in early spring, the residents are commanded by the law to move out of their homes. The reason for this mandated evacuation of Seneca Village is so that a gigantic open park can be built there; a park for the people of Manhattan to enjoy. It is to be called Central Park. This eviction notice is ordered through the legal mandate of "eminent domain" by the Mayor of New York City, Fernando Wood, and has the support of most of the influential figures in the City.

It takes two years to remove the last residents from the Village. With the leadership of Nicole Francis the people put up a fierce fight but, through the machinations of the press and the powers that be, on October 1, 1857 the last remaining residents of Seneca Village are forcibly removed.

The following week the entire village is razed to the ground.

And with that, this wondrous, evolved, and vibrant community founded by African Americans is no more. A community that embraced with open arms members of another group who were experiencing their own anguished travails, simply becomes a footnote of

history. The residents all go their own ways, settle where they can, and pretty much lose touch with one another.

The O'Neill family, now grown to seven members with the addition of two more boys, Owen and Dennis, move to the Westside of Manhattan between 51st and 52nd Streets, along with the Nolan family. The two families live in the same building; a crowded tenement that is wedged in between a tannery and another tenement. Down the block is a slaughterhouse, and the pungent smell of blood permeates the neighborhood night and day. But that's not what troubles the two families.

In their old neighborhood they experienced no discrimination or disdain but in the rest of New York City the O'Neil's and the Nolan's find that that's not the case. Irish Catholics are despised, sneered at, and not trusted at all. Mary and Fiona keep telling William and Daniel Sean, "It will just take some time for us Irish to be accepted as true Americans, you need to be patience and to have a little faith."

Thirty-Five

"You have to look after your brothers, sisters, and your mother. Daniel William, you're the oldest, come this October, you'll be 13 years old and almost a man. I have no choice I have to go and do my duty. I'm an American now and this is my country. Plus I have my own personal reasons to be wanting to go and fight, you see, a black man saved my life years ago and I could not bear to see the likes of him enslaved. And that is exactly what would happen if the Rebels get their way. Not to worry though, nothing will be happening to the likes of me. Ah sure, everyone is saying that 'twill all be over in a couple of weeks anyway."

The news just came in two days ago that the Confederate States have fired the first salvo against the Union in a place called Fort Sumter. America is at war against the treasonous Rebel Army.

Daniel Sean has heard about a group of Irish born Americans who are trying to start up their own regiment to fight for their newly adopted country. It is being touted by none other than the great Irish patriot Thomas Francis Meagher, who was a member of the Young Ireland movement back home in Ireland. He was arrested by the British for treason, sent to a penal colony in Tasmania, escaped from there and then made his way to New York.

Daniel Sean went and heard him speak last night and he was greatly impressed. Meagher declared, "This is our chance to show that we are not only Americans and willing to fight valiantly for this country but we have our own cause back in Ireland that needs the world's attention."

Becoming a part of the Irish Brigade, training and then fighting side by side with fellow Irishmen, Catholics to boot, is truly a remarkable experience for Daniel Sean. It gives him an overwhelming feeling of pride to be in the company of these brave Irish-American men.

For the next two years, Daniel Sean and the 69th New York Infantry Regiment see much action for they quickly prove themselves to be ferocious and fearless in battle. Which is not necessarily true because they are all unnerved and terrified while on the battlefield, surrounded by the horrors of war. But they have one another and they all believe that they have something to prove to the native born Protestant Americans.

Their courage while in battle does not go unnoticed by the top echelons of the United States Army.

Therefore the 69th is sent into one skirmish after another including the Battle of Chancellorsville in Virginia in May of 1863, and the Battle of Fredericksburg in Maryland this past December 1862.

The Irish Brigade suffered horrific casualties in both battles, as more than half of them were killed in action. So fearless were the men of Daniel Seans

regiment that, after the battle of Fredericksburg, the head of the Rebel Army, Confederate General Robert E. Lee, christened them, "The Fighting 69th".

He was reported to have said after another battle, the one at Chancellorsville, "Never has man seen such courage as we have seen today from these men of the Irish Brigade".

But now on this specific day July 13, 1863, Daniel Sean O'Neill has been sent back home to New York City for a call of duty that he, at first, thought would be a godsend for he would spend time with his wife and kids. But there is also a very distressing side to this duty bound relocation as he discovers.

He is crossing Fifth Ave and 48th Street. He is now a member of the newly formed New York City Militia, having been transferred from the Irish Brigade only three days ago. It is a small group of Irish born Americans who have been selected to help 'ease' things over with the New York Irish who have been very rebellious and outspoken about the Draft.

Daniel Sean's transfer came as a precautionary measure due to the possibility of an uprising from the Irish populace in New York City who regarded the Draft as being wholly unfair to the newly landed Irish men.

These new arrivals believe, with some truth to it, that they are being used by the Union Army as nothing more than lambs to the slaughter—canon fodder —and

they were not even born here. And Blacks aren't even a part of the whole draft process which has created a tidal wave of resentment among the Irish. It is ironic because the majority of Black and Colored American men would love to go and fight Johnny Reb.

Daniel Sean is not unaccustomed to the horrors of war. He has been hardened beyond measure by what he has had to perform in the course of his duty, and has distinguished himself in action, being commended, on occasion, for his conspicuous acts of gallantry on the battlefield. So much so that he was promoted to the rank of corporal while still on the battlefield in the middle of a skirmish serving as a private in the bloodletting at Fredericksburg.

Even so, he is more disturbed by what has occurred today than anything that he has ever seen in the war.

One consolation is that a torrential downpour has just started and is putting a temporary pause in the day's goings on. Because of this Daniel Sean has been relieved of his duties and ordered to go home for he will most likely be needed first thing tomorrow.

Looking up at the pouring rain he reflexively crosses himself at the thought of what has happened this day. *Praise God for this miracle of nature, for maybe it will slow down this work of Satan himself. Trying to kill children! Children! Thank God for the New York Police Department, with our little bit of help, we got all of them*

out of harms way. Sweet Jesus! The devil is loose here in the hearts the men and women who are trying to kill children!

It is the first day of the Draft Riots. Daniel was been assigned to the Colored Orphans Asylum, along with other soldiers from the 69th now with the New York Militia and a squad of New York City policemen, to protect the children from the growing mob of Irish men and women who are dead set on attacking the kids.

The Asylum is on 44th Street, right around the corner from where he is now walking. At first it was difficult to keep the rabid mob away from the building, but the New York City Police Department, along with Daniel Sean and his militia, rallied together and were able to hold off the mob long enough to sneak all of the kids from the Asylum out the back door and down the alley to safety.

Crossing over Fifth Avenue, Daniel turns onto 48th Street heading west toward home when he it seems as if the Celtic cross is vibrating against his chest, causing him to glance about. Through the pouring rain he sees two men holding and trussing up a black man in the shadows of a garbage-strewn ally, like a pig about to be slaughtered. His heart stops—he is looking right at a slightly older, grey-tinged haired Jubal. Without hesitating, he walks right up to them, pulls out his Army issue revolver then shoots the two white men, both obviously Irish, in the head, one after another, killing both of them instantly.

He kneels down and cradles Jubal in his arms.

"Can you walk?"

"A little."

Daniel pulls out a knife from his belt, cutting the rope from around Jubal's wrists.

"Lets go. The rain will hide us and help us get out of here."

Out of nowhere a man appears on a horse. He is holding a long rope in his right hand.

"Alright then, I got me the rope for the nigger, you two boyos ready to string him up?" He mistakenly says to Sean and Jubal in the shadows.

Lowering Jubal to the ground, Daniel Sean swivels around and shoots the man, who grabs his chest and rolls backwards off of the horse. With his one free hand, Daniel quickly secures the horse.

"Lets go Jubal, we gotta hurry before anyone else comes along."

Daniel Sean helps Jubal up on the horse then climbs on himself. He kicks the horse, and they head north away from all the action, passing burning buildings as they ride on. Streaking up Fifth Ave, past 55th Street and the construction site that will eventually be St. Patrick's, Daniel Sean touches his cross, saying a quick Ave as they pass by it thinking to himself, *I need to ask for forgiveness for what I've just done as soon as we're safe.*

Because of the rain, thankfully, they don't come across many people, and with Jubal holding on tight to

Daniel Sean's waist, they gallop right into the confines of the not quite finished project, aptly named, Central Park.

Daniel Sean does not break stride. With the two of them concentrating on any noise that they might here, silent and stealthily they keep heading north. Past the herds of sheep sleeping in the meadow, past the swamps, crossing over small granite hills, across a small lake, and into the thickness of a heavily wooded area. Not a word is spoken the whole time, for they are both too scared to talk or stop. Straight north they ride, the horse pressing on and covering ground.

After about twenty minutes of riding in the seemingly deserted soon to be Central Park, Daniel Sean passes right through the ruins of Seneca Village, which has now been plowed over. It is a sight that gives him a feeling of overwhelming sorrow.

He remembers when Mary and him said goodbyes to all of their neighbors as they were all being torn from their homes. This creates a feeling of numbness in his chest as a sense of both sadness and anger swell up in him.

They keep riding hard for another twenty minutes or so, until Daniel Sean slows the horse down to a canter, the animal breathing heavily, and they come to a stop underneath the overhanging branches of a huge oak tree.

They are alone.

Total silence. Then: "Daniel Sean it's mighty good to see you, mighty good. But Daniel, you just shot three people, three of your own kind."

"I put down three mad dogs. That's all. The Lord forgive me for that but I could not let them kill you. You are my brother. And it is mighty good to see you too, Jubal my brother."

Jubal whispers. "Yes, we are brothers."

Silence. One, two minutes pass as they both listen for any sounds of people. They cannot even hear the sound of the rioting way off in the distance. Finally Daniel Sean breaks the silence.

"Do you have a family Jubal?"

"I did. Two children with the best woman that ever did walk the earth." He pauses, then goes on sadly, his voice breaking as he speaks. "Lost all three of them to typhus, just this past year." He looks down at the ground. "They all three died within a month of one another. I was away at the time trying to sign up to go and fight the damned Rebs, so I was not around when they left this world. I ended up getting commissioned to wrangle horses for an outfit in Connecticut. Didn't get to kill no Rebs though."

Daniel Sean pulls out a flask, takes a pull, hands it over to Jubal who takes a swallow.

"Thanks, needed this." He looks at Daniel. "We both done got older."

They both start to laugh, chuckling at first, then segueing into a full-throated guffaw.

"Well me bucko, I reckon it beats the alternative."

"Ain't necessarily so. There's a part of me that is looking forward to leaving this world and seeing my wife and children again."

Jubal looks up at Daniel Sean and smiles broadly.

"Sure is good to see you brother Daniel. Mighty good timing, by the way."

They both take another drink.

"Jubal, the world has gone crazy. By God, I thought what I did and saw at Fredericksburg was bad, fair enough, but what I saw today, sweet Jesus, it's the work of the Devil himself." He shakes his head in shame. "Never thought I'd see sons and daughters of Eire behaving like such savages. Even their children are doing the work of Lucifer." He looks into Jubal's eyes.

"That's why I shot all three of those lads without even thinking. Like mad dogs they were." Daniel Sean pauses, looks away. "I need a minute there now me boyo. All right now?"

Jubal nods.

Falling to his knees, and with a clear open voice, Daniel Sean starts the Act of Contrition.

"O my God, I am heartily sorry for having offended You this very night. I detest all of my sins, I dread the loss of heaven and the pains of hell, but most of all because I have offended you, my God, who art all good and deserving of all my love. I firmly resolve, with the help of your grace, to confess my sins, to do penance and to amend my life."

There are tears in his eyes as he adds, "Please forgive me, know that I had to save your servant Jubal, who loves and fears you as I do. In the holy and blessed name of Jesus, with the intercession of Mary I ask you to forgive me dear Lord."

As Daniel stands Jubal says, "Amen, amen."

They look at one another.

"Lord of Creation, as your servants, the wandering Israelites, who also like my people were once enslaved but through your Grace broke those shackles prayed," intones Jubal, *'May it be Your will, O Lord our God, to forgive all our sins, pardon all our iniquities.'* Amen. And look after my brother Daniel Sean, for The Lord is our Shepard and we shall not want."

They clasp arms like two old Roman or Greek gladiators.

"Wait a minute now, what about you, Danny Boy, you got yourself a family too?"

"Aye, wife and eight kids. I checked on them today, earlier, made sure that they were out of harms way; and I got a lad from the 69th there, guarding them. Along with my oldest son, Daniel William, who is fifteen and who I taught how to use a knife and a gun before I went to war. Probably the safest tenement in all of the West Side with the two of them there. I thank God that none of my boys are old enough to fight in this Civil War that we're having."

"I see you still got that Cross around your neck," Jubal comments, pointing a crooked finger at Daniel

Sean's chest. "Protection from above," he says, redirecting the finger skyward.

"Aye, from above," Daniel Sean nods in agreement.

"We are not far from the Harlem River, Daniel, I can almost smell it." Jubal looks off into the distance, almost smelling it. "I got me a small rowboat hidden in the bushes on the banks of the Harlem, I'm gonna to take it and head back north to Hills in Harrison. It's right near that old campground where we used to live, remember that place, where we first met?"

"Jubal, I will never forget that place, that little slice of heaven where you saved my life. And Jubal my brother. I will never forget you."

"Well Daniel Sean you done saved my life too. And I'll never forget that. Wait a minute now. Did you take care of that blood oath you done tole me about? Don't mean to do no prying or nothing like that, just wondering. So didja?"

Daniel Sean takes a minute to answer.

"I did not," he says with a sigh. "But still plan on doing so, things just have not lined up right for me to do it."

"Well Danny, as soon as this war is over and, if the two of us is still alive, we'll both make that trip out there to Oklahoma together. I been dreaming of heading west these days. Heard tell that there is going to be a lot of opportunities out there after this war is over. The Union must and shall be preserved, as President Lincoln

likes to say. Yessiree, Daniel Sean my brother, I am dying to head on out there to the wildness of the west, see the desert and hear the stillness." He drew out the last word as if savoring it. "I want to be free out there on my own horse and see what's what. And I also want to make sure that you get out to Oklahoma in one piece. But first we got to finish this war and free the slaves down in the south. We got *some* work to do here, but it's gotta be done."

Jubal and Daniel Sean part ways, but not before they exchange addresses so they can keep in touch in the future. They are both determined to head out west together after this war is over. Both watching each others back along the way for there isn't another man on earth that the two of them trust more. It is an unbreakable bond that was forged by the act of saving each other's life.

Thirty-Six

During the Civil War, Daniel Sean had befriended a fellow soldier by the name of William "Wild Bill" Carroll. Like Daniel Sean he was not very tall, but also like Daniel Sean, he was thickly muscled, strongly and compactly built.

It was purported that Bill Carroll had hands like lightening, and that he could knock a man out with one punch—even if that man was twice his size.

Although they were not in the same outfit—Daniel Sean was in the Fighting 69th , while Wild Bill, who was born in Yonkers, New York, was in the Anthony Wayne Guards—they soon crossed paths. Their pugilistic reputations preceded them and, as is the custom with the Irish, a fight was set up. It occurred, of course, between skirmishes with the Confederate Army.

A makeshift ring was set up behind the tents where the upper echelon of the commanding officers should hopefully not witness it. Some of the men watching the fight placed bets as to who would be the victor. Carroll was considered the heavy favorite.

It was a classic knock down drag out fight, each of them, in turns, gaining the advantage over the other, bludgeoning, punching, and grappling each other.

After close to a half an hour of continuously battering one another they stop to catch a breath, look at one another, shake their heads in unison, and then they both start to laugh like crazy. With a twinkle in his eyes and a smile on his face, Carroll reaches out his two arms to O'Neill.

They embrace in a huge bear hug, with Bill shouting out to one and all.

"I say that this is a draw and I salute Danny Boy O'Neill here, and if any of youse don't like it, well you can kiss my royal, red, white, blue, and green Irish-American ass."

That is how the two of them made each others acquaintance and quickly became thick, close friends. William Carroll summing it up with. "The best way to make friends is by having a real old fashioned all American fist fight. It's the only way, ya fight, beat the hell outta one another and in the end ya shake hands and you're pals. No other way."

The war continued on but the South was losing one battle after another and the North was wearing them down, in the process destroying the Rebels morale. One of the biggest turning points was Sherman's March to the sea. His 'scorched earth' tactics, destroying a whole swath of the Southland from Atlanta to Savanah and leaving nothing behind put a knife into the heart of the Confederacy. It was so debilitating to the Rebs and their

supporters that it was really only a matter of time before their inevitable surrender.

Even though there were still some pockets of resistance by the end of April 1865, with close to 800,000 Americans dead, the American Civil War was over.

After they were both discharged from the army in late spring of that year Daniel Sean and William Carroll stayed in touch. It came to pass that 'Wild Bill' Carroll managed to land a job as a police officer in Yonkers New York immediately upon his return to civilian life.

Carroll sent word to Daniel Sean at the end of June and offered him a job in Yonkers as a police officer.

"However the job won't be available until around November but it is yours if you want it," Carrol said enthusiastically.

Daniel Sean is ecstatic but also a little ambivalent about becoming a police officer, happy to have a job but not so sure as to what being a police officer entails.

Daniel Sean and Jubal managed to reconnect, first by mail and then in person as Jubal found his way down to the O'Neill abode. For a couple of weeks starting in May, they have both been working as laborers all around the city, with a number of different crews, allowing Daniel Sean to take care of his Mary and their eight kids.

"Just wait until I start my beat up there in Yonkers, we'll be living the good life, at least I reckon so."

Mary also pulls in a small wage here and there teaching different migrants how to read and write. She has developed a small but thirsty following of people wishing to acquire those skills. Daniel Sean put aside a modest savings from his soldier's salary and pension that he received after being mustered out of the Union army.

Upon hearing about the police job offer, Mary demands that now, with months before he starts his new job, Daniel Sean should make the trek to Oklahoma, so that he can pay his respects and fulfill his blood oath.

"Jesus, Mary, and Joseph, Daniel my love, get it over with so that ya will put my mind at ease. It is hanging over us like a hobgoblin, and this will be the last time that you are able to have a little time to do it." She takes his arm tenderly. "And it gives me great comfort to know that you have Jubal to go with ya now, for there is safety in numbers." Mary smiles at Jubal.

"Daniel my love, he's a great friend to you and me and the kids. I don't think he would let anything happen to you while out there in Oklahoma."

Jubal nods his head at Mary and winks at Daniel.

"God's truth Danny. God's truth."

"Ya never know my love, "Mary says with a twinkle in her eye, "but we may want to have a few more little ones to look after…"

They both smile as she continues in her persuasive way. "I've already looked into it, and Oklahoma is no longer a closed area. It isn't easy but you can travel there now." Mary narrows her eyes at him. "I'll look after

things here, don't' ya be worrying about that. Go on with you now. You have a bit of money that will tide you there and back. My only regret is that I canna go with ya. But I will pray everyday for your safe return and will cry myself to sleep every night missing you next to me."

****

It is four days after a very subdued Independence Day, which was a bittersweet birthday for America, when Daniel Sean and Jubal begin the trip to Oklahoma.

Marking the occasion of the Fourth of July was sweet because the war had ended and the killing is over; and bitter because of the Assassination of President Abraham Lincoln.

Daniel Sean and Jubal take a train to Pittsburgh. Daniel Sean is traveling with a small pack that contains a few changes of clothes, dried beef, a canteen, a buck knife, and some traveling money. Around his neck is his talisman: The O'Neill family Celtic cross.

Hidden in the very bottom is his Starr Army single action revolver which was made up there in Yonkers. The war has made him very wary, and he knows that there are still pockets of Rebels out there who have not finished smoldering over their defeat. With the exception of Jubal and only a few others in his life, he trusts no living man. He will constantly be on his toes and looking over his shoulder at every bend in the road or river.

Jubal has a slightly larger pack, for he has every intention of never returning back East. He packed extra clothes, a skillet for cooking, two pistols, a hatchet, some books which includes a bible, and a small quilt that his wife made for him. This is along with a few mementos, such as a birthday card, and a few small personal items that were given to him by his kids. They will always be with him no matter where he ends up.

The train ride to Pittsburgh is long but pretty much uneventful and smooth. The two of them enjoy the trip west through New York and on into Pennsylvania.

When not looking at the passing scenery or catching a few hours sleep, they pass the time reading the latest novels that have just recently come out, which include Jules Verne's *From The Earth To The Moon*, and Lewis Carroll's *Alice In Wonderland*.

The two of them have both become voracious readers over the years, and even though they are both basically working stiffs, they both read anything that they can get their hands on.

At Pittsburgh, after getting directions to the docks, they grab the first steamer on the Ohio River that's heading southward and begin the second part of their trip. This leg of the journey, to Cairo Illinois, is quite pleasant and relaxing. There they will dock at Fort Defiance, located at the confluence of the Ohio and Mississippi Rivers.

As they travel southward on the Ohio River, Daniel Sean and Jubal exchange stories about their

experiences during the war. Daniel Sean, in a flat, emotionless monotone voice, tells Jubal about the horrors of war that he encountered with the Irish Brigade, not going into any specific details, just giving Jubal the facts.

Jubal, on the other hand, tells Daniel Sean in detail about what he did since the night of the Draft Riots, which was the last two years of the Civil War.

"Well now there Danny boy, ya see I was in charge of our regiment's War horses—that's what we done called them—War horses. Poor creatures didn't know what they done went and got themselves into. And they weren't used just for the boys in the cavalry but also for carrying all the supplies, which included them damn cannons." He shakes his head in disbelief at the memory.

"How much terror and shock those horses went through is impossible to understand. Us humans know what we were fighting for but them War horses, well, it broke my heart to see them so afraid and helpless. And they didn't have nothing to do with this damn war at all.

"Now Daniel Sean this was near the end of the war. We all wanted to go fight them Rebs, brother, all of us wanted to go and get into the mix, but nobody wanted us Coloreds to fight. At least not in the beginning of the war."

Jubal shakes his head at the memory of desperately wanting to fight in the war. "That's right, we weren't allowed at first. Until President Lincoln signed the Emancipation Act, but then it took time for it all to

get organized. So five days after I saw you during the Draft Riots I was on my way to sign up to fight. Once they saw how good I was with horses they put me with a cavalry regiment that also had some heavy artillery. It was an all Colored unit, and let me tell you Danny boy we were as brave as any white man, maybe even more so because we did not want to go back to the way it used to be."

Smiling at Daniel Sean Jubal continues on.

"Still, even though we were doing what we knew was the right thing, I felt awfully sorry for those horses. In fact because of the war, I expect I have a deeper affinity for horses than I do for my fellow man..." He shakes his head and lets out a deep breath. "Hate to say that, but it's the truth."

On this part of their voyage, heading farther into the Southland, they are met with shocked and sometimes hard looks from lots of people that have never seen a white man and a black man together as friends. One couple says something to Daniel Sean about his, "colored man servant," to which Jubal and Daniel Sean are, at first, taken back only to then suddenly break out laughing with Jubal saying to the couple with a fake high brow accent. "No my dear friends, this is my Irish man servant."

After landing they stay the night in Fort Defiance, sleeping on the dock, taking turns keeping watch. The next morning they switch over to another steamer on the Mississippi River, once again traveling southbound.

The first thing they notice that morning at first light, as they depart from the shore in Fort Defiance, is another ship being loaded with men in tattered clothing, some of them with shackles around their wrists. On closer inspection they see that most of them are dressed in old faded Confederate uniforms. It turns out that it is a ship transporting prisoners of war back to their homelands in the South.

Even though they were the enemy just a few months ago, Daniel Sean feels sorry for these poor men who were just caught up in the war. But they were traitors to his newfound country. A country that he loves.

For Jubal there is no sympathy at all for them, none at all.

All along the Mississippi they witness the ravages of the Civil War. Daniel Sean remembers something that he read, something that William Shakespeare wrote, that really has nothing to do with what he is seeing but keeps popping up into his mind. It's from one of his sonnets. "Bare ruined choirs where late the sweet birds sang."

All throughout the Southland, even when they switch steamers off of the mighty Mississippi River to travel westward along the Arkansas River, they see nothing but devastation everywhere. It's as if the Four Horsemen of the Apocalypse; Conquest, Famine, War, and Death, have ridden into the South on their pale horses and wreaked havoc.

But most notable is that there is nary a note of singing, whistling, warbling, chirping, or tweeting

sounds. Once again a line from Shakespeare's sonnet 73 comes to mind for Daniel Sean. "Bare ruined choirs, where late the sweet birds sang."

That is the first thing that they both notice even before they come ashore in Napoleon Arkansas to switch for another steamer: The complete absence of birds and the absolute silence in the air.

It is not just the birds that are quiet, however. As is the case probably with any humans who have lost in war, the people who live in Napoleon seem to go about their business in shocked silence. Still, his heart goes out to them in their misery, for he has also experienced hardship, death, and hopelessness in his life.

When Daniel Sean relates this to Jubal, his reply to Daniel Sean is simple.

"Enslaving another human being is the most evil, diabolical thing in the history of mankind. And if you are even distantly involved, you got to face the wrath of the Creator, for it is a sin against God. Simple as that. I don't argue with God."

Heading west, deeper into Arkansas, on the Arkansas River, closer to Oklahoma and the beginning of the Indian Territory, is when all the destruction and devastation begins to dissipate. The earth, the sky, and the river itself seems to explode in a fusion of life and colors.

It's astonishing to Daniel Sean and Jubal, for they see wildlife that they have never seen before. Birds from the hand of God Himself, including red cardinals, blue

jays, yellow ducks, grey geese, snow white herons, multi-colored hummingbirds, black ravens, golden hued eagles, red tailed hawks, and species of all shapes, sizes, and hues flitting to and fro.

In contrast to what they had observed just two days ago the air reverberates with the sweet sound of trilling, whistling birds!

Along the banks of the river there are white tailed deer, elk, gophers, bobcats, panthers, and other animals that they have never seen before. Even at night they feel surrounded by the comings and goings of bats in the air and raccoons on the shore.

This is when Daniel Sean realizes how beautiful the land called Dixie must have truly been before the Civil War, and why these men who came from there fought so ferociously.

He thinks to himself, that *even though most of those men did not own slaves, by God they still were part of it. And no man deserves to be enslaved by another man. I would rather be dead than be another man's property. Jubal is right—it is a sin against God Himself.*

Thirty-Seven

Fort Smith is located on the border of Arkansas and Oklahoma. When the steamer arrives there the passengers are made to disembark and the boat undergoes an inspection to make sure that there are no Rebels aboard.

The Captain of the steamer explains that there have been a few incidents on the Arkansas River and in the Oklahoma Territory because most of the Choctaw Nation had been Confederate sympathizers during the Civil War.

In fact the Choctaw and the Cherokees had both colluded with the South during the war, allowing the Confederacy to flourish in this area. This is news to Daniel Sean and Jubal, and when they ask one of the passengers, who they have become friendly with, the man explains.

"Some prominent members of the Choctaw Nation owned slaves and were really on the side of the Confederate states. But not all of them."

During the course of the day, as they wait for the inspection to finish, Daniel Sean and Jubal see two Union soldiers on guard here at Fort Smith, both on opposite sides of a large gate.

As he looks at the two of them, the first thing that Daniel Sean notices is their uniforms. The pants are clean and crisp looking, the blue jacket is without wrinkles, their trademark brimmed blue hats are without wear and tear, their swords are impeccably clean as if never used before, and likewise, their bayonetted rifles look almost new.

It dawns on Daniel Sean that neither one of them has been in the thick of combat, and therefore neither has seen the real horrors of war close up.

This deduction is not just the state of their uniforms; it is also the way that the two of them are carrying themselves. They are both too relaxed.

It is obvious that they have not been there in the "blast of war," therefore they have not been there when men are clutching their stomachs, trying to shove their intestines back into their abdomens after being shot in the gut. Nor have they witnessed men who have lost a leg or an arm, with blood spurting up and all over them screaming for their mothers and pleading with God Himself to take away the pain. "Dear Lord God take me away form this place of misery."

Or even, just as bad, neither one of them has ever found themselves in close, chin to chin combat with the enemy, stabbing a stranger with a cutlass or bayonet. It is clear that neither of them have ever experienced this physicality of hand to hand combat; killing young men who are just as god-awful scared as you but you having no recourse but to rip and thrust at his body, oblivious as

to the location; torso, arms, legs, and even the face. For that is a sense memory that never goes away and for those who have had this experienced, well, the residue of the act is always there right under the surface.

After killing another man in close proximity what remains is a numbing sorrow that stays with a man who has a conscious. This is the soul-altering end game of war, when the humanity is displaced, and "I and thou" has become "I and it."

Daniel Sean does not see this indifferent, scabbed -over callousness in the eyes of these two soldiers. Not at all. They both seem…normal. As if they are just doing their jobs.

The soldier on the right is tall and thin, not really young, probably about late twenties, with a laconic, placid attitude about him. His body has taken on a kind of relaxed posture, his eyes glimmer with an almost bemused outlook at his station in life, and while attentive to his surroundings, he is not seeing the broken terrors that always, in this life, lay right below the surface.

Daniel Sean knows from his battle-hardened experience that hell lurks up, down, and all around, with the devil himself ready to rise up and strike when you least expect it.

While An Gorta Mor, The Great Hunger, was a trip to hell, it was not as all consuming as his experiences in the Civil War—when he was starving to death he did not have to kill, not even once.

The other soldier, who is on the left side of the gate, is, in contrast to his compatriot, somewhat short and slightly over weight, soft in the belly, youngish, around twenty years old. He has buck teeth and a furtive look about him as his head darts back and forth, taking in one thing and everything. It gives the impression of his being a close relative of a gopher, or maybe a prairie dog.

The only problem is that he, like his partner, is not seeing what is really going on. He keeps staring at the group of poor, desperate Indians that are on the periphery of Fort Smith, just sitting there in tattered rags, with a small collection of meager possessions.

The two soldiers' eyes wander from the Indians to the shackled Confederate soldiers, and jeer at them. They shake their heads, whisper to one another, quietly laugh, and then point with their chins in a mocking way at the two groups. All the while displaying a complete lack of compassion for any of them.

Daniel Sean knows that most soldiers who have been in the thick of the butchery that really was the Civil War just want to be done with the killing and get on with life. Enough is enough for they have seen enough for ten lifetimes.

If these two men were truly aware, they would know that Daniel Sean is the one right now who is dangerous. He is seething with impatience and disgusted with their complete ignorance of the whole goddamn mess that is war.

With a bristling jaunt to his step Daniel Sean says to Jubal, "be right back", and walks right up to the two soldiers.

After explaining that he too served in the Union Army and where he did battle, he questions them about the whereabouts of the Chief of the Choctaw Nation.

The soldier on the right, the tall, skinny one, tells him, in a Western frontier accent that has a flattened out American twang to it.

"Hell that Injun chief, Chief Peter they calls 'em, full name of Peter P. Pitchlynn in English, or as the Redman say Hootchootucknee—means snapping turtle. Yep, believe it my friend—Snapping Turtle is his Injun name. Don't that beat all?" He grins a foolish sort of grin and shakes his head. Daniel Sean remains expressionless.

"Well he's right here at Fort Smith," the man goes on with his distinctive dialect. "He done come up here from way south in the Injun Territory, down yonder there in Chahta Tamaha—what we call Choctow Town, which is where the Choctaw Nation done got their main base. They brought him up here just a week ago for some kind of powwow with the head honcho here about Injun relationships, or some kind of whatnot. He's heading out in a day or two to go to Mountain Fork, down south in the Injun Territory, which are his happy hunting grounds. So to speak."

He grins over at his fellow soldier and says. "If I had my way I'd hang his half breed neck right here in Fort Smith."

The other younger, shorter soldier, grins back.

"Amen brother. Better to hang the savage than waste our time feeding, and clothing him. It's a waste of our time and money if ya ask me."

They both laugh at this, then the short and chubby man smiles crookedly at Daniel Sean and tilts his head in anticipation.

"Didja kill a bunch of Rebs? Didja see a lot of action? C'mon now tell us, what it was like!"

Jubal, sensing some sort of discord building in Daniel Sean against the two guards, slowly makes his way over to Daniel Sean and takes up a position a couple of feet behind him.

Daniel Sean stands there looking at the two soldiers, calm on the surface but seething on the inside. Finally, he speaks.

"Well now lads, to tell it truthfully, I have seen men just like you two, who were so frozen with the fear that they could not rise up from under the trenches, who instead shite in their pants at the sound of the bugle. Or who shook and whimpered and asked Christ Himself to deliver an angel to take them from this place of slaughter."

As Jubal lounges against a wall watching the goings on with a slight smile on his face, Daniel Sean speeds up in his recollection of battle, shifting focus

back and forth from one guard to the other, taking turns looking each of them in the eye.

" 'Twas the devil's work all in all, and nothing to be proud of doing; but either kill Johnny Reb or be killed by him. And on both sides of the line you came out changed by it all. So much so that for the rest of your life, in the dead of a black silent night, you wake up with a shudder and an icy cold wind whipping through your heart, and you can hear the pleas of men whose throats you slit, or who you stabbed, or shot."

He moves in closer to the men, a grim expression on his face. He looks deeply into their eyes, trying to convey the horrors that he'd seen and experienced since. It appears as if they might see, for their expressions are fraught with fear. Daniel Sean continues, allowing himself to be dark and dramatic for the effect.

"Aye, believe me…you can hear their pleas… mewling like newborn babes, begging you with their dying words to let them live… And it is the dying light in those men's eyes that rise up to haunt your own shattered soul…eyes that you can never erase from your mind. And sleep does not return on such nights when the ghosts of those whom you sent into the next world awaken you."

Daniel Sean looks at them with a challenging look and then points over to the shackled Rebel soldiers.

"Those men over there are now going back to a wasteland. And even though they were all misguided and their cause was treasonous, I wish them all no ill will.

They are just lads, like the two of you, or me. Lads who did what they thought was right. My only hope is that by the grace of God they can find some measure of peace in this broken world. Because they are now once again Americans, and we need to put all this behind us and come together as that."

He pauses and looks at his surroundings, and then points over to the group of Indians.

"And these poor souls, the original Americans, well, they only had their land stolen, that's all. Then were shipped out here like so much cattle."

Daniel Sean clenches his fist and speaks softly through gritted teeth.

"So if either one you has anything to say to one of them, Reb or Indian, say it to me and we'll straighten things out right here and now. Because, even though I'm American all the way through to the marrow, ya got my Irish up now and my fists are just itching, just bloody itching to come to some type of agreement. Ya follow my drift?"

The two soldiers stare at Daniel Sean, not saying a word, both wishing that this day would end. Then, in unison, they glance at Jubal and then back to Daniel Sean. The short one blinks and begins to stammer something, but nothing comes out of his mouth, so he just looks away into the distance, letting his partner handle this dilemma. The tall one looks at Daniel Sean and gazes at his huge clenched fists, knowing absolutely that he does not want to tangle with this crazed, red-

faced madman and his coal black companion. So he salutes crisply and speaks in a clear, but a bit shaky voice, just above a whisper.

"No disrespect sir, what do you need from the two of us?"

Thirty-Eight

They stand in silence. Daniel Sean looks at Peter P. Pitchlynn and thinks to himself that he has never seen anyone who looks so elegant or dignified as this man.

He has long, straight black hair that hangs down to his shoulders. This is accompanied with a strong chin, pronounced dimples on his cheeks, and an aquiline nose that makes him seem aristocratic. There is not an inch of fat on him and his skin appears to be as smooth as alabaster. But it is his eyes that are the most remarkable thing about him. His deep bottomless black eyes exude not only compassion but also an intense, tangible intelligence. They seem to absorb Daniel Sean's sorrow as if empathy is second nature to him, and because of this, a deep sense of peace descends upon Daniel Sean.

The two of them, Daniel Sean O'Neill, formerly of County Kerry in the Southwest of Ireland, and Peter Pitchlynn, current Chief of the Choctaw Nation in the Indian Territory of Oklahoma, are in an unremarkable hallway in the interior of Fort Smith on the eastern border of Oklahoma and Arkansas.

At first they look at one another in a silent haze for Peter knows nothing about the reason for this

meeting. He was simply told that a man has traveled a great distance just to talk to him for a few minutes.

Though he is under house arrest for the time being, he is not in a jail, nor is he chained or bound in any way. He is more a guest of the United States Army than a prisoner.

Jubal accompanies Daniel Sean to the meeting, standing at a respectable distance so that there could be a semblance of privacy. He also wishes to have a few words with Chief Peter, the Snapping Turtle.

After a brief pause the two men shake hands tentatively and then introduce themselves.

"I heard that you came all the way from New York to meet with me. Must say that I am quite surprised at this request to make my acquaintance. Well, well, well, I have no idea whatsoever what this could possibly be about. Okay Mister O'Neill. What can I do for you?"

After another few moments of considered silence, and after staring into Peter's eyes, Daniel Sean finally musters himself together.

"They're all dead…" he says in stops and starts, "every one of them. Two brothers, one sister, my father, my mother…there was nothing that I could do. I didn't even get to bury me mother. But here I am, breathing six feet above the duggened earth. Why? It is only because of the generosity of your people that I am standing before you."

Peter Pitchlynn shakes his head in confusion.

"I don't understand, what do you mean?"

Daniel Sean hold his hands up in front of him in a reassuring way.

"Wait now there, Chief of the Choctaw people, I'm sorry, let me explain why I'm here."

He then tells Chief Peter about An Gorta Mor; his family, leaving his home, the corn meal, and the blood oath along with the trip over from Ireland, along with Mary and his kids. He concludes his little monologue with a prepared statement that fulfills his blood oath. He reaches out his arms in sincere friendship, and warmly clasps both of the Chief 's hands in his own. In a soft voice, but loud enough so that the others around could hear he makes a proclamation.

"On behalf of the Irish race, I give thanks and blessings to the people of the Choctaw tribe for opening their hearts to us in our time of great despair. And may we, the people of Ireland, and the ones that did come here from Ireland and are now Americans, may we one day perform the same heartfelt service to those deserving others that cross our paths and who are also suffering in this world."

Daniel Sean lets go of the Chiefs hands and not able to help himself his eyes start to brim up with tears.

This is not the way that Daniel Sean envisioned the meeting. He thought it would be a fairly formal and simply an obligation necessary to carry out his blood oath. He did not think that it would be chock full of

emotion on his part, or on the part of the Chief of the Choctaw Nation. But it is.

Finally Peter speaks, partly to inform but also to deflect the moment for he can sense that Daniel Sean is slightly embarrassed.

"You don't know this but I'm half Celtic, it's true. You see my father was originally from Scotland but came to America where he and my mother met, fell in love, got married, and had ten children together."

He smiles a big open smile at Daniel Sean.

"I was raised as a full blooded member of the Choctaw Nation, as my father requested. You see he lived with the tribe as an adopted member of the Choctaw people." Laughing he says, "That might seem strange, but the two cultures are not so dissimilar as one would think. Family, honor, loyalty, faith, and most importantly of all, a profound spiritual relationship with nature are central to both the Choctaw and the Celts."

Chief Peter claps his hand to Daniel Sean's shoulder, and they start to stroll on down the hallway.

After a walking down the hall in silence for a short while, he stops walking and turns so that he can look at Daniel Sean.

"I cannot speak for everyone, only my family and myself, but I believe that, just like your people, the Irish, my ties to the Choctaw traditions and its ties to the natural world, plus my faith in Jesus Christ, is what gives me the will and courage to keep moving on. Does that sound familiar to your people?"

They both smile at this and then Chief Peter continues.

"With that said, this is also true: your story and mine are the same. We were both teenagers when we saw those around us starve to death and ..." He stops for a second to collect himself, then starts to speak again. "And there can be almost nothing on earth as horrific as that, for you are powerless to do anything. We both had our own personal Trail of Tears, doesn't matter if it was from Mississippi to Oklahoma or from Ireland to New York. It is the same for all of mankind for..." He pauses to think and then makes his point. "For the Lord giveth and the Lord taketh away. But God, or, if you like, the Great Spirit, is with us all time, until the end of days."

Chief Peter looks up at Jubal and then back to Daniel Sean.

"I see that you have a shadow following you, does he wish to speak to me also?"

Both Daniel Sean and Peter, turn and look up at Jubal with smiles on their faces.

"Yes Chief my friend Jubal does wish to have a word with you if that is okay?"

"Of course, by all means."

Seeing that this is his cue to approach Chief Peter, Jubal ambles over and introduces himself.

"He is my brother from another mother," Daniel Sean adds wryly, "and simply wants to ask you a question."

Jubal looks up and into the eyes of Chief Peter.

"I heard that some of your tribe kept African slaves…did you own any slaves?"

Chief Peter does not waver, and keeps his eyes locked on Jubal's.

"Yes I did. I am guilty of that most horrid deed that did leave the blackest stain on my soul. I believe now with all my heart and soul, that just like John Newton, I was a wretched man, and like him I once was blind and lost, but through an Amazing Grace now I can see and have been found."

He reaches out to Jubal and they embrace. Then with his eyes brimming over, the chief speaks in a voice raspy with emotion.

"A few weeks ago I signed an armistice with the United States government that is the first step in, not only abolishing slavery in the Choctaw Nation, but also in giving the former slaves full autonomy within the tribe, and be referred to as Freed, and honored, members of the Choctaw Nation."

Jubal smiles. "Chief I am glad to hear that. It's just that I was surprised to learn that Indians had slaves —I always thought that only white people owned slaves."

Chief Peter lets out a hearty laugh.

"Jubal there isn't any race of people on earth that has refrained from the evil institution of slavery: Europeans, Africans, Orientals, and us Indians. You name them and it's been done by them. Sad to say but it's the truth. And every race has *been* enslaved one time

or another. Every single one. It is part of history. But you just fought a war; a horrible war that took many lives to end it here in America, a sacrifice by many, both white and black, to rid the country of that evil poisonous trade."

Upon request from Chief Peter, that night Daniel Sean and Jubal eat with him in the canteen, and then sleep on cots in the barracks of Fort Smith as guests of the United States Army.

Over dinner, while discussing their different interests, Jubal waxes on about his love for horses and that he is not going back East with Daniel Sean but rather looking for other horizons out West.

"We have many horses in Chahta Tamaha, or in English, Choctaw Town, which is the new Capitol of the Choctaw Nation," Chief Peter, smiles, then says, "If you want to, Jubal, you can come down there with me and help with the horses. I can guarantee that you will have your own lodgings and a fairly good salary. Not a kings ransom, but a good solid living. We could use some help, as the herd has been growing down there and thriving in the fertile red soil of southern Oklahoma."

He purses his lips together, smiles sadly and continues. "I also have my own reasons for inviting you down there. I think that it would be a really good thing for those who were slaves to meet a real *free* black man, just to show them that I have truly repented. And…" He looks at both Daniel Sean and Jubal and says, "That you and I are friends."

The next day Daniel Sean goes for a long walk with Jubal around the perimeter of Fort Smith. As they stroll along the banks of the Arkansas River, Jubal proceeds to tell Daniel Sean about Joseph, Nicodemus, and Nathanial.

"Joseph and Nicodemus both became pastors and have separate churches someplace upstate, not exactly sure where, but I heard from a mutual friend that they are close and that they are both doing alright. Spreading the Word and living the life. Now, as you know, Nathaniel went and got married to Sugar, but she is no longer called that, she is now going by her real name, which is Miriam. And the two of them have six children, which includes Miriam's little girl, Sherrill, that she had before they met. Well, at least that's the last that I heard. They live out there in Brooklyn and he is working non-stop to support all them kids; concrete work, but I hear tell that he is very happy with his life. He served with a colored regiment from Connecticut during the War and won a couple of medals for bravery on the field of battle. So he is now a well respected man of his community out there in Brooklyn."

The two of them walk in silence for a bit not knowing what else to say.

"I wish the best for you, my brother, and hope that all goes well with you down there with the Choctaws. You think that you will stay there with them for the rest of your life?"

"No I don't see that happening Daniel. I got itchy feet these days. I see myself heading farther west, don't know why but you know that saying, what that newspaper fellow, Greeley wrote: 'Go west young man go west.' Well I do believe that is what I'm a gonna do. I'll stay for a bit down there with Chief Peter but after a couple of months or a little longer, I figure to buy me a horse and head towards the setting sun."

When Daniel Sean and Jubal make it back to the Fort they encounter the Chief with about thirty other members of the Choctaw Nation who have come to take him back to their home in southern Oklahoma. Included in the entourage is a sprinkling of black men and women.

All present are clothed in the same mode of dress, even Chief Peter. This is unlike yesterday, when he was clothed in a more Western style; wearing black pants, black jacket, a white shirt, and a black bolo string tie. Today he is wearing a traditional Choctaw attire: Moccasins that have a red and green ring around the top of them, leather leggings underneath a multi-colored spun breechcloth, around his torso is a loose fitting long sleeved dark velvet colored shirt with a green sash tied around his waist just above the breechcloth, and on his head is a ceremonial multi-plumed feathered headdress.

Chief Peter smiles upon seeing Daniel Sean and

Jubal. "Halito, chum achukma?" Which translates to "Hello, how are you?"

All those present from the Choctaw Nation start to laugh as Daniel Sean and Jubal mutely stand there not knowing what that means until the Chief embraces them saying. "Just a little friendly hello."

Turning to his tribe members he announces to them in their language and then in English. "These are two new friends and this one here," pointing to Jubal, "Is to come to live with us and be afforded the greatest warmth and care for there is much to learn from him. Shackles have been shed by us and I have a strong attachment to him in our mutual pledge of friendship from two free born men."

There is a murmur in the crowd as everyone looks at Jubal, the first time any of them has met a free born black man.

Chief Peter then embraces Daniel Sean and whispers in his ear, "If you desire you can address my people and say anything you like. It would please them immensely."

Stepping away from Daniel Sean the Chief gives him center stage so to speak.

Mute at first, but then after a few moments, Daniel Sean finds his voice and says in as formal a voice as he can muster. "Hunger is something that only one who has lived through it can understand, and only those who have been there know the all consuming state of hopelessness that it creates for along with the pangs of

hunger, the specter of death is its constant companion. Words cannot express the feeling of gratitude that I have for the generosity of the people of the Choctaw Nation. Ah sure but it's not even in the realm of words that can capture…"

He starts to lose his composure and hesitates for a second but then continues. "Ya not only saved the likes of me and my wife but I have eight lovely children that would not be here if not for the likes of youse. So God bless you and keep you. And look after my brother Jubal there while he is in your company."

There is a great whoop from the crowd, almost like a war cry, that is intermingled with the sobs and unabashed weeping of the members of the tribe who still have memories of their Trail of Tears. It is a celebratory moment, one that is shining through their own heartache and loss but also one that illuminates the triumphant of the Choctaw Nations survival. A feat that is being shared with a kindred spirit such is Daniel Sean O'Neill and through him the people of a land far away called Ireland.

An hour later Daniel Sean boards the steamer and starts on his trek that will take him back home.

As the steamer pulls away from the dock at Fort Smith, with the Captain blowing the air horn to signal their departure, Daniel Sean sees Jubal running along the river, keeping pace with the ship and frantically waving his hands to get Daniel Seans attention.

"Good luck my brother," Jubal shouts, "good luck. I shall see you again in the next world. Keep the faith, don't you ever waver now, you hear me boy?"

The ship picks up speed and, even though he is still trying to keep pace with the ship, after a few minutes Jubal is just a dot on the horizon. The whole time Daniel Sean has not blinked or looked away from the vision of Jubal running along the banks of the river.

When he is no longer visible, Daniel Sean has a deep gut wrenching feeling of sadness, but it is also mixed in with a feeling of euphoric expectation for both himself and Jubal. He says out-loud to the sky. "Go west young man, go west."

And despite this sensation of melancholy that has descended down into his chest, the fact is he has finally, *finally* succeeded in fulfilling his blood oath. Because of this Daniel Sean also feels as if a physic weight has been lifted off of his shoulders and carried away, giving him a feeling of clarity and peace.

Because of this he feels exceedingly optimistic and open to any possibilities or opportunities that may come his way that will add to his life with Mary and their children.

As the steamer chugs along shortening the distance between Daniel Sean and his brood, he thinks to himself. *Dear sweet God in heaven but I miss my family and can hardly wait to be with them again.*

Thirty-Nine

One gorgeous, cloudless night on the deck of the steamer that is taking him back home, Daniel Sean recalls something that happened while he was in the midst of battle in Fredericksburg, Maryland in the winter of 1862. It is an almost unexplained event that he had shelved away into the inner corridors of his memory. Something that he had not thought about since it occurred.

Lying there on the deck of the steamer, with a million stars twinkling in the firmament above, heading north up the mighty Mississippi, he vividly recalls being shot in the chest, while running the line straight toward Johnny Reb.

He was thrown to the ground and knocked unconscious as his fellow soldiers ran right into the thick of the battle. Many are mowed down and killed by the constant volley coming from the Confederate Army.

Unconscious and lying there on the frozen ground, Daniel Sean is unaware of the massacre that is unfolding around him.

An hour later he wakes up and finds himself surrounded by the butchery of war. Bodies litter the field, with men moaning in shattered pain. So many are

dead or close to it, yet he, Daniel Sean O'Neill, is still alive.

Shivering with the cold and fear, but pretty much unscathed, he touches his chest to check for bleeding but only finds the family Celtic cross hanging down about his chest at the same spot where the bullet hit him.

The cross is dented in the middle and twisted slightly sideways, showing him that it had taken the force of the bullet that was intended for him, leaving him instead with a bruised chest and nothing more. The Celtic cross, the O'Neill family heirloom that, to him, is now elevated to the stature of relic, has miraculously saved his life!

The next day the battle ends and the Union Army surrenders. That night, on December 14th, in the year of our Lord 1862, there is an almost unheard of cosmic event in the skies overlooking the obscene, horrific killing fields of the Battle of Fredericksburg.

Due to some type of rare solar flare up, the Aurora Borealis—the Northern Lights—appear in all their glory over the blood drenched, scorched earth in and around the city.

It is sight of surrealistic cosmic proportions; beautiful, pulsating, colorful lights casting shadows over the inert misshapen bodies of the dead not yet removed from the hills and fields.

More than one person was convinced that this display from above was a tribute to a Confederate sergeant named Richard Kirkland, who had performed

such an inspiring and selfless act of courage in the aftermath of the battle that he would earn the nickname "The Angel Of Mercy."

Kirkland, upon hearing the repeated pitiful cries and moans of the wounded Union soldiers pleading for help, stood up and slowly and deliberately went out and brought water, bandages, blankets, whiskey and solace to them.

He performed this act of compassion to his sworn enemies unfalteringly, in broad daylight and with no cease-fire.

The General in charge of the Union Army ordered his men to hold their fire when he saw what Kirkland was doing, actually yelling out a thankful and joyous Huzzah to him.

Now, lying on this ship's deck, looking up at the heavens above, I realize that these remembered momentous events in my life are not clouded over with a vague sense of happenstance. But rather something that I now see in its totality with the minute details crystal clear. It is as if the cloudiness of the memory has been cleansed and is now a crystal clear vision of what happened to me back on those shattered killing fields.

From the moment that I took that bullet, to the moment that I woke up and saw all the carnage, to the moment that the Aurora Borealis did her dance in the sky, all of those visions are forever engraved onto my consciousness.

This knowledge of how the Celtic cross—my family Celtic cross—saved my life is something that I will never forget, and something that I can't wait to share with Mary when I am back in her arms again.

It is also something to tell to my children and my children's children—a story to add to the O'Neill's archives, to be shared with my progeny to come. For one thing is certain, one thing is truer than I could have possibly imagined when I was younger and that is this: I am an American, all the way, and I will raise my children to be Americans. But they will all know from whence they came.

As the steamer pushes ever northward, thirty four year old Daniel Sean O'Neill reaches down and clasps the Celtic cross around his neck and thinks to himself. *Remember. Always, remember.*

While he lies there looking up at the vastness of the firmament above, with a million stars shining in the clear black sky, he is touched by the Divine as the chasm of time melts away and the boundaries of the past, present, and future become nonexistent.

All seems fluid, like the river below him. His soul soars upward into the limitless night as he feels a warm, soothing presence all around him.

It is only a fleeting moment, but as the doors of perception open wide, and the spirit of remembrance opens up within his heart, that is when he sees himself, as clear as the night sky above him, in the thatched hut back in Ireland where he grew up.

It is a cold Christmas night the year before the famine began, and Daniel Sean O'Neill is with his entire family. There are his two older brothers, Owen and Dennis, his sister Moira, his father, Conner, and standing center stage is his mother, Florence Rose.

They are not as he last saw them, ravaged with the hunger, but rather as he remembers them on that specific Christmas night so many years ago. Smiling, winking at one another, and celebrating the holiday with affectionate and humorous toasts to the blessings of the holiday. They are so full of life and love for one another that his heart soars with the memory.

This is when he realizes that this moment in time, and therefore all moments, are forever locked into our hearts, for the soul, that part of us that is eternal, is forever unshackled by earthly conventions.

As the image of his family starts to dissolve, and the linear moment of this world starts to come back into focus, the very last vision he sees is his mother's face smiling at him, as if she wills herself to stay behind one extra second to let him know that all is well. That all is as it should be.

**We hope you've enjoyed
An American Canticle
by Robert Carroll**

An author's livelihood depends on his readers.
Please take a moment to post a review for this book on
Amazon, Goodreads and anywhere else you can.
And please spread to word to your friends and relatives.

And now a preview of the next book in the
Celtic Cross Canticle series by Robert Carroll:
BLUE BAYOU CANTICLE

One

Walkabout

Christmas Night, 1969

My parents are having a huge row. As usual, it is about money, or I should say the lack thereof. Specifically, my Mom is upset because nobody really got anything in the way of presents; my Dad just gave each and every one of us a brand new, crisp five-dollar bill, fresh from the bank. And he came home drunk with a big dumbass grin on his happy-go-lucky face as if he didn't have a care in the world, which really pissed off my mother.

As the glaring, red-faced, pitched fevered yelling intensifies, bouncing off of the closed-in claustrophobic walls and ceiling, and just as I am about to scream, "Enough! Shut up, please, just shut the hell up," or else bash my head, in frustration, against the rusty, nonstop hissing radiator that stands right next to the threadbare, worn-out, ugly ass sofa, my older brother, 20-year-old Patrick, goes right up to the family Celtic cross, which is hanging on the wall in between the portrait of John Fitzgerald Kennedy and a brown Byzantium-style

woodblock of the Holy Family, removes it from the wall, kisses it, and places it around his neck.

This Celtic cross has been with our family, the O'Neill's, longer than anyone can remember, going back generation upon generation all the way back to some distant past in Ireland. It is pretty beat-up from age and it is fairly bulky, about five inches long, with the symbols of intertwined life and death, which are Druidic swirls and circles, spiraling up and down the length of it. It is not real comfortable to wear around the neck but one can if he or she desires. But at this point who gives a damn about that, I just want some peace on earth, joy, and goodwill to all or some such holiday stuff.

As if reading my mind, my brother takes me aside saying, "Brendan, get your coat. We're going on Walkabout." I think to myself, *What in the hell is a Walkabout.* But I do as I'm told.

My Mom and Dad have stopped arguing and stare at us as we pull, just like that cartoon character on TV, a Snagglepuss; exiting stage left, out the front door, and down the five flights of stairs to West 48th Street in the bowels of Hell's Kitchen here in New York City.

It has been snowing for hours. There is about seven inches of the white stuff on the ground. A blessing really because we are right in the middle of a mini garbage strike so all the trash is being covered. Last February we had a major sanitation strike for nine days straight, which resulted in mountains of disgusting waste

and trash piling up all over the place, spilling out onto the sidewalks and streets.

The snow is falling nonstop, relentless, with no lulls. The frozen crystals are clean and adhesive. Down through the black night the white snow falls. The huge dry flakes dusting my smiling face as the wind whips about me flapping my limbs, chafing me as it whistles, screeches, and playfully but forcefully slaps me on my naked cheeks, eyes, and forehead, which are the only parts of my body uncovered. The sheer power and vaunt of Mother Nature's frigid breath lifts me up as I lean into the cataract to counterbalance the onslaught. Then it dies down to a doldrums pace and silence reigns, weightily descending over the entire universe while the snow is still coming down, allowing me to nestle in the peaceful solitude of the falling hushed whiteness.

Only the muffled sound of cars, cabs, and trucks remain. All the rest is silence. A few vehicles are whooshing and sliding along the West Side streets. Getting stuck in the snowbanks. The drivers finally giving up, abandoning their cars. The elements showing who is really the boss. Fricking idiots.

I listen to something in the distance. It is the wind beckoning to me. Seeming to whisper to me alone. As my brother Patrick likewise bends his ear to listen, we both swear that we could hear the shuffle of angels' feet. The wind, from afar, racing over the Hudson River, gathers itself into a flying phalanx coming straight toward us—sallying back and forth, to and fro. Like a

winged entity, it is making its way toward us. The nudging vortices gathering in strength, slamming into our bodies. The wind stinging us, causing us both to gasp with the clean ecstasy of nature. Only to fly up, up into the heavens, and with that, all that is left is a blanketed, whispering stillness.

All around the drifts, the mounds pile up, further widening the quietude of the evening. The giant flakes silently washing away all imperfections. Covering my very soul. Patrick and me, like everyone else in Hell's Kitchen, have never owned a pair of boots. Instead we would put plastic bags over our socks, then put our Converse sneakers over the plastic bag. Sure and it works like a charm. It is the same with gloves, we usually use a pair of old socks as gloves over top of plastic bags and tie it to our wrists with a rubber band.

We proceed to walk down Tenth Avenue, completely alone. Just me and my older bro'. Digging the solitude, the beauty of the blizzard that is covering all the filth and grime, the accumulated muck and decay that Hell's Kitchen has started to become in the last few years.

The Christmas lights in the bars and clubs reflecting red, green, and white off the snow reminds me of those stained glass windows in St. Patrick's' Cathedral. I feel that I could, if I listen hard enough, hear a choir singing our Mom's favorite carol, "O, Holy Night."

I take a breath, the air stinging my nostrils, filling my lungs so that they hurt just a little bit. A good hurt. One that's clean and pure in the middle of all the filth.

Little elf hats of snow that are wide on the bottom but narrow on the top cover all the streetlights, fire hydrants, and stop signs.

We cross over 51st Street deciding to head to Eleventh Avenue, down to the piers to check out the river. A rat runs out in front of us scaring the effing hell out of Patrick and me. Walking and walking, we are both enjoying it immensely. No hookers, no hustlers, no junkies, no yelling, none of that nonsense, just the snow and us. We are drifting through the snow when we spy, on the corner, Timmy Quinn. Leaning on a lamppost. What the hell is this idiot doing out here in this snowstorm? Timmy appears to be totally inebriated. Pie eyed. Hammered. Sloshed. Not just from alcohol, this is something else altogether. He is the type of guy who is addicted to everything. Timmy is, also, one of those guys who was born under a bad sign. No matter what happened to anybody, when something happened that was not good, it happened to Timmy first, always.

And right now, something is not right. We watch him for a minute, amazed that he is still standing. He seems to be a contortionist, performing an amazing feat of balance and dexterity while weaving to and fro. Leaning backward one second, then bent over in an impossible position but not falling head first into the snow: Hell's Kitchen Irish yoga.

Patrick finally approaches him. Asks him if he's all right.

Timmy jumps at the sound of Patrick's voice. Nearly falling over. "Is that youse Pat? Thank God it's you, man, Pat, I dunno what's up or down. Hey man, I need your help, or else I'm screwed."

Patrick does not like the sound of this. "What's up, Timmy? Maybe I can help you get offa the streets. You could freeze ta death in all this snow."

Timmy sticks out his tongue. "You're kidding me. It's snowing?"

"Yeah, Timmy, it's snowing. Lemme help ya get back home." He starts to grab Timmy.

Timmy shrugs his hands away from Patrick. "No, man, I gotta deliver this bag over to this bar crosstown."

He is now in no condition to even entertain the idea of going to the East Side. He could just as soon climb Mount Everest as journey to the other side of Central Park. Pat walks back to me. "Ah, man. I can't leave him to his own devices; he's totally wasted, effing hell, fricking stupid dumbass."

Patrick pulls a good old Samaritan, volunteering to mule the dope over to this bar on the East Side. After all, 'tis the season. He tells me to just go home.

I say goodbye to Timmy and start to walk on home, trudging through the snowdrifts not seeing another person along the way. Suddenly, at 48th Street, I say to myself, "To hell with this." I cut over to 50th Street and see Patrick in the distance trudging through

the drifts heading north and east toward Central Park. I
follow him from a distance feeling like a damned private
eye or something, ducking behind snowbound cars
whenever he looks around.

When we get to the park I run up to him yelling,
"Pat, Pat. Wait up." Which seems loud as hell in the
quiet of the storm. He whips around, looking pissed at
first but then his shoulders relax and he says, "You can
walk with me in the Park but when we reach the fricking
lousy-ass East Side, you gotta head on back home." He
mumbles to himself, "I hate the Upper East Side, the
Swells mixed in with the frigging Mick/Kraut Yorkville
trash."

We enter Central Park and it is like being in a
silent frozen magical kingdom or something like that. It
feels as if we are in the mountains of New England,
which I've only seen pictures of because I've never been
anywhere outside of Hell's Kitchen, ever, except here to
the Park. But that was in the summertime and it never
looked like this, so white, clean, and pristine, which
gives me a dash of joy and, strange enough, hope.

The branches of some of the trees are bent over
from the weight of the snow and everywhere, everything
seems to be touched by some peaceful, soothing
invisible hand, making Pat and me laugh at the sheer
beauty surrounding us.

Out of nowhere a guy comes flying by on skis,
silent as a cat crossing the room. Pat points at him and
laughs. "Holy frigging hell, Jesus , Mary, and Joseph!

Look at that! Maybe it's Billy the Kid visiting New York."

"Who's Billy the Kid?"

"Let's see, you are what? Sixteen now, right? You were only eleven then. So. I guess that you don't remember the Winter Olympics in 1964. Billy Kidd won the silver medal in some downhill event. Everyone went ape cuz he was the first American to ever do that. He was raised up there in Vermont someplace."

As we keep on walking, heading north right in the middle of the horse path, we see a few other souls digging the Park, not many but enough to feel the tie of being crazy loons who are out and about in the storm.

We turn east in the very middle of the Park, up a hill past Belvedere Castle, which is covered in a white mantle of snow, making it look and feel like a setting in a Grimm's fairy tale complete with a beautiful Snow Queen ensconced inside sitting in front of a raging fireplace with huge Irish wolfhounds laying at her feet while she is sipping a cup of mead.

The windblown trees swaying back and forth cause drifts of snow to avalanche from the branches onto our faces as we keep sloshing through the drifts, feeling the effort as the snow keeps on piling up underfoot making us work even harder to walk. It is so quiet, so, so hushed. As if in reverence to this absolute silence, not a word is spoken for the rest of the trip. We stop every once in a while as Patrick closes his eyes and sticks out

his arms as if he is meditating. I never felt closer to him than right now, so this night is a great adventure for me.

When we get through the Park to the East Side, Patrick looks at me and says, "A lot of people think that the Big Apple is this amazing worldly, cosmopolitan place but it's really a collection of small villages that all together make up what is known as New York City where most people hardly ever even leave their own neighborhood. In some respects it's pretty cool because you got neighborhoods where you can feel comfortable. Think about it; you got the Barrio, Harlem, Little Italy, Chinatown, hell we even got an area where gay men and women can be with others who are queer too and not get the frigging hell beat out of them just because of who they are. So that's the positive part of the Big Apple, a collection of little ethnic neighborhoods. I mean, how many times have you been out of the Kitchen?"

"I dunno, Pat, a couple, this is my first time to the Upper East Side though."

Pat laughs and says, "Look, this is your first Walkabout, now don't worry you will have many more, maybe you will even get the hell out of the City someday. Who knows?" He pauses, then continues. "In Australia the aborigines do Walkabout to find themselves, to cleanse themselves, and to discover the presence of the spirit. Or something like dat." He looks out toward Fifth Avenue and 79th Street. "Okay, now, get the hell outta here, I gotta go take care of this Timmy Quinn fiasco. See's ya when I see's ya."

I take my time on the way home wading through the snow, which has stopped falling, the whole time thinking about what my brother said, "Maybe you will even get the hell out of the City someday." Yeah right, I could dream I guess.

I have no idea what Patrick is going through since I left him. It turns out that it is a setup, not from Timmy but from a guy named Nunzie, a complete screwup/ druggie who made a deal with some Narcs over on the East Side.

Patrick ends up getting busted, arrested, and spending the night in jail, appearing before the judge the day after Christmas who recommends that he sign up for the Marines or Army in lieu of being busted for possession. Patrick takes the advice of the judge who was a Marine in his younger days and agrees to sign up for the Marines rather than going to jail. The Rockefeller laws are so stringent that the chance of Patrick getting off 'scot free' is zero. He ends up going to Vietnam for an extended tour, kind of messing him up, but in the process, on the up side, he not only gets out of New York for a while but he also rescues and adopts little Bobby while serving in Vietnam and brings him home to be an O'Neill.

This first "urban Walkabout" is followed by many other excursions that awoke in me the feeling of wanderlust, the urge to ramble, the urge to just keep on moving away from all the bullshit and all the filth that is now, at this point and time, what the Big Apple has

become. People tell me that New York City has not always been the hellhole that it is now but I don't believe them because this is all that I know.

      This first Walkabout is also a precursor to the mother of all urban Walkabouts, when, three years later, I walk the entire length of Manhattan.

About the Author

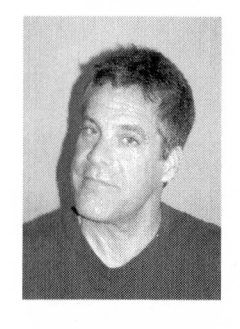

Robert Carroll comes from a large working class but highly educated family of Irish/Welsh descent.

In his early twenties, with three hundred dollars in his pocket, Rob stuck out his thumb and hit the road. For close to three years he worked his way around the States and points beyond that—bartending, doing demolition, stonemasonry, roofing, and even planting trees out west with a crew of hobos who taught him how to "ride the rails." He found gainful employment as a street acrobat, fire juggler, slack rope walker and actor, and lived, worked, or just passed through just about every state, and even lived in a tree house in Hawaii. From Quebec to Key West, to parts of Mexico, the Caribbean, and Ireland he roamed and rambled. But, as Henry David Thoreau did, Robert eventually become a "sojourner in civilized society" again. He now lives in New York City and works as a variety performer and actor, having garnered roles in Joseph Papp's Shakespeare In The Park and Law and Order among others.

This is his first novel, and the first in his Celtic Cross Canticle series.

By Robert Carroll

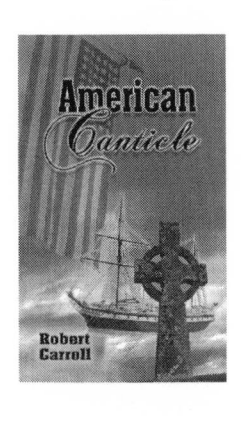

Please check out these other fine books from

Metamorphic Press